P9-CLS-899

Enter the world of Mitford,
and you won't want to leave

❧

"For readers yearning for a cozy,
neighborly read, the town created by
Karon's fine descriptive style
has much to recommend it."
—*Publishers Weekly*

For more information about Jan Karon and her books,
visit www.mitfordbooks.com

Penguin Readers Guide available online at www.penguin.com

At Home in Mitford

**is the first book
in the Mitford Years Series**

THE MITFORD YEARS SERIES

At Home in Mitford
A Light in the Window
These High, Green Hills
Out to Canaan
A New Song
A Common Life
In This Mountain
Shepherds Abiding

PENGUIN BOOKS

AT HOME IN MITFORD

Jan Karon writes "to give readers an extended family, and to applaud the extraordinary beauty of ordinary lives." She is the author of eight Mitford novels, *At Home in Mitford*; *A Light in the Window; These High, Green Hills; Out to Canaan; A New Song; A Common Life; In This Mountain;* and *Shepherds Abiding*, all available from Penguin. She is also the author of *Patches of Godlight: Father Tim's Favorite Quotes; The Mitford Snowmen: A Christmas Story; Esther's Gift;* and *The Trellis and the Seed*. Her children's books include *Miss Fannie's Hat* and *Jeremy: The Tale of an Honest Bunny*. Coming from Viking in fall 2005 is *Light from Heaven*, the ninth novel in the Mitford Years Series.

Now you can visit Mitford online at
www.mitfordbooks.com

Enjoy the latest news from the little town with the big heart including a complete archive of the *More from Mitford* newsletters, the Mitford Years Readers Guide, and much more.

The Mitford Years

At Home in Mitford

JAN KARON

PENGUIN BOOKS

PENGUIN BOOKS

Published by the Penguin Group

Penguin Group (USA) Inc., 375 Hudson Street, New York, New York 10014, U.S.A.

Penguin Group (Canada), 10 Alcorn Avenue, Toronto,
Ontario M4V 3B2, Canada (a division of Pearson Penguin Canada Inc.)

Penguin Books Ltd., 80 Strand, London WC2R 0RL, England

Penguin Ireland, 25 St. Stephen's Green, Dublin 2, Ireland (a division of Penguin Books Ltd.)

Penguin Group (Australia), 250 Camberwell Road, Camberwell,
Victoria 3124, Australia (a division of Pearson Australia Group Pty. Ltd.)

Penguin Books India Pvt. Ltd., 11 Community Centre, Panchsheel Park,
New Delhi - 110 017, India

Penguin Group (NZ), Cnr Airborne and Rosedale Roads, Albany,
Auckland 1310, New Zealand (a division of Pearson New Zealand Ltd.)

Penguin Books (South Africa) (Pty.) Ltd., 24 Sturdee Avenue,
Rosebank, Johannesburg 2196, South Africa

Penguin Books Ltd., Registered Offices:
80 Strand, London WC2R 0RL, England

First published in the United States of America by Lion Publishing, 1994
Published in Penguin Books 1996
This edition published in 2005

1 3 5 7 9 10 8 6 4 2

PUBLISHER'S NOTE

This is a work of fiction. Names, characters, places, and incidents either are the product
of the author's imagination or are used fictitiously, and any resemblance to actual persons,
living or dead, business establishments, events, or locales is entirely coincidental.

THE LIBRARY OF CONGRESS HAS CATALOGED
THE HARDCOVER EDITION AS FOLLOWS:
Karon, Jan, 1937–
At home in Mitford / Jan Karon.
p.   cm.—(The Mitford years)
ISBN 0 14 30.3503 7 (pbk.)
1. City and town life—United States—Fiction.   I. Title.
II. Series: Karon, Jan, 1937–Mitford years.
PS3561.A678A92 1996
813' 54—dc20   95-35716

Printed in the United States of America
Designed by Helen Lannis
Illustrations by Donna Kae Nelson

For Candace Freeland,
my daughter
and friend

Acknowledgments

Warm thanks to Father James Harris, who inspired and encouraged me; to Jerry Burns, who published this book serially in the best of the small-town newspapers, the *Blowing Rocket;* to my doctor, Charles (Bunky) Davant, III, who also doctors all of Mitford; to Bonnie Setzer, Mary Richardson, and Helen Vennard for their support; to my daughter, who laughed in all the right places; to Mary Tarr and the ladies of our volunteer library; to our local police department; and to everyone who buys this book about a small town that does more than exist in the imagination—it really is out there.

Contents

ONE: *Barnabas*   1

TWO: *A Dubious Gift*   23

THREE: *New Possibilities*   45

FOUR: *Company Stew*   58

FIVE: *The Big Six-O*   82

SIX: *Dooley*   99

SEVEN: *The One for the Job*   114

EIGHT: *Golden Days*   138

NINE: *Neighbors*   166

TEN: *A Grand Feast*   188

ELEVEN: *A White Thanksgiving*   212

TWELVE: *An Empty Vessel*   246

THIRTEEN: *Issues of the Heart*   275

FOURTEEN: *Absalom, My Son*   301

FIFTEEN: *The Finest Sermon*   332

SIXTEEN: *A Sure Reward*   347

SEVENTEEN: *A Surprising Question*   380

EIGHTEEN: *Something to Think About*   398

NINETEEN: *A Love Story*   414

TWENTY: *Baxter Park*   447

TWENTY-ONE: *The Bells*   481

TWENTY-TWO: *A High Command*   503

TWENTY-THREE: *Homecoming*   524

TWENTY-FOUR: *In New Life*   541

At Home in
Mitford

CHAPTER ONE

Barnabas

He left the coffee-scented warmth of the Main Street Grill and stood for a moment under the green awning.

The honest cold of an early mountain spring stung him sharply.

He often noted the minor miracle of passing through a door into a completely different world, with different smells and attractions. It helped to be aware of the little things in life, he told himself, and he often exhorted his congregation to do the same.

As he headed toward the church office two blocks away, he was delighted to discover that he wasn't walking, at all. He was ambling.

It was a pleasure he seldom allowed himself. After all, it might appear that he had nothing else to do, when in truth he always had something to do.

He decided to surrender himself to the stolen joy of

it, as some might eat half a box of chocolates at one sitting, without remorse.

He arrived at the office, uttering the prayer he had offered at its door every morning for twelve years: "Father, make me a blessing to someone today, through Christ our Lord. Amen."

As he took the key from his pocket, he felt something warm and disgustingly wet on his hand.

He looked down into the face of a large, black, mud-caked dog, whose tail began to beat wildly against his pant leg.

"Good grief!" he said, wiping his hand on his windbreaker.

At that, the dog leaped up and licked his face, sending a shower of saliva into his right ear.

"Get away! Be gone!" he shouted. He tried to protect the notebook he was carrying, but the dog gave it a proper licking before he could stuff it in his jacket, then tried to snatch it from him.

He thought of running, but if anyone saw him fleeing before a shaggy, mud-caked dog, everybody in town would know it within the half hour.

"Down!" he commanded sharply, at which the dog leaped up and gave his chin a bath.

He tried to fend the animal off with his elbow, while inserting the key in the office door. If he were a cussing man, he reasoned, this would offer a premier opportunity to indulge himself.

" 'Let no corrupt communication proceed out of your mouth,' " he quoted in a loud voice from Ephesians, " 'but that which is good to the use of edifying . . .' " Suddenly, the dog sat down and looked at his prey with fond admiration.

"Well, now," he said irritably, wiping the notebook on his sleeve. "I hope you've got that nonsense out of your system." At this, the dog leaped up, stood on its hind legs, and put its vast paws on the rector's shoulders.

"Father Tim! Father Tim!" It was his part-time secretary, Emma Garrett.

He stood helpless, his glasses fogged with a typhoon of moist exhalations.

Whop! Emma laid a blow to the dog's head with her pocketbook. Then, *blam,* she hit him again on the rear flank.

"And don't come back!" she shouted, as the yelping dog fled into a hedge of rhododendron and disappeared.

Emma gave him her handkerchief, which was heavily scented with My Sin. "That wasn't a dog," she said with disgust, "that was a Buick!"

In the office, he went directly to the minuscule bathroom and washed his face and hands. Emma called through the door. "I'll have your coffee ready in a jiffy!"

"Blast! Make it a double!" he replied, combing the hairs that remained on the top of his head.

As he walked out of the bathroom, he looked at his secretary for the first time that morning. That he recognized her at all was remarkable. For Emma Garrett, full of the promise of spring, had dyed her gray hair red.

"Emma!" he said, astounded. "Is that you?"

"This," she said with feeling, "is the most me you've seen in years. That ol' gray-headed stuff is not me at all!" She turned her head both ways, so he could get the full effect.

He sighed with a mixture of delight and despair. He had hoped this might be an ordinary morning.

❦

Harold Newland had brought the mail earlier than usual and, since Emma had gone to the bank, put it in a neat pile on the rector's desk. At the bottom of the pile, in reverse order of its importance, was the letter from the bishop.

He had asked the bishop to take his time, not to hurry his reply, and he had not. In fact, it had been a full two months since his own letter had been so thoughtfully written and posted.

He stared at the ivory envelope. There was no return address; this was not official stationery. If one did not know that distinctive, looping handwriting so well, one would never guess the sender.

He dared not open it here. No, he wanted complete privacy in which to read it. Would it be in the bishop's own hand? If so, he would then have a precise sense of how seriously his remarks had been taken.

Years ago, his seminary friend had been moved by the Apostle Paul's comment that the letter he wrote to the Galatians was "by my own hand," as if it were an act of great personal sacrifice. As a young seminarian, Stuart Cullen had taken that to heart. Since his installation as bishop, he was known to personally pen all the letters of real importance to his diocese. How did he have the time, people inevitably wondered. Well, that was the whole point. He didn't. Which, of course, made his handwritten and reflective letters a treasure to anyone who received an example.

No, he would not open it, if only to see whether a secretary had typed it. He would wait until evening and the solitude of the rectory, and the peace of his newly dug garden.

After an early supper, he sat on the stone bench that was half-covered with a fine moss, under the overhanging branches of the rhododendron.

He read the letter, which was, indeed, handwritten in the large, exuberant style that demanded space to gallop across the page.

Dearest Timothy:

It is a good evening to sit in this pleasant room and write a letter. Correspondence is, for me, a luxury which stirs my sensibilities, especially if it be with an old friend.

I believe you'd enjoy the way Martha refurbished my disorderly bookshelves, and put this study into working condition. She has even had your favorite rug repaired, so that when you come again, you won't stumble over the torn patch and go reeling headfirst into the armchair!

You ask if I have ever faced such a thing as you are currently facing. My friend, exhaustion and fatigue are a committed priest's steady companions, and there is no way around it. It is a problem of epidemic proportions, and I ask you to trust that you aren't alone. Sometimes, hidden away in a small parish as you are now—and as I certainly have been—one feels that the things which press in are pointed directly at one's self.

I can assure you this is not the case.

An old friend who was a pastor in Atlanta said this: "I did not have a crisis of faith, but of emotion and energy. It's almost impossible for leaders of a congregation to accept that their pastor needs pastoring. I became beat up, burned out, angry and depressed."

The tone of your letter—and I presume you have been forthright with me, as always—does not indicate depression or anger, thanks be to God. But I'm concerned with you for what might follow if this goes unattended.

A few things to think on: Keep a journal and let off some steam. If that doesn't fit with your affinities, find yourself a godly counselor and let me know the cost, for the diocese will willingly cover it.

Your mother, I believe, left a considerable sum, and perhaps you need to use a bit of it for yourself, for something other than the children's hospital you've been so faithful to all these years. I know you well enough to believe I don't have to exhort you to prayer. You always had enormous stamina in this area, and if that has changed, well, then, Timothy, make it right again.

You may not know that you are one of the strongest, most durable links in this diocesan chain. You are important to me, and firsthand inquiry informs me that you are vitally important to your flock. Do not doubt it.

Martha has come in to tell me it is bedtime. I cannot express how wonderful it is to be sometimes told, rather than always doing the telling!

I really never dreamed I would marry, and no one was more surprised than myself when, at the age of 49, I was ready and willing to take yet another lifetime vow. Others found this extraordinary, but I found it the most natural thing on earth.

I cannot exhort you to go out and marry, Timothy, but I will say that these ten years with Martha have brought an ease to the stress which was plundering my own soul. I can't say that the pace is easier—if anything, it has accelerated—but I find the ability to bear it greatly increased.

As I recall from our days in seminary, you and I were much alike when it came to women. You were fairly smitten with Peggy Cramer, but when your feelings for her began to interfere with your calling, you broke the engagement. Even today, I feel confident in having advised you to do it. Yet I wonder—have you ever entirely reconciled this with your heart?

*There she is again, my friend. And believe me, my
wife does not enjoy reminding me twice. That she monitors my energy is a good thing. Otherwise, I would spill
it all for Him and have nothing left with which to get out
of bed in the mornings.*

*I exhort you to do the monitoring you so sorely need,
and hang in there. Give it a year! Or, at most, give it two.
If you simply cannot go the distance, Father DeWilde
will be coming available in the fall and would be my
choice for Lord's Chapel.*

*Timothy, if you have problems with this one-sided
conversation, you know how to ring me up. Please know
that you are daily in my prayers.*

*Ever in His peace,
Stuart*

As the light faded, the chill of the stone bench began
to creep into his bones.

He stood up and looked around the greening yard, as
if seeing it for the first time. There was a certain
poignancy in the shadows moving across the rose bed
he had double-dug twice, and the borders he'd planted,
and the dogwood he had put in himself. He felt at home
in Mitford, completely and absolutely. The last thing he
wanted to do was leave. Yet, the first thing he wanted to
do was make a difference, be productive—and there
was the rub.

☙

Nearly every weekday at 6:45 a.m., he made calls at
the hospital, then had breakfast at the Grill and walked
to the church office. For the rest of the morning, he
studied, wrote letters, made telephone calls, and admin-
istrated his parish of nearly two hundred.

At noon, he walked to the Grill for lunch or, if it was raining, snowing or sleeting, ate half of Emma's usual egg salad sandwich and shared her Little Debbies.

In the afternoon until four he worked on his sermon, counseled, and generally tidied up the affairs of his calling. "A place for everything and everything in its place," he was known to quote from Mrs. Beeton.

At times, he was saddened by never having married and raised a family of his own. But, he had to admit, being a bachelor left him far more time for his parish family.

On Thursday afternoon, he was going home with a basket that a member of the Altar Guild had delivered, containing home-canned green beans, a jar of pickle relish, and a loaf of banana bread. He put his notebook on top, and covered the whole lot with a draft of Sunday's church bulletin.

"Red Riding Hood," he mused, as he took the key from the peg.

He stepped out and locked the door behind him, dropping the heavy key into his pocket. Then he turned around and stared in disbelief.

Coming toward him at an alarming rate of speed was something he hoped he'd never lay eyes on again.

It was the great leaping, licking, mud-caked dog.

For several days, the dog seemed to appear out of nowhere. Once, when he was walking down Old Church Lane to meet the plumber at Lord's Chapel. Again, when he was planting a border of lavender along the walkway to the rectory. Yet again, when he went to The Local to get milk and sweet potatoes. And on two occasions, as he was leaving the Grill.

The meeting in the church lane had been fairly uneventful. After an enthusiastic hand licking and a vigorous leap that had nearly knocked him to the ground, he'd been able to repulse his attacker with a loud recitation of his laundry list. By the time he got to socks—three pairs white, four pairs black, one pair blue—the dog had wandered into the cemetery at the rear of the churchyard, and disappeared.

The meeting at the lavender bed, however, had been another matter.

He was kneeling in sober concentration on a flagstone, when suddenly he felt two large paws on his shoulders. Instantly, such a drenching bath was administered to his left ear that he nearly fainted with surprise.

"Good Lord!" shouted the rector, who had gone crashing into a flat of seedlings. He had not, however, been thrown clear of his trowel.

He turned around and raised it, as if to strike a fearsome blow, and was surprised to see the dog stand on its hind legs with a look of happy expectation.

Spurred by some odd impulse, he threw the trowel as far as he could. The excited creature bounded after it, giving forth a joyful chorus of barks, and returned to drop the trowel at the rector's feet.

Feeling speechless over the whole incident, he threw the trowel again, and watched the dog fetch it back. He was amazed that he was able to stand there and continue such a foolish thing for twenty minutes. Actually, he realized, he hadn't known what else to do.

At the Grill one morning, he asked around. "Has anybody ever seen that big, black dog before?"

"You mean th' one that's taken a likin' to you?" asked Percy Mosely. "We never laid eyes on 'im 'til a week or two ago. A couple of times, he come by here like a freight train. But anybody tries to catch 'im, he's gone, slick as grease."

"We tried to feed 'im," said Percy's wife, Velma, "but he won't eat Percy's cookin'."

"Ha, ha," said Percy, who was working six orders of hash browns.

"You ought to lay hold of 'im sometime when he's chasin' you, and call th' animal shelter," suggested Velma.

"In the first place," said Father Tim, "it is impossible to lay hold of that particular dog. And in the second place, I have no intention of sending him to what could be his final doom." In the third place, he thought, that dog never chased me. I always stood my ground!

"Well, he's sitting out there waiting for you, right now," observed Hessie Mayhew, who had stopped in on her way to the library, with an armful of overdue books.

The rector raised up from his seat in the booth and looked through the front window. Yes, indeed. He saw the creature, staring soulfully into the Grill.

He couldn't help thinking that it was oddly flattering to have someone waiting for him, even if it was a dog. Emma had said for years that he needed a dog or a cat, or even a bird. But no, not once had he ever considered such a thing.

"We ought to call th' shelter," insisted Percy, who thought that a little action would brighten the morning. "They'll be on 'im before you get down t' your office."

The rector discreetly put a piece of buttered toast in a napkin and slipped it into his pocket. "Let's wait on that, Percy," he said, walking to the door.

He stood there for a moment, composing himself. Then he opened the door and stepped out to the side-walk.

The village of Mitford was set snugly into what would be called, in the west, a hanging valley. That is, the mountains rose steeply on either side, and then sloped into a hollow between the ridges, rather like a cake that falls in the middle from too much opening of the oven door.

According to a walking parishioner of Lord's Chapel, Mitford's business district was precisely 342 paces from one end to the other.

At the north end, Main Street climbed a slight incline, and circled a town green that was bordered by a hedge of hemlocks and anchored in the center by a World War II memorial. The green also contained four benches facing the memorial and, in the spring, a showy bed of pansies, which one faction claimed was the official town flower.

Directly to the left of the green was the town hall, and next to that, the First Baptist Church. Set into the center of its own display of shrubs and flowers on the front bank was a wayside pulpit permanently bearing the Scripture verse John 3:16, which the members long ago had agreed was the pivotal message of their faith.

To the right of the green, facing Lilac Road, was the once-imposing home of Miss Rose and Uncle Billy Watson, whose overgrown yard currently contained two chrome dinette chairs which they used while watching traffic circle the monument.

Visitors who walked the two-block stretch of the main business district were always surprised to find the shops spaced so far apart, owing to garden plots that flourished between the buildings. In the loamy, neatly edged beds were wooden signs:

Garden Courtesy of Joe's Barber Shop, Upstairs to Right

Take Time to Smell the Roses, Courtesy Oxford Antiques

A Reader's Garden, Courtesy Happy Endings Bookstore

"Mitford," observed a travel feature by a prominent newspaper, "is a village delightfully out of step with contemporary America. Here, where streets are named for flowers, and villagers can seek the shade of a dozen fragrant rose arbors, spring finds most of the citizenry, including merchants, making gardens.

". . . and while Mitford's turn-of-the-century charm and beauty attract visitors like bees to honeysuckle, the town makes a conscious effort to discourage serious tourism.

" 'We want people to come and visit,' says Mayor Esther Cunningham, 'but we're not real interested in having them stick around. The college town of Wesley, just fifteen miles away, is perfect for that. They've got the inns and guest houses and all. Mitford would simply like to be the pause that refreshes.' "

Going south on Main Street to Wisteria Lane were the post office, the library, a bank, the bookstore, Winnie Ivey's Sweet Stuff Bakery, and a new shop for men's furnishings.

There was also a grocery store, so well-known for its fresh poultry and produce from local sources that most people simply called it The Local. For thirty-six years, The Local had provided chickens, rabbits, sausage, hams, butter, cakes, pies, free-range eggs, jams, and jellies from a farming community in the valley, along with vegetables and berries in season. In summer, produce bins on the sidewalk under the green awnings were filled each day with Silver Queen corn in the shuck. And in July, pails of fat blackberries were displayed in the cooler case.

To the left of Main Street, Wisteria Lane meandered

past the Episcopal rectory, whose back door looked upon the green seclusion of Baxter Park, and then climbed the hill to the Presbyterians.

To the right of Main, Wisteria led only to Wesley Chapel, a tiny Methodist church that stood along the creek bank in a grove of pink laurel and was known for the sweetness of its pealing bells.

The second and only other business block of Main Street was lined with a hardware store, a tea shop, a florist, an Irish woolen shop, and an antique shop, with gardens in between.

Next, Main was crossed by Old Church Lane, rising steeply on the left to Church Hill Drive, where the ruined foundation of Mitford's first Episcopal church stood in the tall grass of the upland meadow near Miss Sadie Baxter's Fernbank.

At the opposite end of the lane was Lord's Chapel, which stood between two vacant lots. After passing the church, which was noted for its fine Norman tower and showy gardens, the lane narrowed to a few comfortable houses on the bank of a rushing stream, where Indian Pipes were said to grow in profusion.

As the streets and lanes gave way to countryside and sloped toward the deeper valley, the rolling farmland began. Here, pastures were stocked with Herefords and Guernseys; lakes were filled with trout and brim; barnyards succored chattering guineas. And everywhere, in town or out, was the rich, black loam that made the earthworm's toil one of unending satisfaction.

❧

On rare occasions, and for no special reason he could think of, he imagined he was sitting by the fire in the study, in the company of a companionable wife.

He would be reading, and she would be sitting across from him in a wing chair.

In this idyll, he could not see her face, but he knew it had a girlish sweetness, and she was always knitting. Knitting, he thought, was a comfort to the soul. It was regular. It was repetitious. And, in the end, it amounted to something.

In this dream, there was always a delectable surprise on the table next to his chair, and nearly always it was a piece of pie. In his bachelor's heart of hearts, he loved pie with an intensity that alarmed him. Yet, when he was offered seconds, he usually refused. "Wouldn't you like another piece of this nice coconut pie, Father?" he might be asked. "No, I don't believe I'd care for any more," he'd say. An outright lie!

In this imaginary fireside setting, he would not talk much, he thought. But now and then, he might speak of church matters, read Blake or Wordsworth aloud, and try a sermon outline on his companion.

That would be a luxury far greater than any home-made sweet—to have someone listen to his outline and nod encouragement or, even, for heaven's sake, disagree.

Sometimes he shared an outline or argument with his close friend Hal Owen, the country vet. But in the main, he found that a man must hammer out his theology alone.

He was musing on this one evening, shortly after he'd been to the garage to give the black dog its supper, when he was surprised by a loud, groaning yawn from the vicinity of his own stockinged feet.

He was astounded to see the maverick dog lying next to his chair, gazing up at him.

"Blast!" he exclaimed. "I must have left the garage door open."

The usually gregarious dog not only appeared thoughtfully serene, but looked at him with an air of earnest understanding. How odd that the brown eyes of his companion were not unlike those of an old church warden he'd known as a young priest.

Feeling encouraged, he picked up a volume of Wordsworth from the table by his elbow.

" 'It is a beauteous evening, calm and free,' " he read aloud.

> *The holy time is quiet as a nun*
> *Breathless with adoration; the broad sun*
> *Is sinking down in its tranquillity;*
> *The gentleness of heaven broods o'er the sea:*
> *Listen! the mighty Being is awake,*
> *And doth with his eternal motion make*
> *A sound like thunder, everlastingly.*

The dog appeared to listen with deep interest. And when the rector finished reading the poem Wordsworth wrote for his young daughter, he moved happily along to an essay.

" 'Life and the world,' " it began without pretension, " 'are astonishing things.' "

"No doubt about it," he muttered, as the dog moved closer to his feet.

Barnabas! he thought. That had been the old warden's name. "Barnabas," he said aloud in the still, lamplit room.

His companion raised his head, alert and expectant.

"Barnabas?" The dog seemed to blink in agreement, as the rector reached down and patted his head.

"Barnabas, then!" he said, with all the authority of the pulpit. The matter was settled, once and for all.

As he rose to put out the lights in the study, Barnabas got up also, revealing a sight which caused the rector to groan. There, on the worn Aubusson carpet, lay his favorite leather slippers of twenty years, chewed through to the sole.

※

"A puppy," pronounced Hal Owen, lighting his pipe. "Not fully grown."

"How much bigger, do you think? This much?" Father Tim extended his hands and indicated a small distance between them.

Hal Owen grinned and shook his head.

"This much?" He held his hands even farther apart.

"Umhmm. About that much," said Hal.

Barnabas had settled in the corner by the rector's desk and was happily banging his tail against the floor.

Hal studied him with sober concentration as he puffed on his pipe. "A trace of sheep dog, looks like. A wide streak of Irish wolfhound. But mostly Bouvier, I'd say."

The rector sighed heavily.

"He'll be good for you, Tim. A man needs someone to talk to, someone to entertain his complaints and approve his foolishness. As far as background goes, I like what E. B. White said: 'A really companionable and indispensable dog is an accident of nature. You can't get it by breeding for it and you can't buy it with money. It just happens along.' "

"Well, he does like eighteenth-century poetry."

"See there?" Hal put on his tweed cap. "You bring Barnabas out to Meadowgate, and we'll give him a good run through the fields. Oh, and Marge will bake you a chicken pie. How would that suit you?"

It suited him more than he could express.

"I'm out of here. Have to check the teeth on Tommy McGee's horses and look up the rear of Harold Newland's heifer."

"I wouldn't want to trade callings with you, my friend."

"Nor I with you," said the vet, amiably.

"Ah . . . what exactly shall I feed him?"

"Money," said Hal, without any hesitation. "Just toss it in there twice a day, and he'll burn it like a stove."

"That's what I was afraid of."

"Tell you what. I'll let you have his food in bulk, good stuff. It'll hardly cost you a thing. About like keeping a house cat."

"May the Lord bless you."

"Thank you, Tim, I can use it."

"May he cause his face to shine upon you!" he added with fervor.

"That would be appreciated," said Hal, pulling on his gloves. "I'll even see to his shots in a day or two."

Just then, they heard the sound of Emma Garrett's sensible shoes approaching the office door. And so did Barnabas.

With astonishing agility, he leapt over the rector's desk chair, skidded to the door on the Persian prayer rug, and stood on his hind legs, preparing to greet Emma.

❧

"The Altar Guild is helpin' plant pansies on the town medium today," said Emma, as he came in with Barnabas on a new red leash.

"Median, Emma, median."

"Medium," she said, brightly, "and they wondered if

you could come out there after while and direct the colors." It certainly wasn't that the Altar Guild couldn't direct the colors themselves, she thought. But he had gone so far as to win some prizes for his gardening skills and had been written up in a magazine put out by the electric co-op.

He noticed Emma was clearly pretending that Barnabas did not exist, which was hard to do in an office with room for only two desks, two chairs, a visitor's bench, four coat pegs, and a communal wastebasket.

"What do you mean, direct the colors?" he asked, sorting through his phone messages.

"Well, you know. Do the yellow ones go in the middle or around the edges or what? And where do you put the blue? Not next to the purple!" she said with conviction.

"I'll take care of it."

She peered at him over her glasses. "You look handsome with that tan, I must say."

"And thank you for saying it. Compared to a golfer's tan, a gardener's tan is not quite so distinguished, but it has its merits. For example, you do not have to wear chartreuse golf pants in order to get it."

Emma howled with laughter. If there was anything she liked, it was a laugh. And frankly, while he was good for a great many things, her rector was not always good for a laugh.

"You don't look as fagged out as you looked there for a while. I thought we'd have to scrape you off the floor a time or two."

"Spring, Emma. It medicates the bones and revives the spirit."

"Well, let's just hope it lasts," she said, eyeing him as if he were a boiled potato.

She went back to posting Sunday's checks. "It rags me good that Petrey Bostic never catches up his pledge," she grumbled.

"You know I don't want to hear that. I don't want to look out in the congregation and see dollar signs instead of souls."

"You know what I think?"

He didn't know.

"I think you live in an ivory tower. It seems to me you'd want to know the nitty gritty of what goes on. You take the Baptists; they keep up with everything."

Emma liked to talk about the Baptists, having previously been one. "Is that so?" he said mildly.

"What comes in, what goes out, who shot Lizzie. You name it, they like to know it."

"Aha," he said. Ever since she got red hair, she had been living up to it.

He turned to his old Royal manual and typed with his forefingers:

> *Dear Walter, thnx yr letter dated march 12. garden going in, through still cold and much rain. preparations for holy week in full swing.*
>
> *hope yr spirits improved. know that He will lead you to right decision. ps. 32:8 promises: i will instruct you and teach you in the way which you shall go: i will guide you with my eye. never doubt it!*
>
> *ever yr fond cousin.*
>
> *p.s. hope to see you this summer. lv to katherine. i keep you always in my prayers.*

As he looked up from the cryptic message to his first cousin and boyhood friend, he saw it had started to rain. All morning, the fog had hung about the village as thick as soup in a bowl, causing him once again to consider buying one of those orange slickers so he could be seen walking in the fog.

"You don't drive a car?" his former bishop once asked, incredulous. Well, and why should he, after all? The rectory was two minutes from the office and less than three from the church. The hospital was only a few blocks away, and one of the finest grocery stores in existence was right across the street.

The old gospel preacher Vance Havner had written about that very thing: "This is the day of the motorist, and anyone who walks is viewed with suspicion. You see a man coming down the road now, just meditating, and you figure he's either out of his head or out of gas. It's such a rarity that dogs bark as though they'd seen a ghost."

Making his rounds on foot kept him fit and positive, if not altogether trim. And, if push came to shove, he could always get the battery charged on his Buick Riviera, back it out of the garage, and go.

Actually, he'd been thinking seriously of getting a bicycle. Only now, there was Barnabas. And a rector in a clerical collar on a bicycle, leading a great, black dog on a red leash? Well, there was no way to bring it off that he could see.

"Peedaddle!" said Emma, as she made an error in her bookkeeping.

Barnabas leaped up and bounded to her desk, where he put his paws on the ledger, leaned over, and fogged her glasses.

"My God!" she exclaimed.

Why was she always saying My God! in a way that had nothing whatever to do with her God? He caught Barnabas by the collar and dragged him into the corner next to his chair.

"I'm tellin' you the truth," Emma said, squinting as she wiped her glasses, "it's goin' to be either him or me." She grabbed her sandwich bag and put it in her desk, slamming the drawer shut.

"Lie down!" he commanded. Barnabas stood and wagged his tail.

"Stay!" he said, as Barnabas ambled to the door and sniffed it.

"Then, sit!" Barnabas went to his water dish and took a long drink.

"Whatever," he muttered, unable to look at Emma.

He sat down and turned to the Gospel reading for Sunday. As he prepared to practice reading it aloud, which was his custom, he cleared his throat.

Barnabas appeared to take that as a signal to stand by his master's chair and place his front paws on his shoulder, giving a generous lick to the Bible for good measure.

He had just read that ignoring negative behavior and praising the positive could be a fruitful strategy. "Whatever you do," the article had implored, "do not look your dog in the eye if you want to discourage his attentions."

" 'And as Jesus passed by,' " intoned the rector, avoiding the doleful stare, " 'he saw a man which was blind from his birth. And his disciples asked him, saying, "Master, who did sin, this man, or his parents, that he was born blind?" ' "

Barnabas sighed and lay down.

He continued, without glancing into the corner: " 'Jesus answered, "Neither hath this man sinned, nor his parents: but that the works of his God should be made manifest in him." ' "

He read aloud through verse five. Then, he stopped and studied Barnabas with some concentration.

"Well, now," he said at last, "this is extraordinary."

"What's that?" asked Emma.

"This dog appears to be . . . ," he cleared his throat, ". . . ah, controlled by Scripture."

"No way!" she said with disgust. "That dog is not controlled by anything!"

Just then, the door opened, and Miss Sadie Baxter helped prove the odd suspicion.

Before she could speak, Barnabas had bounded across the room to extend his finest greeting, whereupon the rector shouted what came immediately to mind, and what Peter had told the multitude:

" 'Repent and be baptized, every one of you!' "

Barnabas sprawled on the floor and sighed with contentment.

"I *was* baptized, thank you," said Miss Sadie, removing her rain hat.

CHAPTER TWO

A Dubious Gift

Miss Sadie Baxter was the last surviving member of one of Mitford's oldest families.

At the age of eighty-six, she occupied the largest house in the village, with the most sweeping view. And she owned the most land, much of it given over to an aged but productive apple orchard. In fact, the village cooks said that the best pies weren't made of Granny Smiths, but of the firm, slightly tart Sadie Baxters, as they'd come to be called.

As far as anyone knew, Miss Sadie had never given away any of the money her father had earned in his lumber operation in the valley. But she dearly loved to give away apples—by the sack, by the peck, by the bushel. Clearly, the only serious maintenance she'd done around Fernbank in recent years was in the orchards, for as anyone could see from the road, the roof that showed itself above the trees was in urgent need of repair. Some said she sat in her living room, surrounded by a regiment of buckets when it rained, and that the sound of it drumming into the pails was so loud you couldn't hear yourself think.

It was, in fact, pouring when she stopped to visit her rector on Tuesday morning. "Mercy!" she said, shaking out her rain hat. "What a day for ducks!"

Father Tim hurried to help with her raincoat and kiss her damp cheek. "What in heaven's name are you doing out in this deluge?"

"You know weather never keeps me in!" she said in a voice as fresh as a girl's.

It was true. Everyone knew that Sadie Baxter would come down the hill in her 1958 Plymouth in a heart-beat—no matter what the weather. Ice, however, was a different story. "You can't predict it," she'd say, "and I dearly love the predictable." So, on icy days, she read, played the piano, sorted through the family picture albums, or called Louella, her former maid and companion, who now lived with her grandson in Marietta, Georgia.

Father Tim could see that Miss Sadie had driven up on the sidewalk, as usual, and parked her car so close to the steps that if he opened the office door all the way, he'd take the paint off her fender.

"Sit down," Emma said, "and have some coffee."

"You know how I like it," she said, settling in for a visit. "Well! Guess what?"

"I give up," said the rector.

"I weigh exactly the same as my age!"

"No!" exclaimed Emma.

"Yes, indeed. I went to see Hoppy for a checkup and I tip the scales at exactly eighty-six pounds. Have you ever?"

"Never!" said Father Tim.

"And you know what else?" she inquired, sitting on the edge of the visitor's bench like a schoolgirl.

"What's that?" he asked.

"Louella is coming to see me for Easter. Her grandson is driving her up here all the way from Marietta! I certainly wouldn't ask her to do the cooking—she's a guest! So I thought we'd just have frozen chicken pies. Don't you think that would be all right, Emma?"

"Why, sure it would. And maybe some fruit cocktail with Jell-O."

"Good idea! And some tea. I can still make tea. Louella likes it real sweet. And let's see, what else?"

Emma thought, tapping her pen on the typewriter. "Ummm . . ."

"Tell you what," said Father Tim, "I'll bake you a ham."

"You would? Oh, Father, that would be so . . . why, bless your heart."

"Don't even mention it!" he said, feeling his heart blessed already.

"Now that's settled, you'll never guess what else, so I'm going to tell you. Yesterday, I didn't go out of the house at all. Why, I hate to say this, but I never even got dressed, isn't that awful? Just went around in my wrapper all the livelong day, my mama would faint. And first thing you know, I was poking around in the attic, looking for an old baby doll I was thinking about, a baby doll that must be eighty years old if she's a day. But we never threw anything away, so I just knew I'd find it. Oh, the dust! Why, I kicked up a regular dust storm!

"And hats! Oh, mercy, the hats I found, why there was a slew of my mama's beautiful hats. I'm going to bring the whole lot to Sunday school one morning and let the children try them on. Would that be too sacrilegious?"

He laughed. "Certainly not!"

"So, then I got to looking for an old picture of Papa, the one with his handlebar mustache, and I was crawling around in there, back in that place where we always kept pictures standing up in little racks, and I was pulling this one out and that one, and the first thing you know, well . . ." Miss Sadie paused and looked at them intently.

"Well, what?" Emma said, leaning forward.

"Well, there was this old painting of the Blessed Virgin and the baby Jesus, that Papa brought back from overseas."

"Aha!" said Father Tim.

"And I want you to have it for the church, Father," she said, "to hang on the wall."

This could be perilous. He remembered two or three other gifts to the church that had caused the widest consternation. One was a mounted moose head, said by the donor to be one of God's creatures, after all, and therefore fit for the parish house wall, if not the nave.

"Maybe I could come up to Fernbank and look at it one day, and we could just, ah, take it from there."

"Oh, no. No need to do that, Father, I've brought it with me. If you'd just step out to the car . . ."

"It's raining cats and dogs, Miss Sadie."

"Oh, I know, so I wrapped it up in a sheet, and then I wrapped that up in some plastic, and I tied it all with a string!"

He found that he was able to open his office door exactly halfway without scraping it on the green Plymouth. Then he maneuvered an umbrella ahead of him, released it outside the door, moved sideways out of the room, drew the umbrella over his head to the drumming sound of a pouring rain, opened her rear car door, and leaned across the seat to pick the heavy painting up with his right hand while holding the umbrella with his left.

He managed to grasp the painting under his arm, shove the car door closed with the heel of his drenched shoe, push open the office door with the toe of the same shoe, then slip the painting through the door ahead of him, lower the umbrella, squeeze through the narrow opening, and stand dripping on the carpet.

"There!" said Miss Sadie with delight, as if she had just fetched the parcel herself.

He leaned the heavy bundle against the wall, quite spent.

"If you have a scissors, Emma, I'll do the honors." Miss Sadie pushed up the sleeves of her cardigan and addressed herself to cutting through several layers of string, cloth, and plastic.

"All right, now," she said, "you look the other way, and I'll say when."

The rector turned and looked out the window behind his desk, and mopped his rain-soaked face and hands with a handkerchief. Emma stoically faced the door to the bathroom, which displayed a bulletin board of parish notices.

Get a move on, thought Emma, who had to coordinate memorials for Easter flowers.

"Now!" Miss Sadie cried.

He turned around and beheld a sight that stunned him.

The painting, in a wide, gilded frame with elaborate carving, was a rosy-hued depiction of mother and child that fairly glowed, even under years of dirt and grime. A faint halo appeared around the infant's head, and the mother looked upon the child in her arms with a wistful tenderness. In the background, moving away from the blue and gold of her gown, was a landscape with a bright stream flowing through open countryside, and above this, a sky that blushed with the platinum, rose, and lavender of an early morning sun.

"Well, now," he said, feeling a sudden desire to cross himself. "This is quite . . . quite beautiful. I wasn't expecting . . ."

"Then you like it?" Miss Sadie's eyes were dancing.

"Like it? I like it enormously! It's a lovely thing to see."

"I cleaned it up," Miss Sadie told him. "Lemon Pledge."

He squatted down for a closer look. "Any name anywhere? Do we know who did it?"

"No sign of a name. I got out my magnifying glass and went all over it, front and back."

The office door swung open suddenly, bringing in a gust of rain and Harry Nelson in a dripping slicker.

"Occupancy by more than three persons is unlawful," Emma said with ill humor. She could hardly bear the sight of the senior warden, and especially not in a wet slicker that was already soaking the thin carpet.

"If we ever get some real money in this place, we'll knock these walls out and add you a thousand square feet," he said with satisfaction.

Over my dead body, thought the rector, who loved the diminutive stone building that the parish had erected in 1879.

Harry Nelson deposited his slicker in the corner, helped himself to a cup of coffee, and joined Miss Sadie on the visitor's bench.

"Okay, Father, here's the scoop. We've looked into it, and it's goin' to make a bloody mess of the sanctuary to tear that cabinet out of there."

As Father Tim and Harry Nelson talked church matters, Emma and Miss Sadie talked Easter dinner. Emma was actually going to bake cloverleaf yeast rolls from scratch, which she hadn't done since Charlie died ten years ago. And Miss Sadie decided she would serve Louella and her grandson on the sunporch, if the weather turned off nice.

"Well, well, well, what's this?" Harry wanted to know, peering at the painting.

"Miss Sadie is making a gift to Lord's Chapel," Father Tim said proudly.

Harry bent over to look closer. As Emma was seated directly behind him, it afforded her such an intriguing idea that she was nearly breathless.

Harry whistled with appreciation. "This looks mighty like a Vermeer to me," he informed the group.

"Why, Harry Nelson, I didn't know you were familiar with Vermeer," said Miss Sadie.

"Familiar! Why, I reckon I am! Shirley and I've had all kinds of classes in art appreciation. Did you know there's only thirty-five Vermeers in the world, except for some Dutchman in the last century who forged a whole bunch of 'em? Baked 'em in the oven to make 'em look like the real thing."

He took his glasses off and squinted at the painting. "Is there a signature on here anywhere?"

"Not that we've been able to find," the rector said.

"If this isn't the real thing, I'll eat my hat. Shoot, I hear that even the fakes bring a bundle. Tell you what, I have a friend who appraises this stuff, I'll just ask him to drive up from Charlotte and take a look. He says some of the biggest art finds in history have come out of somebody's attic."

"That's where it came from, all right," Miss Sadie confessed.

"Well, let me get on the road. I've got to go over the mountain to see some customers. Boys howdy, this coffee'll curl your hair."

"Ah, Harry, about that appraiser, I don't know that this is what we need to do just now. I think we should wait on that."

"Wait? Wait was what broke the camel's back!" Harry grabbed his slicker off the peg, threw it over his head, squeezed out the door, and called behind him, "Miss Sadie, you should have just drove this Plymouth on in the door."

For some reason he couldn't explain, the rector found Harry's plan to involve an appraiser oddly unwelcome. Yet, something even less welcome occurred at noon.

While he waited with eager anticipation for his usual rainy-day share of cream-filled Little Debbies from Emma's paper bag lunch, she said nonchalantly, "Little Debbies? I've given 'em up for Lent."

❧

He had just walked in the door and taken off the tweed cap Hal Owen gave him, when Percy Mosely turned around from the grill and winked. Then, he went back to frying his sausage.

That was odd, thought Father Tim, sitting down at his favorite booth and opening his newspaper. "Percy," he said, "I believe I'll have two over easy this morning."

Velma came to the booth and stood there, grinning. "Gonna celebrate, are you? I'd have two eggs myself, if it wasn't for my cholesterol."

Cholesterol, cholesterol, thought Father Tim. He'd heard more than enough about cholesterol. It was as bad as the Hula Hoop craze.

Velma poured his coffee. He had traveled to many

conferences, retreats, seminars, and workshops, and right here was the best cup of coffee he'd ever had. "What do you mean, celebrate?"

"Well, celebrate over all that money you'll be gettin' down at th' chapel."

"What money is that?" asked Father Tim, dumbfounded.

"That art money. Why, I heard you had a painting over there worth two hundred thousand dollars."

He had just taken a mouthful of coffee and deeply regretted spitting it down the front of his shirt.

"Now, look at you!" said Velma, helping him clean up.

"Velma, whatever you've heard is absolutely untrue. Someone donated a painting to the church and we haven't even had it appraised. It's just a nice painting, that's all."

"We heard it was a Veneer," said Percy, yelling from the grill.

"Yep, that's what we heard," agreed Mule Skinner, who sold real estate around town.

Blast! he thought, completely losing his appetite.

❧

Miss Sadie had delivered the painting on Tuesday. By the end of the day on Thursday, he had received an unprecedented number of calls. Even Emma, who had the day off, called.

In the Grill at eight o'clock, the figure had been two hundred thousand. By three in the afternoon, he had a call from an architect who wanted to submit plans for an addition to the church, and congratulated him on the million dollars Lord's Chapel would be getting from the sale of the old master. At three-thirty, the village newspaper called for a statement.

By four, his stomach felt painful and empty. Bleeding ulcer! he reasoned darkly.

He put the answering machine on, and left.

At five after four, Walter got this message: "Persevere in prayer, with mind awake and thankful heart. This is the office of The Lord's Chapel. Please leave a message at the sound of the tone."

That evening, Father Tim took the phone off the hook, gave Barnabas what was almost certainly his first bath, made a dinner of broiled chicken and packaged spinach souffle, had a glass of sherry, and went to bed.

What if the painting really were a Vermeer? He didn't know much about art, but he did know the work had a certain power, a vitality he hadn't found in just every depiction of the Blessed Virgin and child.

He also knew the turmoil that would ensue if they were actually in possession of such a priceless work. Hadn't he had enough headaches over the seventeenth-century tapestry hanging in the nave? Just getting it insured had been a process that took months, endless costly phone calls, and sleepless nights. In the end, they'd been forced to keep the church doors locked, a thing he roundly despised.

The bottom line, however, was pretty simple. God would, indeed, be faithful to instruct and guide. As the evening progressed, he grew confident that he'd be led to act in the interest of all concerned.

On the way to the church office the next morning, there was a quickness in his step. Of course, he must never tell a soul. But last night, for the first time in his life, he had allowed a dog to sleep on the foot of his bed. And he'd found it an incomparably satisfactory experience.

"There!" said Emma, plunking a box of Little Debbies on his desk. "You weren't the one who gave these up for Lent. You can have my supply." She wondered what he did give up for Lent, anyway, but didn't think it was proper to ask.

He put the box in his top right desk drawer. "You," he said with feeling, "are a pearl above price."

"What happened?"

"It was a landmark day. Petrey Bostick called to say we ought to use part of the money to put air-conditioning in the church."

Emma rolled her eyes. That old business. What was the point of living at an elevation of 5,000 feet if you had to install air-conditioning? Every year, people got lathered up about air-conditioning.

In the course of the morning, a real estate agent called to suggest they buy the property on either side of the churchyard, which would quietly be made available, if they were interested. The rector was not surprised that the price had gone up fifty percent since the vestry made an inquiry just two years ago.

The newspaper called to ask if they could photograph the painting with Miss Sadie standing on one side and Father Tim on the other. The appraiser called and said he'd be there Monday at 9:30. And, they heard that the vestry had scheduled a meeting to discuss the purchase of a steel columbarium painted to look like walnut, brass collection plates instead of the traditional Lord's Chapel baskets, and a floor-to-ceiling stained-glass window for the narthex.

After two parishioners called to remind him of the hungry around the world, another dropped by to remind him of the hungry here at home.

During a lull, he turned to Emma and said simply, "We must not let this destroy the joy of Easter."

"Amen," she said with conviction.

There was only one problem. He couldn't figure out how to prevent that from happening.

❧

A Canadian cold front was sending streams of icy air along the ridges and into the coves surrounding Mitford.

After walking Barnabas through Baxter Park, attending to his hospital rounds, and counseling a parishioner over breakfast at the Grill, he was profoundly ready for a peaceful time at his desk. Now he needed to catch up the loose strings of the two approaching Easter services. Perhaps he could do this, he thought, after the appraiser's visit at nine-thirty. If he had any lingering anxiety about the outcome of the painting's appraisal, he was blessedly unaware of it.

He saw Winnie Ivey sweeping the sidewalk in front of her Sweet Stuff Bakery, as she did each and every morning. It was one of the sights he liked most to see: someone putting their affairs in order.

"Good morning, Winnie!"

Winnie was bundled warmly. He could see only plump cheeks and bright eyes above her scarf. "Father, I'm glad to catch you! I saved yesterday's napoleons just for you!"

Hoppy had recently warned him, "Stay away from that stuff, pal. Carry raisins in your pocket." Raisins, indeed. Worse yet, he'd recently overheard someone refer to him as "that portly priest at Lord's Chapel."

"Winnie," he said, following her inside and taking a deep breath of the cinnamon-scented air, "Hoppy tells me I've got to go easy on sweets."

"He's been telling me that for years, and I sure do

wish I could mind him," she said affably, removing three napoleons from the case.

"Maybe you could give those to Miss Rose and Uncle Billy when they come in."

"Oh, don't you worry about that! They get yesterday's oatmeal cookies. Good fiber, you know."

He wondered why he felt helpless as she handed him the paper bag and patted his arm.

In case Hoppy should drive by on his way to the hospital, he carefully stuffed the bag into his coat pocket. He would not eat one bite, he told himself, not even one. They would go immediately to Emma, who could make her own peace with the seductive charm of Winnie Ivey's napoleons.

As he came within sight of his office, he was startled to see a small group waiting at the door. It appeared to be Harry Nelson, Bud Simmons, and Maude Beatty. Also, two cars were parked at the sidewalk, with their motors running.

He felt a reckless desire to step behind a laurel bush and eat the entire contents of the bag in his pocket.

❧

He was relieved that he'd left Barnabas sleeping in the garage, for the crowd had literally packed the office. He opened the bathroom door, which made room for two, shoved the communal wastebasket under his desk, which made room for another, and let the rest of the group shift for itself.

"Father," Harry said sheepishly, "I know you didn't expect such a big whang-do here this mornin', but we thought the vestry ought to see what this appraiser fellow has to say."

"As you can see, Harry, there's no room left for the appraiser to get in here and say anything."

Harry laughed weakly and stood closer to the wall.

The rector turned on the electric heater, then went about his coffee making. "With patience, forbearing one another in love," he reminded himself. Funny how his morning readings often went out to greet the circumstances of the day.

In a few minutes, the smell of coffee filled the little room and began to warm the hearts of the entire assembly. But since the pot only made four cups, and there were seven people, he proceeded cautiously with the pouring.

Emma opened the front door with a glower and squeezed inside. She did not like cold spring mornings, dimly feeling they were some sort of betrayal.

"Oh, for God's sake!" she said, seeing that Maude Beatty was sitting in her chair like she owned it.

The appraiser arrived at nine-thirty sharp, removed his coat, handed it to Harry Nelson, and went straight to work.

He hummed vaguely to himself and clicked his teeth. No one spoke.

"Hmmmm," he said occasionally.

He took out a magnifying glass and went over every inch of the canvas, which he had propped against a stack of books on the rector's desk.

Then he opened a small black box and removed a pair of pliers and a hammer. "Looking for a signature," he informed the fascinated onlookers.

In a moment, the frame was off, and the appraiser was holding the canvas up to the natural light. "Hmm," he said.

Father Tim thought it a wonderful thing that a man

could say only "Hmm," and gain the fixed attention of an entire roomful of people. Even his pithiest sermons failed to accomplish this.

"Use your bathroom?" asked the appraiser. The two vestry members moved out of the minuscule room, which was scarcely the size of a cupboard, and flattened themselves against Harry Nelson.

The appraiser took the canvas under one arm and went in, searching the walls and baseboards. "Got an outlet in here?"

"You'll have to unplug the heater," said Emma, testily. Why in God's name was Bud Simmons sitting on the recipes she'd torn out of *Southern Living* and put on her desk, was he blind?

The appraiser shut the bathroom door, and everyone looked around with faint smiles.

If there was anything Harry Nelson didn't like, it was a nervous silence. "Did you hear the one about the funeral procession?" he wanted to know.

Oh my aching back, thought Emma.

"Well, this funeral procession was goin' up the hill to the church and the back door of the hearse flew open and out shoots the casket and blametty blam, down the hill it goes through the intersection with horns blowin' and people dodgin' out of the way, and it runs on down the street and jumps up on the sidewalk and busts in through the pharmacy door and shoots down the aisle to the druggist and the lid pops up and this guy sits up and says: 'Got anything to stop this coffin?' "

I wouldn't laugh if my life depended on it, Emma thought, as the appraiser came out of the bathroom.

"This may be a Vermeer," he said dryly. A little gasp went up.

"And then again, it may not. I feel reasonably confident that it could have been painted during the mid-to-late seventeenth century, by any one of a dozen people working under Vermeer's influence.

"There is no signature that I can find and no evidence of restoration. I recommend that the canvas be shipped at once to New York, to a team of experts who can research the matter fully and apply more scholarship than I am able to provide."

The appraiser had finished his report. In fact, he didn't even wait for a response from the astonished gathering, but began to repack his tool box and wind up the cord of his black light.

A murmur ran through the group. Bud Simmons got up, scattering recipes to the floor, and spoke in a low voice to Harry Nelson. The others waited.

"We think it ought to be sent to New York," Harry said, considerably louder than was necessary in the small room.

"Agreed!" said Lester Shumaker, looking around for support.

The appraiser produced a sheaf of papers and had Harry Nelson sign every one. Then, he put on his coat and muffler, wrapped the painting in bubble plastic, slipped it into a large sack, picked up his tool box, bowed briefly from the waist, and was gone.

In a few minutes, so were the others.

"Emma," said the rector, with a trace of weariness, "let's have another pot of coffee."

"Great!" said Emma, who, on those rare occasions when he wanted a second pot, considered it a small celebration.

He looked at the visitor's bench. There, propped against the wall just under the coat pegs, was the empty frame.

He squeezed by Emma, who was measuring out the Maxwell House, and took the frame into the bathroom. It fit perfectly behind the shower stall.

"There!" he said with satisfaction. "Out of sight, out of mind."

At eleven o'clock, he had a welcome phone call.

"Tim, Hal here. I heard what's going on with the painting, and in case you're feeling sick and tired of the whole thing, I'd like to give you a prescription."

He didn't know how he felt about receiving medical care from a vet.

"Here it is: be ready at eight o'clock in the morning and I'll pick you and Barnabas up in the truck. We'll spend the day at Meadowgate, chasing rabbits and looking for woodchucks. For supper, Marge'll make a big chicken pie, and I'll bring you back in time to get your beauty sleep for church on Sunday."

If he had gotten a call to say he'd won the lottery, he couldn't have been happier. Thank heaven he'd worked all week on his sermon, thereby giving him the freedom of an entire Saturday.

He drank two full mugs of coffee, which was unusual, with cream, which was even more unusual, and, according to Emma, spent the rest of the morning "chattering like a magpie."

❧

Meadowgate Farm was situated in one of the most beautiful valleys around Mitford. Just ten miles from the village, the land began to roll steeply, looking like the pictures he had seen of Scotland.

A flock of sheep grazed in one green pasture, across the fence from a herd of contented Guernseys. The white blossoms of wild bloodwort gleamed along the roadsides, and here and there the bank of an old farm-place was massed with creeping pink phlox.

You leadeth me beside still waters! he thought happily. You restoreth my soul!

It was a glorious morning, drenched with birdsong, and as they turned into the drive, a horde of farm dogs came bounding toward the red truck. There was Buckwheat, an English foxhound. Bowser, a chow. Baudelaire, a soulful dachshund. Bodacious, a Welsh corgi. And Bonemeal, a mixed-breed foundling who, as a puppy, had dug up the new tulip bulbs in order to eat the fertilizer.

The rector opened his door cautiously, and Barnabas dived into the barking throng. Was it possible his hearing could be permanently impaired? "Let 'em get acquainted," Hal said.

At the back door, Marge gave Father Tim a vigorous hug, which he returned with feeling.

"Tim! You've got your annual planting tan!"

"And you've got your perennial joie de vivre!"

In the center of the kitchen was a large pine table, bleached by age, with benches on either side. A Mason jar of early wildflowers sat in the center, along with a deep-dish apple pie, fresh from the oven. A dazzling beam of light fell through the windows that looked out to the stables.

Their guest stood transfixed. "A foretaste of heaven!" he said, feeling an instant freshness of spirit.

"Sit," said Marge, whose blonde hair was captured in a bandanna the color of her dress. "We'll start with freshly ground coffee and cinnamon stickies. Then, I've packed lunches, because I hear you guys are going tromping in the woods."

" 'Til we drop," promised Hal, lighting his pipe.

"Tim has some heavy-duty stress to contend with. Holy Week, two Easter services, a Vermeer, a new dog the size of a Buick, fourteen azaleas to get in the ground, and," he looked at Father Tim, "there must be something else."

"A bone spur in my left heel," he said, cheerfully.

At two-thirty, Marge rang the farm bell, and the men came at a trot across the early spring field with Barnabas, Bowser, and Buckwheat dashing ahead. The bell rang only for an emergency.

"Trissie Steven's pony. Caught in a barbed wire fence. Bleeding badly," Marge said in the telegraphic way she had of communicating urgent news to her husband.

"Want to come or stay, Tim? Your call."

"Oh, stay!" said Marge. "We haven't had a good visit in a hundred years. Besides, you've been talking man talk all day. Let's talk peonies and rose bushes, for heaven's sake."

His breathing was ragged from the trot across the field. "Well," he said, lamely, thinking of downing a glass of Marge's sweetened iced tea.

"I'm off," Hal said, kissing his wife on the cheek.

Marge cleared the remains of the pastry she'd rolled out for the pie, while the chicken simmered on the stove. "Sit down and talk to me while I finish up. The tea's in the pitcher, and fresh peppermint. A few shoots are already out; that tall grass by the garden shed kept it protected over the winter."

He poured the tea, got ice from the refrigerator, and sat down in the rocking chair that had belonged to Marge's father.

It was balm to his soul to sit in this beamed, high-ceilinged room, with its wonderful smells and golden, heart-of-pine floors. At Meadowgate Farm, he mused, nothing terribly dramatic ever seemed to happen. Life appeared to flow along sweetly, without many surprises or obstacles to overcome.

Marge sat down on the window seat, and tucked her hair into the bandanna. He thought she looked unusually bright, radiant.

"Did Hal tell you?"

"Tell me? Tell me what?"

Perhaps their Annie was getting engaged, he thought. Or maybe Hal had finally come across with their much-discussed vacation in France, to celebrate her fiftieth birthday.

"I'm pregnant," she said simply, wiping her hands on her apron.

❧

After dinner, which the rector pronounced "the finest yet," the men washed the dishes. Then they all gathered before a small fire on the kitchen hearth.

Hal and Marge sat on the slouchy, chintz-covered sofa, which the dogs usually favored, and held hands like sweethearts. Bowser and Baudelaire slept peacefully by the fire, and Barnabas slept with his head on his master's feet.

The rector lifted a glass of Hal's oldest port.

"To Marge, the bravest of the brave! May you be blessed with a child who is full of grace and merriment, and endowed with the countenance of its lovely mother."

"Thanks, but I'm not brave, at all. I'm scared silly. I keep thinking Hoppy will call and say, 'Ha, ha, just kidding. You can go back to your real life, now.' "

Barnabas gave a little dream bark.

"Chasing squirrels," said Hal. "You know, I think you've got yourself a fine dog, there. His character appears to reveal the wolfhound in him. There's an old story that says a wolfhound can tell by looking on a man's face whether his intentions are good or evil."

"A trait devoutly to be desired by the rest of us," said the rector, with a new pride in his companion.

"Read to us, Timothy. You'll have to be leaving in an hour or so, and you know how I covet a read before you go." Marge fluffed up the pillow behind her and leaned cozily against her husband's shoulder.

She had put several books on the table next to his chair. "First come, first served," he said cheerfully, and opened a volume at random.

" 'Up! up! my Friend, and quit your books,' " he read from Wordsworth, " 'Or surely you'll grow double: Up! up! my Friend, and clear your looks; Why all this toil and trouble?' "

The sun, above the mountain's head, A freshening lustre mellow through all the long green fields has spread His first sweet evening yellow.

Books! 'tis a dull and endless strife: Come, hear the woodland linnet How sweet his music! on my life, there's more of wisdom in it.

As Father Tim read, Barnabas awoke, yawned, and began to listen with rapt attention.

Sweet is the lore which Nature brings our meddling intellect/mis-shapes the beauteous forms of things

we murder to dissect.
Enough of Science and of Art
Close up those barren leaves
come forth, and bring with you a heart
That watches and receives.

Barnabas sighed with what appeared to be satisfaction, and gazed at the reader as if waiting for more.

"Remarkable dog," said Hal.

CHAPTER THREE

New Possibilities

Much to his relief, little mention of the painting came to his ears during Holy Week.

Palm Sunday had been a blessing to the congregation, and on Maundy Thursday, he had truly experienced a deep and enriching mournfulness. On Good Friday he fasted, and on Holy Saturday felt much the better for it in every way.

Easter morning dawned bright and clear. "Dazzling to the senses!" said one parishioner. The beautiful old church was full for both services, and the tremor of joy that one always hoped for on this high day was decidedly there.

Perhaps one of the highest points, for him, had been looking out into the eleven o'clock congregation and seeing Miss Sadie sitting with Louella and her grandson. The countenances of all three were radiant, which created a special pool of light on the gospel side.

After church, Louella grabbed him and gave him a bosomy hug.

"That's some good ham you baked," she said. "We got into it las' night, with the Jell-O. An' Miss Sadie goin' to run it by us again today."

Hal and Marge were there, their good news shining in their eyes.

Emma wore a hat with a Bird of Paradise on one side and was proudly showing off her daughter from Atlanta. And Miss Rose and Uncle Billy, usually partial to the Presbyterians, attended their first service at Lord's Chapel.

He saw faces he'd never seen before, and would never see again, and faces that had become as familiar as his own. It had been a good twelve years in Mitford.

❧

During the days following Easter Sunday, he noticed a certain lassitude of spirit in himself. He would go to his back door and gaze at the azaleas, which he'd left sitting along the bank in their potting cans.

There was still a flat of pansies to be planted, and a dozen rare, pink day lilies.

But the joy he'd felt in gardening, only days before, seemed to have vanished. A letdown was to be expected after the intense activities of high holy days.

He went to the library at noon and sat, idly reading, wanting a nap, forgetting to have lunch. At last, he forced himself to check out the latest Dick Francis, a book on dog breeds, a volume of Voltaire, and Maeterlinck's *Intelligence of the Flowers*. He felt so exhausted from selecting the books that he did something entirely out of the ordinary: he phoned Emma to say he was going home.

"I'm calling Hoppy this minute," she said, alarmed.

"There's nothing to worry about in the least. I'm just a little tired, that's all. I expect to be there bright and early in the morning."

"Well, it's my day off, you know, but I'll come in at ten to check on you. I've found us a new kind of Little Debbies, and I'll bring you a box."

He couldn't summon the energy to argue with her. He also noted, vaguely, that her offer of one of his favorite sweets had no appeal.

By the time he reached the new men's store a block away, he regretted having checked out the books he was carrying, especially the Voltaire, which suddenly felt like the complete works.

❧

Miss Rose and Uncle Billy lived on Mitford's Main Street, in one room of a house that was variously called "a disgrace," "an eyesore," and "a crying shame."

The house had been built in the late 1920s by Miss Rose's brother, Willard Porter, who invented and sold pharmaceuticals.

His biggest seller, a chest rub, had added the second story, the wooden shutters with cut outs of a dove, a wrap-around porch, and a widow's walk. There was an ornate gazebo, large enough for dances, that had commemorated the success of a flavored lip balm. And four sculptured stone garden benches with carved angels' heads, sitting in what once was a majestic rose garden, had marked the debut of a cough syrup containing mountain herbs.

The house had historically been the pride of the village, sitting as it did on the edge of the old town green, across from the war monument, and displaying the finest architecture of its time.

In recent years, however, all that had changed. The stone benches with carved angels' heads were crumbling to dust. Many of the shutters lay in the grass where they had fallen. And Uncle Billy had nailed a *No Trespassing* sign on the widow's walk.

A decorator from Raleigh had often tried to buy the Porter place for a second home, thinking how spectacular it would be for parties. When all efforts to buy it through Mule Skinner had failed, she took it upon herself personally to visit Miss Rose and Uncle Billy, who were sitting in the backyard in two chrome dinette chairs, at a wooden spool previously used to roll up electrical wiring. They were eating bologna sandwiches and drinking iced tea from jelly glasses.

Miss Rose wiped her mouth on a threadbare t-shirt that said *I surfed Laguna Beach.*

"I'm Susan Parnell Phillips," the intruder informed them, with more eagerness than was necessary.

"This is Rose," said Uncle Billy, "and I'm the thorn."

At that, Uncle Billy grinned broadly, showing all three of his teeth, one of which was "covered with enough gold to reroof the house," as a neighbor once said.

Miss Rose glowered at the visitor. "I'm not selling."

"Selling? But how did you—I mean, what makes you think I'm buying?"

"I can always tell," Miss Rose snapped.

Recently, the new men's store had tried to buy the place. And so had a dozen others over the years. But Miss Rose stood her ground.

"Home is where the heart is," she said to one prospective buyer who knocked on their door in January and found her in a chenille robe, a World War II trench coat, a pair of rubber garden boots, a man's felt hat, and what appeared to be Uncle Billy's flannel pajama bottoms.

As far as the frozen caller could tell, there was no heat in the house. Being a caring soul, he inquired around and was told that the Presbyterian church had filled up Miss Rose's oil tank in November, and, on last inspection, it was still full.

Most people knew, too, that the old couple walked to Winnie Ivey's bake shop every afternoon, always hand in hand, to pick up what was left over. Winnie, however, was not one to give away the store. She carefully portioned out what she thought they would eat that night and the next morning, and no more. She didn't like the idea of Miss Rose feeding her perfectly good day-old Danish to the birds.

After their visit to the bake shop, Miss Rose and Uncle Billy, walking very slowly due to arthritis and a half-dozen other ailments, dropped by to see what Velma had left at the Main Street Grill.

Usually, it was a few slices of bacon and liver mush from breakfast, or a container of soup and a couple of hamburger rolls from lunch. Occasionally, she might add a little chicken salad that Percy had made, himself, that very morning.

On balance, it was said, Miss Rose and Uncle Billy fared pretty well in Mitford. And many were pleased to see that they provided for their spiritual nourishment, as well, by going to church on Sunday.

Recently, that very thing had been a matter for conversation around the village, since they'd been over to The Chapel of Our Lord and Savior, as it was properly called, four Sundays in a row, including Easter.

"Are you going to visit Miss Rose and Uncle Billy?"

Emma asked one morning as Father Tim came in with Barnabas.

He hung his hat on a peg. "Do I need to?"

"Well, you usually do go visit after somebody's been to church a few times."

"Yes, I'll do that. Soon. Remind me to do that."

"Don't eat anything while you're there," she warned. "They say Miss Rose cooks, sometimes."

He was going through the mail that Harold Newland, the postman, had just handed him, since the mailbox was too small to hold this morning's bundle. He spied a letter from Walter.

"Are you pale today?" Emma demanded.

"Pale? Do I look pale?"

"As a ghost."

He slowly opened the letter, stared at what appeared to be a blur, then sat down heavily on the corner of his desk.

"Something . . ." he said vaguely. "Something is . . . not right."

Emma rose to steady him. "Don't move," she said, afraid he might crash to the floor. "I'm bringing the car to the door and we're going to the hospital."

❧

"This," said Dr. Walter Harper, who was known to the village as Hoppy, "is where the rubber hits the road."

"Meaning?"

"Meaning the party's over, pal. You've got to make some changes, big-time."

He sighed. Change! If there was anything he didn't like, that was it, right there in a nutshell.

❧

Emma, who had left her glasses at the office, was squinting at cartoons in an old *New Yorker,* when Hoppy and Father Tim came out to the waiting room.

Hoppy Harper was tall, slim, and even handsome with his piercing green eyes, intense gaze, and determined jaw.

Only last September, his wife of sixteen years had died of cancer, and the grief had aged him noticeably. Those who cared about him enough to look closely, and these were quite a few, saw that grief had also done something else. It had deepened him.

"Emma," he said, "let's have a talk."

Oh, God! Emma thought, using the proper meaning of the phrase, Let everything be all right.

"I've already been over this with Tim. But I think someone close to him should also know the score."

"This is a dark day, Emma," said the rector, managing a weak smile.

"Diabetes," Hoppy said. "That's the bad news. The good news is, it's non-insulin dependent. Which means he won't require regular insulin shots. What he will require is a change of diet. Little Debbies, pies, cakes, candy—outta here.

"We stuck his finger for blood sugar, and it's over 350. Not good. And he's got four-plus sugar in the urine. So, here's the scoop."

There was something in the doctor's green eyes that made Emma concentrate on every word.

"Exercise. Jogging is what I recommend. Three times a week, and no less. Morning, noon, night, whenever. But he's got to do it."

The rector looked anguished.

"Less fat in his diet, juice, a lot of fresh fruit. And no skipping meals."

Hoppy grinned and looked at his patient. "Now, the most important thing of all. And that's changing your schedule. You haven't had a real vacation in twelve years, and you usually work seven days a week. I can't tell you how to change that, but it's got to change. Think about it, pal." Hoppy ran his fingers through his unruly hair. Emma thought he looked tired, and wondered who was taking care of him.

&

He had a hurried lunch of Percy's soup of the day, with a salad, and went home to say a word to Barnabas. This took him past the new men's store, which he had failed to stop and inspect since it opened with some fanfare before Easter. The Collar Button, it was called.

It had been a long time, indeed, since he'd gone into a clothing store. In the first place, he didn't like to shop. In the second place, the prices for clothes these days were absolutely—yes, he thought he could honestly say it—sinful. And in the third place, what was the going fashion for a rector who didn't wish to appear conspicuously well-dressed?

He slipped his hand into his jacket pocket, and felt his mended gloves, which he still needed from time to time on cold mornings. He must not get carried away in this place, he thought. He would say he was just looking.

The Collar Button was new, but it seemed old. The walls were dark, burnished panels of mahogany, a low fire burned in a grate, and a large golden retriever, lying by the hearth, opened one eye as he came in.

"Good heavens!" he said with earnest appreciation. This was like walking into a study in some far reach of Cambridge, where he had once gone to research a paper on the life and works of C. S. Lewis.

"Father Tim, I believe!" boomed a deep voice, and from behind a wall of brocade curtains stepped the new proprietor, extending his hand to the rector.

"That's right. How did you know?"

"Oh, I've seen you pass now and again, and I thought to myself, there goes a proper candidate for the Collar Button style!"

"And what, ah, style is that, exactly?"

"English gentleman, country squire, village rector, the man of thoughtful reflection and quiet taste."

"Aha."

"What can I show you? Oh, and would you care for a dash of sherry?"

His head was fairly swimming with the unexpected dazzle of the modern shopping experience.

When he left the Collar Button, he was carrying a large bag with two jogging suits and a box with a new spring sport coat.

For the life of him, he couldn't figure out how it had all come about.

He had mentioned jogging and then, before he knew what was happening, he was standing before a mirror in a turquoise jogging outfit, trying to hold his stomach in.

He had to admit he would need something to run in. He certainly could not do it in a jacket, trousers, and shirt with a clerical collar. As he hurried toward home, clutching his packages, he muttered all the excuses he could possibly think of for having spent such a large sum of money on himself.

❧

On Saturday morning, he put on the forest green running suit and a pair of old Nikes that he'd worn for several years in the garden.

Running shoes was a category he dreaded investigating. Someone had recently told him that shoes these days had parts that you literally pumped up. It was an esoteric realm, and so for now, he concluded, it would have to be his old garden shoes or nothing.

He was smitten at once with the comfort of the new outfit he was wearing. In fact, he praised it aloud.

"Why, this feels just like pajamas," he said into the full-length mirror behind the guest room door.

Barnabas barked and leaped backward when he saw the rector come into the hall.

"You'll have to get used to it, old fellow. If I do what the doctor ordered, I'll be looking like this three times a week. So, pipe down."

Barnabas, however, couldn't contain his excitement over something new in the air. He leaped up and put his forepaws on his master's chest and cocked his head to one side.

" 'Jesus said to the disciples, ' "This is my commandment, that you love one another as I have loved you." ' " The rector looked Barnabas squarely in the eye.

Barnabas sighed heavily and lay down at his master's feet.

"And don't let it happen again," he said, brushing off his new jogging suit.

❧

He knew he didn't want to be seen doing this. First, he wanted to try it out, in a place where there was no traffic. And while he'd seen countless others running heedlessly along Main Street, he felt, somehow, that jogging was an intimate activity, accompanied by snorts, sweating, hawking and spitting, and an inordinate amount of huffing and puffing. Why in the world anyone would want to do that up and down the center of town was beyond him.

He went to the study window at the back of the rectory and peered across his greening yard into Baxter Park. As far as he could see, the coast was clear.

He began in a kind of lope, along the flagstones by his perennial beds, through the space in the hedge and out to Baxter Park, where he turned left and ran close to the hemlock border.

By the time he reached the middle of the park, he was winded. "Take it easy," Hoppy had told him. "Don't try to do Boston the first time out."

He had already broken a light sweat.

A squirrel chattered by one of the ancient park benches. A chipmunk dashed across the grass. And the old fountain, now green with moss and algae, made a sweet, pattering sound.

A bronze plaque on the fountain read: *Given in loving memory of Rachel Livingstone Baxter, 1889–1942.* Miss Sadie's mother, he thought, thankful for such an oasis of peace. He wondered why he hadn't been in this wonderful old park in several years, even though it bordered his yard and he looked into it nearly every day.

Starting again, he jogged over to Old Church Lane. Then, he ran with surprising ease up the hill toward the meadow where the remains of the ruined Lord's Chapel stood.

Panting and soaked with sweat, his heart pounding furiously, he sat on a crumbling stone wall that bordered the old churchyard and saw what lay before him as if for the first time.

It was, he thought, the Land of Counterpane.

The view swept down to a small valley with church spires, orderly farms, and freshly planted fields. Then, the far walls of the valley rose steeply and rolled away to ridge upon ridge, wave upon wave of densely blue, mist-cloaked mountains.

He sat as if stunned for a long moment. Then, he tried to recall when he'd been up here last.

It had been seven or eight years, he figured, since he'd climbed the steep lane with Walter and Katherine and a picnic basket. He wondered who he might share it with now, but could think of no one. Except, of course, Barnabas.

His heart had ceased its thundering, and a light breeze coming up from the valley seemed sweet with the fragrance of earth and manure, leaf mold and blossoming trees.

He got up from the wall, idly wondering how long he had sat there, and began his jog down Old Church Lane.

He was no longer trying to hide himself along the hedges. In fact, he discovered that he was suddenly feeling absolutely "top notch," as Walter might say.

As he ran, he became aware that he was thinking the oddest thoughts. Thoughts of how he might look in his new spring sport coat; about the little girl's pony that had got caught in the barbed wire fence; whether Emma had dyed her hair at home or had it done by Fancy Skinner. Also, he hoped the pink day lilies would not disappoint him and bloom out orange.

He turned out of the bright sun into the cool morning shade of Baxter Park, and paused again to rest at the fountain.

Maybe this jogging business wouldn't be so bad, after all.

New possibilities lay before him, it seemed, though he couldn't yet tell what they were. Perhaps it was time to make some other changes, as well, to do something fresh, something different and unexpected.

The idea came upon him quite suddenly.

He would give a dinner party.

CHAPTER FOUR

Company Stew

In the little village of less than a thousand, everyone's dinner—party or otherwise—began at The Local, unless they wanted to make the fifteen-mile drive to Food Value. Of course, they could go out on the highway to Cloer's Market, but Hattie Cloer was so well-known for telling customers her aches and pains that hardly anyone ever did that.

"See this right here?" she might say, pointing to her shoulder. "Last night somethin' come up there big as a grapefruit. I said, 'Clyde, put your hand right here and feel that. What do you think it is?'

"And Clyde said, 'Why, law, that feels like some kind of a golf ball or somethin' in there,' and don't you know, Darlene took to barkin', and that thing took to hurtin', and I never laid my head on th' pillow 'til way up in the mornin'. Wouldn't you like a pound or two of these nice snap beans?"

Worse than that, according to some, was Darlene, Hattie's Chihuahua, who lay on a sack by the cash register. Every time Hattie rang up a sale, the dog growled and snapped at the customer.

Avis Packard once said that Hattie Cloer had sent more business to The Local than any advertising he'd ever run in the paper.

Two weeks after his first jog up to Church Hill, Father Tim made an early Saturday call at The Local.

Since Barnabas was running with him these days, he found it convenient that The Local had an old bike rack near the front door, where the dog could be tied on a short leash.

He was still out of breath, and Barnabas was panting with some exhaustion himself. The route had by now fallen into place. They ran through Baxter Park and up to Church Hill, then along the quiet road by Miss Sadie's apple orchards, past the Presbyterian Church, three times around the parking lot, down Lilac Road to Main Street, and then to Wisteria Lane where they turned toward home.

"Two miles, right on the money," he discovered with immense satisfaction.

"Mornin', Father," said Avis, who was sitting at the cash register. "How does joggin' compare to workin' up a sermon?"

"Well, Avis, I can't see as there's much difference. I dread both, but once I get started, there's nothing I'd rather be doing."

"We got those fine-lookin' brown eggs you like. And Luther Lovell's boys delivered the nicest bunch of broilers you ever seen. You ought to look at those, and check that pretty batch of calf liver while you're at it."

One thing Father Tim liked about Avis Packard was

the way he got excited about his groceries. He could rhapsodize about the first fresh strawberries from the valley in a way that made him a veritable Wordsworth of garden fare. "We got a special today on tenderloin that's so true to the meanin' of th' name, you can cut it with a fork."

"Well, now, I'm not shopping, Avis. I'm looking."

"What're you lookin' for?" Avis cocked his head to one side like he always did when he asked a question.

"Ideas. You see, I've decided to give a dinner party."

"You don't mean it!"

"Oh, I do. But the thing is, I don't know what to cook."

"Well, sir, that's a problem, all right. I'll be thinkin' about it while you look around," Avis assured him.

A little line was forming at the cash register, so the rector moved away, greeting shoppers as he went.

He stopped to talk to everyone, taking note that four people wondered where his collar was, and only one inquired about the painting, for which he was grateful.

At the produce bins, he admitted he was feeling slightly nervous over his idea. First of all, he didn't even have a guest list.

Of course, he was going to ask Emma, and yes, Miss Sadie. He thought she would make a splendid contribution. Besides, he had heard she once went to school in Paris, and he wanted to know more about it.

Hal and Marge, of course. No doubt about that.

Hoppy Harper, now there was a thought, his wife gone and no one to look after him but that old housekeeper. That made six, including himself.

Six. For the life of him, he couldn't think of another soul that would fit in just right with that particular group.

Perhaps he should invite Winnie Ivey, since she was always feeding everybody else. Maybe he would do that.

Avis came down the aisle with a gleam in his eye. "I turned the register over to my boy. I want to help you get your party goin.' What do you think about beef stroganoff, a salad with bibb lettuce, chickory, slices of navel orange and spring onions, and new potatoes roasted with fresh rosemary? 'Course, I'd put a nice bottle of cabernet behind that. 1982."

❧

He sat with Barnabas one evening with a lapful of cookbooks. As much as he appreciated Avis Packard's menu planning, beef stroganoff seemed too ordinary. He wanted something that spoke of spring, that made people feel there was a celebration going on, and that would fill them up without being too heavy.

"This is a lot of work," he confided to Barnabas, who appeared to understand, "and I haven't even started yet."

He wondered why he had waited so long to entertain. It was clear to him that he had gotten completely out of the notion, although once he had loved doing it. He'd had the bishop and his wife for tea three times and twice for dinner, the vestry had come for a light supper on at least four occasions, and, once, he had the courage to give a luncheon for the members of the Altar Guild, who had such a good time they didn't leave until four o'clock.

Not that he was a great cook, of course. Still, he wasn't half bad at barbecued short ribs, an occasional sirloin tip roast that would melt in your mouth, if he did say so himself, and, in the summer, Silver Queen corn, cooked in milk for precisely sixty seconds. Of course, there was always the economical Rector's Meatloaf, as he'd come to call it, which he usually made at least once a week.

He'd even been known to bake his own bread, but the interest these days somehow eluded him. Gardening had taken over. And where once he had sat and read cookbooks, he now read catalogs from Wayside Gardens and White Flower Farms, not to mention Jackson and Perkins.

"And another thing," he said to Barnabas, who raised one ear in response, "is the cost. Do you realize what entertaining costs these days?"

Barnabas yawned.

"Lamb, I think it should be lamb," he mused to himself after going to bed. And he didn't think it should take the form of anything *nouvelle.*

The thought came to him as he laid his head on the pillow. Company Stew! It was an old recipe, nearly forgotten, but one that had always brought raves.

He got out of bed and put on his faded burgundy dressing gown. Noticing that the clock said eleven, he slipped his feet into the chewed leather slippers and went downstairs to look for the recipe.

The search revealed how vagrant his closets had become, so he began rearranging the one in the hall, which, very likely, his guests might see.

When he finished, he was surprised to find that it was two o'clock in the morning, and he'd collected a boxful of odds and ends for the "Bane and Blessing" sale.

It was rather a free feeling, he noticed, prowling about the house at such an odd hour. To explore this strange freedom even further, he went into the kitchen, made himself a meatloaf sandwich with no mayonnaise,

and sat at the table reading *Bon Appétit,* which he had
bought for ideas and inspiration.

"No wonder I haven't done this sort of thing in
years," he muttered. "It's too demanding."

❧

He was feeling the way he'd felt when they asked
him to be on the Garden Tour.

Though the tour was to be of gardens only, he'd
given the rectory a room-by-room inspection. It was as
if he were seeing it for the first time.

To his amazement, every ceiling corner seemed to
have a spider web, there was clearly a ring in his bathtub, the shower tiles were mildewed, and the kitchen
cabinets were in such a tangle of confusion, it had taken
a full half hour to locate his double boiler.

At what point things had fallen into this state, he
couldn't say. But fallen they had, and by the time of the
tour, he was so exhausted from making both house and
garden ready, that he went to Meadowgate Farm for the
entire weekend, inviting a retired priest from Wesley to
conduct Sunday services.

Now, he found himself compulsively cleaning out
drawers his guests would never open and closets they
would never see, and polishing silver they would never
use. But, he assured himself, it was a perfect time to get
caught up. A dinner party provided the most excellent
of excuses.

"You need house help," Emma had told him, again
and again.

But then, he was often told that he needed one thing
or another: a cat, a bird, a gazebo, earmuffs, English
garden tools, a word processor, a vacation, a bicycle, a
wife, and, until Barnabas, a dog. Several people had

even made the unwelcome suggestion that he get himself a microwave.

When he invited Emma on Monday morning, she was inspired at once to submit plans of her own.

"I'll bring the potato salad," she said happily. "And make a batch of yeast rolls."

"No, you won't bring a thing. This is a bona fide party where all you have to do is show up."

"Why not make it a covered dish? You don't need to do all that cookin' by yourself. Marge could bring her chocolate cake they wrote up in the newspaper, and Hoppy Harper's house help could make somethin' for him to bring . . ."

She was doing it again—treating him like a ten year old.

"Emma, no one is to bring anything. And that's final."

It was indeed final, as she could plainly tell.

He washed the slipcover on the sofa in his study, dusted books on the shelves that were low enough for anyone to reach, ordered four pounds of Avis Packard's valley-grown lamb and two bottles of a ridiculously expensive cabernet, asked Winnie Ivey to bake a special triple-chocolate cake with raspberry filling, hung a new bird feeder outside the dining room windows, and pondered washing the study window that overlooked the best part of the garden. At this, however, he balked.

As he might have guessed, everyone in the village seemed to know about the evening, which was now only a few days away. It amazed him that a man couldn't have a simple dinner party without attracting the attention of everybody from the postal clerk to the dry cleaner. "We hear you're havin' a big blow-out," his barber said, while taking a little more off the sides than they'd discussed. Were people looking at him as if they should have been invited? Couldn't a man have a few friends over without asking the whole blasted town?

Though he still wanted to invite two others, he couldn't decide who they should be. In the meantime, he had ordered for eight and was preparing for eight, and was relieved that everyone not only could come, but seemed pleased at the prospect.

He'd also given some thought to Barnabas. Perhaps he would allow his friend into the study after dinner. Which meant, of course, that Barnabas would need a bath.

At the office one morning, it occurred to him that, instead of bathing Barnabas in the guest room shower stall, he would stop by the hardware store and buy a large tin tub. That way, he could begin the practice of bathing him in the garden and avoid the clean-up in the bathroom.

After a quick lunch with Harry Nelson, who reported that the origin of the painting still hadn't been verified, he went to the hardware.

One of his favorite smells was that of an old hardware store. In fact, it was right up there with the smell of wood smoke, leather-bound books, and leaf mold after a rain. More than that, it unfailingly brought back a rush of memories from his Mississippi boyhood.

As a 4-H rabbit grower for two years, he had often traded at the local hardware for hutch materials and feed. He could even remember the time he picked out six yellow goslings from a box kept warm by a light bulb.

He decided on a tin tub for $22.95, and took it to Dora Pugh at the cash register.

"You want to drive around for this, Father?"

"No, Dora, this is cash and carry."

"I see you walk by here every day and I still forget you don't drive a car. How in the nation do you make out?"

"Not too bad, actually. Nearly everything I could want, and some things I don't, are all right here in these two town blocks."

"I guess you're goin' to tote this tub on your head like in Africa?"

He gave her cash to the penny. "I don't know exactly how I'm going to do it till I get started."

He tried to hold the tub under his arm, but that didn't seem to work, so he took it by one of the handles and was disappointed to note that the rim of it banged against his ankle as he walked to the door.

Turning to say goodbye, he saw that Dora had ducked down behind the pocketknife display case, shaking with laughter.

"Dora, I see you back there laughing! You better quit that and show some respect to the clergy!"

He waved cheerfully and stepped out on the sidewalk, pleased with both his idea and his purchase. He just hoped that people did not think him eccentric. He would far rather be thought ingenious or practical.

By the time he turned the corner at the bank and headed home, he was willing to admit that a car provided something more valuable than convenience. It provided privacy. Otherwise, he reasoned, everyone passing by could stare into your business, which one and all seemed to be doing.

He hurried the last half block to the rectory, set the tub down in a clearing amid some laurel, and unwound the garden hose to make certain it would reach. "Perfect!" he exclaimed, warming to his task on Friday.

❧

On Friday, he left the office early, stopped by The Local, and went home to change into an old t-shirt and khaki pants.

He would get the bath out of the way straight off, he thought, then begin the stew around three, open the wine to breathe at six, and have everything in good order for his guests at seven.

When he opened the door to the garage, Barnabas leaped into the hallway, skidded nearly the length of it on a small Oriental rug, then dashed into the kitchen and hurled himself onto the bar stool, where he began to lick a vinyl placemat on the counter.

The rector put Barnabas on his longest leash. Not only would this give him freedom to thrash about in the bath, it would keep him from bounding into the street if the new setup alarmed him.

Unfortunately, this would prove to be the worst idea he'd had in a very long time.

❧

He was pleased with his location of the tub. The little clearing was shielded from the street by the laurels, and afforded him plenty of elbow room. As soon as Barnabas was bathed, he thought, he'd rub him down with a towel, then lead him into the garage where he could finish drying off and make himself presentable.

Attaching the looped end of the leash to a laurel branch high over his head, he encouraged Barnabas to get into the water, which he'd liberally sudsed with Joy.

Instead, Barnabas hurled himself into the tub with a mighty leap.

Just as quickly as he went in, he came out, diving between the rector's legs. He circled his right leg and plunged back into the water, soaking his master from head to foot.

Then, he leaped out of the tub, raced again between Father Tim's legs, joyfully dashed around his left ankle, and headed for a laurel bush.

It seemed to the rector that it all happened within a matter of seconds. And while his memory searched wildly for a Scripture, nothing came forth.

Barnabas circled the bush at a dead heat, catching the leash in the crotch of a lower limb, and was brought to an abrupt halt.

The tautly drawn leash had run out. Barnabas was trapped on the bush. And each of the rector's ankles was tightly bound.

Shaken, Father Tim observed this set of circumstances from a sitting position, and in the most complete state of shock he could remember.

Miraculously, he was still wearing his glasses.

Barnabas was now lying down, though the leash was caught so tightly in the tree that he could not lower his head. He stared at Father Tim, obviously suffering the misery of remorse. Then, his contrition being so deep that he could not bear to look his master in the eye, he appeared to fall into a deep sleep.

The rector began spontaneously to preach one of the most electrifying sermons of his career.

His deep memory bank of holy Scripture came flooding back, and the power of his impassioned exhortation made the hair fairly bristle on the black dog's neck. In fact, Barnabas opened his eyes and listened intently to every word.

When his oration ended, the rector felt sufficiently relieved to try and figure out what to do.

He could see it now. His guests ringing the doorbell, finally coming inside, searching the house, calling out the back door, and then spying him in this miserable condition, while the stew pot sat cold on the stove.

No wonder so many people these days had heart fibrillations, high blood pressure, and a thousand other stress-related diseases. No doubt all of these people were dog owners.

Lord, be thou my helper, he prayed.

"Father Tim! Is that you back there?"

Avis Packard came crashing through the laurel hedge, looked down at his good customer, and said, without blinking, "I let you get away without your butter. Do you want me to put it in the refrigerator or just leave it right here?"

❧

Fortunately, the washtub incident had put him only an hour off schedule.

The stew was on and simmering, and the fragrance in the rectory was intoxicating. The old walnut dining table gleamed under the chandelier and cast a soft glow over a silver bowl of yellow roses tinged with crimson. The cabernet sparkled in cut-glass decanters, the strains of a Mozart sonata filled the rooms with an air of expectancy, and in the fading afternoon light, the gardens looked fresh and inviting from every window.

He felt rather fresh and inviting, himself, having shaved and showered. Also, he was wearing his new sport coat.

He hadn't come up with two more guests who would perfectly fit in, but he saw this as an advantage. Tonight's little gathering would be relaxed and intimate, like family, and all would get a chance to know each other better.

At 6:45, the bell rang, and while the invitation was for 7:00, he was ready and waiting. He opened the door to see Miss Rose and Uncle Billy, standing on the porch holding hands and dressed in their best finery.

"Preacher," said Uncle Billy, grinning broadly, "we didn't know if you was ever goin' to visit us, so we come t' visit you."

※

Emma arrived at seven sharp, parking her lilac Oldsmobile in the rectory drive. Hoppy Harper's old Volvo station wagon pulled in behind her.

Emma glanced furtively in the rearview mirror to see whether she was wearing enough eye shadow, as Hoppy walked up to open her door. She thought he looked surprisingly boyish in a cotton sweater and khakis.

When Father Tim greeted them on the porch stoop, Emma was so delighted to see her rector in a new jacket that she gave him a big hug and an air kiss that sounded something like "Ummmwah!"

Then she walked into the living room.

There, seated on the antique Chippendale sofa, were Miss Rose and Uncle Billy Watson, sipping a glass of sherry.

Miss Rose was wearing lisle stockings rolled below her knees, a pair of unlaced saddle oxfords, three World War II decorations on the front of her dress, a great deal of rouge, and a cocktail hat with a veil.

Uncle Billy had on a suit that had belonged to his brother-in-law, with a vest and a gold watch chain. A broad grin revealed his gold tooth, which coordinated handsomely.

"Emma, Hoppy, have a chair," said their host, as serene as a cherub. "And will you have a glass of sherry?"

"Make it a double," said the astounded Emma.

❧

Miss Sadie arrived with Hal and Marge, who had fetched her down from Fernbank.

She carried a small shopping bag that contained several items for her rector's freezer: two Swanson's chicken pies, one package of Sarah Lee fruit turnovers, and a box of Eggos. This was what Miss Sadie considered a proper hostess gift when the Baxter apples were not in season.

Marge was busy hugging one and all, including Miss Rose, who did not relish a hug.

Hal was talking with Hoppy and Uncle Billy about baseball, and Miss Sadie was chattering with Emma.

Why, it's a real celebration already, the rector thought happily, seeing two golden finches dart toward the feeder.

"Miss Sadie, your apple trees have been the prettiest I've ever seen," Marge said, taking a glass of mineral water from her host.

"Do you know carloads of people have driven by the orchards this year? They've been a regular tourist attraction! And somebody from over at Wesley stopped to ask if they could get married under the trees that back up to Church Hill."

"What did you say?"

"I said when do you think it might be, and she said she didn't know, he hadn't asked her yet!"

Their host brought in a tray of cheese and crackers. He refused to serve anything that had to be dipped. He thought dipping at parties was perilous, to say the very least. If you didn't drip dip on yourself, you were likely to drip it on someone else. He'd once had a long conversation with his new bishop, only to look down afterward and discover that his shirt front displayed a regular assortment of the stuff, including bacon and onion.

That he did not serve dip seemed especially convenient for Miss Rose, who took two of everything offered, eating one and putting the other in her dress pocket. Uncle Billy, on the other hand, took two of everything and ate both at once.

As he passed around the mushrooms in puff pastry, Miss Sadie was admiring Miss Rose's military decorations.

He had to admit that he'd never given a party quite like this.

❦

The Company Stew, which had simmered with the peel of an orange and a red onion stuck with cloves, was a rousing success. In fact, he was so delighted with the whole affair that he relented and let Barnabas into the study after dinner.

Marge helped serve coffee and triple-layer cake from the old highboy, as the scent of roses drifted through the open windows.

Barnabas, meanwhile, was a model of decorum and lay next to his master's wing chair, occasionally wagging his tail.

"You must have quoted this dog the whole book of Deuteronomy," said Emma, who still refused to call him by name.

"This dog," he said crisply, "is grounded."

"Uh oh," said Hal. "I guess that means no TV for a week?"

"No TV, no pizza, no talking on the phone."

"Ogre!" said Marge.

"What did the big guy do, anyway?" Hoppy wondered, leaning over to scratch Barnabas behind the ears.

"I'm afraid it's unspeakable, actually."

"Oh, good!" exclaimed Miss Sadie. "Then tell us everything."

Miss Sadie enjoyed the bath story so much, she brought out a lace handkerchief to wipe her eyes.

Miss Rose, however, was not amused. "I leave dogs alone."

"Nope, dogs leave you alone," said her husband.

"Whatever," said Miss Rose, with a wave of her hand.

Hoppy set his dessert plate on the hearth, then leaned back and stretched his long legs. He looked fondly at his elderly patient of nearly a decade. "Uncle Billy, I'd sure like to hear a joke, if you've got one."

Uncle Billy grinned. "Did you hear the one about the skydivin' lessons?"

"I hope you didn't get this from Harry Nelson," said Emma, who didn't like Harry Nelson jokes, not even secondhand.

"Nossir. I got this joke off a feller at the Grill. He was drivin' through from Texas."

Everyone settled back happily, and Miss Rose gave Uncle Billy the go-ahead by jabbing him in the side with her elbow.

"Well, this feller he wanted to learn to sky dive, don't you know. And so he goes to this school and he takes all kind of trainin' and all, and one day comes the time he has to jump out of this airplane, and out he goes, like a ton of bricks, and he gets on down there a little ways and commences to pull th' cord and they don't nothin' happen, don't you know, and so he keeps on droppin' and he switches over and starts pullin' on his emergency cord, and they still don't nothin' happen, an' th' first thing you know, here comes this other feller, a shootin' up from the ground, and the feller goin' down says, 'Hey, Buddy, do you know anything about parachutes?' And the one a comin' up says, 'Nope, do you know anything about gas stoves?' ''

Uncle Billy looked around proudly. He would have considered it an understatement to say that everyone roared with laughter.

"I've heard that bloomin' tale forty times," Miss Rose said, removing a slice of cheese from her pocket and having it with her coffee.

Miss Sadie followed her host into the kitchen. "I'm just having the best time in the world, Father!"

"You and me both!" he said, measuring out some more coffee beans.

"I want to have you up to lunch soon. There's something I'd like to talk with you about that's been on my mind for a long while."

It was rare, indeed, for Miss Sadie to have anyone up to Fernbank for anything these days. "It's not another find from your attic, is it?"

"Oh my, no. It's much more important than that!"

"I'll look forward to it," he said, putting his arm around her frail shoulders. "You know, we're supposed to hear something about our painting next week."

"Yes, I know. And I hope you won't think this is awful of me . . ."

"What's that?"

"I dearly hope it's not a Vermeer."

He knew precisely what she meant. Although he'd never said it to a soul, that was his hope as well.

"That was Papa's painting. I remember when he brought it home and we hung it on the wall downstairs. We all stepped back and just stared for hours. It was a real painting from Europe! I'd dearly love to see it on the wall in Lord's Chapel."

"And so would I," he said kindly.

As she went back to the study, Hal joined him, and the two men walked out to the back stoop. The air was balmy, and sweet with springtime.

"Fine dinner, Tim."

"Thanks. It's great to be back in circulation."

"Diabetes seems to be doing you more good than harm." Hal sat on the railing and tamped the tobacco in his pipe. "About that job on the vestry," he said, "let me put it this way: A hundred and seventy acres, a full-time practice, five dogs, two horses, fifteen cows, an old farmhouse that needs a lot of work, and an increasingly pregnant fifty-year-old wife."

"Enough said."

"The timing isn't right . . . and those trips into town at night . . . You know I want to serve, I want to do something more. Just remember that I have in the past and I will in the future."

Father Tim nodded. "When you can, Hal. You know I'd like you to be our senior warden."

Hal puffed on his pipe and nodded thoughtfully. They heard a dog bark in the distance, and a train whistle. "You know that pony that got caught in the fence? We put a saddle on him today."

"Great news! That's been on my mind."

As the coffee finished brewing, they went inside. "You want a good man on the vestry," Hal said with a low chuckle, "recruit Uncle Billy. He'll loosen that crowd up."

Father Tim poured fresh coffee into every cup.

"Miss Sadie," he said, "I've been hoping you'd tell us tonight about your schooling in Paris."

"Oh, do you really want to hear that old stuff?"

"Yes!" said Marge, curling up on the sofa next to Hal. Even Barnabas assumed an air of expectancy. And Emma noticed that Hoppy Harper, who was sitting in Father Tim's wing chair, was as relaxed "as a dishrag," she later said.

"I hardly know where to begin, it's been so long. But, if you're sure . . ."

Everyone was absolutely sure.

"Well, then," she said, sitting even more upright, and squaring her shoulders. "Paris, France, was where I fell in love."

Miss Sadie paused for a moment, her face beaming, and looked around the room. Father Tim saw at once that the truest meaning of the term *captive audience* was being demonstrated right before his eyes.

She sat quietly for a moment, as if she had to summon the memory from a very long distance. "I was sixteen years old when Mama and Papa allowed me to study in Paris," she began.

"Oh, they didn't want me to, not a bit. But Uncle Haywood talked them into it, saying Mitford was just a jumping-off place, that I'd never learn anything worthwhile in Mitford. Wasn't that dreadful of him?

"So off I went with Mama, who was going to take me and spend a month or two near the academy before she came back home. I remember to this day what I was wearing when we left. It was a cream-colored lawn with a georgette bodice worked with seed pearls. And the waist was tied with satin ribbons. Oh, it was lovely!

"Papa took us down to Charleston to catch the boat.

Mama and Papa and I all cried the whole way. We just held on to each other and bawled, because my papa was never afraid to shed a tear, he had the tenderest heart, and he was trying so hard to do what was right.

"And so we got on that old boat, and I had the worst sinking feeling. Why, we never even left the dock 'til we were so overcome with homesickness that we nearly threw ourselves overboard."

"Oh, law!" said Uncle Billy, deeply moved.

"But there were such interesting people on that boat! My, what a collection, and they just took on over me, calling me sweet names and inviting us to eat at their table.

"So by the time I reached Paris, I had quit crying, and I just marched into that academy, and started talking the worst old Southern drawl French you ever heard, why, they nearly fell down laughing at me.

"There was one other girl from home, from Virginia, and I stuck to her like bark on a tree. Mama had to live in this house nearby and could only see me on weekends and every Wednesday. She was so lonesome, and she could only say, *'Oui, oui'* and she'd never spent a single night away from Papa.

"Well, I started learning to watercolor, and recite poetry, and play the pianoforte, and do needlework, and study ancient history, and I don't know what all. They just wanted to make me so fancy! And you know, all I dearly wanted to do was be plain.

"Can you imagine a girl with every privilege in the world, just wanting to be plain? I knew it would be a disappointment to Papa, and to Mama, too, and the heck with Uncle Haywood! I wanted to be back in Mitford, picking up walnuts, and playing in my dollhouse at Fernbank, and sewing doll clothes, and helping China

Mae in the kitchen, and going barefooted under the apple trees with Louella.

"The very first Wednesday, Mama and I were so glad to have our freedom that we both just went skipping down the lane that led to the pastry shop.

"And while we were in there, Mama let me drink real coffee. Oh, it was the thickest, strongest, blackest stuff you ever could imagine! I just loved it! I thought, if Paris, France, was a taste instead of a city, this would be it!"

Miss Sadie's bright eyes appeared to be looking far away. Marge thought this was like opening an old book and reading a fairy tale with faded watercolor illustrations.

"While we were sitting there, we heard this voice. And we looked up, and there was this . . . this handsome young American man, buying a pastry and a cup of coffee.

" 'Listen to him talk!' said Mama. 'Why, he sounds like he could be from Mitford!'

"He was with another young man, oh, they were so handsome and young and carefree, and they were laughing, and it was just music to our ears.

"Mama never met a stranger in her life, although most people thought she was dignified. She just held out her pretty hand to him and said, 'Young man, where are you from?'

"And he said, 'Mitford, North Carolina, ma'am, United States of America.' "

Miss Sadie's audience murmured with amazement.

"I'll never forget how proudly he said that, just like it was the best place on earth. Which, of course, it is," she said, beaming.

"Amen!" Emma fairly thundered.

"He had just moved to Mitford with his family and baby sister from Tennessee, and he was in Paris to show some of his pharmaceutical inventions. Well, I could go on and on, but he invited Mama and me to have dinner with him that very evening, and he gave us his card and all, and Mama felt sure he was a gentleman.

"Every Wednesday after that, he met us for pastry and coffee, and sent flowers to Mama and me, to her rooms in the little pension."

Miss Rose ate a piece of cubed ham and some Havarti from her pocket. Barnabas had gone to sleep, and the doctor, worn from months of unrelieved strain in his growing practice, snored quietly in the wing chair.

"One day, I said, 'Mama, I don't know how to tell you this, but I just hate this place and everything about it. When I watercolor a dog, it looks exactly like an owl, I am still playing "Three Blind Mice" on the pianoforte, and my French is atrocious. I just want to go home and be plain Sadie.'

"Do you know what my mama said? She said, *'Oui, oui!'*

"When the young man learned we were leaving, he sent a dozen yellow roses to Mama and a dozen red roses to me. There was a note attached to mine, which said: 'Someday when I have made my fortune, I would like to ask you to marry me.'

"So we went home, and Papa met us, and I never spoke another word of French in my life. And to this day," she paused and looked around, "I've never forgotten that handsome young man from Mitford."

Marge leaned forward. "For heaven's sake, Miss Sadie, who was he, anyway?"

Miss Sadie looked straight at Miss Rose Watson, whose cocktail hat had tipped forward at a rakish angle.

"That young man," Miss Sadie said, "was Miss Rose's brother, Willard Porter."

❦

Hal, Marge, and Miss Sadie lingered after the others had gone, eating Belgian chocolates. "I've been very, very good all week in order to do this," Marge explained, looking only slightly sheepish as she took another piece off the tray.

The rector had regained his wing chair and put his feet up. "Miss Sadie, in the years I've known you, you've always been a very private person. Why did you tell us that wonderful version of your Paris story tonight?"

Miss Sadie reflected on this. "When I brought you that painting, it started something. I started thinking about things I'd never thought about before. And I decided I was tired of holding on . . . holding on to my orchard, holding on to my possessions, holding on to my memories.

"I have decided," she said firmly, "to start letting go. And that's one reason I'd like to see you next Thursday for lunch at noon, if you can come, Father."

"I'll be there with bells on."

"Swanson's chicken pie?"

"My favorite!" declared her weary, but enthusiastic host.

At one o'clock in the morning, having refused all offers of help, he put away the last dish and went upstairs, thankful that tomorrow was Saturday.

He felt certain there was more to Miss Sadie's story about Willard Porter, but he was even more certain of something else: Considering this party from beginning to end, from the initial idea to the last dried dish, it had occupied exactly six weeks of his life. And while he'd had a wonderful evening, and so had everyone else, he was certain that he didn't want to do this again for a very long time.

He picked up his open prayer book from the night table.

" 'The Lord grants his loving-kindness in the day-time,' " he read from Psalm 42, " 'In the night season his song is with me.' "

CHAPTER FIVE

The Big Six-O

When the appraiser came the following week, the fog rolled in even heavier than it had on his first visit, which did nothing to improve his temperament.

"Is it always like this in June?" he asked with some sarcasm.

"Not always," Father Tim replied, mildly.

According to the rector's wishes, the vestry was to have only one representative this morning, and it was Harry Nelson. Out of respect, Father Tim had invited Miss Sadie, and he and Emma completed the group who would at last hear the news.

If it is a Vermeer, he reasoned, we'll be in the newspapers, and on TV, and the phone will ring off the hook. He had done a bit of studying on the subject himself and read that a small Vermeer had recently sold at auction for over twenty million dollars.

How the church decided to use the money would, of

course, be a topic for the most serious discussion and examination. And, he realized with some regret, at least two of his vestry members would be in deep disagreement over almost any decision.

The little office was fairly bristling with tension and expectation. And, as before, the appraiser did nothing to relieve it.

"Coffee," he said curtly to Emma, removing his jacket and hanging it on a peg.

Just open up your shirt collar, thought Emma, and I'll pour in a whole cupful.

"No cream unless it's the real thing."

Or, she thought, maybe you'd like it in your left ear.

When coffee had been poured all around, the appraiser removed the canvas from its bubble wrap, stacked five books on Anglican church history on the rector's desk, and propped the painting against them.

"This painting has been the subject of grave discussion among the finest Vermeer scholars in America."

"In fact, a paper will be published soon that finely details the depth and distinction of the research it has undergone."

The rector heard himself sigh. Although he'd read that sighing was common to Southern women, he knew for a fact that this unfortunate habit extended also to men.

The appraiser went on for some time, extolling the virtues of the scholarship. Miss Sadie toyed with the diamond cross at her neck. Emma was furious. Harry Nelson could stand it no longer. "Just give us the bottom line!" he blurted.

The appraiser turned to him with a frosty look. "The bottom line?" he asked imperiously.

"That's right," Harry snapped.

"The bottom line is that this painting is not by Vermeer."

"Hallelujah!" shouted Emma.

"Hooray!" said Miss Sadie, clapping her hands.

Father Tim crossed himself, joyfully.

Harry Nelson, however, was devastated. Leaning against the bookcases by the visitor's bench, he brought out a handkerchief and wiped his forehead. Then he sat down, shaking his head. This was a blow. "So who did it and what is it worth?"

"We don't know who did it, but we can safely assume it was done during the time of Vermeer or shortly after his death. It is not one of the famous Vermeer forgeries of the last century.

"As to its market value, we can comfortably expect it to fetch around seven or eight thousand dollars, if properly offered."

"And how much do we owe you for finding this out?" Harry asked, hoarsely.

The appraiser dipped into his jacket pocket and brought forth a crisp envelope, which he handed to the senior warden.

Harry opened it, unfolded the sheet of paper, and read aloud:

"For services of appraisal, as outlined below, four thousand, seven hundred and fifty two dollars and seventy three cents."

"That includes my travel expenses," the appraiser said, adjusting his glasses.

༄

"Thanks be to God!" he exclaimed over and over, as he walked to the Grill the next morning.

He had just come from the hospital, where he had

put his arms around a very ill patient, doing for someone else what God had so often done for him. While some priests, he knew, dreaded their hospital visits, he looked forward to his. It was one of the divine mysteries that he came away feeling stronger, and refreshed in spirit. "My hospital visits," he'd been known to say, "are good medicine."

He was surprised, frankly, that he could fit so much into a morning these days. He was dutifully jogging three times a week and now vowed to increase his schedule to four. Would wonders never cease?

Today, he'd even followed his impulses and worn his new sport coat.

"Got you a new neighbor comin' in next door," Mule Skinner said at breakfast. "Be in there in th' fall sometime."

"Terrific."

"Pretty nice lookin'."

"What does he do?"

"It's a she."

"Aha."

"You remember ol' Joe Whattsisname lived there, that was her uncle, the ol' Scrooge."

"Percy's outdone himself on these poached eggs."

"Blonde, blue eyes," said Mule, looking at the rector. "Real nice legs."

"Who? Percy?"

"Your new neighbor."

He had nearly forgotten about the small house next to him, shielded as it was by the rhododendron hedge. Maybe there would be children in the family, he thought. It would be nice to hear the laughter of children.

Later, as he approached his office, he did hear laughter. It sounded like Emma.

He looked at his watch. Too early for Emma, he thought, opening the door and going in.

There, wearing his mailbag and leaning over her desk, was Harold Newland, the postman. And there, too, was Emma, quite frozen with surprise at the sight of her rector, whom she believed to be in a meeting at town hall.

"Preacher, I mean Father, good mornin'," stammered Harold, blushing like a girl.

He looked at Harold's bare legs. Apparently, it was the season for short pants on mail carriers.

"Good morning to you, Harold! Was there too much mail for the box today?"

"That's right, too much mail," said Harold, backing out the door. "Couldn't get it in the box and had to bring it in. Bye, Father. Bye, Emma. Have a good day."

The rector picked up the very slim packet containing only three letters and a copy of the *Anglican Digest*.

"Aha," he said, with hardly any surprise at all.

❧

"I regret to say that lunch isn't chicken pie, Father."

Miss Sadie searched her rector's face for any sign of disappointment. "It's a sandwich with low-salt ham and low-fat cheese."

He felt a bit disappointed, after all.

"With potato chips!" she assured him.

To say that he was happy to be at Fernbank, at the top of Old Church Lane, was an understatement. He felt as if he'd fled to some other country. Up here, the air was drenched with birdsong, the apple orchards were dappled with sunlight, and the broad, cool porch was as consoling as the nave of Lord's Chapel.

From a cut-glass decanter, she poured her guest a

glass of sherry, which, he thought, tasted precisely like aluminum foil.

"Three ninety-eight at Cloer's Market!" she announced.

From the porch of Fernbank, he had a commanding view of Mitford. It was a toy village that lay at his feet, like something one would find under a Christmas tree, with an electric train running around it.

There was Main Street, which sliced Mitford neatly in half, and the green circle of the town monument at the north end. And, between the shops, the colorful patches of flower beds made it all appear orderly and safe.

He could see the bell tower of Wesley Chapel, the grand bulk of First Baptist, and the empty lots, as green as jade, on either side of the tree-enveloped Lord's Chapel. Away to the west, blue mountains rolled like waves.

"Wouldn't it be marvelous, Miss Sadie, if life could be as perfect as it looks from your porch?"

"I've thought that very thing many times. When Hoppy's wife lay dying, I often looked down at his house and thought, we never, ever know what heartache lies under those rooftops."

"I heard a Mississippi preacher say that everybody is trying to swallow something that won't go down."

"Well, he's right about that."

She had put the glass plates on a green wicker table, with a sprinkle of white lace cloth. There were old-fashioned roses in a vase, and a tall pitcher of sweetened tea. They sat down to lunch, and Miss Sadie held her hands out to the rector.

"At Fernbank," she said, "we always hold hands when we say the blessing."

He prayed with a contented heart. "Accept, O Lord, our thanks and praise for all that you've done for us. We thank you for the blessing of family and friends, and for the loving care which surrounds us on every side. Above all, we give you thanks for the great mercies and promises given to us in Christ Jesus our Lord, in whose name we pray."

"Amen!" they said in unison.

He found, with some surprise, that his sandwich looked remarkably inviting, even though it was on white bread.

After lunch, the two sat on the porch, sipping tea. He had wisely cleared his calendar for the afternoon, wanting nothing to interfere.

"We've got chocolate chip ice cream for dessert."

"I hope it's not that low-fat ice milk stuff."

"When we get to dessert at Fernbank, there's no low anything! My mama taught me that dessert should be high."

"I like your style," he said, getting up to help his hostess.

What he was going to hear today, he didn't know. But he felt relieved that he could trust the content. Curiously, some parishioners brought him the most ravishing morsels of slander, as if it were their bounden duty.

He was sitting on the porch railing, finishing his ice cream, when Miss Sadie finally got down to business.

That he nearly fell backward off the railing when he heard her plan was no surprise. In fact, he told Emma later, if he had fallen off, he would have rolled neatly down her steep lawn, through the apple orchards, and across Church Hill Drive.

Then he would have tumbled down the hill toward town and landed on his barber's rooftop, where he would have jumped to his feet and shouted the good news.

❧

The task at hand was to devise an immediate gathering of the vestry and to make it as splendid as humanly possible.

He ran quickly through his list of things to do. A visit by the bishop. Confirmation services. A wedding. A special outing with the Sunday school children. A parishwide barbecue and car wash. Coordinating new artwork for the church letterhead. Two Sunday services. And now this.

It would be enough to make even Father Roland's head swim. If Jeffrey Roland thought he had his hands full out there in his big New Orleans parish, he should be here in Mitford where a mere 200 souls could occupy every waking moment.

He made a phone call. "Miss Sadie, what is your very favorite thing?"

"Well, let's see. Listening to rain on a tin roof!"

He laughed. "I should have been more specific. What is your favorite thing to eat? Besides chicken pie, that is."

"Why, peanut butter and jelly, I believe. Don't you like that, too?"

For the evening at the rectory, he prepared two platters of peanut butter and jelly sandwiches, cut into small squares with no crust. One platter was crunchy. One platter was smooth.

He set out napkins printed with a drawing of Lord's Chapel. He lined up coffee cups, tea glasses, and dessert plates. He filled a small tray with chocolate chip cookies from Winnie Ivey's, and set a fresh lemon pie from The Local on a cake stand.

He cut several blooms from the fragrant Prosperity, and took a handful of blooms as large as peonies from his clove-scented Sarah van Fleet.

Then he put them in a vase, and waited for what would surely be the most dramatic vestry meeting ever held in the history of his parish. Except the one, all those years ago, when the church leaders had to decide what to do after the hideous fire—the fire that had left only a blackened ruin overlooking the green valley.

Miss Sadie sat in a straight-back chair, in front of the fireplace in his study. She was wearing a cut velvet dress of emerald green, with a high neck, and a brooch hand-painted by her mother. That she made a striking figure was an understatement.

"I know you've wondered why I never gave any money to speak of, all these years."

"No, no, certainly not," someone said.

"And don't say you didn't, because I know you did."

There was a profound silence.

"The reason I haven't given as freely as you thought I should is simply this: I've been hoarding Papa's money." She looked slowly around the room, meeting every eye.

"I've earned interest on the capital and invested the interest, and I haven't spent foolishly, or given to every Tom, Dick, and Harry who held his hand out."

There was a variety of supportive murmurs.

"So, what I'm prepared to do this evening is to give Lord's Chapel a special gift, in loving memory of my mama and papa, and in appreciation for the church I've called home since I was nine years old."

She paused for a moment. "This gift is in the amount of five million dollars."

After a collective intake of breath, a cacophony broke out in the rectory study, something like what was usually heard at the Fourth of July parade when the llamas passed by.

"Shush!" said Miss Sadie, "there's more. This money is to be used for one purpose only. And that is to build a nursing home."

She looked around the room. "But I don't mean just any nursing home. This home will have big, sunny rooms, and a greenhouse, and an atrium with real, live birds.

"It will have books and music, and a good Persian rug in the common room, and the prettiest little chapel you ever saw. I want a goldfish pond, and a waterfall running over rocks in the dining room.

"And above every door, there'll be a Bible verse, and this is the verse that will be over the front door: 'Let thy mercy, O Lord, be upon us, according as we hope in thee.' "

Miss Sadie clasped her hands in her lap and leaned forward.

"There, now!" she said, as radiant as a girl. "Isn't that wonderful?"

Of course, it was wonderful. There was no denying, in any way, shape or form, just how wonderful it was.

She appeared to sit even straighter in her chair. "You understand, of course, that this is only half the plan—but it's enough to get us started."

When the meeting broke up at 9:30, those assembled had drunk two pots of coffee and a pitcher of tea, and had eaten every peanut butter and jelly sandwich on the platters. And though no one had said so, the traveling senior warden had not been sorely missed.

In all, it had felt like a very grand party, with Miss Sadie Baxter the center of attention, the belle of the ball.

☙

Emma had told him over and over again that at one o'clock today, no sooner and no later, a printer was coming to pick up a purchase order for the new church letterhead.

The printer, she said, told her to ask him the following:

Did he want the line drawing of Lord's Chapel printed in dark green or burgundy, or would he like purple, which was always a good religious color and, according to the story of the building of Solomon's temple, one of God's favorites?

Also, did he want the address line run under the pen and ink illustration of the church, or at the bottom of the page, like the Presbyterians did theirs? And did he want a Helvetica, a Baskerville, or a Bodoni like the Baptists?

He felt that, among other things this morning, he should look up the meaning of Helvetica, Baskerville, and Bodoni, and made a note to tell the printer that God also requested purple to be used in the temple Moses built.

It was unusually cool for late June, and he savored his short walk to the office, noticing that he was feeling better than he had in years. He had dashed off a note to Walter after his morning prayers, quoting the encouraging message of Hebrews 4:16: "Let us, therefore, come boldly unto the throne of grace, that we may obtain mercy, and find grace to help in time of need."

Boldly! That was the great and powerful key. Preach boldly! Love boldly! Jog boldly! And most crucial of all, do not approach God whining or begging, but boldly—as a child of the King.

"I declare," Emma said as she made coffee, "you're skinny as a rail."

"That's what I hear," he said, with obvious satisfaction.

"What do you mean?"

"They're not calling me 'that portly priest' anymore."

"I can fix that," she said, and opened her bottom desk drawer to reveal several Tupperware containers. The open drawer also contained a glorious fragrance that wafted upward and soon filled the small room.

"Pork roast with gravy, green beans, candied sweet potatoes, cole slaw, and yeast rolls."

"What in the world is this?"

"Lunch!" said Emma. "I figure if we eat early, it'll still be hot."

Just as his clothes were beginning to fit comfortably again, he saw temptation crowding in on every side. He could outrun Winnie Ivey, but in an office barely measuring ten by fourteen, it looked like it was going to be pork roast and gravy, and no turning back.

"Emma, you must not do this again."

"Well, I won't and you can count on it. You've been meek as any lamb to the slaughter, and I thought a square meal would be just what the doctor ordered."

"Not exactly," said her rector, who enjoyed it to the fullest, nonetheless.

After lunch, Emma went head first into the deep bottom drawer, looking for something. She came up with a large bone, wrapped in cellophane.

"For Barnabas," she said, much to his astonishment. That she had called his dog by name was a landmark event. And to have brought him a bone was nearly a miracle.

"I don't know why you're being so good to me," he said, cheerfully.

She glared at him and snapped, "I just told you, for Pete's sake. Weren't you listening?"

For at least two weeks, he'd noticed that her moods were as changeable as the weather.

"Emma, what is it?"

"What do you mean what is it? What is what?" she demanded, then burst into tears, and fled into the bathroom, slamming the door.

By the time she had mumbled an apology, and they'd decided on Baskerville type, burgundy ink, and where to put the address line, it was nearly one o'clock.

"Put your sport coat on," she said.

"What in the world for?"

"Well, just do it, if you don't mind."

"Isn't this the same printer we've been using? He doesn't wear a sport coat."

"Peedaddle! Just trust me on this, and put your sport coat on. You might comb your hair a little, too."

Suddenly, the office had become so minuscule that he wildly imagined Harry Nelson to be right—what they needed to do was knock out the walls, and add a thousand square feet.

As he put on his sport coat, she looked at her watch. "One o'clock," she announced, crisply. She went to the door, threw it open, and shouted, "Here he comes!"

He stared into a veritable sea of smiling faces. And they were all singing "Happy Birthday."

J.C. Hogan jumped in front of him with a camera, as

Emma led him, dazed, down the step and onto the sidewalk.

To say that he was surprised would have been totally inaccurate. He was astounded. It had slipped his mind entirely that today, June 28, was his birthday.

He saw Pearly McGee in a wheelchair, with a hospital nurse. There was Hoppy Harper towering over the crowd, grinning, Miss Sadie in a pink straw hat. Hal and Marge, with Barnabas on his red leash. Miss Rose and Uncle Billy, holding hands on the front row. And Percy Mosely, Mule Skinner, Avis Packard, and Winnie Ivey.

He saw Andrew Gregory from the Oxford Antique Shop across the lane, Mayor Esther Cunningham, and more than a dozen others. Who in the dickens was running the town?

"Look up!" said Emma, pointing above his head at the front of the stone office building. He did as he was told and saw a large banner strung above the door. *Happy Birthday, Father Tim, the Big Six-O* was printed in bold, red letters.

"What you thought was a squirrel on the roof this morning was Avis Packard on a ladder, hangin' that thing!"

"Way to go, Avis!" The crowd gave a round of applause.

"See why I told you to wear that dern sport coat?" Emma said as Miss Sadie pinned a rosebud on his jacket. "It's got a lapel!"

J.C. Hogan was already on his second roll of TX 400, declaring that this was better than the turnout for the American Legion barbecue.

Then, Hoppy stepped forward with a handshake and a hug for the honoree. He'd come straight from the hospital and was wearing his white coat, which Emma thought looked romantic. "A young Walter Pidgeon!" she whispered to the mayor.

"According to Avis, who takes note of such things," Hoppy declared, "it's been seven years since you gave up your car for Lent."

"Exactly!" he said, able at last to say anything at all.

"Well, we feel that a man of your distinction should have himself some wheels. But unfortunately, this bunch could afford only two."

He heard a loud, explosive sound behind the hemlock hedge in the lot next door.

"Let 'er rip!" shouted Percy, and from behind the hedge roared what someone later called "a sight for sore eyes."

It was Mule Skinner in a double-knit, chartreuse, yard-sale outfit, weaving wildly back and forth across the lane on a red Vespa motor scooter.

Barnabas led the group in scattering to the sidewalk.

"How do you stop this thing?" Mule yelled.

Hal leaped in front of his pregnant wife. "Turn off the key!"

Mule made a wobbly U-turn, turned off the key, dragged his foot to brake the scooter, and glided smoothly to a stop in front of Father Tim, visibly shaken.

To a loud chorus of "For He's a Jolly Good Fellow," led by Esther Cunningham, the astonished rector got on the scooter, a bit pale beneath his tan, and drove with a mixture of excitement and foreboding to the first rose arbor on the lane, then back again.

By the time he parked it on the sidewalk and put the kickstand down, he noticed that he couldn't stop grinning.

"You don't have to make a speech, since you already

make one twice every Sunday," said Mule, slapping him vigorously on the back.

"We know it's not new," said Hoppy, "but it's in great shape. We got it off a little old lady who only drove it on Sundays."

"Nineteen eighty-two, 125 cc, good as new," said Percy, kicking a tire.

"Looky here," Percy said, "you got your horn . . ." He opened up on the horn and everybody clapped.

"You got your high beam and your low beam." He demonstrated, which seemed to be another crowd pleaser.

"And get a load of these turn signals. Ain't that a sight? I rode this thing all the way from Wesley, purred like a kitten."

"Wide open," said Mule, "I followed 'im in th' truck."

Emma cupped her hands to her mouth and made an announcement. "You're all invited in for cake and iced tea. But you'll have to do it in shifts, so step right in and don't tarry. We can take four at th' time."

She had produced a cake from her bottomless bottom drawer, and two gallon jugs of tea with Styrofoam cups.

Hal and Marge filled the cups with ice, and Father Tim cut the cake, as J.C. Hogan shot another roll of black and white, and Esther Cunningham played the kazoo.

The following Monday, the *Mitford Muse* ran two front-page stories on the local Episcopal church community.

A picture of Father Tim on the motor scooter was mistakenly given this bold headline: "Lord's Chapel Rector Receives Gift Worth Five Million Dollars." The story and picture of Miss Sadie giving the rector a cashier's check had no headline at all and referred to the donor as Sudie bixter.

Mule Skinner looked at the front page and sighed. "Law, law," he said, "J.C.'s done it again."

CHAPTER SIX

Dooley

Hay lay in the fields in fat, round bales.

Blackberries were greening on bushes along the roadside.

Lacy elder flowers bloomed in the meadows.

In his opinion, all was right with the world. Except, of course, for the bitter disappointment of his day lilies. While they had been sold to him as rare and peach colored, they bloomed a fatal orange, just like the commoners in the hedge. In fact, he found them a good deal less attractive, for their color was insipidly pale, compared to the bold hue of their country cousins.

He complained to Emma.

"If *day lilies* were all I had to complain about in this world, I'd be a happy woman."

"What *do* you have to complain about, then?" he asked cheerfully.

She gave him a hard stare, and he noticed that her

lower lip trembled. He wisely turned in his swivel chair to face the bookcase, searching, presumably, for a reference work.

That swivel chair was a blessing out of heaven, he mused for the hundredth time. When there was nowhere to go in that infernally small space, one could always swivel in the other direction.

He saw that he was facing a volume on stress in the workplace. He took it off the shelf and opened it at once, daring to hope for a telling insight.

"Well," said Emma, after a considerable silence, "don't you care?" He did not turn around. He was consulting the index.

"Care about what?"

"What I have to complain about."

"I asked you what you have to complain about."

"Yes, but you didn't care."

The rector cleared his throat. He was not accustomed to this sort of thing in his own relationships, although he had seen it in the relationships of countless others.

Slowly, he turned to face his friend and part-time secretary.

"Actually, I am very interested," he said, as kindly as he could.

Tears filled Emma's eyes and splashed down her cheeks.

"Well, then, if you must know," she said, "I'm complaining because I think I'm . . . because I'm falling in love with Harold Newland!"

"Aha," he said, thinking helplessly of Harold Newland's legs in his summer shorts uniform.

"I suppose you're shocked," she said, barely able to speak.

"Not a bit, not one bit. Tell me about it."

She blew her nose on some toilet tissue she'd put in her purse this morning, and composed herself. "Well, whenever I'd get to the office early, he started bringing the mail inside because he saw my car out front.

"Pretty soon, we were talking about this and that, and one evening we went to Wesley to a movie, and then we went to Holding for barbecue, and, well . . . the first think you know, I was . . . I was cooking for him."

Emma inspected her rector's face, and pressed on. "I hate to tell you this, but that big birthday dinner I brought you was leftovers from Harold's supper the night before."

"Two birds with one stone," he said agreeably.

She wiped her eyes. "You know how long Charlie's been gone."

"Ten years."

"Ten *long* years," she said, weeping again.

He waited.

"Harold is such good company. He can fix nearly anything. He even glued three pieces of my good china back together; you can hardly see where. I'd given up ever getting that done! And you know how hard it is to break new ground."

"Oh, I do."

"But he made a little garden out back with nothing but a hoe, and put in a dozen Big Boys."

"That will come in mighty handy around the end of next month."

Emma had warmed to her subject. "And you know those attic stairs that I could never get down? They come down easy as grease, now! Not to mention that he installed new ceiling insulation while he was at it."

"Terrific!" exclaimed her interested listener.

"Plus, he fixed the leak in the basement that mildewed all the clothes I'd saved back for the rummage." Emma wondered if he was getting the point. "You know how things can go down in ten years."

"Around my place, in ten days!"

There was a comfortable silence.

"Does Harold have a church in Mitford?"

"Well, not *right* in. More out. Harold has a farm, you know, eleven acres. He goes to a Baptist church in the country. He said he gave his heart to the Lord when he was a boy."

He had to confess he didn't know much about Harold Newland, since he'd been on their route only a year. Occasionally, if their paths crossed, they'd stop and talk at the mailbox out front.

"Well, then. He goes to church, and knows what for. He owns a farm, he has a job, he's handy around the house, and he likes your cooking. What could you possibly have to complain about?"

Her chin began to quiver. "It's so embarrassing!" she said, wiping fresh tears with the small wad of tissue. "That's why the tomato patch is in the backyard instead of at the side that gets the most sun."

"Whatever can that mean?"

"Well, nobody can see you in the backyard like they can at the side of the house, and I didn't want anybody to see Harold setting out my tomato plants, because . . . well, because . . ."

"Because why, for heaven's sake?"

"Because he's only forty-five!" Emma wailed.

He was quiet for a moment. "Pardon my asking so directly, but how old are *you?*" He thought he remembered that she was two years his junior.

"Fifty-four!"

"Scout's honor."

"Fifty-eight," she said, exhausted by the ordeal of confession.

"I've got an appointment in less than twenty minutes, and I'd like to ask you to think about something."

He looked at her with a gentle frankness. "As Paul wrote to Timothy, 'God has not given us the spirit of fear, but of power, and of love, and of a sound mind.' "

She blew her nose. "Could you write that down?"

"Who's the secretary around here?" he asked, grinning.

✀

One morning in early August, as he was running on Church Hill Drive, Barnabas came to a sudden halt, which caused him to crash headlong into a ditch filled with the last of the summer sweet peas.

When he limped toward the office later than usual, he was inclined to tell Emma a lie about the whole affair.

"What in God's name have you done to yourself?" she snapped.

He couldn't tell a lie. "We were running. Barnabas stopped, I fell over him. Landed in a ditch."

"Barnabas!" she said, with venom. "From the day you let that creature fool you into taking him home, look what's happened! You got diabetes, your day lilies bloomed out orange, and now here you are black and blue, not to mention half-crippled!"

"It goes without saying that it was not a premeditated act." He eased himself into his swivel chair and felt a sharp pain stab his left knee.

"That does it!"

"Does what?" he asked, not really wanting to know.

"That's it, that's absolutely it!"

If she had a gift, he thought, it was for parable and double-talk. And, while showing off Harold Newland in public had recently sweetened her temperament, he could see a real backsliding under way.

"Do you remember how many times we've all tried to make you get house help?"

"Oh, I remember, all right."

"And how many times you have flatly refused?"

"Over and over again, as I recall."

"Well, that dog has just been the cause of you gettin' it, whether you want it or not!"

"What in the dickens does that mean?"

"That means the vestry had a meeting behind your back, to do something you won't do for yourself! You're on medication, you do your own cooking, you've got a big house and a yard and a busy parish and two services on Sunday, and you won't take a vacation, and now this!

"They said just say when, and we'll hire 'im some help. We'll send 'em on over to the rectory every Wednesday and Friday morning at eight o'clock sharp, but we want you to tell him, because we're scared to do it!"

House help! He felt as if he'd just been delivered a blow to the solar plexus.

He could give himself time to think this over, he reasoned, by swiveling around to face the bookshelves. On the other hand, he could call Harry Nelson at once and attempt to overturn the vestry's decision.

Instead, he did at last what Emma Garrett had so often, in recent weeks, made him feel like doing.

He got up from his desk, walked to the door, and left the office without speaking a word.

He walked briskly to the corner and turned right. At

the Oxford Antique Shop, Andrew Gregory invited him in for coffee, but he didn't even slacken his pace. When your vestry goes behind your back and your secretary hates your dog, he thought, there's no place like the Grill to drown your sorrows.

❧

The weather was making it possible for Andrew Gregory to do a thing he liked very much indeed. And that was sit inside the open double doors of the Oxford Antique Shop, on an eighteenth-century bench that was not for sale, and let the breeze drift in while he read from his rare-book collection.

When customers came in, he preferred them to sit on the matching bench as a kind of prelude to the sale, and talk about politics, golf, the gold market, the royal family, Winston Churchill, Italian old masters, and a dozen other subjects that intrigued him.

Without any formal decision to do it, Andrew had become a specialist, not only in old and rare books, but in eighteenth-century partners' desks, English bronzes, hearth fenders, needlepoint chairs, and, for his younger trade, pine farm tables.

He presented these treasures plainly, without even a bowl of potpourri on a table top. Yet, the very soul of elegance pervaded the atmosphere.

The aged, heart-of-pine floors glowed under a regular coat of wax, which he applied himself. And the furnishings got a good rubbing with lemon oil every month, all of which gave the Oxford its seductive signature fragrance.

As a widower, the proprietor of the town's finest antique shop occasioned a good deal of talk. After all, he was attractive, he was trim, he knew how to dress with some flourish, and, because of his early years in Italy, his habits betrayed a certain European gentility.

Also, it did not go unnoticed that he tanned well and was invariably kind to women.

"Five years a widower, and no interest in anybody that we can see. No hope, I'd say," a customer told Winnie Ivey at the bakery.

"There's always hope," said Winnie. Though she was not personally interested, she felt that Andrew Gregory, like her day-old pastries, must not go to waste.

There had once been some talk of Andrew and Emma Garrett, but Emma dismissed it as nonsense.

"Too smart for me!" she said. "And besides, who could live with that ol' dark furniture all over the place?" Emma, who liked sunflower decals on her patio door and kept a vase of artificial tiger lilies on her desk at the office, could not imagine a Georgian highboy in her Danish Modern dining room, or a husband who rattled on about Winston Churchill.

Since he had children in Connecticut, some wondered why he stayed on in Mitford. The truth was, he had grown increasingly happy with his life in the village, and the village was equally happy with him.

It was Andrew Gregory whom the town council sent to visit Myra of Myra's Beauty Bar, to explain why she could not have a shop awning of bubble gum pink instead of the traditional green.

And, when the uproar started over the selling of valley produce through The Local, it was Andrew who was sent to the state capital to set the matter straight.

Still, he was the only Italian in town, and some said, you know how Italians are. They thrive on lots of hugging, kissing, big weddings, and family feasts, hardly any of which was available locally.

Yes, except for those days when he longed for the blue calm of the Mediterranean and a bold sun that made flowers bloom as big as breakfast plates, he was content.

Father Tim was feeling the confusion of too many options in his personal life. For years, he had risen at five, had morning prayer, studied for his sermon, and then made coffee and dressed.

Afterward, he visited the hospital, dropped by the Grill for breakfast, and headed to the office, walking.

It was that simple.

Now, there were decisions to make every new day.

Whether to take Barnabas running if the weather was bad, or leave him at home. Whether to take Barnabas to the office or leave him in the garage. Whether to walk to work or be bold and start riding his motor scooter.

He'd even been considering something he thought would never cross his mind: Whether to start drinking decaf in the mornings.

At his birthday party, Hoppy had reminded him of a tougher decision he needed to make:

When he was going on vacation.

"Go see Walter and Katherine," said his doctor. But he did not want to go to New Jersey, especially in the summer.

"Come out and spend a week with us," said Hal. But he hated to impose for an entire week, with Marge nearly six months pregnant.

He'd never relished planning his own recreation; he simply wasn't good at it. He was prone to turn recreation into something practical, to justify the time and expense, like he'd done with his two-month sojourn in Cambridge. He had intended to make that trip for sheer pleasure, using money from his mother's estate. But he could find no excuse whatever for pleasure alone. So, while he was there, he researched and wrote the paper on C. S. Lewis, which was received with some acclaim.

Recently, he'd heard that the bishop's wife was trying to collect a party to walk a portion of the Appalachian Trail, but since he attracted mosquitoes in swarms, this was not an option.

When he arrived at the office earlier than usual, Uncle Billy was sitting on the single step in front of the door, wearing his deceased brother-in-law's finest three-piece suit, and smelling strongly of mothballs.

When he saw Father Tim approaching, he removed his hat.

"Mornin', Preacher."

"Good morning to you, Uncle Billy. You're out mighty early."

"Me and Rose like to get up with the chickens," he said, his gold tooth gleaming.

Uncle Billy looked carefully at the books that lined the office walls, as the rector made coffee.

"I always did want to git educated," he said soberly. "But I lived down in th' valley and couldn't stay with my schoolin', don't you know. I learned to do sums, and I've drawed a few pictures in m' time, but that's about all."

"What kind of pictures?"

"Oh, dogs and th' like. And mountains. And fields and flowers and orchards an' all. Outdoor things, don't you know, that's what I like."

"Well, sir, I'd be pleased to see some of your drawings when the notion strikes."

"Oh, I've got a few here and there, hid back. I'll bring you some, if you're sure you want t' see 'em. They're not much, they're drawed with pencil, and I've not showed 'em off to any but Rose."

Father Tim poured a cup of coffee and handed it to Uncle Billy. "How is Miss Rose?"

"Oh, well, mean as ever, y' might say."

"Is that right?"

"Mean as all get out, don't you know. But that's 'er illness. Sometimes she's good as gold, and those're the times I live for. When I come up from the valley and found Rose and married 'er, I thought I was one lucky man, and I still do. We been married forty-three years now, and I knowed she was sick. Right off, I knowed what I was gettin' into. I've never spent a night away from 'er, don't you know, she's all I've got, and I'm thankful."

Father Tim knew that Miss Rose was schizophrenic and on daily medication.

"I never went back to m' people after I married Rose, I never scen 'em no more. Maybe I should have went back, but I couldn't leave 'er. The first years, we didn't have a car, I done my work at home, don't you know, canin' chairs, makin' bird houses, paintin' signs. Rose, she had plenty of money comin' in from Willard, but she always said, 'Billy, this ain't your'n, it's mine, don't touch it, you git your own.' She kind of scorned me sometimes, but it was 'er illness.

"Some days, she'd come and set on m' lap an' call me 'er Sweet William. She'd laugh an' go on, and dance to th' radio, an' I'd git s' fired up thinkin' she was well, hit was pitiful. Then she'd turn right around and be like a rattler a strikin'. It's grieved me that she never got better, like I thought she might."

"Is there anything we can do to help, Uncle Billy?"

"Well, sir, I don't know what it would be. The Baptists tried, the Presbyterians tried, the Methodists did their part, don't you know. We've gone around to 'em all, but ain't nothin' worked. I wasn't much on comin' over here because of all th' kneelin' and gettin' up and down and all, but we like it."

"I'm glad to hear that. And you know you don't have to kneel. You can stand or you can sit, just as well. Jesus prayed in both those ways."

There was silence as Uncle Billy took a grateful sip of his coffee, and considered this.

"You know, Uncle Billy, our church can't heal Miss Rose any more than the Methodists or the Baptists can. Only God can heal. But we'll do all we can, you have my word."

"I thank you, Preacher."

Father Tim turned the answering machine on, as he usually did when counseling, and sat down in his swivel chair. "Why don't you tell me what's on your mind?"

"Well, you see, all those years ago when Willard, her brother, died, he knowed his baby sister had a illness of some kind, so he left 'er that big ol' house, don't you know, an' all them fine antiques. An' th' way he left it was, it would all go t' the town when she passed.

"Now what's been worryin' me is that if Rose passes before I do, I won't have no place t' call home.

"Sometimes in th' winter, she won't run the furnace and gits awful sick in the chest, but she won't let me git the doctor. That's when I go to thinkin', I'll be on th' state, I'll be on th' welfare, if she takes a bad turn."

"I see."

"All kind of people want to buy that place, nobody

knows that the town'll get it, except Rose's old lawyer over in Wesley."

"I'm not much at lawyering," said the rector. "But I believe the town could make a special dispensation, if they cared to. I believe there could be a way for you to go on living there, no matter what they decide to do with the property.

"Why don't you let me look into it, and if you'll come back next week sometime and bring me those drawings of yours, we'll talk it over."

"I'd hate f'r word to git out about th' town endin' up with th' place. Rose never did like to talk about that, don't you know."

"Nobody will hear it from me."

Uncle Billy grinned. "Well, Preacher, you've took a load off my mind, and that's a fact. I've been wrestlin' with this f'r a good while, and I'm just goin' to set it down in th' road and leave it."

"That's a good plan, Uncle Billy. God asks us not to worry about tomorrow."

"That's a hard one, Preacher."

"It sure is. And it takes practice. Just stick with today, is what he recommends. Of course, it helps to stick with him, while we're at it."

"I've been stickin' with him for a good many years. Not like I ought to, but I want t' do better, don't you know."

"Why don't we have a prayer?" He put his arm around Uncle Billy's shoulders.

"Father, we thank you for Bill Watson's faith in you, and for his willingness to let you be in control. We turn this matter over to you now, and ask for the wisdom to proceed, through Christ, our Lord. Amen."

"A-men! Y' know, the Lord always has knowed me as Bill instead of Billy, just like you said!"

When the two men parted, he made a phone call to his cousin, Walter, who was also his attorney.

Then he got down to business with his sermon. Oddly enough, his meeting with Uncle Billy had given him just the insight he needed on a certain difficult point.

❧

"Beggin' your pardon, Father, but there's bats in your belfry." Russell Jacks pushed open the door of the office and peered in.

"Ah, well, Russell! It's been that way since an early age. Come in, come in!"

Russell had been the sexton at the Chapel of Our Lord and Savior for nearly twenty years, but, due to a back ailment, had been living in the valley with his daughter for a year.

"I'm mighty glad to see you, my friend," said Father Tim, wringing Russell's gnarled hand with real feeling. "Welcome home!"

"Soon as we get them bats out of there, I'll scrape up th' droppin's and work 'em in th' flower beds."

Russell Jacks was back and, without missing a beat, ready to get on with his work.

"When in the nation is our bells comin' home?" he wanted to know.

"October, November, around then. All the way from England, at last! Its been a long, dry spell with no bells chiming at Lord's Chapel. And it's been a long, dry spell without you, Russell. Tell me about your back. Is it in good working order?"

"I'd do that, Father, but I've got my little granboy

standin' outside." Russell was clasping his hat over his heart, as he usually did in the presence of clergy.

"Let's bring him in, then!" Father Tim stepped to the door and looked out. There, standing at the corner of the stone building, was a barefoot, freckle-faced, red-haired boy in dirty overalls.

I declare, thought the rector. Tom Sawyer!

"His mama's poorly," said Russell, "and cain't half watch after 'im. She kind of looked after me when I was down and out, an' I told her I'd look after him awhile. He's th' oldest of five."

It occurred to the rector that somewhere in his office, though he couldn't recall where, was one last box of Little Debbies. He reached behind a volume of Bonhoeffer's *Life Together,* and pulled out the box of creme-filled cookies.

"What's your grandboy's name?"

"Dooley!" said Russell Jacks with evident pride.

"Dooley!" he called out the door, "Come in and let's have a look at you!"

The boy came and stood on the sidewalk, staring at the rector. Now that he could see him up close, Father Tim was surprised by a certain look in his eyes, a look that made him appear older than his years.

"Ain't this a church place?" the boy asked, skeptically.

"Why, yes, it's a church office."

"I cain't come in, then, I ain't washed."

"You don't have to wash to come in."

"You ain't lyin', I reckon, bein' a preacher an' all."

"No. No, I'm not lying."

The boy bounded up the single step and through the door, searching the room with his quick gaze. "You got any place in here where I can take a dump?"

CHAPTER SEVEN

The One for the Job

It had been a week since Puny Bradshaw had rung his doorbell at precisely eight o'clock in the morning and started taking over his house.

Fortunately, he was just going out the door as she came in, thereby sparing himself the awful trial of having to tell her what to do.

He was humiliated to think that, the night before, he had hidden his laundry in a pillowcase and stuffed it into the back of his closet, like some sneak thief or chicken poacher. What was considerably worse is that she had found it. When he came home around noon to pick up his sermon notebook, she met him in the hall.

"Father," she said, shamelessly holding up the most ragged pair of shorts he owned, "your underwear looks like it's been in a cat fight. How in the world do you preach a sermon in these things?"

He was so stunned by this display that he hadn't been able to reply.

"Don't mind me," she said, seeing that he minded very much. "My granpaw was a preacher, and I waited on 'im hand and foot for years, so you might say I'm cut out for this job. Tell you what, next time I'm at Wal-Mart over in Wesley, I'll get you a dozen pairs, 'cause I'm goin' to use these for cleanin' rags!"

When he arrived home that afternoon at five-thirty, he found a steaming, but spotless, kitchen and a red-cheeked Puny.

"That bushel of tomatoes like to killed me!" she declared. "After I froze that big load of squash, I found some jars in your garage, sterilized 'em in your soup pot, and canned ever' one in th' bushel. Looky here," she said, proudly, pointing to fourteen Mason jars containing vermilion tomatoes.

"Puny," he exclaimed with joyful amazement, "this is a sight for sore eyes."

"Not only that, but I scrubbed your bathroom 'til it shines, and I want to tell you right now, Father, if I'm goin' to stay here—and I dearly need th' work—you're goin' to have to put your toilet seat up when you relieve yourself."

He felt his face burn. A little Emma, her employer thought, darkly. Now I've got one at the office and one at home, a matched set.

He could not, however, dismiss the joy of seeing fourteen jars of tomatoes lined up on his kitchen counter.

❧

On Friday afternoon, he arrived at the rectory to find the house filled with ravishing aromas.

Baked chicken. Squash casserole. Steamed broccoli. Corn on the cob. And frozen yogurt topped with cooked Baxter apples. Oh, ye of little faith, why didst thou doubt? he quoted to himself.

"I know about that old diabetes stuff, my granpaw had it worse'n you," Puny told him with satisfaction. "An' not only can I cook for diabetes, I can cook for high blood pressure, heart trouble, nervous stomach, and constipation."

During the past twelve years, he had sometimes asked in a fit of frustration, "Lord, what have I done to deserve Emma Garrett?" Now, he found himself asking with a full heart, "Lord, what have I done to deserve Puny Bradshaw?"

※

He chose his best suit, just back from the cleaners in Wesley, and hung it on the hook behind his bedroom door. He laid out a pair of brand-new boxer shorts, which Puny Bradshaw had kindly fetched from Wal-Mart, and a shirt she had ironed to perfection. Then he shined his black loafers, put away the kit, and remembered to get a clean handkerchief from his top drawer.

He had already had morning prayer and studied the challenging message of Luke 12: "Therefore, I tell you, do not be anxious about your life, what you shall eat, nor about your body, what you shall put on. For life is more than food, and the body more than clothing.

"Consider the ravens: they neither sow nor reap, they have neither storehouse nor barn, and yet God feeds them. Of how much more value are you than the birds?"

There was not one man in a thousand who considered these words more than poetical vapor, he thought as he dressed. Don't be anxious? Most mortals considered anxiety, and plenty of it, an absolute requirement for getting the job done. Yet, over and over again, the believer was cautioned to abandon anxiety, and look only to God.

Whatever else that might be, it certainly wasn't common sense.

But "common sense is not faith," Oswald Chambers had written, "and faith is not common sense."

He was entering that part of the week in which his sermon was continually on his mind. "Let me say I believe God will supply all my need," Chambers had written, "and then let me run dry, with no outlook, and see whether I will go through the trial of faith, or . . . sink back to something lower."

He put his handkerchief in his pocket, and looked into the full-length mirror on the back of the guest room door.

There. That would do.

He picked up his sermon notebook, went to the garage to say goodbye to Barnabas, and set out walking to his early meeting with Mayor Cunningham.

✼

In her office at the town hall, Esther Cunningham was eating a sausage biscuit with an order of fries and drinking a Diet Coke, which Father Tim found remarkable, considering that it was only 7:00 a.m.

"Top of the morning!" she said, lifting her cup in a grand salute. "Come in, sit down, take a number!"

There were, indeed, a few places to sit in the mayor's office. When she was first elected fourteen years ago, she had rented a U-Haul truck and brought all her den furniture from home, much to the astonishment of her husband. There was a powder blue sofa, a leather love seat, two club chairs, an ottoman, and a Danish Modern cocktail table. None of which did much to conceal the fact that the walls were slowly mildewing from the effect of a roof leak that no one, in as many years, had been able to locate.

"How do you like that fine snap in the air this morning?" he asked, sitting in a club chair across from Esther.

"There's nothin' I like better! Ray and me are takin' the RV and headin' for the first trout stream we can find. Right after the next granbaby, of course."

The mayor was known for her several beautiful daughters and astonishing number of grandchildren, but he could not recall the latest head count.

"And what number will this be?"

"Twenty-three!" she said. A brass band might have struck up behind her.

"Aha!" he said, looking around for a coffee pot. As far as he could tell, there was not a drop in the place. "Esther, your girls are doing all in their power to raise our taxes."

"Don't complain. So far, you've got two garbage collectors, a postman, a bank teller, a policeman, and a park ranger out of th' deal. Not to mention a fireman and a drove of Sunday school teachers."

"How quickly I forget. Well, shall we get right to business?"

"We'd better. I've got a council meeting at eight o'clock about namin' the town flower. They've chewed on this thing 'til I'm about half sick of it, and now the Wesley paper wants a story, and they won't let us alone 'til we announce it."

"Whichever flower it falls out to be, we're goin' to paint it on signs comin' into town, put a plaque at the monument, set aside a special day with a parade, get the governor to come for the ceremony . . . I never saw such a to-do since the Baxter Apple Bake-Off."

"Don't remind me," said the rector, who had personally baked sixteen deep-dish pies last year to raise money for the library.

"What do you think the town flower should be? You're a gardener." She wadded up her biscuit wrapper and lobbed a fine pass into the wastebasket.

"The pansy vote is mighty strong, of course."

"Well, but look at all the rose arbors up Old Church Lane."

"That's right, but they're out of general view. What do tourists see in the window boxes along Main Street? Pansies! Around the town monument? Pansies every year! And the shop gardens? Full of pansies!"

"Would you want to invite somebody to Pansy Day? I mean, think about it, would you call somebody in Raleigh or Salisbury and say come on up for Pansy Day?"

"Ah, Mayor, you've got a point there. I wouldn't have your job for the world."

"I've had it too long, to tell the truth. I wouldn't want you to spread this, but I'm groomin' one of my grans for the next election."

"Imagine that!"

"Now, while I finish my cholesterol fix, why don't you tell me what's up?"

"What if, upon the event of a death, the town were to be given a large home for civic use, and in that home was left a family member with no place to go? The surviving family member is a good sort, presently of sound mind and body, and no trouble to anyone. Do you think the tone of the council would be agreeable, if this came to pass today, to letting the surviving member stay on? It would be legally sound."

"I don't suppose you'd be willin' to mention any names in this scenario."

" 'Drawing on my fine command of the English language,' " he said, quoting Benchley, " 'I'll say nothing.' "

"So, since none of this has actually happened and I don't know doodley squat about who you're talkin' about—I guess you're lookin' for a gut reaction?"

"That's right.

"I'd say if what you tell me is right, and it always has been, we could work it out. We look after our own here in Mitford, that's been one of my big things all along. You know, for example, that we always make sure Miss Rose and Uncle Billy have oil in their tank."

"Good example."

"So," said the mayor, giving him a broad wink.

"So, what's your vote for the town flower?"

"Johnny Jump-Up!" she said, laughing.

"Tell you what. If you can get anybody to drive all the way from Charlotte or Raleigh for Johnny Jump-Up Day, I'll take you out for a big steak dinner in Wesley."

"I'll hold you to it!" said the mayor, vigorously shaking his hand.

❦

When he got to the office after a visit with the seriously ill Pearly McGee, he found Uncle Billy waiting on the step, holding a package wrapped loosely in yellowed copies of the *Mitford Muse*.

"Mornin', Preacher."

"Good morning, Uncle Billy," he said, helping the old man to his feet.

"That ol' arth'r' is gittin s' bad, I cain't hardly git

down, much less up. Pretty soon, you'uns 'll jis' have to stand me aginst th' wall."

"Maybe use you for a hat rack."

"Maybe put a little birdhouse on top and set me in th' yard." Uncle Billy laughed, showing all three of his teeth. Inside, he eased himself onto the visitor's bench, and carefully laid the package across his knees.

Father Tim plugged in the coffeepot and opened the windows. "To get right to it, Uncle Billy, I've done some checking. My attorney is familiar with cases like yours. Legally, a dispensation could be made that would enable you to live on in the Porter house. And while I never mentioned a name, the mayor thinks the council would cooperate whole-heartedly.

"We both know we can't second-guess what tomorrow will bring, or how the town leadership will change, but it seems to me that you have nothing to worry about."

Uncle Billy lowered his head for a moment. When he looked up, there were tears in his eyes. "Thank you, Preacher."

"No, Uncle Billy, thank you. I believe the Holy Spirit has shown me a sermon in your predicament." The disciples had been repeatedly instructed with one simple word: Ask. Uncle Billy, like much of the rest of humanity, had spent precious years worrying instead of asking.

"I hope that's your drawings you've got there."

"I was about not to bring 'em, don't you know. I got to lookin' at 'em an' said, 'Rose, I cain't drag this ol' stuff over to th' preacher.' Well, she got to fussin' an' sayin' how I never did have much belief in m'self. But that ain't right. I know I can cane chairs and make signs as good as th' next feller, and I ain't too bad with a birdhouse, don't you know. But this here is flat stuff."

"And I've been looking forward to seeing it ever since you mentioned it last week."

The old man stood up slowly and put his package down on the desk. Then he began to peel back the brittle newspapers,

Father Tim saw that the date on the *Mitford Muse* was 1952. And then he saw the first drawing.

In stunned silence, he looked at the finely detailed pencil rendering of a bird dog in a cornfield, a sky alive with quail, and, in the distance, a hunter with upraised shotgun against a background of late autumn trees.

"Good heavens," he said quietly.

❧

On Friday, he did something he'd seldom ever done. He took the day off.

After all, the cleaning truck was coming from Wesley, and he needed to go through the pockets of all his suits, and attach notes about simple alterations. He had to go to the barbershop and get his neck "cleaned up" as Joe Ivey always said, take his shoes to be re-soled, and buy something to remove the beer label from his motor scooter helmet.

Because he made his usual trip to the hospital and the Grill before launching these chores, he wasn't at home when Puny arrived at eight o'clock.

She hoped he would have done something with the bushel of Baxter apples still sitting in the garage, and save her the trouble. But there they sat, drawing flies, as she discovered when she opened the door.

As Barnabas came bounding toward her in a frenzy of delight, Puny recited in a loud voice one of the few Scriptures she'd ever committed to memory:

" 'And this is his commandment, that we should believe on the name of his Son, Jesus Christ, and love one another'!"

Barnabas sprawled at her feet and sighed.

"I've never seen anything to beat you in my whole life," she said with admiration. "They should put you on TV."

Puny picked up the bushel of apples and took it to the kitchen, where she washed the fruit in the sink. Three canning jars were all they had left after she had finished the tomatoes. Which meant just one thing: she'd have to bake pies and dry the rest.

"Lord knows," she muttered to Barnabas, "I'm half give out just gettin' started around here!"

She opened the back door for fresh air, and was startled to see a red-haired boy in ragged overalls standing on the step. From what she'd heard, this would be Russell Jacks's grandson. Barnabas barked joyfully and dashed to the door, yelping to get out. "Hush up and lay down! Philippians four-thirteen, f'r gosh sake!"

The boy looked intently at her through the screen.

Puny didn't know which was more noticeable, his blue eyes or his dirty feet.

"I was jis' goin' to knock," he announced. "Are we kin?"

"Not that I know of. What makes you ask?"

"Freckles same as mine."

"We couldn't be kin. You come from down the mountain!"

"Blood travels," he said soberly.

"What can I do for you?"

"Granpaw told me to come an' git th' preacher."

"Father Tim's not here, he's at the hospital."

"What's the matter with 'im?"

"Nothin's the matter with 'im. He goes and calls on sick people and makes 'em feel better."

He looked down at his feet and spoke in a low voice. "My mama's sick," he said.

"Why don't you come in and wait for him? He'll be here in a little bit." As she pushed open the screen door, Barnabas growled.

"Will 'at ol' dog bite?"

"Not unless he has to," Puny said, catching Barnabas by the collar. "Go set down on that stool."

He ran to the stool and tucked his feet on the top rung. "A dog like t' eat me up, one time."

"Based on your overalls alone, this dog won't mess with you," she said with conviction.

"What's your name?"

"Puny."

"Why'd you git a name like 'at?"

" 'Cause when I was born I was all sickly and puny-like."

"How did you get over bein' puny?"

"Hard work, honey, that's how." She started paring the great mound of apples in the sink. "What's your name?"

"Dooley."

"Dooley? Don't you have a real name like Howard or Buddy or Jack or somethin'?"

"Dooley is a real name!" he said with feeling.

There was a long silence as Puny bent to her task.

"Did you ever try stump water?" Dooley asked.

"Stump water! Shoot, I tried everything, but nothin' ever worked."

"I hear if you lay face down in fresh cow dump, 'at works."

She turned around, still peeling the apple. "Did you try that?"

"Nope."

"Me neither, 'cause I heard you had to lay there awhile for it to take."

"Can I have one of them apples?"

"If you'll say 'May I,' you can have one."

"May I," said Dooley.

He quickly put it in his overalls pocket. "My uncle said if you wash y'r face with the same rag you wash y'r feet with, that'll do it."

"I wouldn't try that, if I was you. Besides, I think we ought to be content with what the good Lord gave us. I don't mess with my freckles no more, and I think you ought to stop wastin' your time, too."

He studied his feet, which he was swinging freely now, since Barnabas had fallen asleep. The kitchen was quiet. Birdsong drifted through the open window and a breeze puffed out the curtains.

Dooley decided to eat his apple. "What else you want t' talk about?"

"How old are you?"

" 'Leven."

Puny peeled furiously. "I'm glad I ain't eleven."

"Why?"

"I didn't like bein' a kid. Somebody was always beatin' on you, pullin' your hair, chasin' you around th' house, throwin' mud on you. I wouldn't be your age for all th' tea in China, much less Japan."

"When I'm twelve, I'm goin' t' whip th' horse hockey out of somebody."

"You better not be usin' that kind of language in this house. Nossir, that won't go around here."

He ate his apple. "When's 'at preacher comin'? My granpaw said make it snappy."

"He'll get here when he gets here. What's the matter with your mama?" Puny started slicing the peeled apples. The room was silent except for the slices dropping into the pot. "Well, cat got your tongue?"

"I ain't tellin' you nothin' about that."

"Why not?"

"Because it ain't none of your stupid business."

She turned and looked at him. His face had hardened, and he looked older, like a little old man perched on the stool.

"Let me tell you somethin', then, buster. Don't come in here in my kitchen with them dirty feet, and think you can go sassin' me. I'll pitch your little butt out on th' porch."

He slid off the stool and headed toward the door. "You ol' fat witch!"

She caught him on the back stoop. "Witch, is it? You know what witches do t' back-talkin' young 'uns?" She held him by his galluses and put her face close to his. "They boil 'em in that big ol' pot in yonder."

"Oh, yeah?"

"Yeah!" She bared her teeth at him ominously. "And then . . ."

"And then what?" asked Father Tim, walking into the yard.

"I was jist about t' cook this young 'un alive," she said, "and you come and spoiled everything."

✤

When Father Tim, Dooley, and Barnabas arrived at the side door of Lord's Chapel, Russell Jacks didn't waste time exchanging pleasantries.

He removed his hat, respectfully. "Lock's been broke."

He felt a sudden chill. In the years he had pastored this parish, there had never once been any vandalism, hardly a beer can thrown onto the front lawn.

"Ain't anything else broke, as I can see."

"Dooley," said Father Tim, "I'd like you to do something for me and keep Barnabas company. Just sit here on the grass and I'll put his leash on the bench leg. That way, you two can get to know each other."

Dooley looked suspiciously at the enormous black dog who had tried to lick his face all the way to the church.

"You do what th' Father tells you," said Russell Jacks, holding the door open for the rector.

He walked home, oddly troubled. In the hour they'd spent searching for any sign of harm, they'd found nothing. The priceless tapestry was unharmed, nothing was taken off the altar, nothing was moved or misplaced that he could see. If someone had broken in looking for money, where would they have looked? Emma always carried the collection home and brought it to the office on Monday.

He had checked the drawers in the sacristy, and found $18.34 in an envelope, about the usual amount that was kept around to pay for brass polish or votive candles.

Why would anyone go to the trouble to force an entry, yet disturb nothing inside? He was making too much of the whole thing. It was only a broken lock, after all, nothing more.

Though he didn't consider himself one to rely greatly upon his feelings, he felt uneasy. Perhaps he should call Rodney Underwood, the young police chief, and see what he thought about it.

Some good, however, had clearly come from the bad.

Out there in the grass by the garden bench, Dooley Barlowe had found himself a friend.

✍

When he got home, he went to the kitchen looking for Puny and saw instead an unusual sight in his backyard.

She had discovered an old screen door in the garage, hosed it down, laid it across two ladderback chairs, and covered the screen with apple slices.

"This is our dryin' rack," she said with authority. "Before I leave today, we'll carry it into the guest room. On sunny days, we'll bring it back out again. I know it's extra trouble, but that's th' price you pay for hot cobblers in winter. Meantime, I've got six pies in the oven and six more to go, and I wish to goodness you'd get that boy to wash his feet."

Father Tim was utterly astonished at what he heard himself say: "Puny, do you have any work on Mondays?"

"No, I don't, and I need some."

"Well, then," he said, "you've got it!"

✍

On Saturday morning, he visited the Oxford Antique Shop, carrying an apple pie in a basket.

"Little Red Riding Hood!" said Andrew Gregory, coming from the back of the store to greet him.

The rector held out the basket. "Homemade apple pie," he said, with some pride.

" 'The best of all physicians is apple pie and cheese'!" exclaimed Andrew, quoting a nineteenth-century poet. "What an excellent treat, my friend. Thank you and come in." He took the basket, delighted as a child. "Why don't we just polish off the whole thing right now and you can carry your basket back?"

The two men laughed.

"I'm afraid I'll have to take my basket back in any case, as there's five more to be delivered in it."

"I don't know how you find time to feed your sheep physically as well as spiritually."

"Andrew, Providence has blessed me with the finest house help a man could ever have. Puny Bradshaw is her name, and she not only baked a dozen pies yesterday, she canned fourteen quarts of tomatoes last week."

"Extraordinary!"

They sat down on the matched loveseats at the shop door.

"Here's something even more extraordinary. I've discovered that Uncle Billy Watson is a splendid artist. Uneducated, grew up in the valley, never had training of any kind. 'Rough as a cob,' as he says. Yet, he draws like a Georgian gentleman."

"You always seem to have a Vermeer of one kind or another on your hands."

"The drawings are in my office, and I'd like your opinion. Perhaps you'll stop over on Monday morning. After all, I've been drinking your coffee for years, now come and have a go at mine."

"I'll look forward to it," said Andrew. "And please don't leave yet. I have something to show you."

Andrew went to the back room and returned with two books.

"Just look at this!" he said. "A first edition of the first volume of Churchill's *History of the English-Speaking Peoples*. Something I've wanted for a very long time." He turned to the opening page and read aloud: " 'Our story centres in an island, not widely sundered from the Continent, and so tilted that its mountains lie all to the west and north, while south and east is a gently undulating landscape of wooded valley, open downs, and slow rivers. It is very accessible to the invader, whether he comes in peace or war, as pirate or merchant, conqueror or missionary.'

"Ah," said Andrew, unashamedly beaming. "A prize! I shall read all the volumes over again. Now, for you," he said, with a twinkle in his eyes, "a prize of your own." He handed the rector an early leather-bound volume of Wordsworth.

The rector was touched by the feeling of the softly worn covers against his palm. It was as if the book had belonged to him all along and had at last come home.

Smiling, he turned the linen-weave pages until he found a favorite passage. "Andrew, if you'll permit me, I also would covet a moment to read aloud."

It was Saturday morning in Mitford. The village was up and stirring, yet a slow, sweet peace reigned, a certain harmony of mood and feeling. In the open door of the shop the two men sat, one reading, one listening, and both, for the passing moment, were content.

❧

He was right. While Miss Sadie had lavishly bestowed bushels of apples upon the village populace, no one had thought to carry her a pie this year.

After lunch, he and Barnabas walked up the steep hill to Fernbank. Though the grand old house was showing its age, it was beautiful still, situated proudly at the crest of a hill massed with wild fern.

Miss Sadie met him at the door. "They've brought me two quarts of apple sauce," she reported, "a quart of apple butter, and a dozen jars of jelly. But, oh my, I'm glad to see this pie!"

She talked him into having a piece with her on the porch, and a glass of cold milk.

"This old place is running down so, I can hardly keep it up. Luther has kept busy in the orchard this year, but he's too old to mow and pick apples to boot. It's just catch as catch can around here." Miss Sadie sighed, something he'd seldom heard her do. "What I need is somebody young and stout!"

The walk up the hill had carried fresh oxygen to his brain. "Dooley Barlowe!" he blurted.

"How's that?"

"Miss Sadie, I know a boy who just might fit the bill. Eleven or twelve, I'd say, old enough to push a mower and prune a bush or two if you'd show him how. Shall I look into it?"

"And be quick about it!" she said, beaming.

"Monday morning, first thing. Now, any considerations about the site for the nursing home? I admit to having my own strong opinion."

"Father," she said soberly, "there isn't but one site to consider."

"And what's that?"

"Right down the road where the old church was."

"Precisely! My thinking exactly!"

"Great minds work alike!" she said, clapping her small hands.

"The view . . ."

"Couldn't be better."

"The proximity . . ."

"Absolutely perfect!" she exclaimed.

"And since the money you so graciously donated also covers the cost of land . . ."

"That means the church gets paid for the land, and Lord's Chapel can have a new roof!"

Barnabas looked up at the odd pair, rocking in unison and laughing like children. He yawned hugely.

"I confess I've been concerned about you, giving away all your father's money. I just hope that . . . well, I hope that you haven't strapped yourself."

She looked at him, he thought, almost coquettishly. "Father, what I gave away was only what belonged to Papa. There's still Mama's money, you know."

❧

On Monday morning, Andrew Gregory left the church office with a large, flat package under his arm, just as Russell Jacks arrived.

"Father," said the sexton, making himself at home on the visitor's bench, "my little granboy cain't be took home to his mama yet, and they say school's a startin'. He don't want t' go, it bein' a strange place an' all. I know it's the law for 'im to go and it's right for 'im to go, but I don't hardly know what to do to git 'im started."

School! Well, of course, it was time for school.

"Russell, he'll need to be registered." And, he thought, scrubbed from one end to the other.

"You mean checked in and all?"

"That's right, and we'll need to find out when and how. I believe sometime next week is the first day."

He picked up the phone and called the school superintendent. Then he called the police department.

"Is it all right for two people to ride on a motor scooter over to Wesley?" he wanted to know.

Extra helmet, he wrote on his notepad, as he hung up.

"You may as well git the police back on the line," said Russell.

"Why's that?"

"Because we ain't reported that broke lock, yet. We're supposed t' report a thing like that, git it on th' record."

Ah, thought Father Tim. Much ado about nothing. "I'll take care of that, Russell. Right now, let's get Dooley in school."

❧

At 10:30, he left the office. He had managed to borrow another helmet, and set out for Wesley with an ecstatic Dooley Barlowe behind him on the Vespa.

At two o'clock, they pulled up at the back door of the rectory, with a large plastic shopping bag strapped into the basket. They marched up the steps and stood looking through the screen at Puny, who was rolling dough for a chicken pie.

"Here's a boy who needs cleaning up," said Father Tim. "And here are some clothes for him to wear." He opened the screen door, let Dooley into the kitchen, and handed her their purchases. "I don't know what to tell you to do, but I know you're the one for the job."

Having said that, he left in some haste, leaving Puny holding the bag.

❧

"So I run a tub of hot water," she said, giving her report, "an' handed 'im a bar of soap and said git in there an' soak.

"Well, he went to sayin' how I wasn't 'is mama and couldn't tell 'im what t' do, so I yanked a knot in 'is tail."

He thought she looked very smug and self-satisfied. "And what did you do to yank this knot exactly?"

"That's for me t' know and you t' find out. Not meanin' any disrespect, of course."

"Certainly not."

"So here's what I done. While he was soakin, I washed 'is overalls, and sent 'im home in 'em. I couldn't see dressin' 'im up in new clothes t' go spillin' somethin' down th' front, or settin' in dog poop. I've seen Mr. Jacks's place and it ain't th' Taj Mahal."

"Well done."

"He was mad as fire about it, but Mr. Jacks is bringin' 'im here in th' mornin' and he's gittin' dressed in 'is new stuff, and you can take 'im up to Miss Sadie's. I've cut off th' tags and pressed everything, an' he can wear 'is new blue jeans with that green plaid shirt."

"You're a marvel," he said, sighing with relief.

"What I am is give out, if you don't mind. I declare, takin' care of a preacher is the hardest work I ever done."

"It is?"

"Trust me on this," she said.

❧

"Miss Sadie, I'd like to present Mister Dooley Barlowe! Then what do you say?"

"I say, how d'you do, pleased t' meet you."

"Flawless!"

The sun had come out, and though Dooley had wanted to go by motor scooter, they agreed to walk to Fernbank.

The boy looked so different in his new jeans and plaid shirt, in his fresh socks and Keds, the rector could hardly believe his eyes. He had personally wet Dooley's hair and brushed it, snipping straggly ends with the kitchen shears.

When they reached Fernbank, Miss Sadie was on the porch, waving. A pitcher of lemonade and a plate of store-bought cookies sat on the wicker table.

"Miss Sadie, I'd like to present Mister Barley Doolowe!"

"You got your part wrong," said Dooley.

※

In the few days before school opened, Dooley earned $44.00. As agreed, he came by the church office and reported what he'd done.

"I done this an' that."

"What this and what that?"

"I took out 'er ashes from an ol' stove an' put 'em on 'er 'zaleas. I mowed 'er yard, took goin' over twice, it like to killed me, and hit a nest of yellow jackets."

"Aha."

"I got stung two times, pruned some ol' shrubberies, an' hauled stuff to a wash house. Then I run up an' down them stairs carryin' books to th' attic."

"You pruned shrubbery?"

"Granpaw taught me."

"What else?" the rector asked, genuinely interested.

"I eat some chicken pie an' drunk some lemonade an eat half a pound cake, and pooped in 'er toilet. Doorknob come off 'er toilet door, had t' crawl out 'er window."

"Well done!"

Dooley took the money from his overalls pocket and gave it to the rector, who counted out $40.00 and put it in a box for index cards.

"This will go toward your bicycle. What color did you say you wanted?" He remembered perfectly well.

"Red! Red as a fire engine!"

"Excellent." He took the remaining four dollars and handed it across his desk. "This is for you, just like we talked about. Next week, you can have four dollars again. This after-school work at Miss Sadie's should get that bicycle sooner than we think."

This is too easy, he thought, musing to himself one September evening in his study. For some reason he couldn't explain, he felt like he was waiting for the other shoe to drop.

❧

"Be glad you've never been in love," said Emma.

"Who says I haven't been?"

She stared over her half glasses. "You mean you have?"

"That's for me to know and you to find out."

"I hate it when you talk common." She didn't know which she wanted more, to talk about Harold Newland, or her preacher being in love. She decided to do both. "How bad was it?"

"How bad?"

"Let me put it another way. How good was it, bein' in love?"

"How quickly you forget, Emma. I didn't say I'd been in love."

"I should have known you'd double-talk me blue in the face. He wants me to meet his mother."

"Terrific."

"Terrific? How would you like meeting somebody's mother who's only five years older than you? I could die, I could just die."

"Don't die. Secretary's Day is coming around, and I'm planning to take you to Wesley for dinner."

She brightened. "Really?"

"On my motor scooter."

"I'd give you a good kick if you weren't a priest."

"That never stopped some people," he said.

CHAPTER EIGHT

Golden Days

During the eleven o'clock service, he looked up from the reading in Matthew and found a wife for Hoppy Harper. There, sitting on the gospel side, was one of the loveliest creatures he'd ever seen.

His response was so immediate and overwhelming, he felt certain the inspiration had come from above. What to do about it, however, was not revealed.

From his own observation, matchmaking was more than merely risky, it had proven to be downright disastrous.

Throughout his career as a bachelor priest, people had tried to marry him off. Some parishes had been more intent upon this achievement than others, and the parish of Lord's Chapel had been the worst of the lot.

He had no sooner arrived in Mitford than three vestry members "ganged up," as he called it, and arranged a tea in his honor at the home of a summer resident, Roberta Simpson.

Roberta was so enormously rich that it was beyond his powers of comprehension to imagine the rumored sum.

"You better hook this one," somebody had the gall to say. "You could afford to give up preaching."

After several agonizing meetings, which were manipulated entirely without his knowledge or blessing, Roberta returned to Florida and married her stockbroker. When he met the man the following summer, he could barely resist the impulse to kiss him on both cheeks, after the European fashion.

Then there had been the Becky Nelson Campaign. Becky was a petite and charming widow who played bridge around the clock and thought Wordsworth was a Dallas department store. He didn't like to recall what a fiasco that had been. Talking to Becky Nelson had been precisely like talking to a rock.

It took a full two years for his well-meaning parishioners to throw in the towel. "I give up," he overheard someone declare at a church supper. He had celebrated this good news by eating a second helping of fudge pie.

It was for these reasons, among others, that he refused to play Cupid to any poor, unsuspecting soul, and especially to Hoppy Harper, who had enough worries.

On Monday, Emma was wreathed with smiles. "It worked."

"What worked?"

"Your prayer about me meetin' Harold's mother."

"Never let me say I told you so."

She sat down and put her lunch bag in the bottom desk drawer. "Dottie Newland is a peck of fun. Why, we had such a good time, I think Harold felt left out!"

"Tell me everything."

"We went to Dottie's house and Harold grilled

steaks. She made potato salad and deviled eggs and tea and I brought green beans and a pound cake. I washed, Harold dried, and she put up. Guess what?"

"What's that?"

"She's six years older than me, not five."

"I'm glad to hear it."

Emma unlocked her ledger drawer. "Guess what else?"

"Heaven only knows."

"I think I've found Hoppy Harper a wife."

"No!"

"Did you see that new woman sittin' on the gospel side Sunday?"

"I don't know, I might have."

"Black hair, fair skin, real pretty. Red suit, little hat, black pumps."

"Aha."

"Widow. Just moved to Lilac Road, to her mother's old summer house. Used to come here as a girl. Married a big engineer, bridges or something, who was rich as cream. Killed in a crash in one of those little planes." She looked determined. "I'm goin' to figure a way to get them together."

"Let me know how it works out," he said pleasantly.

❧

In the afternoon, Russell Jacks swung the office door open and stepped in.

"Got my granboy out workin' them bat droppin's in th' flower beds," he said with evident pride. "We'll be havin' us a second spurt of bloom around here."

Russell stood with his hat over his heart, and inspected his shoes.

"Is there something on your mind, Russell?"

"Well, Father, school's startin' tomorrow, y'know. And I'd be . . ." He cleared his throat. "I'd be much obliged if . . ."

"If what?"

"If you'd go with 'im."

"How do you mean?"

"Well, if you'd go sign the papers and git 'im set and all like that." Russell reached into a pocket on the front of his overalls and pulled out a worn ten-dollar bill. He laid it on the rector's desk.

"There's the money t' do it," he said, as if that were the end of the matter.

On Tuesday, he walked with Dooley up Main Street, crossed over Wisteria Lane, and turned right toward the school.

"I'd rather be dead," Dooley said, grimly.

"Aha."

"Laid out in a casket."

"Is that right?"

"With worms crawlin' on me."

"I don't know why. I always liked school."

"You was a sissy, is why."

"Oh, I don't know about that. I was a pretty tough guy."

"They'll be wantin' t' fight me."

"Who's they?"

"Them ol' dump heads from where Granpaw lives at."

"I wouldn't go expecting it, if I were you. That way, you might get it."

"They like to killed me when I come up here, but me 'n Granpaw run 'em off. I busted one ol' boy's nose, and they ain't been back."

"Probably won't come back."

"Yeah, but they'll be waitin' to knock th' poop out of me at school."

"I expect those boys will keep busy getting the hang of things. They won't be thinking about Dooley Barlowe."

"Huh! You don't know how mean people do. Preachers don't know real stuff."

"My friend, if that was a fact, I'd be a happy man."

They turned into the driveway of the old brick school, situated in a grove of oak, blue spruce, and maples showing a faint blush of scarlet. Children with bright clothes and book bags chattered along the sidewalks.

"If you don't mind," said Dooley, "I'd thank you to walk up a ways, 'cause I don't want nobody to think I've got a preacher follerin' me around."

"It might do you some good in the matter that's presently concerning you," said the rector.

❧

In his study that evening, he wrote to Father Roland, in his large New Orleans parish.

"just wanted you to know," he typed with his forefingers, "that the sleepy life you insist i'm living is entirely a product of your 18th cent. romanticism. in two short days, i have run eight miles, washed an exceedingly filthy and enormous dog, counseled a woman in love with our postman, washed two grocery sacks full of collard greens, begun next Sunday's sermon outline, prayed with the sick at our little hospital, read the entire lot of Wordsworth's evening voluntaries (which I heartily recommend to you, my friend), attended a vestry meeting about the building site of our new nursing home, personally registered a boy in school, and worked a bucket of bat droppings into my floribunda beds.

"now," he concluded, "do let me know how you're coming on."

❧

"Lord have mercy!" said Puny on Wednesday. "There's always somethin' to cook around here. Some places you go, all you have to do is clean—it's like a vacation. Come over here, and there's a bushel of this, a sack of that, a peck of somethin' or other."

"I thought you liked to cook." He was sitting at the kitchen counter, having a meatloaf sandwich and a glass of tea.

"I like to cook," she said, crossing her arms over her chest like armor plate, "but not for the entire Russian army."

"Aha."

"Besides, these collards 've smelled up the place 'til it's more'n I can hardly stand."

"Next time, I'll cook the collards and you wash Barnabas. How's that?"

"That dog of yours looks like somethin' the cat drug in. Why you take th' trouble to wash 'im is beyond me, when he just goes out and gets covered with mud again."

"It's the same principle as making the bed. Why do it if you're just going to get in it again? Or, for that matter, why wash the lunch dishes when you're going to use them for supper?"

"That's not the same thing," she said tartly, getting down on her hands and knees with the scrub brush. "Anyway, how did Dooley do on 'is first day?"

"Black eye," he said.

"Oh, law! It's that red hair. I was always pestered for bein' redheaded. Did he whop 'im back?"

"A left to the solar plexus and a right to the nose."

"Hot dog!" she said with evident satisfaction.

"Puny, I know it's none of my business how you conduct your chores here, but I do wish you wouldn't clean the floor on your hands and knees."

"It's the only way to do it right. My mama did it this way, her mama did it this way." She brushed a loose strand of hair out of her eyes. "An' I'm goin' to do it this way."

Little Emma! he thought, finishing his tea.

She looked at him, flushed and beaming. "Did he really get 'im good?"

"I did not press him for the sordid details."

She cocked her head to one side. "Now, Father . . ."

"Oh, well, then, Puny, all right!" He went to the sink and rinsed out his tea glass, so she couldn't see him grinning like an idiot. "Yes! The answer is yes, he got him good."

"I'll bake 'im a cake!" said Puny, scrubbing the worn tiles with renewed vigor.

❧

At the drugstore, he ran into Hoppy Harper, who was buying a bag of jellybeans.

"I overdose on these about twice a week," the doctor said. "I eat the green first."

The rector sighed in mock despair. "You sure cut into my fun. I haven't had a Little Debbie since Easter."

"The trouble with you," said Hoppy, "is that Little Debbies were the only fun you were having."

Hoppy paid for his jelly beans and opened the bag at once, searching for a green. "So when are you going on vacation?"

If Hoppy Harper had asked him that once, he had asked him that a hundred times, he thought. He wasn't proud of the fact that he'd never been good at arranging his own recreation. The trip to Cambridge had been the best of examples.

While the English weather abandoned its usual caprice and offered glorious balm and sunshine, he'd found himself hopelessly plunged into research that confined him for days to the musty, fan-vaulted library.

"There are race horses," a bishop once told him, "and there are plow horses, and the pulpit can make fit use of both kinds."

He didn't try to deceive himself. In his own opinion, he was a plow horse. He set his course at one end of the field, then plowed to the other and back again.

In any case, he felt himself becoming an increasingly dry old crust, and his doctor was profoundly right about his lack of anything even remotely resembling fun.

୧

Autumn drew on in Mitford, and one after another, the golden days were illumined with changing light.

New wildflowers appeared in the hedges and fields. Whole acres were massed with goldenrod and fleabane. Wild phlox, long escaped from neat gardens, perfumed every roadside. And here and there, milkweed put forth its fat pods, laden with a filament as fine as silk.

There were those who were ecstatic with the crisp new days of autumn and the occasional scent of woodsmoke on the air. And there were those who were loathe to let summer go, saying it had been "the sweetest summer out of heaven," or "the best in many years."

But no one could hold on to summer once the stately

row of Lilac Road maples began to turn scarlet and gold. The row began its march across the front of the old Porter place, skipped over Main Street and the war monument to the town hall, paraded in front of First Baptist, lined up along the rear of Winnie Ivey's small cottage, and ended in a vibrant blaze of color at Little Mitford Creek.

When this show began, even the summer die-hards, who were by then few enough in number to be counted on the fingers of one hand, gave up and welcomed the great spectacle of a mountain autumn.

"It is quite a treasure trove," Andrew Gregory told the rector. "Primitive, yes, but with great insight, great depth. There's a winsome quality about them, yet they have surprising polish, too. I'd like to show you how they're looking in the frames."

"I'll drop by around noon."

"If arthritis hadn't caught up with him, who knows what he might have done?"

"And who knows what was lost when Miss Rose set fire to his ink sketches, because he ate her portion of the pickle relish?"

Both men shook their heads with regret.

"I'm afraid our parish hall won't hold a great many people. Maybe we should have the showing in the town hall."

"The mildew will keep the crowd away," Andrew wisely reminded him.

"You're right, of course. Well, then, what about the Oxford Antique Shop?"

"Possibly," Andrew said, thoughtfully. "Possibly. With a little mulled wine, sometime in October?"

"Excellent!"

"Of course, we could sell the whole lot without the trouble of hanging them. Miss Sadie loves art, she'd be good for at least one. And Esther Cunningham would very likely take two for the town hall."

"Hoppy Harper, probably two."

"And your veterinarian friend and his wife?"

"One or two, certainly."

"I'll have a half dozen myself, out of that series he did of the valley."

"How many drawings are there? I keep forgetting the number."

"Forty-three, done over a period of maybe fifteen or twenty years. It's fairly easy to put them in sequential order, his early woodcocks look like mourning doves. And I mistook one of his first bird dogs for a deer."

They laughed agreeably. It gave them much satisfaction that Uncle Billy was not merely an affable, rheumatic village indigent, but a gifted artist.

"I'll have one for my study, of course, and one for Walter and Katherine for Christmas."

Andrew's face lighted up with his well-known smile. "We've sat right here and sold a couple of dozen!" He took a small, black book from the breast pocket of his jacket and consulted it. "Well, then! How about Saturday, October twentieth, around four o'clock in the afternoon? At the Oxford! I'll have a new shipment from England, and a container of books from a Northamptonshire manor house. I'm told Beatrix Potter visited there as a child and scribbled throughout two volumes on moles."

The rector laughed. "I'm astounded that two volumes on moles even exist! Though of course, when they tunnel under my back lawn, I have volumes to say on the subject myself."

As Andrew stood up to go, the rector couldn't help but admire his friend's impeccable tailoring. It was safe to say that Andrew Gregory owned more cashmere jackets than anyone who ever lived in Mitford, all of which were cut so cleanly to his form that a weight gain of barely two pounds would have forced him into another wardrobe. Discipline! That's the ticket! thought the rector, chagrined that he'd slacked up on his jogging.

He stood at the door with his neighbor from across the lane. "I hope business is thriving at the Oxford."

"Better than ever! And a curious thing happened. Over the weekend, I sold half the English pieces to an Englishman! Chap's taking the whole lot back to Ipswich! And your business?" Andrew inquired with a twinkle in his blue eyes.

"Oh, up and down," replied the rector, smiling.

❧

He was sitting at the desk in his study when the phone rang.

"Tim, dear!" said a cheerful voice. "We agree that Barnabas is a wonderful dog and boon companion, but how is it that he so easily replaces two old friends?"

"Marge! I think of you daily, and you and Hal are always in my prayers. But you'd never know it, would you? Please forgive me."

"Forgive you, indeed! Your penalty is a Baxter apple pie, which I hear you've frozen in commercial quantities."

He laughed with the first friend he ever made in Mitford.

"Hal will be in on Friday afternoon to do errands," said Marge. "Why don't you come out with Barnabas and spend the night and most of Saturday?"

"Well, I . . ."

"May he fetch you around four?"

"Well . . . ," said Father Tim, thinking of the rose bushes that needed transplanting, and the English ivy that needed digging up and potting, and the carpet stains he'd sworn to Puny he'd try to remove, and the bath that Barnabas must have at once, and the accumulation of papers and magazines on his desk, and the new helmet he had to order, and the perennial beds that needed attention, and the letters that wanted answering.

His gaze fell upon the open Bible at his elbow. "Thine own friend, and thy father's friend, forsake not," began a verse in Proverbs.

"I'll be ready and waiting," he said.

❧

The next morning, he walked across the plush, green churchyard and rounded the east corner of Lord's Chapel, in search of Russell Jacks. He found the old sexton oiling his push mower.

"Russell, how's the world treating you this morning?"

Russell stood up slowly and removed his battered hat. "Well, sir, there's no rest for the wicked, and the righteous don't need none."

"I'll say!"

"Them leaves 're goin' to be comin' down by the wagon load," he said soberly, looking up at the lacy ceiling of oak and maple branches.

"Let me ask you a favor," said Father Tim. "If you wouldn't mind parting with him, I'd like to borrow your grandboy on Friday afternoon and return him Saturday before dark."

"I'd be much obliged!"

"I'm going out to a farm that has a whole raft of

cows and horses and dogs, and good trees to climb, and I thought Dooley might enjoy it."

"I'd consider it a blessin', to tell the truth. He's about wore me out. Let's just say he's old enough to want t' drive, but not tall enough to reach the pedals, if you get my meanin'."

"You sure don't look any worse for wear," said the rector, noting a new sparkle in the old man's eyes.

He inspected the mulch Russell was putting on the rhododendrons underneath the windows. Where the mulch hadn't yet been spread, he noticed something unusual.

"Russell, this looks like ashes. Are you putting ashes under the mulch?"

"Nope, I ain't."

He was not of the let's-throw-ashes-around-all-the-shrubs-in-the-garden school. He took a spade out of the green wicker tool basket, and scraped the pile of ashes away from the roots. "Looks like somebody dumped ashes out of an outdoor grill."

"No tellin' what people'll do these days."

"If you see any more of it around, let me know. We haven't used the fireplace in a couple of years; I don't know where that could have come from."

He stood up and wiped his hands on a handkerchief Puny had just ironed. "Well, Russell, keep up the good work. You're the one who's made our grounds a regular showplace, and I want you to know we all appreciate it."

Russell put his hat over his heart. "You reported that broke lock yet?"

"The truth will out—no, I haven't." He could tell Russell believed that negligence in reporting this incident to the police would encourage someone to kick the doors in next time. "You rest up, now, while Dooley's off to the farm."

"I'm goin' to cook me a mess of greens and fry out some side meat, is what I'm goin' to do!" he said eagerly. "I'm about half sick of peanut butter and jelly."

❧

When he went home for lunch on Friday, Puny was ironing the shirt and overalls Dooley had left behind when he dressed for Miss Sadie's interview.

"Great farm clothes!" he said with satisfaction. "I wish you were coming with us, Puny."

"I do not like a farm," she said with unusual emphasis. "You have to watch where you step ever' minute."

"I can safely say you'd like Meadowgate."

"Work, that's what farms are! And no letup! Cain't go off to Asheville or down to Lake Lure nor anywhere else, with all them animals hangin' on your dress tail. Women I've seen livin' on farms looks like their granmaw by the time they git my age. No wonder they all run off t' work in the cannin' plant, even if they do come home smellin' like kraut."

"You don't have to preach me a sermon."

She put her hands on her hips and looked at him steadily. "I'll scrub your floors and wash your drawers and put up your tomatoes and feed your dog, but I'll not scrape your shoes after you been stompin' around a farm."

"You have my word. I am not going out there to jump in a manure pile. I am going out there to walk through the woods, read my new book, and help cook dinner tonight. Now, what's so bad about that?"

"An' I'm not goin' to wash Dooley Barlowe if he comes back with farm mess on 'im."

Little Emma! he thought. "It's a deal," he said.

❧

As they approached the farm gate, the resident dogs ran out to meet the red truck.

"Here they come!" yelled Hal over the din. "Open the door!"

Father Tim threw open the door and Barnabas leaped out to greet Buckwheat, Bowser, Baudelaire, Bodacious, and Bonemeal.

"Don't throw me out there!" yelled Dooley, holding his hands over his ears.

"Throw 'im out there!" Hal shouted, taking Dooley by the shoulder.

"No, no, them ol' dogs'll eat me! Don't throw me out there!"

"Oh, all right, then," Father Tim said, laughing. "We won't throw you out 'til we get to the barn!"

As the pickup drove through the stable shed, Dooley saw a bay mare looking soulfully over her stall door.

"Throw me out now!" he cried, enthralled at his first sight of Goosedown Owen.

❧

On his list of favorite things to do, "sit in the kitchen at Meadowgate" was clearly among the top five. This afternoon, however, he might have placed it at the very, very top.

A low fire burned on the hearth, warming the autumn air that, by morning, would cause a heavy mist to rise upon the fields.

The dumpling pot was simmering on the black cook stove, and vases brimming with wildflowers stood on the pine table and along the window sills.

However, there was to be no sitting in the Meadowgate kitchen today. Dooley dragged him out to the stable, saying every step of the way, "I want t' ride 'at horse, I got t' git a ride on 'at horse."

"Dooley, have you ever ridden a horse?"

"Nope, but I know how."

"How?"

"You take it over t' th' house, you stand on th' top step of th' porch, and you jis' jump on it an' go."

"What about a saddle?"

"Don't need no saddle."

"Is that a fact?"

"I've thought about it a million times. It'll work."

He thought Dooley's hair seemed redder, his eyes bluer, and his freckles thicker under the bill of his new baseball cap.

Hal came around the side of the stable from his office, carrying his black O.B. bag.

"Finally got this bag in order," he said. "Let me set it in the truck and I'll join you boys."

"I'd like t' git a ride on 'at horse," said Dooley, following at the vet's heels.

"I think that might be arranged. Ever been on a horse?"

"Nope, but I done it in my mind over and over 'til I know how."

"To tell the truth, that's how I learned to ride a horse. Goosedown has spirit, but I don't think she'll throw you." Hal put the bag through the open truck window and set it on the front seat. " 'Course, there's no guarantee, either."

"I can handle it," said Dooley, putting his thumbs in the straps of his overalls.

☙

The first time Hal walked Dooley and Goosedown Owen around the stable yard, Dooley's face went as white as library paste.

"Stick up there!" said Hal.

The second time around, his color had improved.

"Lookin' good!" said Hal.

The third time, Hal ran, still holding the bridle, and Dooley bounced up and down with glee. "Let 'er go!" he hollered.

Hal let her go.

Goosedown Owen cantered to the hog pen, stopped suddenly at the gate, and threw her rider into a trough of fresh slop.

That it was only apple peelings, sour oatmeal, orange rinds, cabbage leaves, sprouted potatoes, and stale soup was no consolation.

"Slop!" sputtered Dooley, rolling out of the trough and into the mud. "I'd like to half kill 'at horse!"

Goosedown Owen had trotted back to the stable and was eyeing the whole scene from the comfort of her stall. Dooley stood up and shook his fist toward the stable. "I'm ridin' you agin, you mule-headed ol' poop!"

Father Tim strolled over to Dooley, who was climbing through the hog pen gate.

"Do you, ah, know what would happen if Puny Bradshaw could see you now?"

He wiped his hair from his eyes with an arm that was smeared to the elbow. "Yep. I'd be dead meat."

❧

Dinner at Meadowgate Farm was always an event, and tonight was no exception. Marge had baked a savory hen stuffed with sausage, bread crumbs, orange peel, and farm onions, which she served with brandied fruit and a pot of dumplings so splendid that the rector recommended entering the recipe in the county fair.

As the men cleared away the dishes, a three-quarter moon rose and shone through the windows that looked toward the meadow.

Dooley sat on the floor with a jumble of dogs. Bodacious and Bonemeal chewed rawhide strips the size of ceiling molding. Barnabas slept on the hearth by the low, simmering fire. Baudelaire curled up on the chintz sofa and looked doleful. Buckwheat chased his tail and barked, and Bowser sat contentedly in Dooley's lap and licked his face.

Marge eased herself into her father's rocking chair. "Dogs!" she said, with mock disgust. "The baby's first words will be 'woof, woof.' "

"Do you think you'll be game for an art showing on the twentieth?" the rector wanted to know. "Andrew Gregory is framing more than forty of Uncle Billy's drawings."

Marge rubbed her sizeable stomach. "I'm not game for much of anything, Tim dear."

"If she can handle it, we'll be there," said Hal. "Like the rest of us, she has her good days and her bad days."

"I know all about that," said the rector, as the phone rang.

Hal reached into a wooden bread bowl filled with winter squash and plucked out a cordless phone. "Hello! Meadowgate here."

He listened ruefully, holding the receiver away from his ear. Even over the din of the dogs, a voice could be heard shouting.

". . . an' you better come quick, for I don't know how long she's been at it, bellerin' her head off, and me down with the pneumonia and cain't leave the house."

There followed a series of long, racking coughs, explosive hawking, and general bronchial pyrotechnics that made every dog in the room grow silent and stare at the phone Hal now held above his head.

"Is she in the stall?" Hal shouted.

"In the stall tied to 'er feedbox, and it sounds bad t' me. She's kickin' th' wall to beat the band, and if I lose this 'n on top of losin' Mister Cooley, you'll not see no more of me, it'll put me down like a doornail."

"Hold on, Miss Reba, I'll be there in twenty minutes."

"Tell her to have a cup of hot tea with honey, for goodness sake!"

"My wife says have a cup of hot tea with honey!"

This advice was greeted with a coughing demonstration of such force and magnitude that the audience was mesmerized. Finally, Hal came to himself and simply hung up the phone.

"Reba Cooley," he announced, as if that explained everything.

"Rats!" said Marge, as Hal hurried out of the kitchen and took a jacket off the peg in the hallway.

"I like 'is ol' dog," said Dooley, oblivious to anything but Bowser's devoted attention.

Father Tim dried his hands. "I'd like to come with you."

"You're on, pal. Grab a jacket, it's getting cold tonight."

Hal kissed his wife, tousled Dooley's hair, and was gone, the rector beside him in the moonlight that lay like a platinum sheen over the lawn of Meadowgate Farm.

❧

Hal drove a few miles on the moonlit highway, then turned onto a series of narrow roads that wound steeply along the side of a mountain.

"You should drive along these roads when there's no moon," he said. "It's enough to make a man want a chew of tobacco."

They noticed that the higher they went, the lower the temperature dropped.

"I don't mind telling you that this nursing-home business frightens me," the rector said, pulling on a fleece-lined jacket that smelled strongly of horse liniment. "Five million dollars! Sometimes, the enormity of it is overwhelming. It's going to be a huge project to sieve through a little parish.

"It's like that Vermeer fiasco. I was praying it wasn't a valuable painting, as you know, because it would have torn us asunder. I'm not saying we couldn't pull ourselves back together, but I dreaded the . . . well, the violence of the disruption. A small parish is a fragile ecology."

"It is."

"We're close to naming a building committee. And you wouldn't believe the horror stories I've heard about building committees."

Hal tightened his left-hand grip on the wheel. He knew exactly what his rector was working around to. He felt in his pocket for his pipe, which lived in this particular jacket, packed and ready to go during any emergency.

"I'll sit on the committee, of course," Father Tim said, "and I expect Ron Malcolm to be asked . . ."

"A retired contractor," Hal said. "A good man."

"Miss Sadie, of course. Jeb Reynolds." He paused, then plunged ahead. "You know I need you on this committee, even though Marge is only a month away from an event that will change both your lives."

Just then, the truck swung around a bend, and the

lights picked out a small farmhouse and barn, an odd assortment of sheds and chicken coops, great rolls of baling wire, a fleet of rusting tractors and hand plows, and three baying coon dogs standing abreast at the side door of the house.

The porch light came on with such fierce wattage that the rector covered his eyes, then the door banged open as if a gale-force wind had caught it. Reba Cooley peered out.

"We're here," called Hal, "and driving on down to the barn. I'll need a bucket of warm water. I'll send the father back for it."

The rector leaned forward and threw up his hand. To say that Reba Cooley presented a striking appearance would have been an understatement of ridiculous proportions. He thought she looked like a vast boulder, dressed in a chenille robe, that someone had rolled to the door. Her hair was cut short, like a man's, so that he said later he would have sworn it was Mr. Cooley, had he not learned the poor fellow now rested in a plot behind the chicken house.

The cow stall was damp and cold, and he was grateful for the jacket. He couldn't remember when he had last heard the bawling of a cow, but suddenly, the smells and sounds brought back memories of his Mississippi boyhood.

His father had been an attorney in their little town of Holly Springs, with a farm that lay just two miles distant from his office. They'd never kept large animals, as the other 4-H families did. But there were rabbits by the dozens, and flocks of chestnut-colored bantams.

He remembered asking, with immeasurable disappointment, why everything on their farm had to be small.

"This is not a working farm," his father had said with finality, and no amount of pleading by his mother had been able to change his mind.

He remembered Harold Johnson, a strapping boy who was held back in seventh grade for three years running, whom he envied for his knowledge of farm life. "Ol' cow calved last night," Harold might say, smugly. "Dropped a big 'un."

Then there was Raymond Lereaux who showed horses and won blue ribbons that he brought to school for Show and Tell.

It had taken awhile to get interested in something as small as rabbits, but when he did get interested, he was fairly consumed, and it was hardly any wonder that he chose to breed Flemish Giants.

Dark-haired Jessica Raney, who dressed in embroidered pinafores and lived on a dairy farm, was wide-eyed with admiration when he started winning ribbons for his sleek show rabbits. And during the year when disease wiped out his entire herd, she sent a card saying she was sorry. Just that, nothing more. And he'd put it in his sock drawer, where it stayed for a very long time.

The death of the herd, and the shock of seeing them sprawled stiffly in the hutches, had not set well with his father.

"No more," he had snapped, walking briskly from the hutches toward the car. He had run after his father with the taste of iron in his mouth, his heart heavy as a stone. "Wait!" he had cried out to his father, who got in the car and roared down the driveway, not looking back.

He would never forget the agony he felt, as if something of himself had perished with the herd. What he hated most was the way their legs had stood stiffly in the air, a humiliating loss of dignity in creatures whom he'd found to be poised and wise.

Hal Owen inspected his patient carefully, then removed most of the contents of his O.B. bag. Anesthetic, syringe, lubricant, gloves, leg chains, hooks, towels. Father Tim warily laid the cow puller, which he'd carried in from the truck, on a shelf. The cow bawled hideously.

"Tim, might as well go to the house for water now, and I'll see what's up. We may be close to the countdown. Make it warm, it's getting cold as blazes. And bring the bucket full."

He zipped his jacket and headed toward the house, where he was greeted by the trio of baying hounds. They leaped against his chest and legs, barking hysterically, and he was not surprised to find that quoting Scripture did nothing to control the onslaught.

He pounded on the storm door, and waited.

When Reba Cooley threw open the door, he couldn't help but notice that she was wearing overalls under her robe.

"Preacher," she said, "I got a job for you."

In the kitchen, she handed him a flashlight and a bucket of warm water.

"Not one real preacher could I lay hold of t' say a word over Mister Cooley." At this, she coughed so hard that the water splashed on his shoes.

"All I could git was a lay preacher, not hardly more'n twenty year old." She reached into a pocket of her overalls. "Here, this is your'n to go over there and do it right. You know I'd go with you, but I'm a sick woman." He laid the money on the table as they walked out to the stoop. The silvery moon that lighted their path at Meadowgate Farm was not shining at the Cooley's.

"Right over yonder," she said, pointing into the inky darkness. "Go around that balin' wire, on past that tractor, take a left by the chicken coop, and you'll step right on 'is grave."

A fine way to put it, he thought, checking the flashlight. It beamed weakly.

"Hit's a little family plot, about a dozen in there. Mister Cooley's is the fresh 'un, you cain't miss it," she said, overcome with another fit of coughing.

He managed to find his way to the baling wire, and set the bucket by the tractor to pick up when his mission was accomplished. The dogs grew bored with his company and ran ahead.

He beamed the flashlight ahead and picked his way around the huge bale of rusted wire. Surely, this would only take a moment. Best to get it out of the way, then go on to the barn and assist Hal.

"Aha!" he said, expecting to see what he was looking for, as the moon broke through leaden clouds.

In the eerie platinum light, he found that he was, indeed, looking at a graveyard, but not the family kind. As far as he could tell, there were three rusted Chevrolets, a 1956 Pontiac with no hood, a Dodge pickup on blocks, and a couple of Studebakers filled with hay.

"Lord," he said, earnestly, "I don't know where this fellow's grave is, and it's too dark to be stumbling around out here looking for it. Surely I don't have to be standing on it to pray over it. So here goes."

He bent his head and prayed on behalf of the departed.

Then he departed, himself, with great haste, only to fall over the bucket he'd left sitting by the tractor, emptying its contents in the grass.

"Left foot's bent backward," Hal said. "Where the dickens have you been?"

"To a funeral," he said, setting the refilled bucket down.

"I washed up under a spigot I found out front. We've got a little job to do here."

※

It was after two o'clock when they started home in the truck, with the heater going full blast. The moon raced in and out of the clouds, suddenly revealing open meadows and high ridges and cows sleeping under trees in the pastures.

Hal was exhausted, but happy. "Did you see how I turned her to face the calf? Once she licks it, she'll never leave it."

"Tonight ought to be good for at least a couple of sermons."

"Wasn't too much for you, was it? I mean, when I asked you to clean the placental tissue off the calf, you were white as a sheet."

"I beg to differ. When I was doing that, I was merely pale. Turning white as a sheet came when you asked me to help use the cow puller."

"Good, honest work!"

"Let's just say I wouldn't want to swap jobs."

"Me, either, pal. I'd rather reach in a cow's rear end any day than have to deal with a horse's behind."

"Harry Nelson is being transferred to Birmingham," Father Tim said mildly, having saved this *pièce de résistance* for the right moment.

Hal was quiet for a couple of miles.

"Okay," he said, at last. "I'm going to pray about sitting on the building committee, and I want to talk to Marge. I'll let you know next week. Now, lay off, will you?"

Just as he felt a certain warmth in his spirit, he felt the creeping cold in his feet. But it wasn't until later, under the glare of the porch light, that he saw what would have horrified Puny Bradshaw.

Cow manure not only covered his loafers, but the better part of his socks and pants cuffs, as well.

"Lord have mercy!" he said, presumably speaking in the local vernacular, but meaning it quite literally, as well.

❧

He was sitting on the back steps of the farmhouse, a coffee cup beside him, cleaning his shoes. It was a glorious morning, as most mornings had been during this spectacular autumn.

> *Thy bountiful care, what tongue can recite?*
> *It breathes in the air, it shines in the light!*

He sang heedlessly. If there was anywhere on earth he could sing a favorite hymn at the top of his voice, it was here in the sunshine on this very back step.

The screen door slammed. "I want t' ride 'at horse," said Dooley, sitting down beside him.

"You might begin by saying good morning."

"Good mornin', I want t' ride 'at horse."

"Did you know there are cows on this farm? And chickens? And horseshoes and croquet and a grape arbor and apple trees? As I recall, there's even a log cabin down by the creek, built for someone who was once just your age. Would you like to see all that when I finish cleaning these shoes?"

"I would, soon as I ride 'at horse."

"Dooley, you are a man of single purpose, a characteristic which, with proper control, can take you far in this world."

"We're havin' pancakes."

"Wonderful. Who combed your hair?"

"Nobody."

"That's what I thought. What did you do with those clothes covered with slop?"

"I stuffed 'em in a paper sack and put 'em in th' truck. I thought Puny'd wash 'em."

"Ha!" he said, putting the final polish on his loafers.

The two sat in silence for a while, looking toward the barn and away to the steep hill covered with a blaze of autumn maples.

"Do you go t' hollerin' when you preach?"

"Hollering? Oh, not much. Why?"

"Miss Sadie wants me t' go to church with 'er in th' mornin', and if you go t' hollerin', I'll prob'ly go t' runnin'."

"Is that right?"

"I cain't stand a hollerin' preacher."

"Me, either."

"Well, I'll come then."

"Comb your hair first," said the rector.

❧

The morning had continued so fair and golden that, after the service, he greeted his congregation on the lawn. "Did I go to hollerin'?" he asked Dooley.

"A time or two, you had me worried," the boy said.

Miss Sadie gave him the usual bright peck on the cheek. "Louella is coming home to live at Fernbank!" she said, joyfully. "Her grandson's bank has transferred him to Los Angles, and Louella said if she had to live in Los Angeles, she'd kill herself! I'm so happy about this, Father. Could I see you first thing in the morning about some insurance papers? I need your advice."

Harold Newland shook his hand. "If it's all right," he said, blushing, "I'd like to see you sometime in the morning."

The new woman who was sitting on the gospel side these days took his hand and smiled. "Olivia Davenport, Father. I enjoyed the service very much."

"We're glad to have you with us, Olivia. Your hat adds a lovely touch."

"I'm afraid I'm a bit old-fashioned about wearing hats to church."

"No more old-fashioned than I in liking to see them!" Yes, indeed. A perfect wife for Hoppy Harper.

"Would it be possible to have a visit with you in the morning?"

"I'll look forward to it," he said. "Around ten?"

So far, his Monday morning appointments were stacking up like planes over Atlanta.

CHAPTER NINE

Neighbors

"Father, I've come to ask for Emma's hand in marriage."

Having said that, Harold Newland blushed deeply and squirmed like a schoolboy on the visitor's bench. "You see, there's nobody else to ask, and I believe in askin'."

"I believe in it, myself, Harold. And I'm happy you've come. I'd like to say that I think the world of Emma Garrett. She's as dependable as the day is long and has a spirit of generosity that's practically unequaled in my experience. She's been mighty good for me, and I expect her to be twice as good for you."

" 'Course, I'm not takin' her away from you. She'll want to keep workin', and I thought I might get her a four-wheel drive since we'll be livin' out a ways."

"I can see Emma in a four-wheel drive."

"We'll move into my house and sell her place as soon as we can."

"When do you think the wedding might be?"

"Emma thought we ought to wait 'til spring, but I say the sooner the better. And I was hopin' . . ." Harold hesitated, with obvious discomfort.

"What were you hoping?"

"Hopin' that you might be willin' to join with my preacher for the ceremony."

"Well, I don't see why not. The more the merrier!"

Two down and one to go, he thought, as he flushed the toilet in the office bathroom and got ready for his next caller.

❧

The beautiful, dark-haired Olivia Davenport did an odd thing. Rather than use the visitor's bench like everybody else, she walked to Emma's chair, sat down across from him, crossed her shapely legs, and said:

"Father Tim, I'm dying."

He could only trust that his face didn't convey the shock he felt.

"I'm asking you to help me find something to make the rest of my life worth living.

"Mother left me her winter and summer homes, and I have considerable property of my own. That means I could spend these last months being quite idle and care-free, and, believe me, that's tempting. But I did not come to Mitford to join the club and sit by the pool. There's nothing wrong with that, but it's absolutely wrong for me.

"I came to Mitford to do something that will make a difference. And while I'm not smart enough to know what that something is, I believe with all my heart that you can tell me."

The first time he set eyes on Olivia Davenport, he

felt as if the Holy Spirit had spoken to his heart. This time was no different. He sensed at once that Olivia Davenport was the answer to a prayer he'd initiated two years ago.

"Olivia, I'd like to ask you to read something, if you'd be so kind."

He handed her his open Bible, pointed to the twenty-seventh Psalm of David, and in clear, lucid tones, she read:

" 'The Lord is my light and my salvation; whom shall I fear? The Lord is the strength of my life; of whom shall I be afraid? For in the time of trouble he shall hide me in his pavilion; in the secret of his tabernacle shall he hide me; he shall set me upon a rock. Wait on the Lord; be of good courage, and he shall strengthen thine heart. Wait, I say, on the Lord.' "

She let the book rest in her lap.

"If you were ill," he said quietly, "with no one to sit by your bed, to hold your hand when you're lonely, or rejoice with you when you're glad, would there be anything, after all, to live for?"

Olivia looked at him steadily. It was a rhetorical question.

"It would give courage to a lot of people to hear the faith and victory in these words."

She smiled and, without looking at the book in her lap, repeated something she clearly knew well. " 'For in the time of trouble He shall hide me in His pavilion; in the secret of his tabernacle shall He hide me; He shall set me upon a rock.' "

"He has hidden you in His pavilion?"

She smiled, tears shining in her eyes. "And He has set me upon a rock."

"Would you do something to make life worth living

for the patients at Mitford Hospital? Would you be willing to read to them each and every morning? It's a big job."

"He's a big God," she said, with something that seemed like excitement.

In the space of precisely seven minutes, which he reckoned to be the full length of her visit, he had been told a terrible truth, discovered an answer to prayer, helped someone find a ministry, and been unutterably refreshed in his own spirit. Perhaps, he thought, we should all live as if we're dying.

❧

The letter arrived, bearing postage stamps with the queen's likeness. The bells would be delayed again. Perhaps by Christmas . . .

He was disappointed. He had hoped the bells would ring at the time of the Owen baby's birth. Ah, well, perhaps for the baptism, he thought as he walked home.

Tonight he would miss seeing Puny, which he was sure she would think he'd planned. After all, there was that bag of Dooley's laundry that he'd set on the washing machine. As far as he was personally concerned, his own shoes were shining, he had washed out his manure-soaked socks, and cleaned his own pants cuffs. Enough was enough.

He thought, too, of Olivia Davenport. Olivia didn't want to waste time, for she had none to waste. On Wednesday, they would meet at the hospital at seven, and the first patient they'd visit would be the terminally ill Pearly McGee. Finally, there would be more than a pat and a prayer to be distributed along the halls.

He turned the corner toward home and heard the familiar, booming bark from the garage. He felt spare and

light, like the weather, and looked forward to an early
supper of Puny's barbecued ribs.

❧

Recently, he'd dared to let Barnabas off the leash,
though only in his own backyard. Barnabas would dash
to the hedge that separated the rectory from Baxter
Park, do his business, and come bounding back, ready
for a super-size Milk Bone.

Perhaps, just perhaps, he thought, this could become
their bedtime ritual. It would take him out of the house
for a breath of air and a look at the stars, provide Barnabas a moment of diversion, and answer any calls of
nature, as well. It could even, in a pinch, get him off the
hook for the nightly walk to the monument.

It was already dark when he set the dishes in the
sink, and turned the radio to a classical station that was
more static than Mozart.

He stood at the screen door, assessing his companion's mood. If Barnabas was excitable tonight, he'd put
him on a leash, without question. But the dog stood beside him quietly, even reflectively. The strains of a vio-
lin obscured the low growl that erupted just as he
opened the door.

Barnabas seemed to sail through the air, clearing the
steps entirely and landing only inches from a white cat
that was streaking across the yard.

Furious with himself, he watched Barnabas disap-
pear through the hedge that bordered the neighboring
yard, where he was surprised to see the glimmer of
lighted windows.

" 'Blessed be the Lord, who daily loads us with benefits'!" he shouted from a psalm as he raced toward the
hedge.

Barnabas, however, could hear nothing above the din of an old-fashioned cat and dog fight.

Father Tim peered into the yard where the humiliated cat was racing up a hemlock tree. "Barnabas!" he yelled.

Barnabas stood at the foot of the tree, his thick fur bristling, filling the night with a bark that seemed to carry to the monument and echo back along the storefronts.

" 'Be filled with the spirit!' " he shouted. " 'Speak to one another in psalms, hymns, and spiritual songs!' " He never knew which Scripture would float to the surface in such emergencies.

"I'll fill you with the spirit!" a voice announced. Suddenly, the beam of a flashlight shone directly into his eyes. "What are you doing in my hedge?"

"I am trying to retrieve my dog from this yard, what else would I be doing?"

"I haven't the faintest idea," the voice said coldly. "Come, then, and get this beast at once."

The flashlight beam was removed from his eyes and, though he found himself momentarily blinded, he proceeded to shout a thundering verse from Jeremiah.

Barnabas crashed obediently through the rhododendron, and sat trembling at his master's feet. Father Tim grabbed him roughly by the collar.

"I'm very sorry, and I apologize," he stated to the hedge, still unable to see who had spoken.

The new neighbor Mule Skinner had promised finally moved into the realm of her porch light, dressed in a robe and pajamas, and carrying a flashlight that she had mercifully put on low beam.

"Is this going to be the usual behavior of your . . . dog?" She said the word with a tinge of loathing.

"Quite possibly, if your cat continues to tear through our yard, dispensing with any shred of caution."

There was an uncomfortable silence.

Then the woman laughed and extended her hand through a bare spot in the foliage.

"Cynthia Coppersmith," she said, "and you must be Father Tim."

"I am. And I'm sorry we've given you such a poor welcome. I promise I'll make it up." Her hand felt as small as a child's, and warm.

"There's no need," she said. "I'm sorry, too. Nerves, you know. Nothing has gone right with this move! Violet is all nerves herself. You know, cats don't like moving, and I saw this man in my hedge, and Violet up a tree, and a dog the size of my refrigerator, and well . . ."

"I got off lightly, then."

"Yes! You did!"

They both laughed.

"The movers broke my table legs, dashed a French mirror, dented my grandmother's tea service, and heaven knows what other carnage I'll discover when the dust settles."

She peered in his direction over a pair of half-glasses. "I do hope you'll stop in when things are calmer."

"And you must stop in, as well," he said, trying to quiet the whimpering creature at his side.

He took Barnabas to the house, holding on to his collar with great authority. Then he put him on a leash and walked with grim determination to the monument and back, muttering the whole way and unashamedly furious.

He had noted, at some point in their desperate conversation through the rhododendron, that his new neighbor was surprisingly attractive, even with a headful of pink curlers. Tomorrow afternoon, he concluded with neighborly zeal, he would bake a meatloaf and take it over. Better yet, he'd put out a Baxter apple pie to thaw. After all, Mitford was still a bastion of old-fashioned hospitality and generous spirit, and he must not fail to demonstrate this whenever the opportunity presented itself.

"A cat!" he said to himself, as he turned off the back porch light. "Of all things to have right next door, a blasted cat!"

❧

The following evening, he heard a light rap at the back door. "I've come borrowing," Cynthia Coppersmith said with a hopeful expression. "You see, my nephew is coming to help put down my toe moldings, and I thought I'd bake a cake."

She extended a measuring cup.

"Oh, indeed! One must have toe moldings. Come right in, come in!" He couldn't help but notice that Mule Skinner had been dead right—her legs were terrific.

Barnabas skidded into the kitchen, galloped toward Cynthia, rose on his hind legs, and put his paws squarely on her shoulders.

"Oh, my," she said, "and how tall are you? I'm five-two!"

He tackled Barnabas, snapped on the leash, and attached him to the handle of the drawer containing the everyday silverware. "I'm sorry. Really I am." Would this creature forever be fogging glasses, mowing people down in their tracks, muddying their clothes?

"Brown sugar or white?" he asked, breathlessly, taking the cup. "White, I suppose, for a cake."

"White would be lovely. But brown would do just as well. Anything!"

He felt an odd mixture of confusion and delight. Having an unexpected knock at the rectory door was unusual, as he had been given a reticent parish who faithfully called before coming.

"Smells good in here!" she exclaimed, sniffing about with curious pleasure.

"Barbecued ribs," he confessed. Barbecued ribs for a clergyman? It was all a trifle self-indulgent, he thought, but a rare treat after endless weeks of Rector's Meatloaf, which Puny now called Old Faithful.

"Do you know I haven't eaten all day long? I meant to go to The Local, but it was one thing and then another, and I looked a fright, too. The water went off, you know. Something at the water main. But I couldn't bathe, or make coffee, or scrub the cabinets. And Violet deposited a mouse on my kitchen rug."

She seemed a bit worn, he thought. She could do with some cheering up. "A cup of tea would be nice. Or how about a glass of sherry?"

"Both, I think!" said his neighbor.

He had his guest sit at the kitchen counter. Talking happily, she sipped a glass of sherry, drank two cups of Darjeeling tea, ate three cold ribs and sopped the sauce with a poppy seed roll, while he stood by the stove, trying not to look at her legs. If Mule had never mentioned them, he probably wouldn't have noticed, he thought; now he had to make a special effort to look her straight in the eye.

He was thankful that he had made a pan of gingerbread to take to the hospital the next morning, and so was his new neighbor, who devoured a large piece with enthusiasm, and afterward licked her fingers. Clearly, this gesture had not removed the last vestige of the gingerbread, for, afterward, as she reached to pat Barnabas on the head and say goodnight, he leaped to the seductive fragrance on her fingers, hauling the silverware drawer onto the floor and scattering its contents throughout the kitchen and into the freshly waxed hall.

A fork sailed on its backside all the way to the front door.

"Bingo!" exclaimed Cynthia.

They were both on their hands and knees for a full twenty minutes, collecting the muddle of twelve place settings, frilled party toothpicks, and a variety of spatulas and wooden spoons.

When he looked into the bathroom mirror that night, he was humiliated to see that there was barbecue sauce smeared on his chin—barbecue sauce that had, without a doubt, been there during Cynthia Coppersmith's entire visit.

He was so stricken with a vain regret, that he had to step outside for a breath of air.

"Of all things!" he said aloud. "Of all things!"

He had finally decided to tell Emma what had been told him in strictest confidence.

"You know, your role at Lord's Chapel has made you privy to quite a few secrets."

"I'll say! And some I wish to goodness I'd never been told."

"Well, this may be another of that very kind. Have you had any bright ideas about how to make Olivia Davenport and Hoppy . . . an item, as they say?"

"You bet I have, but I've been so busy with Harold Newland, I can't hardly see straight."

"You need to know, and it must never be repeated outside this room, that Olivia Davenport is dying."

Emma sat very still and turned pale.

"I didn't want to know that."

"Well, I didn't want to know it either, and I didn't want to tell you. But it appears to me that the very last thing we should do is try and make Hoppy Harper a widower two times in a row."

Emma drummed her fingers on her typewriter. "How bad is it?"

"What do you mean how bad is it? Dying is dying."

"I mean, how long does she have?"

"Months, she said. She referred to months."

"Oh, well. I thought if it was a couple of years, maybe we could still . . ."

"Emma, you are . . . words fail me."

"But they're perfect for each other!" she persisted. "I just hate this! What's she dyin' from?"

"To tell the truth, I have no idea. That wasn't the way the conversation went. In fact, that seemed the most insignificant detail in the world."

"Boys howdy, I'm glad you're not a reporter on the *Muse*."

"No gladder than I."

"Well," she sighed. "I feel terrible about her. I hope I don't go and be too nice to her now, like I know she's dyin'. You know what I mean?"

"Just try to be your usual aggravating, ill-tempered self, and she'll never suspect a thing."

"Ha, ha."

He looked through his phone messages.

"Did Hal say what he wanted?"

"Just said call him, he's ready to tell you something you've been wantin' to hear."

"Thanks be to God! Evie Adams?"

"Said her mother has started puttin' the wet wash in

the oven; Miss Pattie thinks it's the dryer. She's about to jump out the window."

"Who, Miss Pattie?"

"No. Evie."

"Miss Sadie's nursing home won't get built a minute too soon. I'll drop over to Evie's after lunch. Do you know what the school principal called about?"

"Well, I wasn't going to say anything, but since you asked . . ."

"I can see I shouldn't have asked."

"Dooley Barlowe beat some boy black and blue."

❧

In his mind, he saw exactly how it would go.

He would pick up the phone and do something that, if nothing else, would at least preserve his sanity.

"Hello, Walter? Please ask Katherine to move the Christmas ornaments off the guest room bed: I'm coming up. For how long? Oh, I don't know, a month or two, maybe more! You and I can go fishing, like we've always talked about. Maybe I'll turn loose some of that money you're always claiming I have, and we'll hop over to Sligo and look up our ancestors.

"Yes, that's right. You heard right. No, Walter, do not call 911. I am of very sound mind.

"So, I'll be there tonight around eleven. No, don't bother, I'll take a taxi. Yes, I know a taxi will cost a fortune, but you see, Walter, I don't care! Walter? Walter! Did I hear something crash to the floor?"

He laughed. If he was half the man he liked to think he was, he would make that very call and get away for a while, just like Hoppy kept insisting he must do.

Well, and he *would* get away for a while. Later.

Right now, he had to do something else. He had to

have a talk with Dooley Barlowe about giving Buster
Austin two black eyes, a swollen lip, a bloody nose and
then, heaven help him, chasing Buster into the principal's office with a baseball bat.

❧

Apparently, Buster Austin had broken in line behind
Dooley at the water fountain. While Dooley was bend-
ing over for a drink, Buster slammed him behind the
knees, so that he sank to the floor, hitting his mouth on
the fountain and cutting his lip.

He came up swinging.

"I saw it," said Principal Myra Hayes, standing behind her desk with arms akimbo. "Buster provoked it,
but there are rules, after all, and one does not build character by tearing down rules.

"Of course, what Dooley did at the water fountain
was only half the story! He then grabbed a softball bat
from Willie Bush and chased Buster down the hall into
my office, saying that if he didn't tell me whose fault it
was right then, he'd meller his head."

"Aha," said Father Tim. Why did she have to frown
so? It wasn't the end of the world.

"He'll be severely punished, and so will Buster. And
if this sort of thing happens again, we're prepared to
take more drastic action. You understand."

"Oh, I do."

He felt she might be considering some special punishment for the offense of even knowing Dooley Barlowe.

At three-fifteen, he met Dooley at the corner and
walked with him toward the church, where Russell
Jacks was transplanting hydrangeas.

" 'at principal preached me a sermon t'day," said
Dooley.

"Good! That'll save me the trouble."

They walked awhile in silence. Leaves had drifted in deep banks of gold and crimson along the curbs and whispered under their feet. Ah, to be as young as Dooley Barlowe, with countless autumns ahead!

"You like Goosedown Owen, don't you?"

"Better'n snuff," he said, using one of Russell Jacks's favorite expressions.

"You got over being thrown in the slop pretty quick."

" 'at ain't nothin'. She was jist playin'. I'm goin' t' ride th' hair off 'at horse next time."

"Let's talk about next time."

They crossed over Old Church Lane and went to the office.

"Got any homework?"

"Just some dumb ol' book t' read."

"Your grandpa will be around for you in an hour." He opened the windows and turned on the fan in his bookcase. The answering machine light was blinking, but that could wait. "I've been thinking," he said, sitting on the corner of his desk. "All of us need a change of scenery now and again, and it occurred to me that some of the best scenery around is at Meadowgate Farm."

The boy's face brightened.

"Let me ask you something. How would you like to learn how it feels to have a horse of your own?"

Dooley was so astounded at this extraordinary thought, he was unable to speak. Instead, his eyes spoke for him.

"Let's say that you and I make it a point to go out there once a month. And that you learn to groom Goosedown, and feed her, and take care of her tack, the whole works. However," he said, as Dooley leaped off the bench, "there's only one way we'll be able to do this."

"What's 'at?"

"You can no longer let Buster Austin or anybody else tempt you to fight." He let that sink in. "Do you understand?"

Dooley looked at the floor. "I reckon."

"Tell me what you think I'm saying to you."

"I can have me a horse, kind of, and take care of 'er an' all, but I cain't whip Buster Austin."

"Nor anybody else."

"N'r anybody else."

"We're going to talk in a little bit about what you can do if Buster . . . or anybody else . . . tries to get you to fight. In the meantime, are you willing to do what it takes to have yourself a horse once a month?"

"I'm willin'."

"Can you do it?"

"I can do it!"

He stood up and took Dooley's money box off the shelf. "Well, then, we'll talk more later. Do you want to work tomorrow? You've got eighty-eight dollars in your bicycle account."

"I don't want t' work tomorrow n'r any other day. I'm tired of haulin' them ashes out of th' basement and cleanin' out all that ol' junk. We filled up Luther's truck three times." Dooley went into the bathroom and slammed the door.

Lord, the rector prayed, I am not very good at this. Thank you for being this boy's Father, and teach me a trick or two, while you're at it. One thing he needed to do right away, he realized, was get Dooley enrolled in Sunday school, in Jenna Ivey's class.

He heard the toilet flush, and Dooley threw open the door. "You know what was in my poop jis' then?"

"I cannot imagine," he said, gruffly.

"Corn. Big whole pieces of that corn I eat for lunch. That reminded me of what I'm goin' t' do for 'at ol' horse."

"Really."

"I'm goin' to clean out 'er stable. There's no tellin' how long she's been steppin' in 'at stuff."

❧

Esther Cunningham called before he left the office.

"I was goin' to ask you to come by in the mornin' for coffee and a sausage biscuit, but the dern mildew's so bad in here, I'm thinkin' of movin' to the fire depot. Anyway, I've got big news."

"Let me have it before J.C. Hogan gets it crossways and backwards."

"You'll be proud to know you've been elected to officiate at . . . tah dah! . . . The Festival of Roses!"

"What happened to the pansies and the hollyhocks and all that crowd?"

"Outvoted! Here's the deal. We rope off Main Street, put a big garland of roses around the town monument, make speeches—that's where you come in—invite the governor, have house and garden tours—oh, and yours is on, by the way, just say yes—and sell potpourri and rose bushes and have flower arranging, and quilts, and I don't know what all. Not to mention food, of course— box lunches, cakes, pies, Winnie's doughnuts, you name it."

"You people sure don't mind shoveling out a load of work for the rest of us," said the rector.

"Honey, wait'll you hear what some folks are gonna be doin'. You got off light. Now, you're in big with Miss Sadie, and we'd like to use her house for a tour, but not one of us has the guts to ask."

"What makes you think I have?"

"Let's just say I'm countin' on you, Father. Anyhow, it's a long way off, not 'til next summer. Be thinkin' of somethin' good to say in your speech, an' I gotta go, Ray's out here blowin' the horn, got supper cookin' at the house."

One thing he could say for Esther Cunningham. She made people feel almost good about being harassed, talked down to, and generally bossed around.

❧

"You go and get house help and that's the last we see of you," said Percy Moseley, wiping down a booth table. "One of my best reg'lars has fell off to a total stranger."

The rector sighed. "But what's a man to do? When you've got somebody at home three days a week cooking and baking and making a fuss over you, you don't walk home anymore, you run. That is, if you've got the sense God gave a billy goat."

"You missed my latest special. Had it on the menu so long, it's about to go off."

"Bring it."

"But I ain't even told you what it is."

"Surprise me. I need more surprises in my life."

As he sat down and opened his sermon notebook, he heard two women enter the booth behind him.

"Well, of course, I love it here, but there's never anything to do!"

"Do you know this little town has more bachelors than practically Miami Beach?"

"Oh, sure. And where are they? Listed on the war monument?"

"There's J.C. Hogan, you know . . ."

"Too fat!"

"And Andrew Gregory. He's *Italian!*"

"Too old!"

"What about Harold Newland?"

"Too bashful. Besides, he's taken."

"Maybe Avis Packard, then. He could teach you how to flambé something. Or roast a goose."

"Ha! I roasted my own goose when I moved to this hick town."

"Marlene, bein' picky is no way to find somethin' to do around here. What about that rector over at Lord's Chapel? He's kind of cute."

"Too short!"

"OK, OK! I've got it! Here's one to die for. Hoppy Harper!"

"Too handsome."

"Too handsome? Are you *crazy?*"

"Good-looking men are always stuck on themselves."

"Marlene, one of these days, you'll have nothin' to hold on to but your convictions!"

"What in the world are you laughin' at?" asked Percy, setting a plate in front of him.

Father Tim looked down at his meal with genuine alarm.

Liver!

"Why'd you stop laughin'?" Percy wanted to know.

❧

"How do you like your new neighbor?" Emma was putting on her lipstick to meet Harold Newland at the hardware, where they would pick out brass towel rings to give her condo more appeal when they put it on the market.

"Oh, fine, just fine."

"What does she do?"

"Do? I haven't the faintest idea. She has a cat."

"Does she work?"

"I don't know, she didn't say."

"Well, she sure can't be rich, livin' in that little house not big enough for a doll and a tea set. So she must work."

"Like I told you, I don't know."

"What does she look like?"

"Short, I think. Small."

"Short, small, has a cat. You're a fount of information!" She looked in a compact and pressed her lips together. "And you still don't know what's killin' Olivia Davenport?"

"No, I do not. Olivia Davenport is highly involved in living, not dying, and we do not discuss it."

"How's she doin', readin' the Bible to sick people?"

He hadn't felt particularly well this morning, in addition to having some guilt about how slack his running schedule had become.

"Emma," he said crisply, "you are the one who should have a reporter's job on the *Muse*." And perhaps you'd like to go and inquire about a position this very day, he thought, yanking the cover off his typewriter.

He was following Miss Sadie along the upstairs hall at Fernbank.

"I don't know when I've been so excited!" she said, moving quickly in her tennis shoes. "Having Louella come and live with me will be the best medicine in the world. Did you know they say people who live alone die earlier than people who don't? Now, here, this is the first room I want you to look at and see what you think."

The years had definitely taken their toll on the former

glory of Fernbank. The rooms smelled musty and airless, and wallpaper was peeling in great patches. Still, it was hard to dim the beauty of Mitford's grandest house.

"This little room was Mama's sewing room. Look at all the good light it gets, and the view. Don't you love this view? Step right up to the window and you can look down on Mitford. See? There's your office! We could put the bed over there, Dooley could help, and the dresser here. What do you think?"

"How far down the hall is it from your room?"

"Oh, a good ways down."

"Let's look at the room right next to yours," he suggested.

There he found a sitting room with large, airy dimensions, a loveseat and two comfortable chairs, a single bed, a warm rug for winter, and a view of the orchard through the tall windows.

"Miss Sadie, I think you and Louella need to be next door to each other."

"Well, if that's what you think," she said, "that's what we'll do. You know, Father, I've decided to stay right here in Papa's house, no matter what. We'll just fall apart together, and when I die, I'll leave it to the church, like I always planned, and let you fix the roof and patch the walls."

He wondered how much more of Miss Sadie's generosity Lord's Chapel could stand.

"Now I ask you," she said, shaking the dust out of a needlepoint pillow on the loveseat, "how many ladies have a priest who'll come and say which room to put somebody in?"

He laughed. "I try to be versatile."

"Since we're up here, would you like to see another painting Papa bought in Europe?"

"Maybe I should be getting back . . . ," he said, heading for the stairs.

"Now, Father, this is no pretend Vermeer. This is a real Monet!"

He followed Miss Sadie into her bedroom, where he admired a small, vibrant oil that depicted a party of bathers. But what intrigued him more were the old photographs in tarnished silver frames, which sat on a table in front of the windows.

A very striking, dark-haired woman with luminous eyes looked out at him. "Why, how extraordinary! This woman is the very image of Olivia Davenport!"

"That was my mother," said Miss Sadie, "and when I met Olivia Davenport several Sundays ago, I was nearly speechless. I felt as if I were a little child again, looking at my beautiful mother. It was such a queer sensation that I was a bit shaken by it. I think it is the eyes, especially. There's an attitude of . . . of . . ."

"Victorious overcoming!"

"Why, yes. That's the very thing I was trying to say!"

The man in the photograph next to Rachel Livingstone Baxter was strikingly handsome and intense; in his twenties, perhaps.

"May I ask who this is?"

"That was the young man I met in Paris. That was Miss Rose Watson's brother, Willard Porter."

❧

They descended Fernbank's broad staircase, hand in hand.

"I had hoped to walk down these stairs in my bridal gown," she said, "and be taken into the parlor on Papa's arm. I imagined it so clearly, for so long, that years later I would sometimes forget, and think it had really happened.

"In my mind, Willard was standing at the fireplace in the parlor, which Mama and China Mae had decorated with white hydrangeas in silver urns. I liked to imagine that Papa had gotten up on the ladder and strung wild grapevine around the archway, and that I'd twined it with tea roses from the garden."

When they reached the landing, she turned to him.

"In all these years, I've never told anyone my love story. I know that I don't want to die without sharing it with someone. And I've been hoping, Father, that you'd be the one."

"I'd look upon it as a privilege."

"Considering my age, perhaps we shouldn't wait too long," she said, smiling. "So, one day, when you've nothing to do but listen to an old lady ramble, perhaps some rainy day when you've no heart for your chores, well then . . ."

"I'll remember," he said.

"When I've finished telling you my story, you'll be the only other living soul who knows what really happened the night of that terrible fire."

He felt a chill. And though it passed quickly, it was a feeling he didn't like.

CHAPTER TEN

A Grand Feast

"I wish I could make you some cornbread," Puny said, wistfully. "I just crave to do that."

"And you don't know how I appreciate it, and thank you for the thought," he said, eating a tuna sandwich made with whole wheat, and no mayonnaise. "But I can't eat cornbread because of this aggravating diabetes."

"I could leave out th' bacon drippin's, and use vegetable oil. But it wouldn't be no good."

"That's right!"

"If my granpaw didn't git cornbread once a day, he said he couldn't live. I'd bake him a cake at night, he'd eat half of it hot. Then he'd git up in the night and eat what was left, crumbled up in milk."

"Really?"

"Stayed a string bean all his life, too. He said preachin' the word of God kept the fat wore off."

"It has never served me in that particular way, I regret to say."

Puny filled the scrub bucket and went to work with her brush.

Seeing her scrub the floor on her hands and knees continued to be among his least favorite sights. "Puny, may I be so bold to ask why someone with your fine abilities has never married?"

"Th' good Lord ain't sent the right one, is why."

"And your family, is there family?"

She looked up. "My daddy died when I was little, and Mama raised me and my two sisters 'til we was all in junior high. My twin brothers went off to live with my aunt, 'cause she could send 'em to school. After that, Mama took sick and lingered.

"She said she lingered for one reason only, and that was to prepare us for life."

Puny sat back on her heels.

"She knowed she was dyin', and ever' night after we done our schoolwork and got th' supper dishes washed, Mama would call us in to set on her bed.

" 'Tonight I'm goin' to talk to you about hard work,' she might say. 'I've only got one thing to say about it, and that is—don't be afraid of it.'

"That was all the lesson on hard work, and she'd lay back and we'd brush her hair and paint her nails and just kind of play with 'er like a doll.

"She liked that, and would fall off to sleep that way, with us pettin' 'er. Another night, she might say, 'Girls, I'm goin' to talk to you about men, and here's what I've got to say: Don't let a man pick you. You do the pickin'.'

"You know, if that's all somebody has to say about somethin', you'll think about it more'n if they rattle on and on."

He thought she had a point.

"Mama always told us, 'I don't want to look down from heaven and see my girls makin' fools of theirselves.' "

"Well, I'm sure she's pleased, Puny, for you're a hardworking, good-spirited young woman who'd make any mother proud."

"After Mama died, th' church took my sisters, sent 'em hither an' yon, an' I quit school to go look after granpaw. Lived all by hisself out in th' country, but he had a pretty little place, neat as a pin, wouldn't hardly a leaf fall in th' yard till he was out there sweepin' it up. He was tough as a old turkey gobbler, but I liked 'im. He could preach up a storm! Make the windows rattle!" She looked at him soberly. "How's your preachin'?"

"There's any number of opinions on that subject," he said, laughing. "You'll just have to come and see for yourself."

☙

Puny had left baked chicken and green beans cooked with new potatoes, one of his favorite meals. He laid a tray, and took his supper into the study to watch the news. World events continually reminded him of how blessed he was to live and work in the peace and tranquillity of Mitford. It was only by the grace of God, some said, that their village was still largely unspoiled.

A lot of the credit, of course, belonged to Esther Cunningham. The mayor was like a great, clucking hen, sitting on a nest which was the fragile ecology of their little town, and she was ready to defend it to the death.

Still, development had sprung up around the edges, like weeds encroaching on a garden. Just beyond the big curve from Lew Boyd's Esso was the bright yellow motel with a huge green cactus outlined in neon. There was growing pressure for a shopping center, and a food store chain was pawing the very ground where the town limit sign was erected. It was only a matter of time, was the general consensus at the Grill. "Over my dead body," said Esther, who stood firm on three Churchillian words: Never give up.

After the news, he put the dishes in the sink and went to his desk to make notes on his sermon. He was considering what J. Hudson Taylor, the English missionary to China, had said, in reflecting on the verse from Matthew: "Where could we get enough bread in the wilderness to fill such a great multitude?"

"What God has given us," Taylor had written, "is all we need; we require nothing more. It is not a question of large supplies—it is a question of the presence of the Lord."

That was a sermon that was almost unpreachable in today's world. Why take off along that narrow and difficult path, when wide boulevards were generally more inviting to a congregation?

Barnabas barked gruffly, then leaped across the study floor and into the kitchen, where he put his front paws on the back door and barked again.

He heard a small knock.

"Your sugar!" Cynthia Coppersmith said when he opened the door. He was holding Barnabas firmly by the collar.

"You shouldn't have bothered. Really! I'm just finishing up some notes, and we were going to settle in for a bit of Wordsworth . . ."

"I love Wordsworth!" she exclaimed, handing him the cup of sugar.

He was unable to think of anything to reply, when

years of social training came to his rescue. "Won't you come in?" he blurted, much to his surprise.

"Well . . . yes! Yes, I will, if you're sure you don't mind."

Blast! he thought, tucking his shirttail in with one hand and holding Barnabas with the other.

As he almost never had unexpected company in the evening, he hardly knew how to proceed. A drink? Didn't people offer drinks? Well, he didn't have any to offer. It would have to be sherry, perhaps, or tea, and a plate of . . . what? Shortbread.

Giving himself time to think it through, he took Barnabas to the rear hedge, leaving his neighbor happily inspecting his bookshelves.

When he returned, she was sitting on the study sofa, poring over a book of lectures by Oswald Chambers and appearing oddly at home among the jumble of worn, needlepoint pillows.

She looked up, quoting the Scottish teacher who happened to be one of his favorite writers. " 'Faith by its very nature must be tried,' he says. Do you agree?"

He sat down in his wing chair, suddenly feeling more at home with his company. "Absolutely!"

"I've never been one for physical exercise," she said, "but what God does with our faith must be something like workouts. He sees to it that our faith gets pushed and pulled, stretched, and pounded, taken to its limits so its limits can expand."

He liked that—taken to its limits so its limits can expand. Yes!

"If it doesn't get exercised," she said thoughtfully, "it becomes like a weak muscle that fails us when we need it."

He felt himself smiling foolishly, though his question was serious. "Would you agree that we must be willing to thank God for every trial of our faith, no matter how severe, for the greater strength it produces?"

"I'm perfectly willing to say it, but I'm continually unable to do it."

"There's the rub!"

When he went to the kitchen to make a second pot of tea, he was astounded to find that it was eleven o'clock. That hardly anyone in Mitford stayed up until eleven o'clock was common knowledge.

⚬❧

At noon, he walked briskly from the church office to Lord's Chapel, with Barnabas on his red leash.

He had a pile of correspondence to tend to and another visit to make to the hospital in the afternoon. That's why he'd brought a sandwich made from last night's chicken, which he'd put in the parish hall refrigerator early this morning.

The sky was darkly overcast, but he hardly noticed the weather. He was thinking of last night's unexpected caller and the visit that ensued.

He turned the key in the lock, and went in the side door of the old parish hall. Though it was barely large enough for a party of fifty, they often squeezed in seventy-five or more for coffee after the late service.

Three walls displayed a collection of framed needlepoint that had been worked by parishioners since 1896, and included embellished crosses, a view from the ruined church on the hill (the first Lord's Chapel), a crown of thorns, and his personal favorite: a mass of roses framing the Scripture from Psalm 68: "Blessed be the Lord, who daily loadeth us with benefits."

The fourth wall contained a series of mullioned windows that looked out to the finest of the Lord's Chapel gardens. As he passed the windows, he saw the rain begin.

He opened the refrigerator, but didn't see his lunch bag. "Odd," he said aloud to Barnabas, "I put it right here with the wine." With some bewilderment, he noted that the sacramental wine was also missing, a fact that was easy to establish since there was nothing in the refrigerator but two containers of half-and-half, and a jar of Sunday school apple juice.

"Did I dream we walked over here this morning and left that sandwich?" Barnabas yawned hugely and lay down by the kitchen worktable. "That's the darndest thing. What in the world . . ."

Perhaps the Altar Guild had come in and cleaned out the refrigerator. But it was already clean. Feeling stupid, he looked in the broom closet, and inspected the contents of the drawers. After all, he had once put a package of butter in the oven while wrestling with the idea of a sermon on greed.

The lunch bag was nowhere to be found. "Well, then," he said, irritated. "We'll give our business to Percy."

As he locked the door, he thought he heard the barest whisper of singing, a mere wisp of last Sunday's anthem. He listened, but heard nothing more.

"Angels!" he said, as they set out in a light autumn rain.

❧

"I've found out all about your neighbor," Emma announced.

"Really?"

"She's an artist and a writer. Paints watercolors for

th' children's books she writes. That white cat she has? That's the star of her Violet books. *Violet Comes to Stay, Violet Grows Up, Violet Has Kittens, Violet Goes to England.* You name it, that cat has done it." She paused, hoping for some response, but got none.

She selected another choice piece of information, as one might poke through the caramels to find a chocolate. "She used to be married to somebody important."

"Is that right?"

"A senator," she said grandly.

"Aha."

"Her uncle gave 'er that little house. Remember him? The old scrooge!"

He remembered well enough. He'd tried to be friendly, and had even regularly prayed for his unkind neighbor, seeing that he needed it. Nothing he'd done, including the delivery of an apple pie, had softened the old man's heart toward him. Then, two years ago, his neighbor had died, leaving the little house empty and unkempt.

"It wasn't actually the uncle who gave it to her," said Emma. "It was her uncle's daughter. Called her up, said she didn't want it, thought Cynthia should have it. Said Cynthia was the only one her old daddy ever liked."

"Um," he said, looking through his phone messages.

"Never had any kids. Kind of adopted her husband's nephew."

She waited, having gone nearly to the bottom of her information barrel. "Drives a Mazda!" she said at last.

"With such vast reportorial skills, you might talk to J.C. Hogan about working at the *Muse*."

"That's more than you'd ever find out in a hundred years!"

"You're right, as usual," he said, dryly. "I think it's

especially fascinating to know what kind of car she drives."

Emma pursed her lips. Down deep, she could tell he was thrilled she'd found out all this stuff.

He finished putting his phone messages in order. "And how did you learn all this, exactly?"

"I did what anybody would do. I asked her!"

He queried the sexton when he came by to collect his check. "Russell, did you go in the church yesterday?"

"Nossir, Father, I didn't. I was goin' to heat up some soup in th' kitchen, but th' rain looked like it was settin' in for th' day, so I went home and fried me some liver-mush. Dooley come home on th' bus."

"The Altar Guild wasn't in there, either. It's a mystery, all right."

"How's that?"

"Yesterday morning, I put a sandwich in the refrigerator, and when I went to look for it, it was gone, along with a bottle of sacramental wine."

Russell scratched his head. "I was in th' churchyard 'til around noon or so, when I seen you leave out to Main Street. I didn't lay eyes on another soul."

The rector shook his head. "Ah, well! Do you think you can get to those broken flagstones before winter?"

"I'm workin' on it, Father," he said, as the phone rang.

"Father," said Olivia Davenport, "Pearly McGee just died."

"I'll be right there," he said.

As he hung up the phone, it rang again.

Marge Owen had delivered a healthy baby girl. Seven pounds, eight ounces. Rebecca Jane!

Sorrow and joy, he thought, so inextricably entwined

that he could scarcely tell where one left off and the other began.

※

He had taken particular pains about dressing for the art show at the Oxford. For one thing, he felt it would demonstrate respect for Uncle Billy. Here he was, dressed in his second new jacket purchase of the year, a circumstance he found just short of miraculous. If there had ever been a year in which he'd bought two jackets, he couldn't remember it.

Of course, there was no way he could have resisted this particular jacket. Not only was it a color that Emma told him would be flattering, but it was comfortable, fit perfectly, would go with everything, and was on sale. So, what was he to do?

"English Copper!" the Collar Button owner said, grandly describing the color. "It will look stunning with your black clericals."

Stunning? He wasn't at all certain that this was how he wanted to look.

※

The Oxford was wearing its signature fragrance of floor wax, lemon oil, old wood, and worn leather. Andrew had even gone to some pains to buy flowers at Mitford Blossoms and arrange them himself in an ancient silver wine bucket, which he placed on a hunt table newly arrived from Cumbria.

Fortunately, there was one thing a host could count on in Mitford. Villagers arrived early or on time, and everyone, to a person, left at a decent hour.

When he appeared at five minutes after the specified four o'clock, the tea table was already surrounded.

He greeted Esther Cunningham, who was enjoying a large slice of Brie, and shook hands with her husband, Ray. Then, as he turned to look at the drawings, he observed quite another show. It was Miss Rose Watson, dressed to the tee in a green taffeta evening gown, a moth-eaten plaid velvet cummerbund, elbow-length satin gloves, a World War II officer's cape, and saddle oxfords without laces.

She held several tea sandwiches in one gloved hand, while graciously extending the other. "How do you do," she said to the rector, who no longer felt conspicuous in his new jacket, much less overdressed.

❧

The beautifully framed drawings hung in a long, chronological line along the left wall, beginning with Uncle Billy's rendering of three deer in a copse of spruce, drinking from the basin of a waterfall. Seeing them framed and hanging was unexpectedly impressive.

"Eloquent, aren't they?"

Cynthia Coppersmith was standing by his side, dressed in a sweater and skirt the color of periwinkles, and holding a cracker on a napkin.

"Indeed!" he said. "I knew they were well done, but this, well this is . . ."

"Extraordinary!" she said helpfully.

"Emma tells me you're an artist and writer."

"I earn part of my way with a brush, yes. But I don't call myself a true artist. I can't draw people, you see. I'm best at animals, and especially cats."

Someone slapped him on the back so hard, he nearly went reeling into a drawing of a quail on her nest.

"I see you're learnin' to love your neighbor as yourself!" said Harry Nelson. "This is the last I'll be seein' of you. Shirley and I have the car packed and we're headed out behind the movin' van."

"Don't take any wooden Vermeers," said Mule Skinner, who had joined the group.

❧

Uncle Billy was seated in a Chippendale wing chair, balancing a plate of cheese and grapes on his lap, with a paper napkin stuck into his shirt collar.

J.C. Hogan was writing in a notebook with his left hand, and mopping his forehead with his right. "When did you say you started drawin'?"

"Oh, when I was about ten or twelve, m' uncle was a railroad man and ever' time he come through the valley, he'd blow th' whistle startin' up around Elk Grove, and by th' time he got over t' Isinglass, don't you know, I was standin' by the track, and he'd th'ow somethin' out t' me.

"Sometimes, it was a sack of licorice candy, or horehound, and one time it was a little ol' pack of pencils, real wide pencils with a soft lead, don't you know. My daddy said that was a foolish thing to give a boy who couldn't write, so I took to drawin'."

"Did you ever use ink?" J.C. asked.

"Well, sir, I used it some, but I eat up a jar of pickle relish Rose said was hers, and she burned th' whole stack of m' ink pictures."

"No!" exclaimed Winnie Ivey, nearly moved to tears.

"I'd a clapped 'er upside th' head," said Percy Mosely, with feeling.

Miss Rose rustled by in her taffeta gown. "Don't be tellin' that ol' tacky story, Bill Watson! I've heard it a hundred times, and it's a lie."

"No, it ain't," said Uncle Billy, grinning.

"It most certainly is. It was not pickle relish. It was chow chow." As she turned on her heel and walked away, the rector couldn't help but notice the Ritz cracker that fell out of her cummerbund and rolled under a chair.

"I hear you've quit drawin'," said J.C. "Why's that?"

"Arthur," said Uncle Billy.

"Arthur who?"

"Arthur-itis. But that ain't hurt my joke tellin' any. Let me give y' one t' go in th' paper."

"We don't print jokes in the *Muse*," J.C. snapped.

"If that ain't a lie!" said Percy Mosely, who was thoroughly dissatisfied with a recent editorial.

❧

At the food table, he visited with Rodney Underwood, who was Mitford's young new police chief and a deacon at First Baptist.

"My granddaddy and my daddy both were police chiefs in this town. An' bad as I always wanted to work at th' post office, I couldn't do it. No way. After four years of bein' a deputy over in Wesley, I give up an' let th' town council hog-tie me."

"Well, I imagine it's a good life. I hardly ever see any crime reported in the *Muse*."

"It's around, though, don't kid yourself. You don't know what goes on behind these rose arbors . . ."

No, indeed, he thought, moving away. And I don't want to know, either.

"Hello again, Father," said Cynthia, holding what appeared to be the same cracker on the same napkin. "I've been meaning to say you look stunning in that copper-colored jacket."

He felt the color rise to his face. Stunning! He knew he should have bought the navy blue.

❧

"Well, what do you think?"

Andrew Gregory sat on one of the Queen Anne dining chairs that someone had placed in a neat circle around Uncle Billy.

"A smashing success!" said the rector. "Undeniably! How many have we sold?"

Andrew's pleasure was visible. "Twenty-seven!"

He saw Hoppy Harper come through the door with Olivia Davenport. There was a flush in her cheeks, and her violet eyes sparkled. From what he could see, Hoppy looked more rested than he'd looked in months. Green jelly beans! he thought. That'll do it every time.

"Well, I must be off," said Andrew. "Miss Rose and the mayor have eaten all the Brie and I have to dash to The Local and replace it with cheddar!"

Cynthia Coppersmith sat down where Andrew had gotten up. "This is my first social occasion in the village. Except, of course, for visits to the rectory."

He could not think of one word to say.

"Violet ran away today," Cynthia said matter-of-factly.

"She did?"

"But she came back."

"Good! I hear you write and illustrate books about your cat."

"Yes. *Violet Comes to Stay, Violet Goes to the Country* . . . oh, and *Violet Has Kittens,* of course. To name only a few!"

"What a full life! How old is Violet, anyway?"

"Just two."

"Two! And she's done all that?"

"Well, you see, this is Violet Number Three. I have to keep replacing my Violets. The original Violet was seven when I got her, and I painted her for two years before she died of a liver infection.

"Then there was a very haughty Violet, which I found through an ad. Oh, she was lovely to look at, but unaccountably demanding. There were three books with that Violet, before she took off with a yellow tom."

"Aha."

"I was sent scurrying, as you can imagine. A contract for a seventh book, and no model!"

"Couldn't you use a cat of another color, and just, ah, paint it white in your illustrations?"

"No, no. I really must have a Violet to do the job. And not every white cat is one, of course."

"Of course."

"So, we were all looking for another Violet, and the newspaper got wind of it and the first thing you know, fifty-seven white cats turned up."

He had a vision of Barnabas set free in the midst of fifty-seven white cats.

"Then, the eighth Violet story won a book award— the Davant Medal. It's the most coveted award in children's literature, and the whole thing absolutely took my breath away! Suddenly, all the books started selling like . . ."

"Pancakes?" he asked. Blast! He'd meant to say hotcakes.

"Yes! And now I have my own true home after years of apartments, and a bit of money, too. It's a miracle!" she said in the earnest way that made her eyes seem bluer still. "But I must admit I'm weary of Violet books.

Perhaps next time, I'll do something with . . . oh, maybe
with moles!"

His worst enemy! Why, every blessed spring in Mitford, a man could step into a hole up to his knee. If there
were any more detestable creatures in the animal king-
dom, he could not think what they might be.

"If it's moles you're after, you can find all you'll
ever want right next door. In my lawn."

"You're fun when you laugh," she said, smiling
frankly.

"Thank you. I'll have to laugh more often."

"You've been so kind to me, I was hoping you might
be able to come for dinner next week. I think I'll be settled by then."

He stood up. "Well . . ."

"Good!" she said. "I'll let you know more."

Andrew Gregory approached, buttoning the cashmere jacket across his trim midsection, and looking
even more tanned and vigorous than he had an hour ago.

"Twenty-nine!" he said expansively to Father Tim,
and then turned to Cynthia. "If you're ready, I'd like
you to see the books Miss Potter is said to have made
notes in."

As they walked away, the rector suddenly felt short,
pale, overweight, and oddly suspicious that his jacket
contained more polyester than wool.

❧

"Why haven't you told me about this woman?"
Hoppy wanted to know, as they stood outside Andrew's
rear office and waited for the rest room.

"What was there to tell?"

"That she's lovely, new in town, goes to Lord's
Chapel, I don't know. I'm walking down the hall last

week, and I see this angel sitting by Pearly's bed, reading from the Psalms. I'll never forget it. 'Thou art my hiding place and my shield. I hope in thy word,' she said. It struck me to the very marrow."

And no wonder, thought the rector, whose own marrow had been struck by the depth of her feeling.

"I've been away from church so long . . . so long away from . . . believing." Hoppy leaned against the wall, avoiding the rector's gaze. "I've been very angry with God."

"I understand."

"He operated without anesthetic."

He looked at the man who had lost his wife of sixteen years, and saw the sure mark that bitterness and overwork had left. Yet, something tonight was easier in him.

Percy Mosely came out of the rest room. "You better watch it," he said, "there's a real loud odor in that pink soap."

He insisted that Hoppy go ahead of him and wandered into Andrew's comfortably untidy office. He sat in a wingback chair next to Andrew's desk and looked at the collection of paintings on the walls, at the jumble of books and magazines spilling from baskets and shelves. He idly turned his attention to a fragment of newspaper, protruding from beneath a leather blotter on the desk.

"Jewels Missing from Museum Exhibition," he read silently, without any special interest. "Last night, as the fund-raising gala got under way in the new wing of the Sonningham, an armed guard discovered that a priceless array of antique royal jewels had been stolen while he stood within feet of the glass case.

" 'I stepped away for perhaps a minute and a half, to

see what was making a rattling noise in the skylight,' said Nigel Hadleigh, 62, of Armed Forces, Inc., a private security firm. 'When I looked back at the case, the jewels were gone.'

"Investigators so far have no clue to the theft, nor any suspects. There were no fingerprints on the case, which, until 9:30 p.m. on the first night of the museum's fund-raising effort, contained rare jewels from all of the British Isles, including a necklace once worn by Princess Louise.

" 'We're dreadfully embarrassed,' said Museum Director Wilfred Cappman. 'Whatever will we say to the queen?' "

Ah, there's the rub! thought the rector.

Hoppy came out of the rest room and peered into the office. "I need to talk to you pretty soon. But this time," he said, "I'll let you write the prescription."

Strike while the iron is hot! he thought. "How about Thursday at the Grill? That's Percy's day for salmon croquettes."

"Don't be late," warned the village doctor, grinning.

As he finished washing his hands, he heard laughter on the other side of the restroom wall. It was Cynthia Coppersmith. Obviously, she found moles very, very amusing, which was the oddest mark of character he had recently observed.

❧

When he came home, he discovered one of his pie plates on the back step, and in it, a square envelope.

It contained a watercolor of Barnabas, which was so lifelike it might have barked. A note tucked into the envelope read, "Thanks so much for the kindness you've shown a stranger in your midst. Cynthia."

"Truly amazing," he said, looking at the watercolor with rapt fascination.

☙

"Your sermon was real good yesterday," Emma said on Monday morning.

There's obviously no accounting for tastes, thought the rector, who recalled that a baby cried throughout the service, a squirrel chewed something behind the wall, and a lens from his glasses had dropped into the Bible as he read the gospel message.

"I saw you at the art show," she said, "but when I finally got over to where you were standin', you'd up and left."

"Yes, well . . . how's Harold?"

"Work, work, work. Do this, do that. Fix the roof. Paint the porch. Change the oil. Mulch up his corncobs. That's the way the Baptists do, you know."

"Is that right?"

"You don't ever see Episcopalians mulching up their corncobs."

"Don't have any to mulch up."

"I guess."

Emma took her ledger out of the top drawer, along with a locked box containing Sunday's offering.

"Seems to me your new neighbor was on your heels at the art show."

"My neighbor . . . oh, yes, you mean Miss Coppersmith."

"I do mean her, that's right. Everywhere you turned, she turned. It was like ice dancin'."

"Didn't you have anything better to do than watchdog your preacher?"

"First thing you know, there'll be more of those cat

books in the stores. Like, *Violet Goes to Church, Violet Visits the Rector* . . ."

"Emma, don't push your luck."

"Didn't Miss Rose look tarted up?"

"Quite."

"And Uncle Billy, what's he goin' to do with all that money?"

"Hard telling."

A sudden wind moaned around the little stone building, rattling the windows. They looked at each other.

"They're calling for snow tonight," he announced.

"Maybe I should marry Harold before spring, after all," she said.

❧

Before Pearly McGee died, she had given him a check for $1,456.00.

"Use it to make somebody happy," she had told him. "That's what I want, is somebody to be happy."

He thought it would make one Dooley Barlowe very happy, indeed, if his red bicycle could be sitting under the Christmas tree.

Dooley had earned a hundred and eight dollars, and needed that much again to pay the layaway balance on the red mountain bike.

Perhaps what he should do, he mused, is give fifty-four dollars of his own money and match it with fifty-four from Pearly's "discretionary fund."

He mentioned it to Emma.

"I don't know about that. Maybe he ought to work for the whole thing."

"Why?"

She shrugged. "He's hot-headed. Workin' for it might cool 'im off."

After Emma left, he called the bicycle store in Wesley. Yes, they could make a delivery to Mitford before Christmas.

When he told Puny that the red bicycle would be coming to hide in the garage, he thought she'd be delighted. She wasn't. "I hope you know what you're doin'," she said, flatly.

❧

On Tuesday, he had breakfast with Olivia Davenport, and allowed her to drive him to the office in a rain so heavy they could scarcely see the lights of oncoming cars along Main Street.

"Did you hear what happened at the lay readers meeting last night?" Emma asked as he removed his raincoat.

"Esther Bolick did her impersonation of the bishop?"

"Worse than that. Somebody stole her famous orange marmalade cake out of the parish hall fridge."

"Stole it?"

"Just cracked open that cake carrier and cleaned it out, crumbs an' all."

"I don't understand."

"Everybody brought a little somethin' for refreshments. After meetin' in the nursery where it was warm, they went to the kitchen to pour tea, and the cake was gone. Hilda Lassister said she'd been waitin' two years for a taste of that marmalade cake, and when they couldn't find it, she said she like to cried."

He scratched his head. "I don't understand why they couldn't find it."

"The point," she said impatiently, "is that it wasn't in the refrigerator where Esther left it. It was gone. Kaput. Zip. Outta there."

"They put the cake in the refrigerator and went back after the meeting and it was gone?"

"That's what I'm tryin' to tell you. But whoever stole it didn't even touch Marge Houck's pineapple upside down."

"Now there's something I can understand," he said.

On Wednesday evening, he took a shower and dressed, and prepared to visit his new neighbor in her tiny house next door. Cynthia Coppersmith had done as promised and invited him to dinner. And the invitation, it seemed to him, was perfectly timed.

The last of his Rector's Meatloaf was gone, and good riddance. To his chagrin, he'd used more oatmeal than before, which resulted in the most unsavory concoction he'd tasted in years. But he had soldiered on and eaten the entire loaf over a period of several days. He was so ashamed of it, he had hidden it at the back of the refrigerator, where he hoped Puny wouldn't find it.

Every light in the small house glowed warmly through the heavy mist that lay upon the village.

"Pleasant!" he said, aloud. "A small house for a small person." He lifted the old brass knocker and rapped three times.

There was no answer to his knock, so he tried again. Nothing.

Since callers occasionally had to go to the back door of the rectory to rouse him from his study, he thought the same might apply in this case. He stumbled around the side of the house, over broken flagstones, toward a light shining above the back door.

He knocked and waited. Not a sound.

He cautiously opened the door and peered into a minuscule but inviting kitchen.

A broiling pan sat on the stove, containing a blackened roast. Next to it, a pot had boiled over, and a tray of unbaked rolls sat disconsolately on the countertop. "Hello!" he called.

A white cat leaped onto the breakfast table, looked at him curiously, and began cleaning her paws. "Violet, I presume?" He had never been fond of cats.

He heard her coming down the stairs, then she appeared at the kitchen door, her eyes red from crying.

"I've done it again," she said, sniffing. "I can never get it right. I sat down at my drawing table for just one minute. One minute! An hour later, I looked up, and the rice had boiled over and the roast had burned, and well, there you have it."

" 'Whatever your hand finds to do, do it with all your might'!" he quoted cheerfully from Ecclesiastes. "You must have been doing something you liked."

She sighed. "I was drawing moles."

Moles again! That explains it, thought her caller. "Look here," he said, "if you don't mind, let me experiment with this." He made a broad gesture toward the ruined dinner.

"It will take a miracle," she said flatly.

"I'd be very open to a good miracle. Where's your carving knife?"

He drew the sharp knife across the end of the roast, and a thick slice peeled away neatly. "Well, now! Just the way I like it. Overdone on the outside and rare in the middle." He carved a sliver and handed it to his hostess on the point of the blade. "See what you think."

Cynthia eyed it suspiciously, then did as he suggested. "Delicious!" she declared with feeling. "It *is* a miracle!"

He lifted the lid on the pot that had boiled over on the burner, and stirred the contents with a wooden spoon. "It's stuck on the bottom, but I think it's just right. Yes, indeed. Wild rice. A favorite!"

"You really are infernally kind," she said tartly.

"Not kind. Famished. I ran today and missed lunch entirely."

"Well," she said, the color coming back into her cheeks, "I did make a crab-meat casserole for the first course. That worked! And there are glazed onions with rosemary and honey that appear edible." She took two fragrant, steaming dishes out of the oven and set them on the counter.

"I hear you like a drop of sherry now and then," she said, and poured from a bottle with a distinguished label. She handed him a glass, and poured one for herself.

"You've prepared a grand feast!" exclaimed her guest.

"Cheers!" said his relieved hostess.

CHAPTER ELEVEN

A White Thanksgiving

Thanksgiving came to the village, along with a deep and unexpected blanket of snow.

"A white Thanksgiving comes to Mitford," wrote *Muse* editor J.C. Hogan, "and a lot of turkeys have been careening down Baxter Hill on biscuit pans."

Winnie Ivey, wearing last year's Christmas muffler, walked with a heavy basket and a light heart to her brother's rooms over the barbershop.

Miss Rose and Uncle Billy put on their boots and went to the All-Church Feast, with Miss Rose carrying quantities of wax paper in her pockets, for wrapping take-outs.

Miss Sadie, fearing there might be ice under the snow, chose to stay home, eat a Swanson's chicken pie, and make a list of things to do for Louella's arrival the week after Christmas.

Puny Bradshaw roasted a turkey and went to visit her sisters.

And Russell Jacks baked a hen, cooked a mess of collard greens, and made a cake of cornbread. When villagers saw smoke boiling out of the Jacks chimney, and his scrap-metal graveyard obscured by a mantle of fresh snow, they were fairly enchanted.

Before attending the All-Church Feast, held this year at First Baptist, Father Tim put two pies and a pan of Puny's sausage dressing into a basket and walked with Barnabas to Little Mitford Creek.

When he reached Winnie Ivey's cottage by the bridge, he turned left and headed far along the creek, into the snow-silent woods.

Here and there, limbs fell with a soft thud onto the white crust of the forest floor, which caused Barnabas to leap with a mixture of joy and alarm at the end of his red leash.

What, he wondered, had he ever done without Barnabas? Without the long, companionable walks, the pleasure and the aggravation of a living creature to care for, the growing empathy between them, and yes, the delight?

"Son of consolation" was the meaning given to the name Barnabas in the fourth chapter of Acts, and he was all that and more.

Barnabas had even done for him what nothing else had ever done. This great, black, maverick dog had somehow made him feel twenty years younger.

They followed fresh tracks to a low point on the creek bank and crossed the creek on a series of large boulders. On the other side, the tracks led to the door of a ramshackle house, sitting near a derelict bridge.

The chimney sent up billows of fragrant wood smoke, and from inside the dwelling, which was scarcely bigger than a tool shed, came the sound of laughter.

"Come in, come in!" said Samuel K. Hobbes, as he opened the door and limped aside on his crutch. "Come in and warm yourselves by th' fire!"

Barnabas bounded in to shake his wet fur on all assembled, then lay down by the glowing wood stove. The rector was pleased to see that every church denomination in town was represented in that small room, and each had come with a bag or basket for Homeless Hobbes.

Homeless moved nimbly on his battered crutch, pouring coffee for every guest.

"You could use another chair in this place," suggested a Methodist deacon who was standing in a corner.

"Nossir, I couldn't," said Homeless, setting the empty pot on a shelf. "Mr. Thoreau himself had two and often regretted it. Fact is, m' two pairs of pants is one too many."

Father Tim unwound the wool muffler from around his neck. "What about these two pumpkin pies? You want me to take one back?"

"No, my good Father, I do not. Pants and pies is two different things."

"You got that right!" said Rodney Underwood, who had brought a pie himself.

Homeless hitched up his suspenders and surveyed the little table. "Lookit this bounty! Two, three, four, five . . . seven pies. Scandalous! Far too many pies for ol' Homeless. And a big, fat hen, and a sack of ham biscuits, and a quart of collards, and a fine mess of sweet potatoes . . ."

"Don't forget th' bag of grits and a ham hock for soup," said Rodney, who was a stickler for accuracy.

"And Puny Bradshaw's sausage dressing," said the rector.

Homeless surveyed the gathering. "Well, boys, much as I 'preciate all this, I've got to tell you the gospel truth."

"What's that?" the deacon asked, suspiciously.

"I'm goin' to give the best portion of these eats to folks who're worse off than me."

"I didn't know there was anybody worse off than you," said young Jack Teague from the Presbyterians.

"That's what you think, son. You head up the hill from this creek, and all back in there, you'll find 'em worse off than me. With little young 'uns, too."

"Do what you want to with it," said Rodney. "It's yours in th' name of the Lord."

"And I thank you for it," said Homeless.

Rodney passed a basket of ham biscuits his mother had sent. "Let's bless these ham biscuits, boys," he said, and launched into a prayer covering world hunger, food stamps, stray animals, firewood, the Baptist conference, Little Mitford Creek, Big Mitford Creek, the sick, the unsaved, an unwelcome forecast for more snow, the town council's decision on sidewalks for Lilac Road, the president, the Congress, the Senate, the House of Representatives, and the local fire and police departments.

"Amen!" said Homeless. "That ought t' last me 'til this time next year."

"Mr. Hobbes," said Jack Teague, "I hear tell you used to live in New York City."

"That's a fact. Had a big, fancy office on Madison Avenue, and an apartment right on the Hudson River."

"No kidding!" said Jack, shaking his head in amazement. "And how long have you been homeless . . . sir?"

"My friend, as you can plainly see, I am not homeless in the least." He indicated the wood stove, a rickety table covered with oilcloth, two shelves, a kerosene lamp, a chair, a cot, a sink, and a toilet that was partially hidden by a red gingham tablecloth looped over a wire.

"The way I'm able to live today is not only one hundred percent stress-proof, it is guaranteed recession-proof. No matter which way the economy goes, it don't affect me one way or th' other.

"To tell th' plain truth, this is th' finest home I ever had, and I've lived in high style from New York City to Dallas, Texas, not to mention one stint in Los Angelees, California."

"Wow! What business were you in?"

"Advertisin', my boy!" said Homeless, with a wicked grin. "Advertisin'!"

❧

On Saturday morning, Mitford woke to a second blanket of snow, so Father Tim canceled his trip with Dooley to Meadowgate Farm. Instead, he had lunch at the Grill and went shopping with Uncle Billy.

"Rose needs somethin' to wear," said his friend, who had decided to spend some of the proceeds from his art show. "I'm not a proud man, Preacher, but that ol' army stuff she drags out'n the closet nearly shames me t' death.

"Th' dress she wore t' the drawin' show, she hauled that out'n th' dumpster on Forks Road—seen th' tail of it hangin' over th' side, don't you know, when we was th'owin out some dinette chairs."

"I don't know how much good I can do you, Uncle Billy. I've never in my life shopped for women's clothes. It's all I can do to shop for myself."

"Well, but you're a preacher, and you know what's right for Sunday morning." Uncle Billy flashed his gold tooth in a winning smile. "I'd be beholden to you."

"Done, then!" said the rector, and they set off in heavy boots and coats toward the dress shop across from the war monument.

❧

He was deep in thought as he walked with Barnabas on Saturday afternoon to Lord's Chapel. His shopping trip with Uncle Billy had been a thorough success, and he could hardly wait to see Miss Rose on Sunday, decked out in the black suit that was forty percent off, and a fuchsia wool coat they landed for half price.

The only trouble was, there was no ladies' shoe store in Mitford. That meant that Miss Rose might very well show up in her brother's army boots with the heavy latches.

The second snowfall had muffled the everyday sounds of the village, so that all he heard as they walked was the crunch of their footsteps in the untracked blanket that covered the sidewalk.

Along the way, Barnabas felt compelled to melt the snow in several places, after which he dashed on eagerly, pleased with the accomplishment.

"Recession-proof!" he muttered aloud, thinking of Homeless Hobbes's comment about his bare-bones existence. If only the rest of Mitford could claim that privilege. In recent months, he had not had to turn on the news to learn the deepening impact of the recession— he could read it in the faces of the town merchants.

As he came by the drugstore, he hoped to wave at Sparks through the window, but saw Hoppy Harper instead. Getting his green jelly bean fix, he thought. It pleased him immeasurably that Hoppy had done more than agree to be on the building committee. He said he'd be taking part, once again, in the life of the church.

Passing the window, he saw Olivia Davenport, muffled in fur, approach Hoppy with a radiant smile.

Like an image caught by the click of a camera shutter, the scene flashed upon his consciousness and was gone. Yet, he'd clearly seen something that troubled him. He'd seen a look of unmistakable happiness on his friend's face, a look of tenderness as he gazed down upon Olivia Davenport, who was dying.

At the church, he found the door unlocked and, coming inside in his snow-encrusted boots, was greeted by the lush, alluring fragrance of flowers. Their fresh scent spoke at once to his heart and lightened his sober thoughts.

He looped the red leash around a chair leg and took off his boots as Barnabas lay down contentedly. Apparently, the Altar Guild had been in to arrange the flowers and had forgotten to lock the side door. He must speak to them about it, of course.

Not that he didn't like an unlocked church. No, indeed; he preferred it. If there was anything disheartening, it was to seek out a church for prayer and refreshment and find its doors barred.

But the Mortlake tapestry, woven in 1675 and now hanging behind the altar, was of such extraordinary rarity that the insurance company not only demanded a darkened room and locked doors, it stipulated the type of locks.

It was unusual for him to visit Lord's Chapel on Saturday, but today he was seeking special refreshment of his own. Who was there, after all, to counsel the counselor? He crossed himself. "Revive me, O Lord," he prayed, "according to thy word."

For days, he had felt weighted and heavy, but not from the holiday turkey and dressing. If anything, he had been more careful of his diet than ever. It was his spirit that was heavy, at a time when church events were in full force and Advent preparations were hurling him madly toward Christmas.

Yet it wasn't the escalating rush of daily life that concerned him. What concerned him were his sermons.

In recent weeks, they had been tepid and controlled. Barren, somehow. It was as if the Holy Spirit had taken his hands off and was standing back, observing, watchful.

He sighed as he opened the door into the nave, and noted that he must stop doing that. Sighing was not becoming to anyone, much less to a rector. Perhaps he could put the burden on Emma, saying, "Emma, I have this bothersome habit of sighing, as you no doubt have noticed. From now on, tell me when I do it, and I'll put a dollar in the thank offering box."

A dollar! he thought. The very stiffness of the penalty should resolve the problem.

Before he prayed, however, he wanted to complete a chore. It had always been his habit to do a chore when he came to the church on Saturday.

Today he would pay some overdue attention to the columbarium, where six ash-filled urns were hidden away in a closet on the parish hall corridor.

He located the key on the top of the door frame, unlocked, and turned on the light.

It wasn't much of a final resting place, he thought. His own wish was to be buried in the old-fashioned way, with birds singing and roses blooming over him.

He moved the 1928 prayer books that someone had piled onto the shelf next to the urns, and partially filled a wastebasket with the glass ashtrays they'd used in the parish hall before the blessed relief of the smoking ban. Rummage sale!

He dumped two arrangements of plastic poinsettias into the wastebasket, lest anyone should find them and use them again, and followed that with a stack of hymnals so badly worn that the covers were off. Recycling bin!

Feeling warmly satisfied with the results of twenty minutes' effort, he went to the kitchen for cleaning rags and returned to dust off the remains of Parkinson Hamrick.

"Gone to Glory!" he said with a smile, remembering the kind man who had sung like an angel.

Parkinson's ashes rattled dully as he set the urn down. Though he had never looked into one of these morbid containers, he'd been told by Father Roland that bits of charred bone were mixed with the ashes, which caused the rattle.

"Lydia Newton," he murmured aloud, lifting her urn. Lydia Newton, herself widowed, had come with her widowed mother-in-law to Mitford, where the two had lived happily for years. "Where thou diest," Ruth had said to Naomi in the Bible story, "will I die, and there will I be buried; the Lord do so to me, and more also, if anything but death part thee and me." It was one of the loveliest passages in Scripture, mistakenly used, he thought, in Protestant weddings.

The musty little closet was, in a sense, coming alive. And he was feeling better already. Then he picked up the next urn.

While the other urns had rattled dully, he found that the remains of Parrish Guthrie rattled differently. Again, he held up the bronze urn and shook it.

Odd. Not at all like the sound of the others. There was a brighter rattle, as of something small and hard, like pebbles.

He was curious. After all, he'd never seen inside one of these things. He looked up at the dim, bare bulb, and decided to move the urn into the kitchen by the big window over the sink.

He took a tea towel from the rack by the sink and applied some pressure to the top of the urn. It wouldn't budge. Need one of those rubber things that unscrews jars, he thought, trying again. The urn rattled brightly. Seashells, he thought, remembering his time as a child at the gulf shore. It sounds like a jar of small seashells.

Then, the top of the urn gave way and unscrewed as if it had been oiled.

He turned the open mouth of the urn toward the light and peered in. Something gleamed.

"I hope that's not the old boy's gold tooth!" he said aloud.

He spread the tea towel on the counter top, then turned the urn on its side and shook it gently. Something loosely wrapped in cloth appeared, and tumbled onto the towel.

When he untied the string, the bright, faceted gems came rolling out like so many peas.

"Good Lord!" he croaked, hearing his voice fail.

The winter light coming through the window struck the stones at playful random. Some, shaped like tiny globes, radiated a scarlet glow that was utterly bewitching. Others, the shape of teardrops, seemed to burn with a green and living fire. Still others were as darkly blue as distant mountains.

He stood by the sink, unaware that he was holding his breath. He could see that the jar contained more of the loosely wrapped parcels, and he was seized with such anxiety that he felt a heaviness in his chest.

"Father, something is out of order here. I need your

wisdom. Help me think this through . . ." He let out his breath, and sat down on the stool by the telephone. His knees were weak.

Trouble! What he was looking at was trouble. Before he even began to think it through, he was convinced of that.

He had personally attended these urns about three years ago; the date would be in his journal on the shelf at the office. At that time, Parrish Guthrie's rattle had been no different from the rest. So, the jewels had been put into the urn since then.

Scarcely anyone ever went near that closet. Someone would occasionally open the door, throw in a bit of rubbish and depart. Once, a Sunday school class had been shown the closet, in a teaching about death. "Gross!" said a ten-year-old. If there was a neglected, seldom-used part of the church, the closet was it. A perfect place, then, for someone to hide what he'd just found.

But had he found anything of real importance? Were these the genuine article? He knew nothing about jewels. As payment of a legal fee, his attorney father had once come into possession of some uncut diamonds, which he'd considered dull, gray, and uninteresting. But once they were cut, they flashed like fire. What a marvel!

No, he had no knowledge of jewels. But something told him that these were the real thing. He had seen that same vibrant, indescribable fire in the cut diamonds.

Now what? He moved off the stool and paced the kitchen.

The proper thing, he thought, was to call Rodney Underwood, who would conduct endless questions, investigations, and fingerprinting, just like on TV.

Rodney, always overzealous, would have his small force swarming—yes, swarming—over the place, and here it was nearly Christmas, with new music for the choir to practice, and the special musicale and concert reading coming up within the week, and the Festival of Lessons and Carols. Clearly, the beauty and holiness of a time already fractured by stress and distractions would be further eroded.

Then there was J.C. Hogan to consider.

J.C. would run a front-page story, colored by the usual inaccuracies. He'd very likely have an interview with Emma Garrett, Russell Jacks, the vestry, and whoever had an opinion at the Grill, which was everybody.

Worse than that, J.C. would camp out at Lord's Chapel and the rector's office for days on end, looking for a "scoop" and eating countless bags of M&Ms, a great number of which would end up on the floor, smashed underfoot.

The other course, then, was to let sleeping dogs lie, and wait until after Christmas to call Rodney Underwood.

He didn't think twice about what he did next.

He put the jewels back into the cloth, tied the string and placed the parcel in the urn, screwed the top on, folded the tea towel and replaced it on the rack, walked down the hall and put the urn on the closet shelf exactly where it had been, dusted the other three urns, turned off the light, carried out the full wastebasket and the dust rags, locked the door, put the dust rags under the kitchen sink, stored the wastebasket in the rummage room, and checked on Barnabas before he went to the nave to do what he had, after all, come to do:

Pray about his anemic sermons.

As he paused to let his eyes adjust to the dimness of

the nave, he heard a strange sound. Then, toward the front, on the gospel side, he saw a man kneeling in a pew. Suddenly, he leaned back and uttered such a desperate cry that the rector's heart fairly thundered.

Give me wisdom, he prayed for the second time that morning. Then he stood waiting. He didn't know for what.

"If you're up there, prove it! Show me! If you're God, you can prove it!" In the visitor's voice was a combination of anger, despair, and odd hope.

"I'll never ask you this again," the man said coldly, and then, with a fury that chilled his listener, he shouted again, "Are . . . you . . . up . . . there?"

With what appeared to be utter exhaustion, he put his head in his hands as the question reverberated in the nave.

Father Tim slid into the pew across the aisle and knelt on the worn cushion. "You may be asking the wrong question," he said, quietly.

Startled, the man raised his head.

"I believe the question you may want to ask is not, 'Are you up there?' but, 'Are you down here?' "

"What kind of joke is that?"

"It isn't a joke."

The man took a handkerchief from his suit pocket and wiped his face. He was neatly dressed, the rector observed, and his suit and tie appeared to be expensive. A businessman, obviously. Successful, quite likely. Not from Mitford, certainly.

"God wouldn't be God if He were only up there. In fact, another name for Him is Immanuel, which means 'God with us.' " He was amazed at the casual tone of his voice, as if they'd met here to chat for a while. "He's with us right now, in this room."

The man looked at him. "I'd like to believe that, but I can't. I can't feel Him at all."

"There's a reason . . ."

"The things I've done," the man said flatly.

"Have you asked Him to forgive the things you've done?"

"I assure you that God would not want to do that."

"Believe it or not, I can promise that He would. In fact, He promises that He will."

The man looked at his watch. "I've got a meeting," he said, yet he made no move to leave. He remained on his knees.

"What business are you in?" It was one of those questions from a cocktail party or Rotary meeting, but out it came.

"Shoes. We make men's shoes. I was on my way to a sales meeting in Wesley when I saw this place and I came in. I didn't mean to do it, I just couldn't help it. I had to come in. And now I don't know what I'm doing here. I need to get on the road."

Still, he made no move to rise from his knees.

It was an odd thought, but the rector pursued it. "Let's say you need to move into another factory building. Trouble is, it's crowded with useless, out-of-date equipment. Until you clear out the rubbish and get the right equipment installed, you're paralyzed, you can't produce."

"How did you know we're looking for a new factory?"

"I didn't know. A divine coincidence."

There was a long silence. A squirrel ran across the attic floor.

"You can keep the factory shut down and unproductive, or you can clear it out and get to work. Is your life working?"

"Not in years."

Somewhere in the dark church, the floor creaked. "There's no other way I can think of to put it—but when you let Him move into your life, the garbage moves out. The anger starts to go, and the resentment, and the fear. That's when He can help get your equipment up and running, you might say."

"Look, I don't want to wallow around in this God stuff like a pig in slop. I just want some answers, that's all."

"What are the questions you want answered?"

"Bottom line, is He up there, is He real?"

"Bottom line, He's down here, He's with us right now."

"Prove it."

"I can't. I don't even want to try."

"Jesus," the man said, shaking his head.

This was like flying blind, the rector thought, with the windshield iced over. "I get the feeling you really want God to be real, perhaps you even want to be close to Him, but . . . but you're holding on to something, holding on to one of those sins you don't think God can forgive, and you don't want to let it go."

The man's voice was cold. "I'd like to kill someone, I think of killing him all the time. I would never do it, but he deserves it and thinking about it helps me. I like thinking about it."

The rector felt suddenly weakened, as if the anger had seeped into his own bones, his own spirit. He wanted the windshield to defrost; where was this going?

"Do you like the fall of the year?"

The man gave an odd laugh. "Why?"

"One of the things that makes a dead leaf fall to the ground is the bud of the new leaf that pushes it off the limb. When you let God fill you with His love and forgiveness, the things you think you desperately want to hold on to start falling away . . . and we hardly notice their passing."

The man looked at his watch and made a move to rise from his knees. His agitation was palpable.

"Let me ask you something," said the rector. "Would you like to ask Christ into your life?"

The stranger stared into the darkened sanctuary. "I can't do it, I've tried."

"It isn't a test you have to pass. It doesn't require discipline and intelligence . . . not even strength and perseverance. It only requires faith."

"I don't think I've got that." There was a long silence. "But I'd be willing to try it . . . one more time."

"Will you pray a simple prayer with me . . . on faith?"

He looked up. "What do I have to lose?"

"Nothing, actually." Father Tim rose stiffly from the kneeler and took the short step across the aisle, where he laid his hands on the man's head.

"If you could repeat this," he said. "Thank you, God, for loving me, and for sending your Son to die for my sins. I sincerely repent of my sins, and receive Christ as my personal savior. Now, as your child, I turn my entire life over to you. Amen."

The man repeated the prayer, and they were silent.

"Is that all?" he asked finally.

"That's all."

"I don't know . . . what I'm supposed to feel."

"Whatever you feel is exactly what you're supposed to feel."

The man was suddenly embarrassed, awkward. "I've got to get out of here. I was on my way to a meeting in

Wesley, and I saw this old church and I . . . things have been, I've been . . . I've got to get out of here. Look, thanks. Thank you," he said, shaking the rector's hand. "Please . . . stay in touch."

He stood at the door for a moment and watched him go. There was so much he hadn't said, so much he'd left out. But the Holy Spirit would fill in the blanks.

As they were leaving the church, Barnabas looked up, sniffed the air, and began to bark wildly at the ceiling. His booming voice filled the small nave like the bass of an organ.

With some difficulty, he unglued his charge from the narthex floor, and pulled him along on the leash.

It seemed years ago that he'd come in this door, he thought. Yet his watch told him he'd been at Lord's Chapel only a little more than two hours.

He felt strangely at peace, following the man's footprints along the snowy path to the street.

❧

As Christmas drew nearer, sleep became more elusive. For hours, he'd lie awake while Barnabas snored at his feet. He had tried without success to put the jewels completely out of his mind.

Catching himself pondering the imponderable, he'd toss this way and that, until the bed was a scramble of sheets and blankets and Barnabas had gone to the kitchen for a snack, which he crunched loudly enough to wake the neighbors.

He wondered briefly how his neighbor was doing, anyway. He thought he'd seen Andrew Gregory's gray Mercedes parked in front of her house recently, but he couldn't be sure, as he'd never been good at identifying cars.

Was she going out with Andrew Gregory? Was he coming over for dinners of blackened roasts and burned rolls? He remembered Cynthia's silvery laugh behind the rest room wall, and his odd sense of feeling fat, short, and boring, compared to Andrew. He had not liked that feeling.

He sat up on the side of the bed.

It had just occurred to him that there were no ashes in Parrish Guthrie's urn. No ashes had spilled onto the white tea towel, and, clearly, no ashes had marred the sparkle of the jewels, which had been only loosely contained in the porous cloth. Well, then, where were the ashes of the departed?

Ashes. Ashes. Something dimly tried to get through to him, but he couldn't summon it. Also, he seemed to remember reading about stolen jewels.

He got up and walked to the window and looked down on Cynthia Coppersmith's house. He wondered how she was getting on, she and Violet, and if she was happy in Mitford. There were lights on, though it must easily be midnight. And he saw the tiny white lights she'd strung for Christmas, winking on the bushes by her front steps. A comfort to have someone in that house!

He sat down in his wing chair and picked up the *Observer*, but couldn't read it. Stolen jewels. He'd read something somewhere. . . .

The newspaper article, sticking out from under the ink blotter on Andrew Gregory's desk! Jewels! Stolen from under the guard's nose. Something about the queen being upset.

No, he thought, those were necklaces that royalty had worn, not loose stones. Ah, well.

Ashes, he thought, again. But almost immediately, he dozed off in his chair.

❧

Olivia Davenport opened the office door and said brightly, "Knock, knock!"

She was wearing an emerald-colored suit with black trim, and carrying a Bible under her arm. All in all, he thought, a lovely sight.

"Sit down, Olivia, and bring me up to date."

"I'm excited, Father! We're organizing a reading at the hospital. Isaiah. Ruth. Psalms. Portions of the Gospel of John. I'm hoping you'll join us, be a reader. Will you? You have such a beautiful voice. Oh, and then we're taking it to Wesley, to the hospital there."

Olivia's cheeks were flushed, and her violet eyes sparkled. Whatever her illness may be, her new mission was obviously good medicine.

"Count me in!" he said. "Just give me the schedule and I'll try and work it out."

"Wonderful," she said, getting up to go. "I was just dashing to The Local . . ."

"Olivia . . . ?"

"Yes?"

"Would you mind staying a moment?"

She smiled and sat down again.

He didn't want to do it, but it had to be done. "Olivia, what exactly . . . is going on?"

Her violet eyes were perplexed. "What . . . exactly do you mean?"

"Something tells me, and it isn't Hoppy, I assure you, that he's growing . . . shall I say . . . fond of you."

She stared at him, unspeaking.

"This troubles me," he said simply.

"It troubles me as well."

"Does he know?"

"He does not."

"I'd be grateful if you would tell me everything. It goes without saying that it will be held in the strictest confidence.

"You say you're dying. But why are you dying? Why do you appear so very healthy? What course will this . . . illness . . . take? Are you suffering?" He paused. "These are serious issues. But perhaps, for me, the issue is this: If you're dying, I can't bear to watch a friend who was lately grief stricken by his wife's death form an attachment that—"

Olivia stood up. "Please! I understand." She looked suddenly drawn and pale. "I'm going to tell you everything. You really should know, and I apologize. It's just that, when I moved here, I wanted to try and forget it. I wanted to . . . live without thinking of dying."

She was silent for a moment. "Before I say more, I'd like to ask you to do something for me."

"Consider it done," he said impulsively.

"When I've explained it all to you, I'd like you to tell him everything."

He was silent.

"I tried once," she said, "but, after all, he has said nothing to me of his feelings. It may seem shameful, but I'm too proud to say, 'Look, you appear to be falling in love with me, and you mustn't.' What if he isn't falling in love with me, what if I've guessed wrong, and we're both humiliated?"

"You haven't guessed wrong."

"You'll tell him, then?"

"I will. But I'd like you to do something for me, as well."

"Anything," she said with sincerity.

"This will be his second Christmas alone, and I feel

he still has some sorrow to work through. To tell him now would . . . complicate things unduly. You'll probably see him at church, of course, and even at the hospital. But I'd like you to avoid him as graciously as you can. Then, after the holidays, I'll tell him."

"I can do that," she said slowly. "I care for him very much. He's a wonderful man."

"He is, indeed."

"Well, then," she said, sitting down, again. "I suppose I can't put this off any longer."

❧

After Olivia Davenport left, he sat in silence, staring at the door. Then, he cleaned off his desk and typed an overdue letter to Walter, in which he quoted Romans 8:28: " 'We know that all things' (*all* things, Walter!) 'work together for good to them that love God, to them who are called according to His purpose.' Please bear with Katherine on this."

He was typing with more than usual dexterity when Russell Jacks pushed open the door.

"Russell! Come in and sit. Have some coffee." He got up and poured a cup for the old man who, he thought, looked gaunt and tired. "How are you pushing along, Russell?"

The sexton launched into a racking cough. "No rest for th' wicked," he said, grinning.

"How's Dooley doing? We missed our trip to Meadowgate because of the snow, and with Christmas on us, it'll be January before we get out there."

"Well, Father," said Russell, rolling his hat between his palms, "mournful is the word for that boy."

"Mournful? Dooley?"

"Yes, sir. That's th' word."

"What's the trouble?"

Russell hesitated, looking at the floor. "Well, Father, it's 'is mama. He's bad homesick."

"Can't he go home to visit? I've been meaning to ask that."

"I reckon he could . . ."

Father Tim waited.

"But t' tell th' truth, I reckon he cain't . . ."

Another silence.

"What is it, Russell? You need to share the truth with me, if you will. What exactly is wrong with your daughter?"

"Nerves," Russell mumbled.

"Nerves?"

The old man looked up. His face was sad. "Liquor, t' tell th' truth. His mama lays drunk."

"I'm sorry."

"She let all 'er young 'uns go, all five. Jus' give 'em out like candy. I'd've took two, if I could, but . . ." He shrugged, then coughed again. "Th' boy was th' oldest, been takin' care of them little 'uns all 'is life, nearly. They were snatched up like a bunch of kittens in a box, one give here, another give yonder, it's an awful bad thing for th' boy."

"I'm sorry. I didn't know." He felt immeasurably sad for Dooley.

Russell held his hat over his mouth as another fit of coughing overcame him. When it was over, his face was ashen.

"What are you doing for that cough, Russell?"

"A little of this an' a little of that, you might say."

"How's your Christmas looking?"

"Oh, we'll get by, me 'n th' boy."

"I'd like to see you do more than get by." He pulled

out his upper right-hand desk drawer and felt for the packet of bills. He had banked a thousand dollars of Pearly's "happiness" money and kept some cash for times like these.

He handed Russell a crisp hundred-dollar bill.

"In the name of the Lord, Russell, get the boy a tree, and string some lights, if you can."

"I thank you, Father," Russell said, looking embarrassed and relieved. "Do you reckon th' Lord would mind if we had a nice ham out of th' change?"

"Mind? Why, I think He'd mind if you didn't! And here, this is for that cough." He took a twenty-dollar bill out of his pocket.

The sexton folded the bills respectfully and tucked them into his overalls pocket. "I thank you, Father. We finished mulchin' them rhododendrons before it snowed, I thought you orght t' know."

Rhododendrons. Mulch. Ashes!

He remembered the fall day he'd gone around to the side door where Russell was mulching. He'd found ashes that looked like somebody had cleaned out their barbecue grill. He remembered asking Russell where the ashes came from, and then he'd borrowed Russell's gloves and worked the ashes into the soil.

Suddenly, he knew it just as sure as he was sitting there. He'd buried the remains of the double-dealing Parrish Guthrie in the church rhododendron bed.

❧

In the fall, somebody had emptied the ashes out the side door. Then, he reasoned, they'd put the jewels in the clean urn, where they thought they'd be safe. In most churches, columbariums were not often moved about, and their own had not been touched in fully three years.

He was horrified to think it was a parishioner. Yet, who else but a parishioner would know about the closet, and know that the door was scarcely ever opened. He found he was going over and over the list of members, questioning each name. It was a process that left him angrily depressed. The discovery of those stones had been a wicked intrusion that had robbed him of peace and tranquillity during a season, in which both were greatly longed for.

The concert reading and musicale drew a packed house, and the choir had, in his opinion, reached a new pinnacle of praise. After the event at church, the choir proceeded out the church doors and along Main Street, caroling in the chill evening air, carrying lanterns. They made a glowing procession along the old street, stopping here and there in an open shop for hot cider and cookies.

A tenor and a baritone broke away from the choir and went along the dark, cold creek bank, to the little house of Homeless Hobbes, where they warmed themselves by the wood stove and lustily sang, together with their host, as many carols as they had strength left to deliver.

The rector had the caroling choir finish up at the rectory, where he laid a fire in the study and spread out a feast that Puny had spent days preparing. Curried shrimp, honey-glazed ham, hot biscuits, cranberry salad, fried chicken, roasted potatoes with rosemary, and brandied fruit were set out in generous quantities.

The little group gathered around the roaring fire and, as the last carol of the evening, sang something they knew to be their rector's great favorite.

"In the bleak mid-winter," ran the first lines of Christina Rossetti's hymn, "icy wind made moan, earth as hard as iron, water like a stone . . ."

Then, the poignant last verse: "What shall I give him, poor as I am? If I were a shepherd, I would bring a lamb; if I were a wise man, I would do my part; yet what I can I give him . . . give my heart."

That's the key! he thought, as they pulled on heavy coats and gloves, mufflers and boots. Then, with much laughter and warm hugs, they trooped out the door and into the biting wind.

"The Lord be with you!" he called, his breath forming gray puffs on the stinging air.

"And also with you!"

For a long time afterward, he sat by the fire, feeling the joy of Christmas, and knowing with unsearchable happiness that Christ did, indeed, live in his heart. Not because he was a "preacher." Not because he was, after a fashion, "good." But because, long ago, he had asked Him to.

❦

He was working on his homily, which he intended to deliver on Christmas morning, glad to be by the study fire instead of out in the howling wind. He was glad, too, for the soup Puny had left simmering on the back burner, for it gave the house not only a mouth-watering fragrance, but a certain cheer.

When his mind wandered from the homily, he admired the tall spruce, garlanded with strings of colored lights like he remembered from his childhood in Holly Springs, and hung with ornaments that, somehow, had made it through dozens of Christmases past.

There was such a quantity of gifts stacked under the tree that he was mildly embarrassed.

Walter and Katherine had sent what he foolishly believed to be an electric train. Miss Sadie had given him a very large package tied with a red bow. Dooley had made him a present in school. Winnie Ivey wrote on hers: *I didn't bake this, but I hope you enjoy it anyway.*

Emma, who always liked to reveal the identity of her presents, had given him a gift certificate from the Collar Button, with which he planned to buy the first new pajamas he'd owned in years.

On and on, the presents went. And who was there to open them with him? There was the rub for a bachelor.

Occasionally, he would go to the garage and stand looking at the red bicycle. None of the presents under his tree inspired the excitement he felt in helping give Dooley Barlowe the desire of his heart.

He had tied a huge bow on the handlebars and made a card which read: *To Dooley from Dooley, and also from his friend, the preacher. When you see this, please don't go to hollerin'.*

When he heard the knock, he thought it was Barnabas scratching.

Then, he heard it again.

Dooley Barlowe stood at the back door, out of breath and shivering in a thin jacket.

"Granpaw's bad off sick," he said, looking desperate. "You got t' come."

He gave the boy a down jacket, gloves, and a wool hat, and, with the icy wind scorching their faces, the two sped off on the motor scooter toward Russell Jacks's house.

This time next year, he thought, I'll be driving my car again. It is eight long years since I gave it up for Lent, and that's long enough.

❧

"Pneumonia," said Hoppy.

The rector wasn't surprised.

When he and Dooley arrived at Russell's house, they had found the old man in bed, scarcely able to breathe and with a frightening rattle in his chest. He had stoked up the embers in the stove, covered the sexton with blankets from Dooley's cot, and, because there was no telephone, rode to the hospital where he ordered the ambulance to fetch his friend, along with the frightened boy.

Hoppy had come on the run from his house three blocks away. "We've got our work cut out for us," he said. "He's in bad shape. Has the boy got a place to go?"

Father Tim looked at Dooley, whose face was ashen. "He'll come home with me."

"Are you two on that bloody motor scooter?"

"We are."

"Park it in the hospital garage, for God's sake. I'll send you home with Nurse Herman."

"You really don't . . ."

"Oh, but I really do! It's twenty degrees and dropping, and if I'm going to be a church regular, I'd like to have a live preacher in the pulpit."

When they came home from the hospital, Barnabas bounded to the back door, put his front paws on Dooley's shoulders and licked his face with happy abandon.

" 'is ol' dog's got bad breath."

"He spoke well of you," replied Father Tim, helping Dooley out of the down jacket.

"Is granpaw goin' t' die?"

"I don't think so."

Dooley took off his hat and gloves, dropped them on the floor, and walked away.

"Dooley . . ."

He looked up at the rector.

The rector looked down at the hat and gloves.

A long moment passed before the boy sighed heavily and picked them up. "Stayin' around here ain't goin' t' be any fun," he muttered.

"If I were you, I wouldn't make that decision just yet. Put your hat and gloves right here in the bin. Hang your coat on this peg. Then I've got something to show you."

When they stepped into the study, which was still warm from the fire on the hearth, Dooley saw the fragrant spruce that reached all the way to the beamed ceiling. It twinkled with hundreds of colored lights, and underneath were presents, dozen upon dozen. "Maybe stayin' around here ain't goin' t' be 'at bad," he said.

❧

Dooley stepped into Father Tim's pajama pants, pulled the drawstring tight, and rolled the legs above his ankles. Then he buttoned the top over his undershirt, and pulled on a pair of green socks. Over this, he put a burgundy terry cloth robe which just touched the floor, and tied it with a sash.

"Well, what do you think?" asked the rector, who had also changed into a robe and pajamas, and was filling soup bowls at the counter.

"It's good you're short," said Dooley, pointing to the hem of the robe. " 'is ol' thing's jis' right on me."

The phone rang.

"Looks like viral pneumonia," said Hoppy. "That's a tough one, because it doesn't respond to treatment with antibiotics. We're giving him oxygen, and we've removed a piece of lung tissue, so we'll know more tomorrow. I'll call you."

"You're in my prayers."

"That's a good place to be," said Hoppy, hanging up.

"Is granpaw goin' t' die?"

"I don't think so."

"Let's eat, then," said Dooley.

❦

Sometime in the early morning, he woke up. While Barnabas snored, he stared at the ceiling, praying for Russell Jacks and Hoppy Harper, for Cynthia Coppersmith and Homeless Hobbes, and anyone else the Holy Spirit called to mind.

At times like these, his mind let down its daytime defenses, and the names of people whom he hadn't remembered in months or even years came before him.

Suddenly, he sat straight up.

The red bicycle!

It was standing in the garage, in plain view of anyone who cared to look.

He crept out of bed, slid his feet into the old leather slippers, and quietly put on his robe. "Stay," he said to Barnabas, who opened one eye, closed it again, and beat the bed with his tail. He did not want an alarmed Barnabas barking his head off and waking Dooley.

The street lamp shone through the wide hall window and was the only light he ever used to go downstairs at odd hours.

He padded softly down the steps and along the hall, then opened the garage door and turned on the light.

The bicycle stood next to his long-unused car. With its vast red ribbon and handmade card, it had transformed the garage into something quite magical.

What if the boy had seen it standing there in broad daylight? All those carefully laid plans—dashed!

He took several blankets from a storage cabinet and wrapped them around the bicycle. Then he gently laid the bicycle on its side, in the corner, and out of sight from the study door. On top of this bundle, he placed stacks of the *Mitford Muse*.

"Excellent!" he said, standing back to survey his camouflage.

He turned off the light, walked quietly to the stairs, and started up. He had nearly reached the landing when he felt a sudden and violent explosion in his head.

As he reeled backward in a half-circle and slammed against the stair railing, he saw a blinding light that was followed by a shooting pain in his temples, and then, everything went black.

&

When he came to, he was sitting on the stairs.

Dooley Barlowe was crying and staring urgently into his face. Barnabas was licking his ear.

"What in God's name . . ." he began, weakly.

"I didn't know it was you!" Dooley sobbed. "I thought it was a dern burglar tryin' to git me!"

He felt exactly as if a train had struck him, but it was only Dooley's tennis shoe, one of the very pair, ironically, that he had bought the boy before school started.

"One time, a burglar broke in my mama's house and it was jis' us young 'uns by ourselves, an' you sounded jis' like 'im, a creepin' up the stairs in th' dark." Dooley's fear suddenly gave way to a rising anger.

"How come you t' creep up your own dern stairs, anyway? How come you couldn't jis' walk up 'em, like anybody else, so this wouldn't 've happened?"

Later, drifting toward a restless sleep, he murmured a deep truth. "It's different having a boy in the house."

❧

Tell Rodney about jewels—after Christmas.

Talk to Hoppy about Olivia—after Christmas.

On his list of things to do, these delicate issues hung suspended like icicles from a limb.

The day following the incident on the stairs, Mitford was enclosed by a thick blanket of fog and rain. And since his parishioners were obviously busy with other affairs, he left the office early and went home. Even with the Tylenol, his head pounded furiously.

"Dadgum!" Percy said with admiration, when he stopped at the Grill to pick up a cup of soup. "Somebody busted you good."

"I'll say."

He paid $1.69 for the soup, which he thought was outrageous, and left without giving Percy the details. As he passed the window, he saw Percy standing at the cash register with a hurt look. If there was anything Percy thrived on, he mused, it was details.

At four o'clock, he helped Dooley with his homework and put a cold washcloth on the enlarging bump that was slowly turning black, blue, and chartreuse.

"I'm sorry," Dooley said, miserably.

"No sorrier than I. But all in all, I think you were brave."

"You do?"

"Indeed I do. I have only one complaint."

"What's 'at?"

"You might have looked before you struck. There was, after all, some light on the stairs, so you could have seen the top of my head shine."

"I seen it shine! But you ain't th' only man in the

world gittin' bald-headed, y' know. Burglars git bald-headed, too."

❧

At nine o'clock, they had a report on Russell Jacks. Not faring well, but resting. Age was against viral pneumonia, Hoppy said. While Dooley took a bath, the rector made two calls asking for prayer, and gave Miss Sadie an update.

Then he stretched out before the flickering fire and closed his eyes. Puny hadn't come today, which always made an astonishing difference. He was growing to depend on her, he knew that. And a dependable one she was.

He would slip a crisp hundred-dollar bill into her Christmas envelope. And it would be out of his own happiness fund, not Pearly McGee's. He realized that, in the space of a few days, he would have given out two bills of that stellar denomination, and decided he liked doing it. Very much.

Dooley came into the room, smelling of soap, with Barnabas at his side.

He looked at the pair, feeling a certain contentment. "Are you taking over my dog?"

" 'is ol' dog follers me ever' where I go. It ain't my fault he likes me."

"Well, go up to bed and read your book. I'll come in a bit and say goodnight."

"I'm about give out," Dooley said, sighing.

"You and me both, pal."

At the door, Dooley turned around and looked back. "When you come up them steps tonight . . . ?"

"What about it?"

"Don't creep. I cain't stand creepin'."

That boy needs a lot of teaching, he thought, putting his feet up. Starting tomorrow, we're going back to something I hardly ever hear these days. We're going back to "yes, sir" and "no, sir," not to mention "thank you" and "please." Driving that home ought to be at least as much fun as pulling teeth.

He thought he might lie down and enjoy looking at the tree lights. But then, he'd be fast asleep in minutes, with Dooley waiting upstairs. He went into the kitchen instead, and turned the burner on under the tea kettle.

There was a small, delicate rapping at the door.

No rest for the wicked, he thought, quoting Russell Jacks.

It was his neighbor, dressed in a yellow slicker streaming with rain.

"Just one minute," she said, "that's all it will take. May I come in?"

"Well, absolutely! Do come in."

"Here, I'll just stand right here on the mat, so I won't drip all over the kitchen. I just wanted to give you your Christmas present!" She had one hand tucked inside her slicker.

"You shouldn't have!" he exclaimed, truly meaning it. For heaven's sake, why had he impulsively sent all those Belgian chocolates to the nurses at the hospital, when he might have kept a pound or two at home for emergencies? "I was just going to have a cup of tea, and I hope you'll join me."

"Oh, I'd love that," she said, with unabashed enthusiasm, "but I can't. I finished your present a few minutes ago, and I couldn't wait to give it to you." He saw that earnest look in her blue eyes. "I hope you'll open it tonight."

"Well, yes," he said, feeling a bit rattled, "but wouldn't you like to come in by the fire, and I'll open it while . . ."

"I promise I can't. I must run. Here!" She withdrew her hand from the wet slicker, and gave him a flat manila envelope. "Oh, good!" she said, looking at the envelope. "Dry as a bone!"

She turned and bolted out the door. In the glow of the porch light, he saw her dash across the yard and through the hedge, water splashing around her boots.

"Merry Christmas!" he called. But she was gone. And she hadn't even mentioned the gruesome, multicolored bump on his head.

CHAPTER TWELVE

An Empty Vessel

The news from the hospital was not good. Russell Jacks was stable, but not improving.

"Pneumonia takes a lot of forms," said Hoppy. "For a man Russell's age, this is the worst form. We're doing all we can, and there's still hope, but it's like swimming upstream."

Russell's name was listed on the prayers of the people at Lord's Chapel and put on a community-wide prayer chain. Father Tim wasn't surprised to see the concern of his parishioners. They cared about the taciturn old man whose tender heart was revealed only in the showy perennials, elaborate paths, and manicured borders of the church gardens.

Food poured into the rectory, to assist with the unexpected duty of having a boy to feed.

"Growin' boys is bottomless pits," said Percy, who sent fresh potato salad and pimiento cheese.

Winnie Ivey delivered doughnuts, cream horns, and a coconut cake.

Miss Sadie had Luther drive over with a bag of Swanson's chicken pies and a Sara Lee pound cake, and the Altar Guild brought a roasted turkey.

"I ain't never seen nothin' like 'is," confessed Dooley, who was able to choose from more than a dozen lunch options.

"I ain't . . . I've never seen anything like it myself, and that's a fact," said Father Tim, as they sat at the kitchen counter.

Soon, he would have to deal with Dooley's English, but as he'd just begun dealing with "please" and "thank you," he didn't want to push his luck.

His eye fell on the manila envelope that Cynthia Coppersmith had delivered several evenings ago in a drenching rain, and which he'd tucked among the books he kept on the counter.

"I hope you'll open it tonight!" she had said. He was deeply ashamed that he'd forgotten. How could he have forgotten? He had stuck it between a couple of books on the shelf so he wouldn't spill tea on it, thinking he'd take it up to bed. Then, he'd forgotten it completely. Whatever might be inside, he clearly didn't deserve it.

He slipped the gift from the envelope and removed the wrapping paper so it wouldn't tear. "You know how I could tell I was getting old?" his mother once said. "I began to save used wrapping paper."

It was a matted watercolor of a furry creature dressed in a dark suit with a clerical collar, and horn-rimmed glasses perched on the end of its nose. The little creature had small toes on its furry feet, a very large smile, and a pair of engaging eyes.

"Father Talpidae," read the caption at the bottom.

" 'at's funny," said Dooley, peering over his shoulder.

The rector thought it was the most charming creature he'd seen in years; better, even, than Beatrix Potter might have imagined.

"Father Talpidae," read a legend on the back, "is the good rector of a small parish, located under the green grass of Father Tim's rectory garden in Mitford. Fr. Talpidae says he's happy to announce that his congregation is growing, and that he has absolutely no plans to retire."

"Mole," Webster informed him, or "L., talpidae." He laughed as heartily as he'd laughed in a long time.

"It ain't that funny," said Dooley.

"That's your opinion."

"I like it when you laugh," said Dooley. "It makes it more fun around here."

"Then I'll try to laugh more often," he said, still chuckling. Hadn't he recently promised Cynthia Coppersmith that very thing?

❧

That evening, he and Dooley walked Barnabas to the monument and looked in all the shop windows. Boxwood wreaths hung on the doors, and windows were garlanded with tiny, winking lights.

Mitford at Christmas was a fairyland. If only their Christmas snow hadn't fallen at Thanksgiving!

Dooley examined the displays in every window, from cuff links and sports jackets at The Collar Button to iron skillets, fishing tackle, and tree stands at the hardware.

As they turned the corner and headed home, he was sure he saw Andrew Gregory's gray Mercedes parked in front of the little house next door.

"Hot chocolate?" he asked Dooley, when they'd taken off their coats. He felt oddly absentminded, unable to concentrate. He'd recently seen Andrew's car parked in that precise spot at least five times.

"No."

Maybe six, he thought, setting the saucepan on the stove. "No, thank you. Milk and fruitcake?"

"No."

"No, thank you. What, then?"

"Nothin'."

Dooley had recently turned mournful, as Russell called it. "You know what I'd do?" Puny had said on Wednesday. "I'd give 'im a swift kick. Just say bend over, honey, and whop, you'd see a diff'rent young 'un. My granpaw wouldn't n' more let me git away with bein' ill to him than he could fly. Blam, he'd yank me up and preach me a sermon that'd scorch the hair off my head."

"I have great respect for that approach, but it's not one I could administer effectively."

"You'd git along better if you was part Baptist."

"You may be interested to know that I'm precisely one-half Baptist."

She looked at him suspiciously.

"My mother was a fervent Baptist, and my father was . . . a lukewarm Episcopalian."

"Lukewarm! I don't even like my dishwater lukewarm!"

"Puny, what if Russell Jacks doesn't make it? What would we do with Dooley?"

"Did you ever find out what's th' matter with 'is mama?"

"Alcohol. I don't know the whole story. She let all five of her children go."

Puny was silent for a long time, as she cleaned the silver and put it in soapy water. "Well," she said, "maybe he don't need a kick in the tail, after all."

"Oh?"

"Maybe what he needs is jist . . . a whole lot of . . . lovin'."

Now, there! he thought. There's an idea I can get my teeth into, in a manner of speaking. "Puny," he said, "that is splendid thinking. So splendid, in fact, it deserves special recognition. Please dry your hands."

He went into the study and took the cream-colored envelope from his desk drawer, and gave it to her at the sink.

"Merry Christmas!"

She looked in the envelope, saw the hundred-dollar bill, and burst into tears, just as Dooley came in with Barnabas.

"Poop on 'at ol' puzzle you're makin' me do," he said, glaring at Puny.

Father Tim saw the color rise in her cheeks.

" 'at's th' stupidest thing I ever seen," said Dooley. "I th'ow'd it in th' trash."

"You know what I'm goin' to do to you?" she snapped.

"What's 'at?"

"I'm goin' to jerk a knot in your tail!" She moved toward him, with fire behind the fresh tears in her eyes.

Dooley backed into Barnabas, who yelped and fled down the hall.

"But you know what I'm goin' to do, first?" She grinned wickedly at Dooley, whose eyes were wide with alarm. "I'm goin' to grab you and give you a great big hug!"

"Oh, no you ain't!"

As he pounded up the stairs, Puny turned to the rector. "There," she said, looking triumphant. "That'll fix 'im for a while."

❧

On the afternoon of Christmas Eve, Father Tim and Dooley planned to visit Russell, who was sitting up and no longer needed oxygen.

"Let's drop by Mitford Blossoms," said Father Tim, "and take Russell a gloxinia."

On the way, they stopped at the drugstore, where he bought a bag of jelly beans for Hoppy and a Reese's Cup for Dooley.

When they walked in the florist shop, he was surprised to see Hoppy standing at the counter, dressed in a hospital scrub suit, his navy pea jacket, boots lined with sheepskin, a worn khaki raincoat, and a cap with ear flaps.

"Left the hospital on the run," he said, grinning.

"My friend, it looks like you were dressed by Miss Rose Watson."

Hoppy laughed. A glorious laugh, thought Father Tim, and one he hadn't heard in far too long.

"These are the best we have," said Jena Ivey, as she came out of the cooler with a bucket of roses. "Hello, Father! Merry Christmas! Merry Christmas, Dooley!"

" 'at's my Sunday school teacher," Dooley whispered to the doctor.

Jena proudly set the bucket on the counter.

"What do you think, pal?" asked Hoppy. "You're the rosarian."

Jena's roses were grown in Holland, a fact that made them considerably more expensive, but they never drooped their heads after a day in the vase, and they always smelled like roses. He nodded his strong approval.

"Two dozen!" Hoppy said, taking out his wallet. "And, Jena, please deliver them right away. You know the house."

As Jena arranged the stems in a long, pink box, he turned to the rector. "She's practically quit speaking to me," he said.

"She?"

"You know, Olivia."

"Aha."

"From cool to freezing."

Father Tim felt his heart beat dully. He had an impulse to take Hoppy across the street to the church office, and tell him the truth at once. But no, he had made a promise, and the promise was to tell him after Christmas—after the joy and trepidation of sending two dozen splendid roses, after Olivia's delight and sorrow in receiving them. Good Lord, why did this have to happen to two of the finest people he knew?

"You're mighty quiet. Do you know something I don't know?" asked Hoppy.

The rector reached into his jacket pocket. "All I know is, this bag contains at least eleven green jelly beans, as I counted every one I could see through the wrapper. Merry Christmas!"

Hoppy laughed as he opened the bag. "Are you going to see Russell?"

"We are."

"My car's out front, I'll give you a lift."

As they were leaving with the purple gloxinia, Dooley tugged at Father Tim's sleeve. "Wait a minute," he said, and went back to the counter where he handed Jena Ivey his Reese's Cup.

At the hospital, they stood outside Russell's open door, and talked.

"It's a bit of a miracle," said Hoppy. "I think he may pull out of it, but there's another problem."

"What's that?"

"He could be down for months. The best way to recover from this is to get plenty of bed rest. That means he won't be able to care for the boy. In fact, he's going to need some care himself."

"Well," said Father Tim, at a loss for words.

Dooley stood by the bed, looking anxiously at his grandfather. The old man was weak and spoke with his eyes closed.

"Dooley, are you behavin' yourself?"

"Nope."

"Don't shame me, boy. You hear?"

"All right, Granpaw, I won't."

Before he left, Dooley took his grandfather's hand. "Granpaw," he said, "don't die!"

Russell Jacks opened his eyes and looked at his grandson with a faint smile. "All right, boy, I won't."

❧

According to parishioners, the Christmas Eve masses at Lord's Chapel were more beautiful, more powerful, more stirring than ever before.

Candles burned on the window sills, among fragrant boughs of spruce and pine. Fresh garlands wrapped the high cedar beams over the nave. A glorious tree from Meadowgate Farm stood near the pulpit, and a lush garden of creme-colored poinsettias sprang up around its feet.

In the midnight service especially, there was an expectant hush that went beyond the usual reverent silence before the service, and someone said that, for the first time in her life, she had felt the sweet savor of the Christ child in her heart.

"Once in royal David's city stood a lowly cattle shed, where a mother laid her baby in a manger for his bed . . ."

Someone who was out walking in the balmy air heard a great wealth of music pouring from the little stone church, music with a poignant clarity and purpose.

". . . This child, this little helpless boy, shall be our confidence and joy . . ."

"Hark! the herald angels sing, glory to the newborn King!"

Miss Rose came on the arm of Uncle Billy, wearing her new black suit and fuchsia coat, and a pair of red and navy argyles with unlaced saddle oxfords.

"We're gittin' there," Uncle Billy said to Father Tim after the service. "You might say we got a pretty good ways past the head, but we ain't made it to th' toe."

As he headed home with Dooley at nearly one-thirty in the morning, he felt deeply grateful, but uncommonly fatigued.

❦

He had never been able to decide when to open his gifts. He could hardly do it on Christmas Eve, when he arrived home past 1:00 a.m. after preaching two services. And on Christmas morning, conducting two masses kept him at Lord's Chapel until well past noon.

"I play it by ear," he once told Emma, who couldn't imagine not opening presents anytime she felt like it, starting on or before December 15.

At nearly two o'clock in the morning, they sat on the floor with hot chocolate and Winnie's doughnuts, and he gave Dooley his presents from Miss Sadie, Puny, Emma, and one from himself: a wool scarf from The Collar Button.

Miss Sadie had sent two pocket handkerchiefs, a pair of shoe laces, and a five-dollar bill wrapped in aluminum foil and tied with a red ribbon. Puny had given him a yellow windbreaker, and there were two dozen Reese's Cups from Emma.

Dooley sat mournfully in the midst of his gifts. "I wanted 'at ol' bicycle."

"The way your earnings are piling up, you'll have it before long. Now, I'd like to open your present to me."

"Wait 'til mornin'. You ain't goin' t' like it, anyway."

"I'd appreciate making that decision myself."

"Wait 'til morning. I'm give out," Dooley said, irritably.

It was two-thirty when the pair trudged upstairs, well behind Barnabas, who was already sprawled at the foot of the bed and snoring.

On the landing, he put his hand on Dooley's shoulder. "I'll be awake before daylight, preparing for two services, and you may definitely expect to hear some creeping on the stairs. But if I catch you coming after me with a shoe . . ."

"I'll be dead meat."

"Precisely!"

At six-thirty, he and Barnabas woke Dooley.

"I don't want t' git up!" he wailed. "You done wore me out goin' t' church. I ain't never been t' s' much church in my life. I didn't know they was that much church in th' whole dern world."

"My friend, you will be pleased to know that Santa Claus visited this humble rectory last night and left something in the study for one Dooley Barlowe."

"They ain't no Santy. I don't believe 'at old poop."

"Well, then, lie there and believe what you like. I'm going downstairs and have my famous Christmas morning casserole."

Barnabas leaped on Dooley's bed and began licking his ear.

" 'is ol' dog is th' hatefulest thing I ever seen!" Dooley moaned, turning his face to the wall.

"Come, Barnabas. Leave him be."

Barnabas lay resolutely on Dooley's bed and stared at his master.

Barnabas, at least, was determined to execute Puny's good idea.

❧

He set two places at the counter and took the bubbling sausage casserole from the oven. There would be no diet this day. Then, he turned on the record player and heard the familiar, if scratchy, strains of the *Messiah*.

Dooley appeared at the kitchen door, dressed in the burgundy robe. "Sounds like a' army's moved in down here."

"My friend, you have hit the nail on the head. It is an army of the most glorious voices in recent history, singing one of the most majestic musical works ever written!"

Dooley rolled his eyes.

"I believe you've been asked to sit with Jena Ivey and your Sunday school friends this morning, is that correct?"

"Yeah."

"Yes, sir."

No response.

Directly after Christmas, he would deal with this pigheaded behavior to the fullest.

"I ain't feelin' too good."

"Is that right? What's the trouble?"

"I puked up somethin' green."

"Really?"

"It had a lot of brown in it, too."

"The walk to church will revive you. You've been going pretty strong, keeping to a rector's schedule. Why don't you look in the study and find out what Barnabas is up to?"

He followed the boy into the study, to see what he'd been imagining for weeks:

The look of joyful astonishment on Dooley Barlowe's face.

ॐ

Dooley really hadn't seemed well, he concluded, as he walked home from church. He'd promised to stay right there on the study sofa, looking at his new bicycle and drinking 7-Up.

Though he'd received three invitations to Christmas dinner with parishioners, he wanted nothing more than to go home and crash. Later, if Dooley felt up to it, they'd take the new bike to the school yard and over to the Presbyterian parking lot.

There was only one problem with that plan.

Dooley could not be found in the study, nor anywhere else in the house. And neither could the new red bicycle.

The down jacket was missing from the peg, and the gloves weren't in the bin. And while he easily located the handkerchiefs and shoe strings from Miss Sadie, the windbreaker, the five-dollar bill, and the Reese's Cups had vanished.

Nurse Herman said she hadn't seen Dooley, and no, she wouldn't mention this call to Russell.

He drove the motor scooter through the school playground and then to the Presbyterian parking lot.

He rode up and down Main Street twice, circled the war monument and checked the lot behind the post office. There was hardly a soul to be seen on the streets, though Christmas lights in the shop windows winked cheerfully. He slowed at the corner of Old Church Lane, then turned left at his office and headed up the hill to Fernbank. Perhaps the boy had taken the bike to show Miss Sadie, he thought, but there was no sign of a visitor at the silent white mansion, nor even Miss Sadie's car.

Coasting down the hill in the increasingly chill wind, he came to a single, desperate conclusion: Dooley Barlowe had run away.

❧

Rodney Underwood answered the phone over the uproarious giggles of his three small daughters. "Aw, he's just gone out for a little spin," said the police chief. "Maybe he went out to Farmer on all them dirt roads."

The rector was convinced that Dooley Barlowe would not take his new red bike on a dirt road. The boy was gone. He could feel it in his bones, and he knew he could trust the feeling.

Rodney said he'd personally file a missing persons report and send an officer out in a cruise car. "Don't you worry, Father. You can't lose a red-headed boy on a red bicycle. We'll find 'im."

After he talked to Rodney, he went to the hospital, where Russell Jacks was sitting up and, with some effort, eating a bowl of soup.

"Dooley wanted to come, Russell, but early this morning, he . . . ah, threw up."

"Puked, did he?" the old man asked, with evident pride.

The heat in the small room was stifling. Father Tim removed his jacket and sat down by the bed. "You know, Russell, I've been wondering about his mother. Has she had any help?"

"Gits food stamps an' all, and I've tried to help."

"I understand. But help with her drinking . . ."

"Went off to Broughton one time t' dry out. Come back, started up again." His hand shook, so that soup spilled down the front of his hospital gown. Father Tim felt miserably guilty about asking such questions on a day when the sick needed special cheering.

"What is your daughter's name, by the way, and where does she live?"

" 'er name's Pauline, married a fella Barlowe worked on the new highways they put through here. Give 'er five little young 'uns in a row, got them highways built, then jumped on one and went. Didn't come back."

He had never ceased to be astonished by the weight of sorrow in the world. "A vale of tears," the poet had called it, and rightly so.

"And she's still down in Holding?"

"I hope t' God she is."

"Has a warm place to live, I expect."

"Ol' trailer over behind Shoney's. She worked there awhile 'til they run 'er off for drinkin on th' job."

There. That was enough to go on. He'd call Rodney from the phone in the waiting room.

"Russell," said the rector, brightening his tone and changing the subject, "if you could have just one Christmas wish, what might it be?"

Russell pushed the soup bowl away and wiped his

mouth with a trembling hand. He lay back on the pillow and closed his eyes, so that Father Tim thought for a moment he hadn't heard the question.

Then he said, "I wish Ida was still livin'; she'd be a blessin' to th' boy . . . an' I wish th' rhododendrons would set their buds real good so we git a nice show of bloom, come spring."

❧

He liked it to be where he could reach for it and find it immediately. Yet he could not find his small, worn, leather-bound Bible with his name stamped on the cover.

He turned on the lights above the pulpit and, once again, searched the empty shelf.

He walked angrily back to the office. That Bible contained marginal notes and special references that were irreplaceable. Who would have been so thoughtless to move it, and where did they move it, and why?

"Missin' Bibles, missin' cakes, missin' boys," Emma said, as if she were filing a report.

"Has Rodney called?"

"Not since he talked to you at ten o'clock."

On Christmas afternoon, Rodney had notified the Holding police, giving them Pauline Barlowe's name and the location of the trailer. Holding had called back to say the trailer had been moved, and they were continuing to investigate.

We're going into the third day, he thought anxiously.

Emma fielded the phone calls. "No, we don't know a thing, yet. Thank you for calling, we appreciate it, we have no idea. Yes, we'll let you know."

He noticed she'd begun dabbing at her eyes with that wad of toilet tissue she always carried.

"Are you all right?" he asked.

That was when she finally said it:

"That poor little orphan, gettin' somethin' he wasn't responsible enough to own! I hate to say I told you so!"

He turned and blurted angrily, "Then for God's sake, don't say it!"

When he went home for lunch, Puny was back from her holiday with a sister. He told her about Dooley.

Her face went white. "I could've told you so," she said.

Ah, the everlasting smugness of people! He might have sighed, but thought of the thanks box which now contained eleven dollars' worth of his infernal sighing.

"Dadgummit," said Puny, as he left for the office, "I'm worried sick about that little poop-head!" She burst into tears and ran down the hall to the kitchen.

According to Puny, who later saw Emma at The Local, he had "picked at his lunch like a bird, and looked kind of gray-colored."

"Humph," snorted Emma, who was still nettled from her brush with the rector. "If you ask me, he's actin' exactly like he did before he got diabetes."

"Well he cain't be gittin' it again if he's already got it."

"So maybe he's gettin' somethin' else," Emma said, airily.

❧

"Nothing is more wearying," Agatha Christie had said, "than going over things you have written and trying to arrange them in proper sequence or turn them the other way round."

He couldn't agree more, he thought, as he struggled with his sermon. Directly after the meeting with the stranger in the nave, his sermons had seen a definite up-turn; he was nearly jubilant afterward. Then, suddenly, he felt that he was right back where he started.

"The trouble with you," Walter had said in a recent phone conversation, "is that you're too prepared. You don't give the Holy Spirit room to do wondrous things. You need to take risks now and then—that's what makes life snap, crackle, and pop."

Snap, crackle, and pop? Not only did people love saying they told you so, they were infernally full of advice.

He looked at the calendar clock on his desk. If the boy didn't turn up in the next few hours, he and Miss Sadie had agreed to drive to Holding, where they'd go over the town with a fine-tooth comb.

"I've got new tennis shoes," she told him. "I'll go up one side of the street and you go up the other!"

"Listen to this," the rector said to Barnabas, who was sprawled at his feet. As he read the first draft of his ser-mon, Barnabas listened with sincere interest.

Actually, he found his dog more attentive than many of his congregation. On the other hand, none of the con-gregation ever openly engaged in vigorous scratching. So it was a wash.

He got up and walked to the tall spruce with its twin-kling lights, and looked at the array of gifts still lying beneath it. He had lost the heart to finish opening them, somehow, though he'd torn right into his cousin's gift and discovered that it was, indeed, an electric train. As soon as Dooley comes back, he thought, we'll set it up. Surely, Dooley would be coming back.

Suddenly, he remembered the present Dooley had made for him and found it lying near Winnie's bulky gift.

He opened it eagerly.

A glasses case, made at school. Two pieces of leather, glued together on three sides, and monogrammed with the aid of a stencil. *FT* was printed on one side, *DB* on the other. "I put my initials on it," Dooley had scrawled on a piece of notebook paper, "so you won't firgit me."

Forget Dooley Barlowe? Never!

Many boys who'd been raised like Dooley, he reasoned, would be good for nothing. Dooley, he was convinced, was extraordinarily good for something. It only remained to be seen what it was.

He wished he had someone in the house to talk to about this disturbing turn of events. Like Walter, with whom he'd shared nearly every confidence since he was a boy.

He put the glasses case in his shirt pocket, and walked back to his desk. "Talk to Hoppy. Tell Rodney. Thank Cynthia" were scrawled across the top of his desk calendar.

He decided to work his list backward.

§

Cynthia, he thought, did not have much trouble making herself at home. When he'd called to thank her for the mole watercolor, she'd suggested tea, and he said he had just put the kettle on. In barely two minutes, she had "popped through the hedge," as she liked to say, and curled up on his study sofa, helping herself to a piece of shortbread. He was intrigued to see that another of her pink curlers, obviously overlooked, adorned the back of her head.

"I'm so sorry," she said, when told about Dooley. "I always thought runaway boys came straight home when they got hungry."

"Yes, well, that is complicated by the fact that this is not his home."

"Has anyone seen him?"

"Rodney says he was seen by three different people on his way down the mountain. They remembered the red bicycle."

"Did they say anything else?"

"They said he was . . . ah, flying."

"Flying! Oh, dear."

There was a thoughtful silence.

"I've never raised a boy," said Cynthia.

"That makes two of us."

"But I do try to understand their feelings. I always pretend I'm a child when I write Violet books, and then I write exactly what I want to hear."

Is that the way he should write his sermons? Saying exactly what he would like to hear?

"A publisher who looked at the first manuscript said, 'Oh, we can't print this, it's far too silly.' But the next publisher understood, and there have been eight since then. All silly!"

"And all successful, I believe."

"Well, yes, and then the Davant Medal was announced, and we went into second and third printings of everything. But my point was, let's try and put ourselves in his shoes, even if it seems silly. It might work! Let's see . . . if I were a boy with a new bicycle, where would I go?" She stared intently at the fire, wrinkling her forehead.

"We think he's gone to his mother, but we can't trace her."

"Where does she live?"

"She had a trailer down in Holding, but it's been moved."

"We could go and ask around the neighborhood where she lived. Somebody would know something."

"The police are doing that. They haven't turned up anything."

"I hate this," she said.

"I hate it more."

How, he wondered, could he be sitting here by a warm fire, when a fatherless boy was out there somewhere, almost certainly cold and hungry?

There was a knock at the back door. His heart pounded as Barnabas leaped from his place in front of the fire and skidded into the kitchen. Rodney! Surely it would be Rodney with some news.

When he opened the door, Dooley Barlowe looked him straight in the eye. "My mama tol' me to come back."

"Come in," the rector said, hoarsely.

There was an ugly welt on the boy's face. Barnabas licked it while Dooley silently removed his gloves, the down jacket, and the yellow windbreaker. He dropped the gloves in the bin and hung the jackets on the peg.

"Come and say hello to Miss Coppersmith."

Dooley met Cynthia's gaze without wavering. "Hey," he said.

"Hey, yourself."

His face was red from pedaling in a chill wind, and he trembled slightly from the cold.

"It might be good if I made some hot chocolate to warm you up," said the rector.

But Dooley was headed toward the stairs, Barnabas hard on his heels. "I cain't stand here talkin'," he said over his shoulder, "I got t' take a dump."

The rector looked at his neighbor, coloring furiously.

"Don't look at me," she said. "I never raised a boy!"

❧

Before he called Rodney about the jewels, he called Walter.

"You're in possession of stolen goods," said Walter.

"Good Lord!"

"I doubt if Rodney will press any charges, but you ought to know where you stand by failing to report what you found."

"I knew I should have reported it. It's just that the choir was rehearsing three different performances, and I was busy with Lessons and Carols, and Rodney would have conducted a lengthy investigation, and . . ."

"Believe me, I understand. But it was still a damn-fool thing to do," Walter said.

He sat for a moment after talking with Walter, with his head in his hands. Then he called Rodney.

"I've got something I want to show you. How about this morning, at Lord's Chapel?"

"Let me stop by the Grill and get a coffee to go, and I'll be right over."

He felt sick. In possession of stolen goods! A fine thing for a man of the cloth, for heaven's sake. If there were any punishment, it was the nauseating humiliation he felt, which was surely punishment enough.

"You look like somethin' the cat drug in," said Emma, coming through the door.

"That's a fine greeting."

She sighed. "Dooley Barlowe is doin' you about as much good as a case of diabetes, if you ask me."

"He came back last night."

"What a relief! I wish you'd called me!"

"I did. No answer."

"Oh, yes, well . . . I was at Harold's mama's and we worked on my suit."

"Your suit?"

"That I'm gettin' married in. Red. Black buttons. Peplum. High neck."

"I see."

"Black patent shoes. Black hose. Pearl earrings. Where was he?"

"His mother's, like we thought. She sent him back, told him she couldn't care for him."

"Breaks my heart," said Emma.

That's encouraging, he thought.

"But mostly, it makes me mad."

Aha! Here it comes.

"You get house help, change your diet, get you a nice dog for company, start feelin' better, and what happens?"

He was so astounded to hear Emma refer to Barnabas as a nice dog that he was speechless.

"What happens is, you get a boy who runs you down, wears you out, and worries you half to death, and you're right back where you started. I declare, I've seen diabetes make you look better than you look this mornin'." She caught her breath and plunged ahead. "Do you know how old you are?"

Remind me! he thought, enduring her assault.

"Not twenty-five! Not thirty-two! Sixty! You're too old to be takin' on a boy, plus do your preachin', and go to the hospital, and visit the elderly, and go to meetin's, and read in that program with Olivia Davenport, not to mention the bells comin' in, and the nursin' home startin' up, and that old mangy dog to wash . . ."

Now his nice dog was old and mangy.

As she continued her oratorical massacre, he came to a sober realization. He would certainly never tell her so, but he had to admit one thing:

She was right.

❧

"Dark in here," said Rodney. "But it smells good."

"It's the old wood, and years of incense and beeswax and flowers and lemon oil and dried hydrangeas. It's a wonderful smell!" he agreed as he switched on the lights. "Come down this way. What I want to show you is where we keep the ashes of the departed."

They walked down the hall and stopped at the closet, where he removed the key from above the door.

Rodney adjusted his holster. "Is somethin' goin' to jump out of there?"

"I fervently hope not."

He opened the door and turned on the light, relieved to find that everything was as orderly as he'd left it. No one had tossed in any plastic flowers or worn hymnals.

"Now," he said, carefully picking up the bronze urn which was sitting third from the left, "this is Parrish Guthrie. Remember him?"

"Ha! How could I forget th' old so-and-so? I wasn't th' only one that got a deep breath when he went to his grave . . . or whatever that thing is."

"This is an urn. After the body is cremated, the ashes—which are mostly bits of bone—are interred here."

"Bits of bone!" Rodney said, shuddering. "I like th' old-fashioned way—pushin' up daisies."

"Lets take this urn and walk on back to the kitchen." His heart was pounding. Oh, how he hated to tell the bitter truth about his wrong behavior.

He stood at the sink and unscrewed the cap of the bronze urn, which came off more readily than before. "I'm going to show you something very . . . what is the word? Something that grieves me." With his other hand, he took the white tea towel from the rack and spread it on the drain board. Then he gently shook the urn, so that the contents would spill out.

Nothing tumbled to the mouth of the urn.

He shook it again, and turned the urn nearly upside down. There was no rattle, as of seashells in a jar, and nothing came rolling onto the towel. He realized there was a good explanation for this:

The bronze urn was empty.

He felt strangely light-headed and confused. "I don't understand," he began.

"What's the deal?"

The rector shook the urn. "I don't know. I'm . . ."

"Somethin' was supposed to be in that jar. Right?"

"Jewels," he said weakly. "Jewels that I found in this very urn sometime before Christmas."

"I don't get it."

"Let's sit down."

Rodney sat on the stool by the wall phone. Father Tim sat on the old pine table in the center of the room.

"Before Christmas," he confessed, "I was cleaning up that closet, throwing things out. I picked up Parrish's urn and it rattled strangely. I remembered I'd never seen the contents of an urn, so, out of curiosity, I brought it back here to the kitchen, and opened it. There were little cloth sacks full of jewels in there, cut jewels."

"Maybe it was another jar you brought back here."

"No. It was definitely Parrish."

Rodney rested his hand on the butt of his pistol. "So, why didn't you report it?"

There! There was the question he was dreading.

As he explained why, Rodney took off his hat and scratched his head.

"I don't know," said the chief, "I never run up against anything like this. When you found 'em th' first time and didn't report it, you were in possession of stolen goods, I know that."

"So I'm told by my cousin, who's an attorney."

"But now that there's nothin' here, well, there's nothin' I can see to charge you with. Maybe we ought to look in th' other jars."

The rector shrugged. He didn't think it would do any good.

❧

"This is creepy," said Rodney, peering into the urns and stirring their contents with a bread knife from the silverware drawer. "I wish to th' Lord I'd brought me a chew of Red Man."

When they finished an hour later, they'd found nothing amiss. "I'm just goin' to write up a report, and then you sign it, and I'll file it."

"Where? Where will you file it?"

"In my right-hand drawer over at th' station."

"Aha! I thought you might file a report with J.C. Hogan."

"Not, by dern, if I can help it," said Rodney.

He felt faint with relief.

❧

He had thanked his neighbor for her imaginative gift.

He had confessed his unfortunate discovery and equally unfortunate behavior to Rodney.

And now there was only one thing left to do on his list, and that was to talk with Hoppy Harper.

He felt like calling the airline immediately and flying nonstop to Shannon, then renting a car and driving to Sligo. There, he'd spend at least four weeks in a remote inn, riding a bicycle along narrow lanes, and tapping his foot to fiddle music played in thatched cottages.

Instead of calling the airline, he called Hoppy.

"Harper."

"Your good rector here," he said, not feeling very good at all. "How's Russell?"

"It's amazing the way the infection is reversing. Not typical in cases like this. How're you? Are you running?"

"Slacked off."

"I've got three words to say to you, pal: Just do it."

"OK. You're right, and I will. Let me ask you something. I need to talk with you about . . . an important matter. Your place or mine?"

"Mine, if it's OK with you. Everybody from here to Wesley and back has upper respiratory infections. I can't leave."

"Say when."

"Around six."

"I'll be there."

He put the phone down. It was the first time he'd had a moment to catch his breath, and the jewels came instantly to mind.

Why were they gone from the urn? Why would they have been moved? Did someone know he'd found them? He felt an odd chill, and he did not like the feeling.

✺

"Viral myocarditis!" Hoppy looked as if he'd been struck. "Good God," he said quietly, and sat back in his chair.

Father Tim looked at the notes he'd taken while Olivia told her story. The condition was complex, and he'd tried to assemble the facts accurately.

The doctor leaned forward. "Tell me everything she said."

"It began with what she thought was flu, about two years ago."

"No energy," said Hoppy. "Shortness of breath, chest discomfort."

"That's right. She said she felt like she was falling apart. She went to the doctor, took antibiotics, accelerated her vitamins, got plenty of rest, but nothing worked. They gave her a battery of blood tests and didn't find anything."

"Typical."

"Finally, they did an EKG and saw some abnormalities. Then an echocardiogram, which showed an enlarged heart."

"Then the biopsy," said Hoppy.

"Right. Viral myocarditis."

The doctor looked ashen.

"The symptoms waxed and waned. She would have perfectly normal times, just like she's had since coming to Mitford, then severe flare-ups when she could hardly breathe, and scarcely walk for the edema in her legs."

"The flare-ups are totally unpredictable. Who's her doctor?"

"A man from your old alma mater, Mass General."

"Leo Baldwin, I hope."

He checked his notes. "Exactly! Leo Baldwin."

"The best. I know him. Stunning credentials. What happened when she had the tissue biopsy?"

"Cocksackie B, she said. They tried medication, but the side effects were gruesome. Affected her blood count."

"You've seen termites in action?" Hoppy asked.

"Yes. Right under my back steps, more's the pity."

"Cocksackie eats away like that, at the heart muscle. Vile, insidious, incurable. Why hasn't she had a transplant?"

"You understand the chances of finding a donor with a normal blood type."

"Seventy-five, a hundred to one."

"Add to that the chance of finding a donor with B blood type."

"Thousands to one."

"And then the chances of getting the heart to the patient with the right kind of timing."

Hoppy removed his glasses and rubbed his eyes. "Crap," he said softly.

✄

He called Walter.

"Not there? You mean just . . . vanished?"

"The urn was empty."

"Look, Timothy, you've been pressing hard. You haven't had a vacation in years and—"

"No, I am not seeing things, and it was not my imagination. The jewels were there before Christmas. I only opened one little sack, there must have been fifteen or twenty stones in it, and I could see there were others, other little cheesecloth sacks just like it." He sighed. "There is, however, one comfort in all this."

"Which is . . . ?"

"I'm no longer in possession of stolen goods."

CHAPTER THIRTEEN

Issues of the Heart

"He's hardly speaking to me," said Olivia.

Percy came over to their booth, wiping his hands on the worn apron. "I don't b'lieve I've had th' pleasure," he said to Olivia.

"Meet Olivia Davenport," said Father Tim. "Olivia Davenport, Percy Mosely, the owner of this venerable establishment. When we were in for breakfast, he was out with the flu."

She smiled and extended her hand. "I hear your calf's liver with onions is four-star."

"She didn't hear it from me," said the rector.

"Well, th' Father here don't like it, n'r Miss Rose, but th' rest of us ain't so hard to satisfy."

"I look forward to deciding for myself."

"For you," said Percy, obviously enchanted, "we can have it back on th' specials by Tuesday."

"Well, then, look for me at noon on Tuesday!"

Percy went away in such ecstasy that the rector feared for his angina condition.

"Barely speaking?" asked her rector.

"I know what it is, of course. He's afraid."

"Yes, of course. And he's ashamed."

"What do you mean?"

"I mean that he wants very much to be brave, to let his feelings for you grow. But, as well as fearing the pain, I believe he's ashamed of the fear."

Olivia's brow furrowed as she considered that. "Yes. Yes, I understand that."

"Also, I feel that Hoppy is . . ."

"Is what?" she asked eagerly.

"Is thinking."

"Thinking?"

"He knows your doctor."

"No! Leo? He knows Leo?" She was obviously thrilled with this news.

"Hoppy interned at Mass General."

Olivia laughed with unbridled warmth. The sparkle danced again in her eyes. "Mass General is like home! I've spent so much of my life there, why, just talking about it makes me suddenly . . . almost homesick. And Hoppy . . . he interned there, and knows Leo." She said this softly, as if it gave her great comfort.

"I believe Hoppy may be thinking of how you could . . . that is, what he might do if . . ."

"A transplant? No. It's too much. I've given up. The chances, the risks . . . nothing is in my favor. Father, I promise you—I can't do it."

"Well, Olivia, all I can say to that is: Philippians four-thirteen."

She laughed easily. "I love it when you talk like that!"

❧

Emma handed him the phone, looking tentative. "Harold's preacher," she said.

"My good brother," said the voice on the line, "this is Absalom Greer—orchard keeper, general-store operator, pastor of three little churches, and all-around worker in the vineyards of the Lord."

"Pastor Greer!" said the rector, instantly attracted to the tone of his caller's voice. "What can I do for you this morning?"

"Well, my friend, since we're to perform a ceremony together, I'd be beholden to you if we could have a mite of fellowship!"

"Consider it done," he said with warm anticipation. "Consider it done!"

❧

"I declare," he told Puny on Wednesday, "if Dooley and I don't get out to Meadowgate soon, Rebecca Jane will be in college."

"When's the baptizin'?"

"Two weeks hence. The weather has been so variable, with rain or snow nearly every Sunday, that I've never laid eyes on her."

"I'd like to hold a baby," Puny said wistfully.

"Well, then, young lady, go find yourself a husband."

"Ha! There's not a soul out there I'd pick."

"How can you know that when you've limited the picking to Mitford and Wesley?" That was a good question, he thought.

"Mama said you don't go huntin', you let 'em kind of go by you in a parade."

"Yes, well, that may be. But have you seen any parades going by lately?"

She sighed. "What d' you want for supper?"

"You're asking me?"

"Well, for a change I thought I'd ask, instead of leavin' a surprise."

"Puny, please do not try to fix a thing that ain't broke."

She stared at him. "What kind of talk is that?"

"I mean that I fervently beseech you to keep doing exactly what you're doing. Your surprises are my unending delight."

She smiled gratefully, but a little weakly, he thought, as she paired his clean socks.

"Puny," he said, "I faithfully pray for you each day. But I believe I'm going to add something to that prayer. I'm going ask the Lord to start the parade!"

Puny blushed, and lowered her eyes. He was astounded to see a tear creep down her freckled cheek.

Without knowing why, it touched him so deeply that he turned away. He heard her blow her nose.

"Cornbread!" she suddenly said, with great feeling.

"Cornbread?"

She flew to the stove drawer. "I'm goin' to make you a cake of cornbread, I don't care what your doctor says! And I'm puttin' salt in it, and bacon drippin's, and fryin' it in Crisco, 'cause I'm tired of holdin' back on my good cornbread."

"Well, then!" he said, with admiration. "Just do it!"

❧

The weather on Thursday morning was grim. He'd been aware of rain all night long, and sometime around four o'clock, Dooley crept into his bedroom. On hearing a noise, he and Barnabas sat straight up, seeing only a silhouette in the doorway. Barnabas growled darkly.

"Oh, shut up!" said Dooley, "I ain't no burglar. I come t' say I'm freezin' m' tailbone in there."

He got up and turned the thermostat to sixty, and Dooley stomped back to bed. The floor was like ice, and the rain beat against the windows in sheets.

At five, just before he was to get up for morning prayer and study, the wind began. It lashed the trees outside his bedroom window, groaned around the rectory, and made him recall the ominous forecast that ice would coat the streets like glass by midmorning. He remembered, too, that this was the day Louella was to arrive in Mitford and begin life again at Fernbank.

He went to the window and looked down at the little house next door. A lamp burned in an upstairs window, a pool of warm light in the dark and pouring rain.

"Well, then, Lord," he said aloud as he stood there. "Is this another memo from you about taking my car to Lew Boyd, so I can start driving again? How will the boy get to school in all this? And how can I make it to the hospital in this downpour?"

He heard a sound behind him.

"Is that you talkin' in here?"

"It is."

"Well, it sounds creepy with this ol' storm a blowin' and you settin' in here in th' dark, yammerin' to yourself."

"Yammerin', is it?"

"It jis' kind of sounds like yammer, yammer, yammer, yammer."

He looked down at the boy's anxious face, and put his arm around his shoulders.

"Dooley?"

Dooley hesitated. Then he said it. "Yes, sir?"

"What if we do something different today?"

"What's 'at?"

"What if we stay home and play with that train my cousin sent?"

Dooley hollered so loud that Barnabas leaped off the bed and ran into the hallway, barking at his shadow on the wall.

" 'at's a great idea! Boy, 'at's a great idea!"

"Would you be willing to admit, then, that preachers can occasionally have a great idea?"

"Yeah! Yes, sir! Boys howdy!"

"And while we're at it, why don't we have some of our favorite things, like hot chocolate with three marsh-mallows, and chili, and—"

"Popcorn, an' apple pie with ice cream—"

"And a bit of Wordsworth . . ."

"Yuck!"

"And stay in our robes and pajamas."

"Cool!"

"At eight-thirty, I am going to call your school and say, 'Dooley Barlowe is not sick today, but if he came out in this weather, he would surely get sick, so look for him tomorrow.' "

Without a word, Dooley took the rector's hand and shook it vigorously.

❧

Early the following morning, the leaden skies cleared, the sun came out, and the village stirred briskly. After his hospital visit, he made a phone call to Lew Boyd, who agreed to do whatever it took to get his car running.

Then, he drove to Wesley on his motor scooter, took

the drivers' license test, and, by grace alone, he later said, passed it.

Lew Boyd was looking out the window when he saw the rector walking past the war monument, toward the station. "Here 'e comes, boys," he said, cutting himself a plug of tobacco.

"Been twenty year since he's drove a car," announced Coot Hendrick.

"No, it hain't," said Bailey Coffey. "Hit's been fourteen, maybe fifteen."

"Ain't none of you got it right," said Lew. "Th' last time he drove that Buick was eight years ago. I looked up where I drained th' fluids."

"Time flies," said Coot, dumping a pack of peanuts in his bottled Coke.

"Boys," said Father Tim, coming in the front door, "she looks good."

Lew went down his list. "We washed 'er, waxed 'er, put on y'r radials, put in y'r fluids, give you a batt'ry, vacuumed 'er out, spot cleaned y'r front seat, warshed y'r mats, filled 'er up, run 'er around th' block, honked th' horn, and tried out th' radio."

"I heard my fav'rite song," said Coot, " 'If You Don't Stand F'r Somethin', You'll Fall F'r Anything.' "

"We just all piled in and rode around, if you want to know th' truth," Bailey Coffey confessed.

"Here's th' bill," said Lew, "and I don't mind tellin' you it's a whopper."

Coot patted the dinette chair next to his. "You better set down, is all I can say."

"Four hundred eighty-six dollars and seventy-eight cents?" the rector asked.

"That includes y'r Peaches an' Cream deod'rant spray."

"A bargain!" he declared, and shook Lew's hand with enthusiasm.

They followed him to the car. "Boys," said Lew, as the rector started the ignition, "since he ain't drove in a good while, I'd step back if I was you."

They stood watching as the car cruised around the monument and disappeared down Main Street, where several people turned and stared in complete disbelief at the sight of the local priest driving a car, apparently absorbed in his own thoughts, but actually listening intently to the country-and-western station on his radio, which was playing a number called "I Bought the Shoes That Just Walked Out on Me."

❧

During the service the following Sunday, he asked the congregation if anyone had seen his Bible, which he described in minute detail.

Black. Embossed with his name in gold. Leather. Worn. Small. Red-letter edition. Marked in the margins.

Not a soul raised a hand, stood up, confessed, or otherwise gave any indication of its whereabouts.

He didn't know why such a thought occurred to him, but he felt he should search the church. The basement, the attic, that sort of thing. Too many things were missing; something felt oddly out of place, like a picture hanging crooked on the wall.

It was after dark when he walked to Lord's Chapel, noticing the sign on the front door of the Oxford as he passed. "Away," it read, which was Andrew's unique language for "Closed." He'd heard that Andrew had left last week on his biannual trip to England to buy antiques and meet with a society that collected Churchill memorabilia. The gray Mercedes would not be parked at the curb for a while, which gave him a puzzling sense of relief.

Arriving at the church, he turned on all the lights and went first to the basement. He searched the sprawling, unfinished room thoroughly, even looking into the surplus food cabinets where they stored canned goods for church suppers. On the few occasions he'd looked in this cabinet, he'd seen it full, as Esther Bolick was the major-domo of all kitchen activities and a real cracker-jack at keeping supplies on hand.

This time, it was nearly empty; they were even low on toilet paper. "Have you ever tried to go to the johnny over at the Baptists'?" Esther once said. "They never have any toilet paper. You have to use the Kleenex in your pocketbook, if you're lucky enough to have any!" It had been a particular ambition of Esther's never to run out of this commodity at Lord's Chapel.

On entering the parish hall, he was surprised to smell the unmistakable odor of chicken noodle soup. He would know that smell anywhere, having lived off that particular soup during his early years in the priesthood.

There was no indication that anyone had been in the church. No meetings were scheduled. Altar Guild never worked on Sunday, having a tradition of cleaning up on Monday. And Russell lay sick in the hospital.

He felt a sudden foreboding. Something was wrong, very wrong. He could sense it, and he didn't like it.

At the left of the altar, he reached up and pulled the chain that brought down the attic stairs.

Why in heaven's name anyone would have put attic stairs near the altar was beyond him. However, the chain did make a fine place to attach a flower basket during spring and summer services.

Chicken noodle soup! As he turned on the attic lights and climbed the creaking steps, he smelled it more distinctly than before.

In his twelve years at Lord's Chapel, he had been in the attic only once, and found it as large as the loft of a New England barn. According to Miss Sadie, they had built the church with room for growth of the Sunday school. As his eyes came level with the floor of the loft, he saw nothing but a vast, empty space filled with shadows.

It was strangely restful to stand in this place, without the fret and clutter of "things."

He noticed something lying near the window in the corner. But when he walked over to it, he saw that it was only a candy wrapper. Almond Joy. One of his favorites.

He picked it up. He could smell the tiniest scent of chocolate on the wrapper.

He put the wrapper in his pants pocket and walked to the door that opened into the nearly empty belfry. Three of the enormous bells were gone from their oak mountings. The fourth, the great and solemn "death bell," as it was called, stood silent in the corner of the Norman tower.

What was he looking for, anyway? he asked himself. Perhaps he hoped the jewels would turn up again somewhere on the premises, and Rodney Underwood would take them away, and the whole incident would be off his mind and out of his hands. After all, wasn't it possible that whoever put them in the urn might have moved them to another hiding place in the church?

If nothing else, he was able to see the pristine condition of the old building, even in the poor light from naked bulbs.

He closed the door to the belfry, and walked to the stairs.

Very likely, he thought, the theft of Esther Bolick's marmalade cake had been an inside job, a practical joke by one of the many fervent admirers of that famous cake. And his Bible would turn up in some unexpected place that, after all, would make perfect sense.

The jewels, however, were another matter. He had hoped to come up from the basement or down from the attic feeling some sort of peace. But the matter of the jewels would give him no peace at all.

❧

When he went home from the office on Monday, Puny was standing at the door, waiting. He could see the fire in her eyes before he opened the screen.

"This is a pleasant surprise," he said, seeing that it wasn't going to be pleasant at all. "You're usually gone when I get home."

"Are you still prayin' that parade prayer?" she demanded, as he came in with a quart of milk and a loaf of bread.

"Parade prayer?"

"You know, th' one that asks th' Lord to let th' parade begin'?"

"Aha! Well, yes. Yes, I am."

She glowered at him. "If you don't mind, I'd appreciate it if you'd tell th' Lord to stop th' parade!"

"Well, now," he said, putting the grocery bag down and sitting on his counter stool. "What's going on?"

"Th' very day we talked, I went to th' Local to get those nectarines Avis was ravin' about, and I'm standin' there by the produce, and this ol' coot walks up t' me an' goes, 'Well, little lady, where you bin at all my life?'

"He had his jaw stuck s' full of tobacco, it would've gagged a billy goat. He follered me around 'til I had to nearly smack 'im to get 'im to leave me alone.

"Th' very next day," Puny continued, quite red in the face, "I was mindin' my own business at th' mall, tryin' to buy you some wash rags, and this big galoot slithers up t' me like a snake and says, 'Want t' go git some chicken fingers at th' arcade?'

"Chicken fingers! I showed 'im chicken fingers!"

"Puny," he said, "when you go to a parade, do you like every float that passes?"

"I like some better'n others," she said grudgingly.

"Well, then."

"I don't know. I think you should pray some other prayer. This'n scares me t' death."

"You wait," he said, mildly. "This is only the start-up. We haven't got to the drum and bugle corps yet, much less to the marching bands!"

"Whatever that's supposed to mean," she said, thoroughly disgusted.

♨

That evening before dinner, he built a fire. Dooley made popcorn, and Barnabas did his business at the hedge with great expediency. He was as glad as a child for the comfort of home, and rest, and peace.

For what he estimated to be the fourth or fifth time, he picked up the *Mitford Muse,* which by now was four days old, and tried to read Esther Cunningham's editorial on the July Festival of Roses. J.C. had done it again. "Festival of Ropes Will Transform Main Street," said the headline.

Dooley answered the ringing phone in the kitchen. "Rec'try. Yep, he's here, but he don't want t' talk t' nobody."

Dooley put his hand over the receiver and yelled, "It's y'r doctor!"

"Hang up," he said, and lifted the cordless by the sofa. "Got anything for exhaustion, sleeplessness, and general aggravation?" he asked.

"I was calling to ask you the same thing."

"The blind leading the blind. How are you, my friend?"

"This place is eating me alive. I've got to get out of here for a while, and the kitchen said they'd make me a plate. I wondered if I could bring it to your place. Dining out, it's called."

"Of course!" he said, trying to conceal the weariness in his voice.

"I'll bring you a plate, too."

"I don't know," said the rector, with some caution. "What do you . . . ah, think it might be?"

"God only knows."

"I've had that a few times. Bring it on, then. I need more surprises in my life."

"Yuck," said Dooley, "don't give me any of that stuff. I eat somethin' off granpaw's plate th' other day at th' hospital, an' it like t' gagged me."

"Thanks for reminding me."

"I'll jis' have me some popcorn, peanut butter an' jelly, an' fried baloney."

"Yuck," said the rector.

❧

"When in heaven's name are you going to get some help?" he asked his doctor. They were sitting by the fire with trays on their laps.

"Soon."

"That's what you always say. And soon never

comes. Here you are, a Harvard medical school graduate who could practice anywhere in the country, and you've chosen our obscure little village and the work of three men."

"A man from Wesley will be spending a couple of afternoons with me, starting soon. Good doctor. Wilson. You'll like him. Young."

"A lamb to the slaughter."

Hoppy grinned. "So, what do you think of the cuisine?"

"Well, now . . . words fail me."

"Come on. We're talking Chicken Cordon Bleu here."

He laughed. "If that's what you're talking, my friend, we are clearly speaking two different languages."

Hoppy gulped down his food, a habit encouraged by overwork and understaffing, and leaned back in the wing chair. "I need you to check me on something," he said, looking into the fire.

"Proceed."

"I don't know where I'm going with this. Maybe nowhere." He was silent for some time, as the fire crackled. Barnabas got up from his master's feet and went and lay next to Hoppy's. This act of simple consolation was only one of the reasons Father Tim admired his dog's character.

"When Carol was dying, there was nothing I could do. All I could do was control the pain. It was . . . hopeless."

"Yes. It was. It was hopeless."

Hoppy turned from the fire. "Severe myocarditis isn't hopeless!" he said, with feeling.

"Keep going."

"Which means I'm not helpless!"

"I hear you."

Hoppy stood up and paced the floor. "I'm scared out of my mind. I hardly know this woman. We spent some time at the art show, I see her at church, we've had coffee in the staff room. And of course, I see what she's doing for my patients. She's the best medicine we've got up there."

Father Tim heard Dooley running his bath water upstairs.

"Track me here, and see if I'm making sense."

"I'm with you."

"Severe myocarditis is not hopeless for one reason only—transplants. But this option is complicated by her blood type. Who knows whether we could find a compatible donor in a hundred years? And when we found one, would she be in stable enough condition to receive the heart? Another thing, it can't be just anybody with her blood type, it will take someone who's about her same weight. It's scary business, but what I'm saying is this . . ."

He stood in front of the fire, his tall, lanky frame cast into shadow. "I hardly know this woman, but . . . I feel something for her that's so strong, so . . . compelling . . . that I want to help her. I want to stick my neck out and help her. I want her to have a heart that works. I want . . ."

"What do you want?"

"I want her to live," Hoppy said softly.

"I want that with you."

"Get behind me in prayer, will you?"

"I will."

"You'll think I'm crazy, but I've been running down all the scenarios. I've got a friend in Wesley who's a pilot. He's not always easy to find, but we're twenty minutes to his plane. And if I can't find Millard, there's a little charter service at the same strip, with a couple of Cessnas.

"Wherever they harvest the heart, it could be put on ice until we arrive. Or, it could be packed in ice and flown to Boston. I'm going to talk to Leo Baldwin at Mass General."

Father Tim felt strangely shaken and joyful.

"We can get her on a national waiting list, and if her blood type comes up, we'd have to move immediately. She'll have to wear a beeper, and . . . I'd like you to have one, too. When that thing goes off, pal, we're talking on your knees."

He felt the sobering impact of such a plan. It would mean they would all have to be accessible, every hour of every day.

"The call could come anytime, from anywhere," said Hoppy. "We may even be able to keep the donor alive, keep the heart pumping until we get her wherever we have to go."

"Would that be desirable?"

"The longer it's in the physiological state, the better."

"I see."

Hoppy rubbed his eyes and sat down again, wearily.

"What do I tell her?" he asked his concerned host. "That I'm willing to go out of my way, complicate my life, turn my practice upside down for God knows how long, just because I'm a nice guy? How do I keep . . . what would she think my reasons are for getting involved like this?"

Father Tim sat forward on the sofa. "I suggest you don't concern yourself with what she thinks. You're a doctor. Your business is saving lives."

"But according to you, she's turned off the transplant idea completely. Leo Baldwin has probably walked her through all these scenarios; she's considered them seriously, and dumped the option. Period. So, who's going to sell her?"

"Probably not me, probably not you."

"Who, then?"

"God," he said, simply.

"Tell me more."

"If we're going to be a team, my friend, we must think like a team. And to do that, we need to agree in prayer."

"Count me in."

"Neither you nor I may be able to convince her about this transplant, but if God thinks it's best for her, it's just a matter of time."

"Let's go for it," Hoppy said.

The two men bowed their heads, and Barnabas rested his on the doctor's foot.

❧

After his friend left, he sat for a while on the sofa. Then he went upstairs, said goodnight to Dooley, and took a hot shower. But an hour after getting into bed, the adrenaline was pumping so fast and furiously, that he lay sleepless until three o'clock. At four, he awoke exhausted, and lay staring at his moonlit window until dawn.

He wondered about his recent, creeping fatigue. His running had been sporadic, and he'd let a few taboo foods slip back into his diet. But his indiscretions had been minor in that regard, no more than a piece of cornbread, a sliver of chocolate.

Dear God, what a hideous feeling to go down for the

count, when he'd spent most of his life in glowing good health. He wondered, as he lay there, about the helplessness of the elderly, about people who couldn't move their limbs, or walk to the barbershop, or get up and go to the toilet.

He had devoted his life to intercessory prayer, asking little for himself, trusting in God's provisions, and seeing that trust confirmed on every side. But he lay, now, feeling that his very essence was somehow draining away, and prayed fervently for his own strength, for wisdom, and renewal.

❧

The baptism was truly a blessed event. When he held her in his arms and said, "Rebecca Jane, you are sealed by the Holy Spirit in baptism and marked as Christ's own forever," a great warmth flowed through him, and the infant stirred in his arms and looked into his eyes.

At the reception in the parish hall, they were standing in line to hold the amiable Rebecca Jane, whose green eyes, stand-up strawberry hair, and dimpled chin were melting hearts by the score.

Though Dooley didn't attempt to hold her, he stayed by the side of anyone who did, looking at her intently, and marveling.

"I like 'is baby," he told Father Tim. "I like 'is baby better'n' . . ."

"Better than snuff, I suppose?"

"Nope. Better'n Goosedown Owen!"

"That's quite a compliment."

"But 'er hair's funny. It looks kind of like a stump full of gran'daddy spiders."

"Every baby is special," the rector told Marge, who had finally reclaimed her daughter from the eager parishioners. "But there's something quite different about Rebecca Jane. I sense a spirit that's very rich with God's promise."

"I sense that, too," she said, kissing her baby's downy head.

🌰

It was inspiring to see Louella's broad, mahogany face smiling at him these days from the gospel side. Her presence brought something nourishing to the spirit of the congregation, like raisins added to bread.

She also made an addition with her fruity, mezzo voice, which she lifted with surprising strength in the Anglican hymns, learned as a girl in this very church.

"She makes me feel young," said Miss Sadie, when Father Tim visited Fernbank for lunch. "When I'm around Louella, it's like being close to Mama, all over again!"

"Did you know Miss Sadie rock' me in her arms when I was a baby?" Louella said, proudly. "So, when I'm aroun' Miss Sadie, I feel young myself!"

"We don't know who raised who!" said the mistress of Fernbank.

A very nice kettle of fish, thought the pleased rector.

🌰

On Thursday evening, it occurred to him that he had never invited his neighbor to attend a service at Lord's Chapel. What kind of hospitality was that, he asked himself, as he dialed her number.

"I don't mind telling you," he confessed, "that I've been wanting to invite you to a church service, but, well, I keep forgetting to do it. And I apologize!"

"Do you soak your beans?" asked Cynthia.

"Why, yes. Yes, I do," he said, taken aback.

"I just love to cook a pot of beans. But you will never guess what I did a few days ago, speaking of forgetting."

"I can't imagine," he said, which was the truth if he'd ever told it.

"I was soaking a big pot of beans, and I put the lid on the pot, and set them on the stove, and a week later, there was this horrible smell, I thought something had died in my kitchen, that Violet had, well, you know . . ."

"Killed a mouse?"

"Exactly! But guess what it was? It was those beans! I'd simply forgotten they were in the pot, and they'd just . . . well . . ."

"Spoiled."

"Exactly! So, don't feel bad if you can't remember to ask me to church."

"Well, then, I won't feel a bit bad. But whenever you'd like to come, please know you'll be welcomed by one and all."

"I've been going to the Presbyterians," she said, "but yes, I will come soon!"

After the invitation to his neighbor, he called the hospital to check on Russell.

Nurse Herman said he had sent his dinner back, barely touched, insisting that he could have cooked it better himself, so she figured he was improving, and could the rector please bring a pound of livermush the next time he came to the hospital, as it wasn't something they ordinarily bought, and Russell said he would give a war pension for some.

"He also insisted," reported Nurse Herman, "that he would go down to the kitchen and personally fry it himself, and Dr. Harper said fine, fry him some too. Can you imagine?"

"LIVERMUSH," Father Tim wrote on his list of things to do.

❧

After a useless and frustrating meeting on Friday afternoon, he decided to take Barnabas on a long walk. When Dooley left on his bicycle to do Fernbank chores, he headed toward Little Mitford Creek with Barnabas straining at the leash.

The wet winter promised a glorious spring, and here and there, pushing through sodden leaf mold, were furtive shoots of green that gladdened his heart. He loved the smell of the woods, and the damp alluvial soil that covered these mountains like a blanket.

Smoke was boiling out of the chimney, the great aluminum tub that Homeless used for bathing was hanging on the side of the house, and a colorful wash was on the line. Homeless answered the door, leaning on his crutch and swaddled head to foot in a worn Indian blanket.

"Well, sir, if it ain't the clergy! Come in, come in, make yourself at home!"

The rector and his dog discovered a roaring fire in the old stove, a soup pot simmering on top, and a book open on the little table where an oil lamp burned against the fading afternoon light. In the corner stood the neatly made cot, with two worn quilts folded at the foot.

"I declare, Homeless, I could move in here and be happy as a clam."

"Happy as a hog in slop, is what I am. Set down right here," he said, offering his only chair to the rector, who took it, knowing that it pleased his host to offer him the best seat in the house.

Homeless settled on the wood box between the table and the stove.

"My friend," said the rector, "I'm feeling the ills of the world these days. I thought I'd come and visit a man with some plain sense."

"You're visitin a man s' plain, he's settin' here with no britches on. One pair is hangin' on th' clothesline, and I give th' other pair away. Fella lives up th' creek yonder was too ragged t' look for work, so I stepped out of m' pants, an' he put 'em on and headed to town. You prob'ly don't want to get that plain, yourself."

"No. No, I don't. You're right. That's too plain for me."

"Sometimes you have to gag on fancy before you can appreciate plain, th' way I see it. For too many years, I ate fancy, I dressed fancy, I talked fancy. A while back, I decided to start talkin' th' way I was raised t' talk, and for th' first time in forty years, I can understand what I'm sayin'."

They laughed easily.

"Right here is the way I talked for a lot of years," said Homeless. "You might have thought I had a degree from some fine college. It was a real paste-up job, you might say." He grinned. "Well, that's the end of my demonstration on talking fancy . . ."

"I'd find it interesting to know what you did all those years in advertising." Leaning against the wall in a straight-back chair gave the rector an odd sense of relief, as if he'd run away to the creek and left his worries behind.

"I was what you call an account man. Toothpaste, beer, and automotive was my categories, with a little stint on bankin' and breakfast cereals. It was when I went on breakfast cereals that liquor got me. If I'd've been around when that oat bran thing hit, somethin' worse than liquor might've got me."

Homeless stood up and opened the stove door, and

poked the logs with a stick. The blanket shifted and slipped toward the floor but he grabbed it, adjusted it, and sat back down, grinning broadly. "There's every temptation in th' world for me to get another pair of pants, but I'm fightin' it."

Father Tim laughed heartily.

"Th' bottom line is, I was drunk for thirty years. Thirty years! It astounds me to this very day. I signed contracts, made presentations, drove cars, flew planes, directed meetin's, and stayed half-shot th' whole time.

"I lost three wives, nine jobs, four houses, two kids, and one foot. Th' only thing I didn't lose was m' self-respect, and that's because I didn't have any."

Barnabas listened intently.

"You might say I did everything I could to earn th' name Homeless and live up to it. And now that things are diff'rent and I've been sober for nine years, I don't try to dodge m' name. It reminds me of what I was. Homeless! Sick! Slobberin' in th' gutter! God A'mighty."

"What brought you back here?"

"I asked myself where I'd been th' happiest, and it was right here, back home where I was raised. They were hard times when I was comin' up, but they were good times. And I'd got to th' place where I'd seen it all. I'd made the big money, had th' big expense accounts, th' whole nine yards. I turned myself in to dry out, and I stayed dry. I sold everything, paid my debts, and turned up in Wesley with sixty bucks in m' pocket."

"Did you ever look back?"

"I never looked back."

The fire crackled in the stove.

"I don't mind telling you I'm curious about the kind of terms you're on with God."

"We talk," said Homeless. "We're definitely on speakin' terms. I'm no all-out pagan, by a long shot. I was raised in th' church, and baptized as a boy. But there's somethin' lackin' and I don't know what it is. It's like somethin's itchin' me, won't let me be. I cain't name it, and t' tell you th' truth, I don't want to think about it.

"You know how th' town churches do, bringin' me this t' eat and that t' eat, tryin' to get me in a pew. You people come back in here to th' creek, an' make me feel like a frog you're tryin' to gig."

The rector had fished a stick out of the wood basket. It was a comfort to turn it in his hand, to look at the knots and the grain. He felt the urge to whittle on it with a knife, but no urge to speak. Homeless was right.

"Now that's a hateful thing for a man t' say, but I can talk to you, I can level with you."

"I appreciate that, my friend. Once in a while, I need to talk to somebody I can level with, myself."

"You can level with me any time. But right now," said Homeless, picking up his crutch, "I'm goin' to jump in here and lay on some supper, and give *you* somethin' t' eat, for a change!"

He lifted the lid on the soup pot, and out of it wafted a fragrance so heavenly that his guest was transfixed.

"I'm afraid I won't be able to stay. I've got a boy who'll be wanting his dinner."

"I've got a nice, big ham bone down in here for ol' Barnabas," said their host, stirring the soup with a long-handled spoon.

Barnabas beat the floor with his tail.

"You don't know how we'd like to stay, but the boy . . ."

"How old's this boy?" asked Homeless, setting a cast iron griddle on the stove top.

"Dooley's eleven."

"When I was eleven, my daddy had a big farm th' other side of Wesley. From th' time m' mama died, I got up at four ever' mornin', made breakfast for three little young 'uns, milked th' cows, cleaned up th' kitchen, and walked t' school. If that boy can't make hisself a jam san'wich . . ."

"Set me a place," said Father Tim.

❧

"I got a deal with Avis," Homeless confided, ladling a second helping into his guest's bowl. "All he throws out, I go through. But don't worry that y'r soup's not sanitary. I brought th' cabbage home and washed it good. I cleaned th' potatoes with a scrub brush, cut the soft spots off th' onion, gored a bad place out of th' rutabaga, and put it all on t' boil after I took m' bath and done m' washin'. I keep busy. I'm not one t' lollygag."

The rector thought this might be the best soup he'd ever put in his mouth, and he didn't even like rutabagas.

Homeless waved his hand over their supper, which included mugs of steaming coffee, and the hot, day-old bread he'd toasted on the griddle and buttered. "I paid for th' coffee and th' butter, but not another morsel. There's prob'ly less 'n twenty-five cents in this whole deal!"

"That's a deal, all right."

"Come spring, I won't even be payin' for th' coffee. I'm goin' t' dig a mess of chick'ry, roast th' roots, and grind 'em up. You boil that of a mornin' and drink it, and it'll set y'r feet on th' floor."

"All things considered, my friend, I count you among the richest folks in Mitford."

Homeless winked and laughed his rasping laugh.

"That man is th' richest whose pleasures are th' cheapest!"

"Thoreau," said Father Tim.

"Dead right," beamed his host.

❧

When he and Barnabas came out into Lilac Road at Winnie Ivey's cottage, he felt as if he'd been away on vacation.

"Why pay a fortune to fly to Sligo for a month," he asked aloud in the gathering dusk, "when I can spend an hour or two on Mitford Creek?"

He hardly noticed the car that drove slowly toward them across the narrow bridge, its lights on low beam, but Barnabas did. He barked viciously, lunging with all his might as the car slowed down and seemed about to stop.

Just then, one of Rodney Underwood's men came down Lilac Road in a patrol car.

He could barely control the furious energy straining at the leash, as the rusted Impala gunned the engine and shot past them, belching fumes of noxious exhaust.

CHAPTER FOURTEEN

Absalom, My Son

When he arrived at church the following Sunday, he found his missing Bible lying open on the pulpit. He was flooded with relief, as if a picture hanging crooked on the wall had been set nearly straight again.

Rodney Underwood called on Monday afternoon.

"I've just read an in'erestin' article, says a ring of English antique dealers has been shippin' jewels over here in holler table legs and secret desk drawers. Says, ah, let's see, says three English dealers are currently under suspicion of shippin' rare stolen gems and antique jewelry in furniture transported by ship in sealed containers. So far, authorities have not been able to seize a shipment, as those destined recently for America were diverted to other, unknown ports.

"You don't reckon your jewels could have anything to do with this, do you?"

Please don't call them my jewels! he thought. "I

don't think so. Fact is, I just searched the church, thinking that . . . well, in any case, I didn't find anything. Nothing but a lone candy wrapper, to tell the truth."

"Candy wrapper? What kind of candy wrapper?"

"Almond Joy."

"Where'd you find it?"

"In the loft. It was absolutely the only thing up there, as we never use that space at all."

"What would it be doin' up there?"

"I haven't the vaguest idea." He felt a creeping alarm that Rodney might deploy fingerprinting crews over the entire church grounds, on account of a harmless candy wrapper.

"You better let me look at that wrapper," Rodney said.

"If you want to run by the house and ask Puny to look in my brown pants pocket, I think that's where I put it."

"I'll send over a cruise car," said Rodney, seemingly pleased with this turn of events.

❧

The police chief called back in an hour. "You sure you searched th' church good? Did you look in behind things?"

"I went over it with a fine-tooth comb. Of course, I didn't pry up any floorboards or look behind the bookcases."

"We got th' wrapper, and th' candy on it's still fresh. You say nobody ever goes in th' attic?"

"Nobody."

"Well, th' wrapper's covered with prints. But since you handled it, we'll have to come and take a set of your prints to see what's what and who's who."

Here we go, he thought.

❧

"Nobody's prints but yours," said Rodney, when he called the rectory in the evening. "But I'll tell you one thing."

"What's that?" he asked, sitting down on his study sofa with the cordless phone.

"No other fingerprints means that whoever eat that Almond Joy was wearin' gloves. Y'see what I mean?" he asked the rector, who clearly didn't. "Anybody wearin' gloves to eat a candy bar is up t' no good."

"Aha."

"What I'm sayin' is, I believe I better come down there tomorrow with th' boys and go over th' place."

Well, and why not? Perhaps the whole thing could be laid to rest.

"Come ahead," he said.

❧

When he arrived at the office the next morning, the phone was ringing.

"Father!" said the caller, "Pete Jamison."

"Pete Jamison?"

"You know, Father, the man you saved."

The stranger in the nave! "Let me say at once that it was not I who saved you, Pete—that power belongs only to God. How are you, my friend?"

"Coming along, I think. When I get your way again, I'd like to drop by and see you. Right now, I'm calling from a coffee shop in Duluth, Minnesota. I just wanted to say thank you. Thank you for being there. May I call you again?"

"I'll be disappointed if you don't," said the rector, who heard an unmistakable difference in Pete Jamison's voice.

❧

Throughout the day, Rodney, Joe Joe Guthrie, and another officer searched Lord's Chapel. They looked for floorboards that might have been freshly pried up. They pounded on walls, searching for unexpected hollows. They peered under rugs in the nursery, examined the ceilings for loose tiles, removed the covers of heating vents, and generally raised a cloud of dust that caused the rector to cough and sneeze throughout the day.

They looked in the gardens for any sign that might indicate the planting of something other than bulbs. They put on gloves and masks to remove strips of insulation in the loft. They shone flashlights into the belfry, searched under the kitchen sink of the parish hall, and peered behind the doors of the retable.

Their search, however, revealed nothing more than a long-lost prayer book that had belonged to Wilma Malcolm's grandmother, a box of Palm Sunday bulletins from 1947, and several squirrel nests containing a store of pecans from trees at the rear of the church yard.

"Dadgummit!" said Rodney, with considerable feeling.

Toward the end of the afternoon, the rector felt like walking to The Local and buying a box of Little Debbies, any variety, and devouring the entire contents in the privacy of his kitchen. Nor would he wait for the kettle to boil for tea.

❧

In the fading afternoon light, Absalom Greer's slim frame might have been that of a twenty-year-old as he hurried down the steps of the old general store.

"Welcome to God's country!" he said, opening the door of the Buick. "Get out and come in, Father!"

The rector was astonished to see that the face of his eighty-six-year-old host was remarkably unlined, and, what was more astounding, he had a full head of hair.

"I was looking for an elderly gentleman to greet me. Pastor Greer must have sent his son!"

The old man laughed heartily. "I can still hear an ant crawling in the grass," he said with satisfaction, "but there's not a tooth in my head I can call my own."

The country preacher led the village rector up the steps and into the dim interior of the oldest store in several counties.

Father Tim felt as if he'd walked into a Rembrandt painting, for the last of the sunlight had turned the color of churned butter, casting a golden glow upon the chestnut walls and heart-of-pine floors.

"My daddy built this store when I was six years old. It's got the first nails I ever drove. It sold out of the family in 1974, but I bought it back and intend to keep it, though it don't do much toward keeping me.

"Let me give you a little country cocktail," said his host, who was dressed in a neat gray suit and starched shirt. He selected a cold drink from an ice box behind the cash register, opened it, and handed it to the rector.

"You're looking at where I do my best preaching," he said, slapping the worn wood of the old counter. "Right here is where the rubber hits the road.

"Like the Greeks said to Philip, 'Sir, we would see Christ.' If they don't see him behind this counter six days a week, we might as well throw my Sunday preaching out the window. Where is your weekday pulpit, my friend?"

"Main Street."

"That's a good place. Some soldiers set around and

smell the coffee and watch the bacon frying, but the battle is waged on your feet."

"Absalom," said a quiet voice from the back of the store, "Supper's ready. You can come anytime."

A door closed softly.

"My sister, Lottie," the old man said with evident pride. "She lives with me and does the cooking and housekeeping. I can assure you that I never did anything to deserve her ministry to me. She is an angel of the Lord!"

His host turned the sign on the front door to read "Closed," and they walked the length of the narrow store on creaking floorboards, passing bins of seeds and nails, rows of canned goods, sacks of feed, thread, buttons, iron skillets, and aluminum wash tubs.

Absalom Greer pushed open a door and the rector stood on the threshold in happy amazement. Before him was a room with ancient, leaded windows gleaming with the last rays of sunlight. In the center of the room stood a large table laid with a white cloth and a variety of steaming dishes, and on it burned an oil lamp.

In the corner of the room, a fire crackled in the grate, and books lined the walls behind a pair of comfortable reading chairs. A worn black Bible lay on the table next to one of the chairs, and an orange cat curled peacefully on the deep windowsill.

He thought he'd never entered a home so peaceable in spirit.

A tall, slender woman moved into the room from the kitchen, wearing an apron. Her blue dress became her graying hair, which was pulled back simply and tied with a ribbon. She smiled shyly and extended her hand. "Father Tim," said Absalom Greer, "Lottie Miller! My joy and my crown, my earthly shield and buckler, and my widowed sister."

"It's my great pleasure," said the rector, feeling as if he had gone to another country to visit.

"My sister is shy as a deer, Father. We don't get much company in here, as I do all my pastoring at church or in the store. Why don't you set where you can see the little fire on the hearth, it's always a consolation."

After washing up in a tidy bathroom, Father Tim sat down at the table, finding that even the hard-back chair seemed comforting.

❧

"I left school when I was twelve," said Absalom Greer over dinner, "to help my daddy in the store, and I got along pretty good teaching myself at night. One evenin', along about the age of fourteen—I was back here in this very room, studyin' a book—the wind got to howling and blowing as bad as you ever heard.

"Lottie was a baby in my mother's arms. I can see them now, my mother sitting by the fire, rocking Lottie, and humming a tune, and I was settin' right there on a little bed.

"My eyes were as wide open as they are now, when suddenly I saw a great band of angels. This room was filled with the brightness of angels!

"They were pure white, with color only in their wings, color like a prism casts when the sun shines through it. I never saw anything so beautiful in my life, before or since. I couldn't speak a word, and my mother went on rocking and humming, with her eyes closed, and there were angels standing over her, and all around us was this shining, heavenly host.

"Then, it seemed as if a golden stair let down there by the door, and the angels turned and swarmed up that staircase, and were gone. I remember I went to sobbing, but my mother didn't hear it. And I reached up to wipe my tears, but there weren't any there.

"I've thought about it many a time over the years, and I think it was my spirit that was weeping with joy."

Lottie Miller had not spoken, but had passed each dish and platter, it seemed to the rector, at just the right time. He had a second helping of potatoes that had been sliced and fried with rock salt and chives, and another helping of roasted lamb, which was as fine as any lamb he'd tasted in a very long time.

"It's a mystery how I could have done it, but I completely forgot that heavenly vision," said the preacher, who was buttering a biscuit.

"Along about sixteen, I got to feeling I had no soul at all. They'd take me to hear a preaching, and I couldn't hear. They'd take me to see a healing and I couldn't see. My daddy said it was the name they'd put on me—Absalom! A wicked, rebellious, ungodly character if there ever was one, but my mother was young when I was born, and heedless, and she liked the sound of it, and I was stuck with it. Later on, when I got to reading the Word, I got to understanding Absalom and his daddy, and that pitiful relationship, and the name got to be a blessing to me instead of a curse, and, praise God, some of my best preaching has come out of my name.

"Well, along about twenty, I kissed my mother and daddy goodbye, and my baby sister, and I walked to Wesley and took the train and I went out West carrying a cardboard box tied with twine.

"Times were so hard, I couldn't get a job. I ended up

putting the cardboard from that box in the bottoms of my shoes. A fella told me the bottom of one foot said Cream of Wheat, and the other said This Side Up.

"I walked on that box for three months 'til I got work in a silver mine. Way down in that mine, in that deep, dark pit, I heard the Lord call me. 'Absalom, my son,' He said as clear as day, 'go home. Go home and preach my Word to your people.'

"Well sir, I didn't know his Word to preach it. But I up and started home, took the train back across this great land, got off at Wesley, walked twelve miles to Farmer in the middle of the night with a full moon shining, and I got to my mother's and daddy's door right out there, and I laid down with the dogs and went to sleep on a flour sack.

"I remember I told myself I'd never heard the Lord call me in that mine, that I'd just been lonesome and was looking for an excuse to come home.

"I went on like that for a year or two, went to church to look at the girls, helped my daddy in the store. But that wasn't enough, something was sorely missing. One day, I commenced to read everything theological I could get my hands on.

"I drenched myself in Spurgeon, and plowed through Calvin, I soaked up Whitefield and gorged on Matthew Henry, as hard as I could go. But I was fightin' my calling, and my heart was like a stone.

"One day I was settin' in the orchard I planted as a boy, and the Lord spoke again. 'Absalom, my son,' He said, clear as day, 'spread my Word to your people.'

"It made the hair stand up on my head. But in five minutes, I had laid down in the sunshine and gone to sleep like a lizard.

"I went on that way for about three years, not listening to God, 'til one night He woke me up, I thought I'd been hit a blow on the head with a two-by-four.

"It was like a bolt of lightning knocked me out of bed and threw me to the floor. Blam! 'Absalom, my son,' said the Lord, 'go preach my Word to your people, and be quick about it.' "

"I got up off that floor, I ran in here where it was cold enough to preserve a corpse, I wrapped up in a blanket and lit an oil lamp, and I got to reading the Good Book and for two years I did not stop.

"Everybody who knew me thought I'd gone soft.

" 'Absalom Greer has got religion,' they said, but they were only partly right. It was religion that had got me, it was God Himself who had me at last, and it was the most thrilling time of my life.

"The words would jump off the page, I would understand things I had never understood before. I could take a verse my tongue had glibbed over in church, and see in it wondrous and thrilling meanings that kept the hair standing up on my head.

"I would go out to work at the lumber company and take it with me. I would set on the toilet and read it. I would walk to town reading, and I'd be so transported I would fall in the ditch and get up and go again, turning the page.

"I felt God spoke to me continuously for two transcendent years. Glory, glory, glory!" said the old preacher, with shining eyes.

"One Sunday morning, I was settin' in that little church about three miles down the road there and Joshua Hoover was pastoring then. I remember I was settin' there in that sweet little church, and Pastor Hoover come down the aisle and he was white as a ghost.

"He said, 'Absalom, God has asked me to let you preach the service this morning.'

"I like to dropped down dead at his feet.

"He said, 'I don't know about this, it makes me uneasy, but it's what the Lord told me to do.'

"When I stood up, my legs gave out under me, I like to fainted like a girl."

Lottie Miller laughed softly.

"I recalled something Billy Sunday said. He said if you want milk and honey on your bread, you have to go into the land of giants. So, I went into that pulpit and I prayed, and the congregation, they prayed, and the first thing you know, the Holy Ghost got to moving in that place, and I got to preaching the Word of God, and pretty soon, it was just like a mill wheel got to turning, and we all went to grinding corn!"

"Bliss!" said the rector, filled with understanding.

"Bliss, my friend, indeed! There is nothing like it on earth when the spirit of God comes pouring through, and he has poured through me in fair weather and foul, for sixty-four years."

"Have there been dry spells?"

The preacher pushed his plate away and Lottie rose to clear the table. Father Tim smelled the kind of coffee he remembered from Mississippi—strong and black and brewed on the stove.

"My brother, dry is not the word. There was a time I went down like a stone in a pond and sank clear to the bottom. I lay on the bottom of that pond for two miserable years, and I thought I'd never see the light of day in my soul again."

"I can't say my current tribulation is anything like that. But in an odd way, it's something almost worse."

"What's that?" Absalom Greer asked kindly.

"When it comes to feeding his sheep, I'm afraid my sermons are about as nourishing as cardboard."

"Are you resting?"

"Resting?"

"Resting. Sometimes we get so worn out with being useful that we get useless. I'll ask you what another preacher once asked: Are you too exhausted to run and too scared to rest?"

Too scared to rest! He'd never thought of it that way. "When in God's name are you going to take a vacation?" Hoppy had asked again, only the other day. He hadn't known the truth then, but he felt he knew it now—yes, he was too scared to rest.

The old preacher's eyes were as clear as gemstones. "My brother, I would urge you to search the heart of God on this matter, for it was this very thing that sank me to the bottom of the pond."

They looked at one another with grave understanding. "I'll covet your prayers," said Father Tim.

ॐ

As the two men sat by the fire and discussed the Newland wedding, Lottie Miller shyly drew up an armchair and joined them. She sat with her eyes lowered to the knitting in her lap.

"Miss Lottie," said Father Tim, "that was as fine a meal as I've enjoyed in a very long time. I thank you for the beauty and the goodness of it."

"Thank you for being here," she said with obvious effort. "Absalom and I don't have supper company often, and I'm proud for my brother to have an educated man to talk with. It's a blessing to him."

An educated man! thought Father Tim. It is Absalom Greer who is educating me!

❧

"Take home a peck of our apples." Lottie handed him a basket of what appeared to be Rome Beauties.

"If you like 'em," said her brother, "we'll give you a bushel when you come again!"

"I'm deeply obliged. We have quite an orchard in Mitford, as you may know. Miss Sadie Baxter is the grower of what we've come to call the Baxter apple."

A strange look crossed Lottie Miller's face.

"Miss Sadie Baxter," Absalom said quietly. "I once made a proposal of marriage to that fine lady."

❧

Rain again! he thought, as he put the tea kettle on. But every drop that fell contained the promise of another leaf, another blossom, another blade of grass in the spring. Better still, it would help make Russell Jacks's wish come true, for the buds forming on the rhododendron were as large as old-fashioned Christmas tree lights.

Though it was fairly warm, he had laid a fire, thinking that he and Dooley might have supper in the study. But when he looked in the refrigerator, he found little to inspire him.

"Scraps!" he said, as the phone rang.

"Hello, Father!" said his neighbor. "I remembered that Puny isn't there on Thursdays, and I've made a bouillabaisse with fresh shrimp and mussels from The Local. May I bring you a potful?"

Providence! he thought. And one of his favorite dishes, to boot. "Well, now . . ."

"Oh, and crab meat. I used crab meat, and I promise it isn't scorched or burned."

He laughed.

"I could just pop through the hedge," she said.

"Indeed, not. I'll ask Dooley to come for it. And I have two lemon pies here that Puny baked yesterday. I'll send one over."

"I love lemon pies!" she said.

"Of course, we'd be very glad to have you join us here. Dooley will be getting his science project done on the floor of the study, so if you wouldn't mind a bit of a muddle . . ."

"Oh, but you should see the muddle here! I'd be glad to exchange my muddle for yours!"

"All right, then, fish stew and lemon pie it is! Give us an hour, if you will."

"I will! And I look forward to it," she said.

He couldn't help thinking that his neighbor sounded like a very young girl who'd just been invited to a tea party.

❧

While he was shaving, the phone rang.

Dooley appeared at the bathroom door, and handed him the cordless. "It's a woman," he said, and sat down on the closed lid of the toilet seat to listen.

Father Tim held the phone away from the lather on his face. "Hello?"

"Father, this is Olivia."

"Olivia! You've been much on my mind."

"I could feel it. I've strongly felt your prayers. Something odd seems to be happening."

"I'm all ears." And all lather, he thought, noting that he'd gotten a great deal of it on the phone.

"I feel I'm being released from the fear of seeking a transplant, it has just . . . I feel the fear is being lifted, somehow. You know I've pored over every possibility, every hazard, I've done my homework—it doesn't make sense to consider a transplant, even Leo finally agreed with that. I thought it was all settled, and now . . . and this is the oddest thing of all, there's a sense in which I'm afraid of losing the fear."

"Fear is one of the Enemy's deadliest strategies. Fight this fear, Olivia."

Dooley watched him.

"But how strange that I might be having . . . a change of heart," she said.

"Have you told this to the one who wants to hear it even more than I?"

"No," she said, "I just don't feel sure enough, I feel confused. Will you pray for me to have wisdom in this? I don't want to die, Father. I thought I was resigned to it, but I'm not. I'm not!"

"You know I love it when you talk like this," he said.

"Pray for me," she said, and the lightness of her voice touched him.

"You sure git a lot of calls from women," Dooley said sullenly, taking the phone. The rector noticed that the boy's cowlick was standing straight up.

"My friend, a priest gets a lot of calls from everybody. In fact, there are times when I'd like nothing better than to open the window and throw the phone in the yard!"

"I could tell 'em you ain't here."

"Aren't here."

No response.

"That, however, would be a lie, wouldn't it?"

"I reckon."

"No reckon about it. It would be a lie, and a lie is a hateful thing."

"Why?"

"For one thing, telling a lie is like eating peanuts. One leads to another. In no time at all, you've gone through a bag full."

He rinsed the razor under the tap. "Worst of all, you become a slave to something that isn't real."

"We been readin' about slaves. I wouldn't want t' be one."

"Let me say again that lying will make you a slave, for whoever tells a lie is the servant of that lie. I hope you'll hide that in your heart, son." He put his hand on the boy's shoulder. "Now, why don't we do something with that cowlick before company comes?"

❧

Cynthia arrived, wearing a pair of blue oven mitts and carrying a large stew pot.

She set the pot on the stove and handed Dooley the book that was tucked under her arm. "This is for you. It's my latest book, and it has a boy with red hair in it."

Dooley looked at the cover. " 'is ol' Vi'let stuff's f'r babies," he said, offended.

"It most certainly is not! It's for readers up to ten years old!"

"I'm eleven," said Dooley, "but I'm grown for my age."

A likely story! thought the rector.

"Okay, do this," said Cynthia. "Read it. And if you don't like it, you never have to read another Violet book as long as you live."

"Dooley has been known to make up his mind in advance of the facts."

"I understand perfectly. I was afflicted with that very trait for years on end."

"Are we havin' hot chocolate tonight?" Dooley asked.

"We are, as soon as you've finished your science project. Double marshmallows for you. While I'm in the kitchen, why don't you poke up the fire for Miss Coppersmith?"

"Call me Cynthia," she said to Dooley.

"Would you like to see our train?" asked Dooley.

"Oh, I would! I love trains."

Was there anything his neighbor didn't love, he wondered.

"What's 'at smell?"

Father Tim took the lid off the steaming pot, and the aroma lifted from it like a fragrant cloud. "This, my friend, is a delicacy of the rarest sort. In plain language, fish stew."

"Yuck! I'm not eatin 'at stuff."

"Thanks be to God! There'll be more for the rest of us."

"You don't know what you're missing," said their neighbor with some asperity. "There's octopus in here."

Dooley looked at the pot with alarm.

"Not to mention good old scrod."

"Scrod?"

"And fish eyes. Mmmmm. Delicious! My favorite! So tender."

"Yuck! Gag!" said Dooley, fleeing to the study.

Cynthia laughed with delight. "I hope you'll forgive an innocent lie."

"Well," he said, grinning, "but just this once."

❧

"I done read half of that book," said Dooley, who had finished eating his fried bologna sandwich and was

working on his science project. "I read it while you all
was in th' kitchen."

"And what did you think?" asked Cynthia.

"Cool."

"Thank you," she said, obviously pleased.

The table had been moved from the bookcase to the
fireplace, and covered with a damask cloth that had
come with the rectory. Dooley had lighted a green
Christmas candle and set it in a saucer and, overall, the
effect was so festive that they lingered over the lemon
pie and coffee.

"Again, your bouillabaisse was outstanding."

"I'm glad you liked it." She smiled, almost shyly.

"Gross!" said Dooley.

"By the way," said his neighbor, "if you catch any
moles this spring, I'd truly like to have one."

The idea was so grisly that Barnabas, who was lying
by the fire, caught the sense of it and growled.

A dead mole! He'd never had such an odd and un-
wholesome request in his life.

"I'm about t' puke," said Dooley, vanishing into the
kitchen.

"I suppose you think Beatrix Potter drew her creatures from imagination, or from one fleeting glance at
something scampering across the path?"

"You mean she didn't?"

"Of course not! She drew from life. Or death, if you
will."

"You're by far the most unusual, that is to say,
unique person I've had the privilege of meeting in
years."

"You're only too kind to call me unusual. I've been
called worse!"

He smiled. "You don't say!"

"Peculiar . . ."

"No!"

"Curious . . ."

"Certainly not."

"And even eccentric . . ."

"Entirely inaccurate!"

She sighed.

"There are those," he said, "who call me odd, as well, so I understand. I was without a car for nearly eight years, and took up with a maverick dog who's disciplined only by the recitation of Scripture."

"How I wish that all of us might be disciplined that way."

There, he thought. What a grand thing to say.

"How did you become an artist?"

"My mother was artistic, my father too. And I was an only child. They taught me to see. Yes, I think that's the very best way to put it. I didn't just look at a painting or a picture, I looked at every single facet of it. And a tiny flower that most people tread underfoot, well, we'd look at it very closely, and find such extraordinary detail."

" 'To see the world in a grain of sand, and heaven in a wild flower,' " he quoted from Blake.

" 'Hold infinity in the palm of your hand, and eternity in an hour,' " she replied.

"For that alone, you deserve a mole. I can't bring myself to make any promises, but I'll see what I can do."

She laughed. "I've learned not to live on any promises other than God's, actually."

"That's wisdom, indeed. The kind one usually comes by the hard way."

"It was hard, all right. I was married for many years to a man who became . . . an important public figure.

I'm perhaps the least public person on earth. That's a terrible kind of division to have in a marriage. And he wanted children, he was desperate for children, and I couldn't give them to him. I learned he had at least three, all by different women."

Her eyes, which he always found so vividly blue, appeared oddly gray.

His mother's death had been the keenest pain in his memory, and his conflict with his father had refused to give him any lasting peace. Yet, compared to the grief and heartache revealed to him by others, he felt he had lived a nearly idyllic existence.

"I must tell you," she said, "that I never dreamed I'd be sitting here now—alive. And happier than I've ever been or ever dreamed of being. Successful in my work, with my own home and no mortgage, and a gracious neighbor who's gone out of his way to make me feel welcome."

"I must admit something."

"What's that?"

"I haven't gone out of my way in the least."

"Oh, rats!" she said, laughing. "I was hoping you had!" Her eyes were blue again. "But what about you? Have you ever had a broken heart?"

One thing he could say for his neighbor. She caught one off-guard. While several had asked if he'd ever been in love, no one had ever directly inquired after his heart.

"Dooley," he called to the kitchen, without taking his eyes from Cynthia, "isn't it about time for hot chocolate?"

❦

He made the hot chocolate with milk, put three mugs on a tray, and walked back to the study, where he found his neighbor on her hands and knees with Dooley, waiting for the train to come through the tunnel.

Rain pattered on the roof, the boy looked happy and confident, there was laughter in his home, and, as he set the tray on the table, the fire crackled invitingly.

He wasn't unaware that it all combined to give him a feeling of unutterable pleasure.

✺

A renewed running schedule had increased his energy. He had finished his Lenten homilies, and Dooley Barlowe had said "thank you" all of four times.

Evie Adams's mother had stopped putting the wet wash in the oven. And the nursing-home building committee had chosen an architect. What did it matter that the bells were once again delayed, when so many other things were chiming along nicely?

On Sunday morning, as he and Dooley were starting out for the eight o'clock service, he saw his neighbor walking briskly up the sidewalk. She was wearing a small hat and navy suit and looking, he thought, quite a picture.

"Good morning!" he called out.

"Good morning to you! Hi, Dooley! You look terrific in suspenders! I thought I'd just pop over to your early service and see what's up with the Anglicans before I go along to the Presbyterians."

"We'll be thrilled to have you."

"Thanks! It's such a beautiful morning, I thought I'd get there a bit early and enjoy the calm."

As she said that, he, for some unexplainable reason, looked down at her shapely legs, which brought her feet into view.

Seeing what must have been a bewildered look on

his face, she also looked down. She was still wearing her terry cloth bedroom shoes with the embroidered violets.

"Oh, no," she said, miserably. Without another word, she turned and fled into the little house.

" 'at was funny," said Dooley.

He hated even to think it, but he could understand perfectly why she should never have been a senator's wife.

☙

"Peedaddle!" said Emma, attempting to total the first quarter's offerings. "We didn't collect a hundred and *eighty* thousand! It was only *eighteen* thousand!"

"Decimals can be tricky," he said. "However, that's not bad, considering the recession."

"What recession?"

"I know you've been busy with your wedding plans, but do you mean to say you didn't know we're in a recession?"

"All I know is, the post office has cut back so far, Harold has to bring his own toilet tissue to work."

"No!"

"Yes, can you believe it? And with stamps gone up, to boot."

The phone rang, and Emma listened patiently to the caller before handing the receiver to Father Tim. "Evie Adams," she whispered.

"Hello, Evie. How are you?"

That, thought Emma, is not a good question to ask Evie Adams.

"Is that right? You don't say! Aha. I understand. I'm sorry. Well, then . . . I'll come by right after lunch. Yes, of course, I'll pray for you."

He hung up and shook his head. "Last week, Miss Pattie took her bath while holding an open umbrella over her head."

"No!"

"Well, there *was* a drip in the shower nozzle."

"That explains it," said Emma.

"And when Evie had a bridge luncheon yesterday, Miss Pattie made a centerpiece out of Evie's red pumps and filled them with daffodils."

"That sounds kinda cute. I wouldn't mind tryin' that."

"Well, we'll see what your new husband would think of such a thing."

"My new husband!" Emma said, almost rapturously. "Do you know he begged me last night to do it at the courthouse, he's so bashful about this big weddin'. Dottie told him no way am I wearin' that red suit with the black trim to the courthouse. We have slaved over that outfit."

"I can imagine."

"I saw your neighbor comin' out of the early service on Sunday."

"Really?"

"And I saw Hoppy Harper drive off with Olivia Davenport after the eleven o'clock."

"Is that right?"

"Is she still dyin'?"

"She is still living. Which is more than I can say for most people."

"Well, you don't have to get huffy about it," she replied.

He opened a letter containing photos of a former parishioner's new grandchild. Amazing! The infant looked precisely like Dick Satterfield, wearing a crocheted hat.

"You know what you ought to do?" Emma asked suddenly.

"I can't imagine."

"You ought to get out more. Take Dooley to a movie in Wesley. Boys like movies."

He continued to read the letter that came with the photos.

"Or," she said, peering at him over her glasses, "take your neighbor."

He swiveled in his chair to face the bookcase.

"Harold and Dottie and I saw a great movie the other night. The, ah, something, something, something was th' name. You know, everybody's talkin' about it."

"Is that right?"

"Oh, peedaddle! I can't think of th' name to save my life. You know what it is. Th' something, something, something."

"Who's in it?" he asked, tepidly.

"Oh, ah, what's his name. You know."

He did not know and did not want to know.

"Can't you think?" she asked. "It was all over TV, sayin' it was comin' to a theater near you." She furrowed her brow. "Seems like it starts with a B. Th' something, something, B-something."

"Aha."

"This just drives me crazy. Don't you know all those clips of it on TV, there's this woman with long, black hair, kind of like Loretta Young, and this man that looks like Caesar Romero but it's not. I know you know who I mean, kind of tall."

Dear God, thought Father Tim, when You made Emma Garrett, You broke the mold.

"Well, anyway," she said, "you ought to go see it. It's at th' Avon over in Wesley. It's that new place over around the Farmer's Market. You know. You make a turn somewhere around there, I can't remember if it's left or right, and then there's a tire store maybe on the corner.

"Oh no, I think that's a launderette. Well, anyway, you can't make a U-turn there, so I'd go on down to the post office and turn around in their parking lot—that's what Harold does.

"I think it's the post office—it might be the library— and then in a block or two, you're there. Can't miss it."

Is there no balm in Gilead? he wondered.

&

He still wasn't sleeping soundly. Recently, he not only had trouble falling asleep, but staying asleep. In the night watches, as the psalmist had called them, he found himself wondering again and again about Andrew Gregory and the hollow table legs Rodney had mentioned and the newspaper clipping he'd seen at the Oxford.

He was relieved to discover that he couldn't imagine Andrew doing such a thing as trafficking in stolen goods, jewels or otherwise. Andrew Gregory breaking into the church and hiding jewels in a closet he very likely knew nothing about? Andrew Gregory in his beautiful suits and cashmere jackets, stumbling around in the dark like a common thief? No. It wouldn't work. Never! Andrew Gregory could not possibly be involved, thanks be to God.

After such thoughts, which he went over again and again, he would drift off to sleep, only to awaken with fresh concerns.

While the stolen jewels mentioned in the clipping had been in necklaces and such, couldn't those same jewels have been taken from their mountings, to prevent a link to the museum theft? And could it be that those very jewels were put into the leg of an English farm table, perhaps, and shipped to Andrew in one of those vast containers he received twice a year? And if the authorities had linked the thefts to antique dealers, wouldn't he have removed the jewels from his own premises at once? And possibly into a church, where no one would ever think of looking?

For God is not the author of confusion, but of peace, he reminded himself more than once, as Paul had reminded Corinth. Confusion was ungodly, the hour was ungodly, and Barnabas had lately begun to snore in an alternate bass and baritone.

He would drift off to sleep again, only to wake and look at the clock. Andrew Gregory, the very soul of graciousness, a lover of rare books—of Wordsworth, for heaven's sake? No, not Andrew. Never.

❧

On Saturday, after Dooley went to Meadowgate for the weekend, he turned off the telephone and lay down on the study sofa where he slept for ten hours under the crocheted afghan Winnie had given him for Christmas. He was awakened by barking in the garage and was bewildered to see that it was nighttime.

After taking Barnabas to the hedge and feeding him, he lay down again in the study, exhausted, and waited for the eleven o'clock news.

He should have visited Russell Jacks today, gone to see Olivia, bathed Barnabas, cleaned up the garage, vacuumed his car, shined his shoes, bundled up the newspapers for recycling. How very odd, he thought, to have slept through an entire day, something he couldn't remember ever doing before. He felt strangely disoriented and feebly guilty, and for a moment could not remember the crux of his sermon for tomorrow.

At a quarter of eleven, the phone rang.

"Father," said Hoppy Harper, "Olivia is in trouble."

❧

At Olivia's home on Lilac Road, Hoppy opened the door. "You're not going to like this," he said.

"What won't I like?"

"The way she looks. You'll be . . ."

"Shocked?"

"Very likely."

"I've been shocked before, my friend."

Hoppy ran his fingers through his disheveled hair. "I've talked to Leo Baldwin. Last week, I took a risk and put her on the national waiting list. She doesn't know I did that."

"Good! The nick of time," he said, observing his friend's anguished look. As they walked down the hall, he laid his hand on Hoppy's shoulder. "Whatever we do, let's remember who's in control here."

Olivia's housekeeper, Mrs. Kershaw, stood outside the bedroom door, wiping her red eyes with a handkerchief and lustily blowing her nose.

As they went into Olivia's bedroom, he saw only a large, high-ceilinged room with softly colored walls and a deep carpet. Silk draperies began at the ceiling and cascaded to the floor. Lamps glowed here and there in the room, creating pools of warm light. Even in view of the circumstances, he sensed that he'd stepped into a treasury of calm and peace.

"Hello . . . Father," a voice said breathlessly. He turned and saw Olivia in a silk dressing gown, sitting in a chair. Tears sprang at once to his eyes, and he was glad for the dimness of the light. For all his priestly experience with sorrow and with shock, nothing had prepared him for this.

"Father . . . ," she said, lifting her hand slightly from her lap. She was so swollen that he wouldn't have recognized her. And her alabaster skin, always such a stunning foil for her violet eyes, was an alarming shade of yellow. He called upon every professional strategy he knew to appear composed.

"Olivia," he said, simply, taking her hand. He didn't recognize his own voice.

"Shock . . . ing," she said, gasping for the breath to say it.

He looked at her feet, which were propped on a footstool. They were more than twice their normal size. He couldn't help but notice that a pair of bedroom slippers beside the footstool looked foolishly small.

"It's the congestion," Hoppy said. "It's backing up from around her heart and enlarging the liver. I'm putting her in intensive care for a couple of weeks, using some IV drugs to move the fluid around. Mrs. Kershaw, have you packed her things?"

Mrs. Kershaw was now weeping openly, without the formality of a handkerchief. She picked up the blue suitcase standing by the bedroom door and carried it into the foyer.

Olivia's desperate struggle for breath created the most agonizing sound the rector had heard since his mother's harsh illness.

He dropped to his knees by her feet, and taking her hands in his, began to pray.

❧

"Socks," Hoppy said. "Is there a pair of socks she can wear?"

"Socks?" asked Mrs. Kershaw with dignity. "Miss Olivia does not wear socks!"

Mrs. Kershaw tenderly wrapped her mistress's feet in scarves, and took a dark mink coat from the closet, as insulation against the night air.

Hoppy bent over and put one arm behind Olivia's shoulders and another under her knees. Carefully, he picked her up from the chair. "She can't lie down in the ambulance because of her breathing, and there's nothing they can do for her. We'll take her in my car."

It was precisely twelve midnight when the doors swung open to the emergency hall, and Hoppy carried his patient inside.

The doctor came swiftly along the corridor, carrying a woman wrapped in scarves and fur, whose dark, unbound hair swept over his arm like a mantilla.

"Get the drips started," he said to a nurse, who was wheeling a stretcher toward them. "Oxygen. EKG. The works."

As he laid her on the stretcher with pillows under her head, Olivia looked at the rector. She was fighting for air like a fish stranded on the beach. "Philipp . . . ians four . . . thirteen, for . . . Pete's sake," she said, and smiled.

"Hook her up," said the doctor.

❧

"How did she get so . . . stricken?" the rector asked, as they stood outside Olivia's room in the Intensive Care Unit. "I knew she wasn't feeling her best, but she assured me it was nothing. I saw her only days ago."

"It flares up without warning, and she couldn't face that it was happening. She's been well-compensated for several months, and she let herself believe . . . the unbelievable. When the relapse came, she let it go too long. Mrs. Kershaw was under strict orders not to call me."

"What next?"

"God knows. She could arrest at any time."

"What does that mean exactly?"

"She could die." Hoppy snapped his fingers. "Just like that."

"I see."

"Pray for me when I tell her I've put her on the list."

"That prayer may already be answered. She's been considering that, but didn't want you to know until she came to a firm decision. Where do we go from here?"

"I'll keep her a couple of weeks, at least, then we can let her go home . . . if all goes well."

"It will go well," Father Tim said, with unusual conviction.

Hoppy took off his glasses and rubbed his eyes. "You need to know that a third of the patients on the waiting list will die while waiting."

"That means," the rector replied, evenly, "that two-thirds of them will not die while waiting."

Hoppy looked at him for a long moment. "You're a good guy," he said.

When he arrived home at two o'clock, after looking in on Russell Jacks, he hurried to Dooley's room to see if he was sleeping soundly, then remembered the boy was at Meadowgate.

He sat on the side of his bed in a daze until nearly

two-thirty, when he finally undressed and lay down, taking care to set the alarm for five.

He was surprised and dismayed that he did something he hadn't done since childhood:

He wept until he fell asleep.

CHAPTER FIFTEEN

The Finest Sermon

On Sunday morning, he made entries in the loose-leaf book provided for prayers of the people. Under prayers for the sick, he wrote the names of Olivia Davenport and Russell Jacks, Miss Sadie who had a sore throat, Rebecca Jane who had the colic, Harold Newland who had cut his hand on a saw blade, the Baptist kindergarten who was having a measles epidemic, and Dooley Barlowe who had come home from Meadowgate this morning with a fever.

Lord, he had prayed on the way to the church at seven o'clock, keep that boy in bed and out of mischief.

While he ordinarily trained his eyes on Miss Sadie's painting at the rear of the nave, he allowed himself a quick search of the congregation. Hal, with his pipe sticking out of his jacket pocket. Emma in a leopard-skin hat. Louella with Esther Bolick. And yes, there was his neighbor, sitting on the gospel side, looking happy and expectant.

As he offered the prayer before the sermon, he heard a harsh, grating noise somewhere behind him in the sanctuary. When the prayer ended, he saw the entire congregation sitting with open mouths and astonished faces, gazing toward the ceiling.

It was, perhaps, his dysfunctional sleep pattern that caused such an odd storm of feeling. He turned around with a pounding heart, to see that the attic stairs had been let down and that someone in bare feet was descending.

He heard a single intake of breath from the congregation, a communal gasp. As the man reached the floor and stood beside the altar, he turned and gazed out at them.

He was tall and very thin, with a reddish beard and shoulder-length hair. His clothing fit loosely, as if it had been bought for someone else.

Yet, the single most remarkable thing about the incident, the rector would later say, wasn't the circumstances of the man's sudden appearance, but the unmistakable radiance of his face.

Hal Owen stood frozen by his pew on the epistle side.

"I have a confession to make to you," the man said to the congregation in a voice so clear, it seemed to lift weightlessly toward the rafters. He looked at the rector, "If you'd give me the privilege, Father."

As Hal Owen looked to the pulpit, Father Tim raised his hand. Let him speak, the signal said.

The man walked out in front of the communion rail and stood on the steps. "My name," he said, "is George Gaynor. For the last several months, your church has been my home—and my prison. You see, I've been living behind the death bell in your attic."

There was a perfect silence in the nave.

"Until recently, this was profoundly symbolic of my life, for it was, in fact . . . a life of death.

"When I was a kid, I went to a church like this. An Episcopal church in Vermont where my uncle was the rector. I even thought about becoming a priest, but I learned the money was terrible. And, you see, I liked money. My father and mother liked money.

"We gave a lot of it to the church. We added a wing, we put on a shake roof, we gave the rector a Cadillac.

"It took awhile to figure out what my uncle and my father were doing. My father would give thousands to the church and write it off, my uncle would keep a percentage and put the remainder in my father's Swiss bank account. Six hundred thousand dollars flowed through the alms basin into my uncle's cassock.

"When I was twelve, I began carrying on the family tradition.

"The first thing I stole was a skateboard. Later, I stole a car, and I had no regrets. My father knew everybody from the police chief to the governor. I was covered, right down the line.

"I went to the university and did pretty well. For me, getting knowledge was like getting money, getting things. It made me strong, it made me powerful. I got a Ph.D. in economics, and when I was thirty-three, I had tenure at one of the best colleges in the country.

"Then, I was in a plane crash. It was a small plane that belonged to a friend. I lay in the wreckage with the pilot who was killed instantly, and my mother and father, who would die . . . hours later. I was pinned in the cockpit in freezing temperatures for three days, unable to move."

George Gaynor paused and cleared his throat. He waited for a long moment before he continued.

"Both legs were broken, my skull was fractured, the radio was demolished. Maybe you can guess what I did—I made a deal with God.

"Get me out of here, I said, and I'll clean up my act, I'll make up for what my father, my uncle, all of us, had done.

"Last summer, a friend of mine, an antique dealer, had too much to drink. He took me to his warehouse and pulled an eighteenth-century table out of the corner, and unscrewed one of its legs."

Father Tim's heart pounded dully. He could feel it beating in his temples.

"What he pulled out of that table leg was roughly two-and-a-half-million dollars' worth of rare gems, which were stolen from a museum in England, in the Berkshires.

"I'd just gotten a divorce after two years of marriage, and I'd forgotten any deal I'd made with God in the cockpit of that Cessna.

"The bottom line was that nothing mattered to me anymore."

George Gaynor sat down on the top step leading to the communion rail. He might have been talking to a few intimate friends in his home.

"I discovered that thinking about the jewels mattered a great deal. I was consumed with the thought of having them, and more like them.

"The British authorities had gotten wind of the stuff going out of England in shipments of antiques, and my friend couldn't fence the jewels because of the FBI.

"One night, I emptied a ninety-dollar bottle of cognac into him. He told me he had hidden the jewels in

one of his antique cars. I stole his keys and went to his
warehouse with a hex-head wrench. I lay down under a
1937 Packard and removed the oil pan, and took the
jewels home in a bag.

"I packed a few things, then I walked out on the
street and stole a car. I changed the tag, and started driving. I headed south."

He paused and looked down. He looked down for a
long time. A child whimpered in the back row.

He stood again, his hands in the pockets of the loose,
brown trousers. "I hadn't spoken to God in years. To tell
the truth, I'd never really spoken to God but once in my
life. Yet, I remembered some of the language from the
prayer book.

" 'Bless the Lord who forgiveth all our sins. His
mercy endureth forever.' That's what came to me as I
drove. I pulled off the road at a rest stop and put my
head down on the steering wheel and prayed for mercy
and forgiveness.

"I'd like to tell you that a great peace came over
me, but I can't tell you that. I just started the car and
drove on.

"There was no peace, but there was direction. I
began to have a sense of where I was going, like I was
attached to a fishing line, and somebody at the other end
was reeling me in.

"I stopped and bought a box of canned goods and
crackers . . . candy bars, Gatorade, beef jerky, so I
wouldn't have to stop so often to eat and risk being
seen.

"One morning about two, I hit the Blue Ridge Park-
way and stayed on it until I saw an exit sign that said
Mitford. I took the exit, and drove straight up Main
Street, and saw this church."

His voice broke.

"I felt I'd . . . come home. I had never felt that before in my life. I couldn't have resisted the pull God put on me, even if I'd tried. I broke the side door lock, Father."

The rector nodded.

George wiped his eyes with the sleeve of his shirt.

"I brought my things in . . . a change of clothes, a flashlight, a blanket, and my box from 7-Eleven. Then I parked the car several blocks away and removed the tag. No one was on the street. I walked back here and started looking for . . . a place to rest, to hide for a few days."

George Gaynor moved to the lectern, and gestured toward the attic stairs. "I've got to tell you, that's a strange place to put stairs."

Welcoming the relief, the congregation laughed. The placement of the stairs had been a parish joke for years.

"That's how I came to live behind the death bell, on the platform where it's mounted. I didn't have any idea why I was in this particular place, as if I'd been ordered to come. But just before Thanksgiving, I found out.

"I kept my things behind the bell, where they couldn't be seen. But I put the jewels in an urn in your hall closet. The closet looked unused, I figured nobody went in there, and I didn't want them on me, in case I was discovered.

"During the day, I lived in the loft over the parish hall. I exercised, sat in the sun by the windows—I even learned a few hymns, to keep my mind occupied. On Sunday, I could hear every word and every note very clearly, as if we were all sitting in the same room.

"At night, I roamed downstairs, used the toilet, looked in the refrigerator, found the food supplies in the basement. And I always wore gloves. Just in case.

"One day in December, my shoes fell off the platform and landed at the bottom of the bell tower." Grinning, he looked at his feet, then at the congregation. "Every time a box came in for the rummage sale, I was downstairs with my flashlight. But I've yet to find a pair of size elevens."

A murmur of laughter ran through the congregation. Hal Owen continued to stand by his pew, watching, cautious.

"One afternoon, I was sitting in the loft, desperate beyond anything I'd ever known. It made no sense to be here when I could have been in France or South America. But I couldn't leave this place. I was powerless to leave.

"I heard the front door open, and in a few minutes, a man yelled, 'Are you up there?'

"I was paralyzed with fear. This is it, I thought. Then, the call came again. But this time, I knew the question wasn't directed to me. It was directed to God.

"There was something in the voice that I recognized—the same desperation of my own soul. I told you the sound from down here carries up there, and I heard you, Father, speak to that man.

"You said the question isn't whether He's up there, but whether He's down here."

Father Tim nodded.

"He told you that he couldn't believe, that he felt nothing. You said it isn't a matter of feeling, it's a matter of faith. Finally, you prayed a simple prayer together."

Remembering, the rector crossed himself. A stir ran through the congregation, a certain hum of excitement, of wonder.

"That was a real two-for-one deal, Father, because I prayed that prayer with you. You threw out the line for one, and God reeled in two."

The congregation broke into spontaneous applause. The rector noticed that Cynthia Coppersmith was letting her tears fall without shame.

George Gaynor came down the altar steps and walked into the aisle. "After I prayed that prayer with two people I had never seen, to a God I didn't know, I came down, Father, and stole your Bible."

He looked plaintively at the rector, who smiled at him, and nodded.

"As I read during the next few weeks, I began to find the most amazing peace. Even more amazing was the intimacy I was finding with God—one-on-one, moment by moment."

The man from the attic moved to the first pew on the gospel side and leaned on the arm rest.

"I come to you this morning, urging you to discover that intimacy, if you have not.

"I also come to thank you for your hospitality, and to say to whoever made that orange cake—that was the finest cake I ever ate in my life."

Esther Bolick flushed beet red and put her prayer book in front of her face, as every head in the congregation turned to look where she sat in the third row from the organ.

"Father," said George Gaynor, "thank you for calling someone to take me in."

The rector looked at his senior warden. "Hal, go over to First Baptist and get Rodney Underwood." Then he looked at his congregation.

"Let us stand, and affirm our faith," he said, "with the reading of the Nicene creed."

❧

After the confession of sin, Father Tim saw Hal, Rodney, and two officers walk in and wait at the rear of the nave. The rector knew his senior warden would not come forward with the police until the signal was given. How grand to have a man like Hal Owen by his side, he thought. Harry Nelson would have had the entire force storming the aisles with cocked revolvers.

During the final hymn, he went to George Gaynor, who was sitting in the front pew, and took his hand. Together, they walked down the aisle behind the crucifix, toward the rear of the church.

Ron Malcolm, head of the nursing-home building committee, stepped out of the pew in his sock feet and handed George Gaynor his shoes.

A look passed between the two men as George took the loafers. He put them on without a word. They appeared to fit perfectly.

At the rear of the nave, the rector turned and proclaimed: "Go in peace, to love and serve the Lord!"

"Thanks be to God!" chorused his amazed congregation.

❧

While Father Tim, Hal Owen, and one of the officers drove George Gaynor to the Mitford jail, Rodney and another officer collected his things from the bell tower, including a Gatorade jug containing the jewels.

J.C. Hogan, who heard the news from a breathless Lord's Chapel member at Lew Boyd's Esso, rushed to the church, but found it was already locked. He arrived at the jail as lunch was being served.

"Is that him?" J.C. asked Joe Joe Guthrie. J.C. had

one eye on the prisoner, who was sitting in a cell with Father Tim, and one eye on the rolling cart that contained Sunday lunch.

"That's him, all right."

"Fried chicken?" asked J.C.

"Fried eggplant," said Joe Joe.

J.C. took out his handkerchief and wiped his face. "I was goin' to see if you had extras today, but I just got over it."

"Eggplant's all right if you soak it," said Joe Joe, who was leaning against the wall in a straight-back chair the department had bought at a library yard sale.

"I hear this guy's been hidin' in the church attic over at Lord's Chapel."

"Had a big job in economics. Turned hisself in during church service, preached 'em a good sermon."

"What's th' deal?" asked J.C. "I hear he stole some jewels worth th' moon."

"Four or five million is what I hear," said Joe Joe, taking a meal off the cart as it passed. He took the plate with both hands, held it under his nose and smelled it, then looked it over carefully. "Checkin' t' see if there's any onions in this deal. I'm goin' out tonight."

"Who with?" asked J.C.

"That's for me t' know and you t' find out, buddy."

Rodney came down the hall, adjusting his holster. "J.C., how can I he'p you?"

"I'd like to talk to your prisoner, if it's all right with you."

"Well, it ain't all right with me, number one. Number two, this is a federal offense, and he's not in my jurisdiction. Go talk t' somebody who was at Lord's Chapel this mornin', that's a whopper of a story right there."

"Maybe I'll just wait for the father."

"I wouldn't do that if I was you," said Rodney, without explanation. "If I was you, I'd talk to Ron Malcolm. He gave th' prisoner th' shoes off his own feet. That's a human-interest angle."

"This town is full of human-interest angles. I'm lookin' for hard news," said J.C., who turned on his heel and left, slamming the door.

"I'd like to give 'im some hard news," said Joe Joe.

❧

He was sitting with the prisoner in a small cell that was spotlessly clean, containing a bed, a chair, a floor lamp, a sink, a toilet, a hooked rug, and a table with an orderly stack of *Southern Living* magazines.

"I didn't know you'd found the jewels in the urn. I kept moving them around, just in case. But the day you came up to the attic, I could sense trouble.

"I'd been sitting in the loft, reading your Bible, when I heard you pull the stairs down. I was scrambling for my place behind the bell, and the wrapper dropped out of my pocket. When I got to the door of the tower, I turned and looked back, and there was the wrapper in the middle of the floor. It looked as big as a football."

"I like Almond Joy, myself," the rector said, agreeably.

"A lot of the time up there, I was starved for a decent meal. The box from 7-Eleven emptied fast, then I found the canned stuff in the basement. All those stewed tomatoes got to me after awhile. Then, around Christmas, your coffee hour picked up for about a month. I remember coming down one Saturday night and sliding the top layer of pimento cheese sandwiches right off the platter, clean as a whistle.

"For Thanksgiving, I ate a jar of pickles and a can of stewed okra. For dessert, I mixed a pint of half-and-half with Sweet 'N Low. I came down from your attic with a new heart and a cast iron stomach."

The rector laughed. "A priceless combination in today's world."

"I have a great feeling for Lord's Chapel. Strange as it seems, it was a true home to me, in many ways. Since I could hear what went on in the church and parish hall through the heating vents, I began to feel close to the people. It was like family."

"The Holy Spirit moved and worked through you in a wonderful way this morning. It was the finest sermon He's delivered to Lord's Chapel in a long time."

"Will I see you tomorrow?"

"Tomorrow and the next day and the next. For as long as you're with us."

"I'd like to be baptized."

He embraced the man from the attic. "Consider it done," he said.

❧

"Where you been at?" A glowering Dooley Barlowe was sitting on the study sofa, wrapped in a blanket.

"At the jail."

" 'is ol' phone's rang off th' hook. I like to th'owed it out th' window."

"Help yourself."

"I ain't had a bite t' eat."

"Feed a cold, starve a fever is what I've been told."

" 'at's easy f'r you t' say."

He took off his jacket and sat on the sofa. Barnabas sprawled at his feet. "Who called?"

"Y'r doc."

"What did he want?"

"Said come up there when you can."

"Who else?"

"Walter."

"And?"

"Said call 'im up tonight after some ol' TV show."

"*60 Minutes.* What else?"

"Y'r neighbor. Cynthia."

"What did she say?"

"Call 'er up. Ol' cat's stuck in th' basement."

Come here. Go there. Do this, do that.

"What do you want to eat?"

"Baloney."

"Baloney, yourself," said Father Tim, getting up from the sofa.

❧

On Monday, he made breakfast, got Dooley off to school with a bag lunch and thirty-five cents for juice, and greeted Puny, who appeared to be all smiles. He gave her a quick recap of Sunday's great drama, and, since he had seen nearly all of the hospital patients on the previous afternoon, he walked quickly toward the office with Barnabas on his red leash.

At the Oxford Antique shop, Andrew Gregory was just opening up.

"Andrew, my friend!" said the rector, with unmistakable joy. He proceeded to give the antique dealer a great slapping on the back and a vigorous, interminable handshake. "I can't tell you how glad I am to see you! You will never, ever know how glad."

What a homecoming! thought a pleased Andrew, as the welcome fragrance of his shop greeted him at the door.

❧

He had seldom been happier to lock up the office.

The phone hadn't stopped ringing the livelong day. J.C. Hogan had dropped by twice, and the Associated Press had called after a parishioner had given the story to the editor of the Wesley *Weekly.* The Wesley TV station had prowled around the village all day, asked him to open the church for tape footage, and trained glaring lights on the Mortlake tapestry.

Puny had called to say the sink had stopped up and Dooley was "ill as a hornet."

He had visited George at the jail, Olivia and Russell at the hospital, and feebly attempted to work on his sermon.

For a change in their routine, he and Barnabas crossed the street and walked past Mitford Blossoms in the deepening gloom. As they approached the corner, the street lights came on. Easily an hour early, he thought, looking at the overcast sky.

Suddenly, Barnabas growled viciously and lunged at a car that had slowed down in the lane next to them. It was the only car on the street, and they were the only pedestrians.

Before he could take it all in, someone opened the back door of the car and grabbed Barnabas by his collar, yanking the leash from his hand. "That'll learn you to steal our dog, Preacher Man!"

An arm shot through an open window and struck him in the chest. He reeled away as Barnabas was dragged into the back seat and muzzled.

He grabbed for the door handle, but he was shoved again, so violently that he crashed against the lamppost and fell to the sidewalk.

"VAT," he read on the license plate, as the car roared away. He tried to rise, but the breath had been knocked from him.

CHAPTER SIXTEEN

A Sure Reward

The rector nodded to the police chief, who hitched up his holster belt and took a deep breath. "I present George Gaynor," he said in a loud voice, "to receive the sacrament of baptism."

"Do you desire to be baptized?" the rector asked the freshly shaven prisoner.

"I do."

"Do you renounce Satan and all the spiritual forces of wickedness that rebel against God?"

"I renounce them."

"Do you renounce the evil powers of this world which corrupt and destroy the creatures of God?"

"I renounce them."

"Do you renounce all sinful desires that draw you from the love of God?"

"I renounce them."

"Do you turn to Jesus Christ and accept Him as your Savior?"

"I do."

"Do you put your whole trust in His grace and love?"

"I do."

"Do you promise to follow and obey Him as your Lord?"

"I do."

Father Tim turned to the police chief, Joe Joe Guthrie, and two other officers. "Will you who witness these vows do all in your power to support this person in his life in Christ?"

"We will!"

After the thanksgiving over the water, George dropped to his knees on a braided rug.

Father Tim cupped his left hand and filled it with water from a pitcher. "George Gaynor," he said, spilling the water over the prisoner's head, "I baptize you in the name of the Father, and of the Son, and of the Holy Spirit. Amen."

"Amen!" chorused the Mitford police force.

Following the prayer, the rector came to the part of the service that, in all his years in the priesthood, had never failed to move him deeply.

Placing one hand on the prisoner's head, and, with the other, marking his forehead with the sign of the cross, he said, "George Gaynor, you are sealed by the Holy Spirit in baptism and marked as Christ's own forever. Amen."

Marked! Forever. He felt the certainty of it.

❧

After baptism, the prisoner received the Eucharist. Then, he received Esther Bolick's cake.

"Looky here," said Rodney. "Miz Bolick done brought you her knockdown, drag-out cake."

Joe Joe Guthrie stepped forward with a box from The Collar Button. "Me 'n the boys went in and got you a shirt and a pair of pants. Fifty percent off. We don't want any thanks."

Another officer pulled a pair of socks from his pants pocket. "Here," he said, shyly, "they're not new, but my wife washed 'em, seein' as you needed 'em."

George stood in the middle of the floor, speechless, tears splashing down his cheeks.

"This feller," Rodney said to the rector, "is bad to bawl. He's about had me doin' it a time or two."

"The Holy Spirit tenderizes the heart."

"You know I don't want to mess with the work of the Holy Spirit," said Rodney, "but we ought to get this cake cut."

❧

Before he left the jail, he placed a cross on a silver chain around the new communicant's neck.

"I'm sorry about your dog," said George.

My dog! He'd been able to forget this sorrow during the baptism service. He instantly felt the pain around his heart. "Pray for me," he said simply.

Rodney met him in the hallway. "We're doin' everything we can. You cain't lose a black dog th' size of a Buick like you could one of them little bitty Chihuahuas. He'll turn up, and you can mark my word."

Barnabas missing! It was unthinkable. He still couldn't believe it. It was a fact that simply would not take hold, except at night, when the foot of his bed felt empty as a tomb.

In recent months, it seemed that a lot of important things had ended up missing. But there was one comfort he clung to: Everything that had ended up missing—jewels, Bible, Dooley—all had come back, all had been restored. It was this thought, and this alone, that kept him going.

Joe Joe Guthrie ran ahead of him to open the door.

"We're real sorry to hear about your dog, Father."

"I appreciate that, Joe Joe."

"My grandmother thinks th' world of you."

"And I think the world of the mayor. She's the finest."

"Yes, sir," said Joe Joe, grinning.

J.C. Hogan caught up with him as he crossed the street at The Collar Button. "Find out anything?" J.C. asked. The editor's briefcase came open suddenly, spilling papers onto the sidewalk.

"The prisoner has been baptized," he said, kneeling down to help pick up the jumble of papers.

J.C. stuffed the papers back in the case and took out his handkerchief. "I cain't go on that," he said, wiping his face. "I got to have more."

The two men walked on. "The only more is that Esther Bolick brought him a marmalade cake and the men on the force gave him a new shirt and pants."

"What else?" said J.C., keeping to the rector's brisk pace.

"Not another crumb or scrap that I can think of."

"I'd like to get out of th' newspaper business," snapped J.C.

They walked on in silence. "What about your dog?" J.C. asked, with sudden enthusiasm. "You want me to run a picture?"

"Excellent! Thank you for thinking of it, my friend."

"Get a picture up to the office today and I'll run it Monday."

He realized he didn't have a picture. He hadn't owned a camera in years.

"I don't have a picture. Could you describe him, instead? You know, you could create a wonderful description of Barnabas. You're a fine writer when you put your mind to it."

"My mind is currently elsewhere," J.C. said, huffily, as he left Father Tim and crossed the street.

There, thought the rector, goes a man who's standing in the need of prayer.

❧

"And what are you still doing here, young lady?" he asked Puny when he came home at five o'clock.

"Fluffin' up this place," she said, grinning. "I never saw a place to need so much fluffin' up."

"What exactly do you call fluffing?"

"Air th' pillows, wash th' mattress covers, soak your seeds . . ."

"Soak my seeds?"

"If you want tomatoes th' size of dinner plates, like you been sayin', you have to soak th' seeds an' then plant 'em in indoor pots."

"Is that right?"

"I hope you don't think you just set them little seeds out in th' ground to make it on their own."

"I never thought about it. I never raised tomatoes before."

"I've raised bushels!" she said happily.

The rector opened the refrigerator. "What's this?"

"Cinnamon chicken salad, out of that diabetes book.

I tasted it, and it's delicious, has almonds in it, and grapes."

"What would I do without you, I wonder?"

She giggled. "I don't wonder. I know!"

He shut the door. "Do I detect something . . . different about you? Anything like . . . oh, maybe there's been a parade by here recently?"

"Ha!" she said, blushing.

He raised his eyebrows and smiled. "Well, well."

"Well, well, yourself!"

"I don't suppose you'd care to tell me what's going on?" he asked casually, washing off a carrot at the sink.

"Not meanin' any disrespect," she said, "but that's for me t' know and you t' find out."

※

"What can I do?" asked Cynthia, who was standing on the other side of the screen door. "I know there must be something I can do."

"About . . . ?"

"Why, about Barnabas, of course! Are you putting it in the paper?"

"J.C. said he would run a picture, but I don't have a picture."

"Why, you most certainly do!" she said, offended. "I gave you one in that pie plate, remember?"

Of course! A watercolor of Barnabas that was so realistic, so natural, that it might have barked.

"Cynthia, you are . . . ," he searched for a word, "terrific."

Her eyes seemed very blue as she laughed. "Whenever possible, I like to work ahead of the need," she said.

※

"I need me some shoes," said Dooley, coming in the door and slamming his books on the kitchen counter.

He looked up from the counter, where he was working on his sermon. "That," he said evenly, "was no way to speak to me. At any time or in any place."

Dooley met his gaze with defiance. "I still need me some damn shoes."

He felt the wrenching impact of Dooley's hostility, and it was a feeling he did not like. Boys, unfortunately, did not come with owner's manuals, and to fairly address the issues this particular boy raised would be equal to rebuilding the motor of his Buick. In fact, though he had never done more than raise the hood and stare impotently underneath, he believed he could more easily rebuild a motor than instill respect and obedience in Dooley Barlowe.

"Dooley," he said, "there's something in your voice that makes me feel . . . indifferent to your need. Perhaps you could go out and come in again."

Dooley stared at him blankly. In a family of five children, with no money and no stable center, there were a lot of ways to get attention, hostility being only one of them. That this strategy would not work here was a point he must drive home, at all costs.

There was a cold silence.

"Actually, I do recommend that very thing. Why don't you go out the door and come in again? You might say something like, 'Hello' or, 'What's up?' Anything civil.

"Then you might like to come and tell me all about the shoes you need. You can be assured," he said, looking into the boy's eyes, "that I will listen intently."

Father Tim could feel the undercurrent in Dooley's hesitation. He knew he was considering what he was hearing. And he knew he was also considering the alternative.

Dooley stepped back and cursed with such vehemence that the rector stared in disbelief. Then the boy ran up the stairs and slammed his bedroom door.

Good Lord! He felt his heart seized with a sudden, thundering fury. He forced himself to sit where he was, until the feeling passed.

He shut his sermon notebook, removed his glasses, and rubbed his eyes. There was Dooley's own notebook which had skidded across the counter. He saw that the boy had written his name many times on the cover, over and over. Trying to make himself real, thought the rector.

He picked up the notebook and held it next to his own. Two notebooks. Two people trying to make sense out of life.

An odd thought occurred to him. The boy had lived here for weeks without uttering such words. Given his background, wasn't that, after all, an extraordinary accomplishment?

He spoke aloud to himself: "Think on the accomplishment, Timothy. Then act on what just happened."

A Scripture from the Psalms came to him: "I will instruct you and teach you in the way which you shall go. I will guide you with my eye."

He felt the peace of that promise, and went upstairs. He knocked, but there was no answer. "Dooley?" Silence. Of course, there would be silence.

He opened the door.

Dooley sat on the side of the bed, sobbing. His whole body seemed given to grief, frustration, and rage.

My heart, thought the rector, feeling it wrench with sorrow. I have never had so many sensations of the heart in one short span of time.

He sat down beside Dooley Barlowe and held him. He held him tightly, as if to say, Hang on, hang on. I won't let go.

❦

"I want me some onions, don't you?" asked Dooley, whose face, though red from weeping, was relieved. It was among the few times the rector had seen Dooley looking only eleven years old.

The hamburgers sizzled in the black iron skillet. "Indeed, I do. Mayonnaise?"

"Mayonnaise, ketchup, mustard, relish, pickles, th' works."

"The works, is it?" He didn't know when he'd heard the boy call for the works on anything. "Somebody needs to tell you, by the way, that crying is a good thing. I hope you will never let anyone convince you otherwise." He moved to the stove to turn over the hamburgers.

Dooley said nothing, but the rector knew he was listening.

"Gives you a fresh start, you might say. And speaking of fresh starts, I want you to know that I appreciate and accept your apology. That apology gives you and me a fresh start."

Dooley was setting plates and silverware on the counter. "D' you cry?"

"Sometimes."

"Did you cry about y'r ol' dog gittin' stole?"

"Not yet, but I've felt like it."

"I did. I cried about 'at ol' dog. I miss 'at ol' dog, even if he has got bad breath. I don't care if 'e's got bad breath. It don't matter none t' me, I wish 'e'd come back, I'd give 'im a big ol' bone or . . . or my hamburger, even."

The rector swallowed hard.

"Can I ask you somethin' else?"

"Ask away."

"If you're a preacher, how can you git away with lyin'?"

"Well, first of all, no one ever really gets away with lying, preacher or no preacher. What have I lied about?"

"About me an' Goosedown Owen. You said we was goin' out there ever' month, and Goosedown could be kind of like mine if I wouldn't git in fights. You an' me ain't bin out there any, and I jis' bin one time. So, that was a dern lie."

It was and it wasn't. Circumstances alter cases, his Uncle Chester always said.

"When I told you that, I meant it sincerely. Then, for weeks on end, the weather was bad on Saturday, and there was no use to go to the country to sit around in the house. Then Christmas came, and there was the baptizing, and then the Owens had company, and . . . well, and you ran away. So, you see, circumstances alter cases."

Dooley furrowed his brow. He was wearing a red shirt and clean blue jeans, and his cowlick was lying down. "It seemed like a lie."

"I understand. And so I won't make any more promises. I'll just take you when I can. How's that?"

"This weekend?"

"If we can get your grandfather settled in with his nurse, that could be. Let me look at my calendar. But right now, let's look at some hamburgers."

"Cool," said Dooley, as the rector set the hot platter on the counter.

"I've got to take Dooley out to the Shoe Barn at four o'clock." He was putting the change from his pockets into the blue thanks offering box.

"Now what?" demanded Emma. "You just got him shoes."

"Boys are hard on shoes."

"What kind are you gettin'?"

"Pumps," said the rector, feeling foolish.

"Pumps!"

"That's what they're wearing these days."

"Pumps?" Emma was astounded.

"Yes, and I'm thinking of getting a pair for myself while I'm at it." There. It was done. Hadn't the bishop said he should do something special for himself?

"I'm speechless," said Emma.

Alleluia, thought the rector.

"You know, you don't look so good to me. Are you takin' your medication?"

"I have to get it refilled. I'll do that today."

"Are you, ah, seein' much of your neighbor?"

He could hardly believe what came out of his mouth. "Not nearly enough!" Where had such a remark come from? His words seemed to hang frozen in the air. He swiveled to the bookcase, feeling his face flush.

"You could fix that," Emma said reasonably, much to his surprise. "I hear she cooks, she ought to have you over." There was a meaningful pause. "Or, since you cook, why don't you have her over?"

It gave him some pleasure, however small, to know that Emma Garrett was considerably behind the times.

❧

When he made his now-daily visit to the Mitford jail, he noticed a stack of boxes near the front door.

"Shoes," said Rodney. "We've had shoes pourin' in here from all over th' county. Old shoes, new shoes, black shoes, blue shoes. We're run over with shoes. Th' FBI's goin to have t' take George back t' Connecticut with a U-Haul."

"Tell 'im about the casseroles," said Joe Joe.

"Seven casseroles," said Rodney, reading from a list, "two blueberry pies, a pound of sliced turkey because he missed 'is Thanksgivin' dinner, and a box of bridge mix from th' drugstore. Let's see, we've got cream horns and doughnuts from Winnie, a coconut cake from the help up at Miss Sadie's, and a Bible from ah . . . what's that name, Joe Joe?"

"Looks like Cynthia . . . Coppersmith."

"We need a check-in counter," said Rodney.

A clean-shaven George Gaynor was dressed in his new shirt and pants, sitting on the cot, writing. He stood up and smiled at the rector.

"How do you like that shave an' haircut I give 'im?" asked Rodney, who was unlocking the cell door.

"You could put Joe Ivey clean out of business."

"I'm glad to see you," said George, who shook the rector's hand with both of his own. He was looking very different from the gaunt, bearded man who had come down from the attic. "Any word on your dog?"

"Not a word."

"I'd like to put up a reward, if Rodney will let me have my money. I had about two hundred dollars in my wallet."

"Thank you, George. Thank you."

"Make that two twenty-five," said Joe Joe Guthrie, taking out his billfold.

"Why don't we just get up a big reward fund, and I'll

keep it in my drawer," said the police chief, hitching up his holster. "Money talks, you know."

❧

Before he made a visit to The Local, he made a call.

"Ron, we need to take care of Russell Jacks. Betty Craig has offered to nurse him in her home, which is good, and I expect he'll need attention for at least three or four months. Whatever you can send, I'll match."

"You've done your share of matching," said Ron Malcolm. "Let me know what it takes, and you'll have it."

"You're a prince, my friend. Thank God for you! When do we look at renderings?"

"Could be summer before we see anything. The architect meets with Miss Sadie on Tuesday. Sometime in July, we ought to get a rough idea of square footage, how it'll be sited, that kind of thing. Before it goes fast, Father, it always goes slow."

"My love to Wilma," said the rector.

❧

On the way to The Local, he stopped by the Grill. "We're gettin' up a reward," said Mule Skinner, who was sitting at the counter, counting. "Sixty-five, seventy-five, ninety-five, a hundred. . . ."

Esther Cunningham, who was having a cup of coffee and a piece of lemon pie at a table, raked through a large knitting bag for her checkbook. She gave Mule a check for fifty dollars. "In Mitford, we take care of our own," she said proudly, reciting her long-established platform.

"You might as well put your money back in your pocket," said one of the loan officers from the bank across the street. "That dog is long gone over the state line, if you want my thinkin'."

"I personally don't want it," snapped Percy. He turned to Father Tim. "We're goin' to get ol' Barnabas back, you just wait'n see."

❦

He found Avis Packard behind the meat counter, wearing a butcher's apron that read *The World Famous Local: Fine Wines and Premium Meats.*

"Avis, how's that duckling you told me about at Uncle Billy's art show?"

"You're lookin' at it," said Avis, who reached into his meat case and held up a duckling. "Less grease, more flavor, corn fed, no chemicals. And there's a big, fine liver in here to make you a pâté as smooth as silk."

The bard of foodstuff, that was Avis Packard.

"Four point two pounds. Just right for two people. And if I was you," said Avis, speaking confidentially, "I'd put a nice, crisp champagne behind this dinner."

"Wrap it up," said the rector, who felt dimly troubled that he hadn't yet extended his proposed invitation for Saturday evening.

❦

He'd seen Olivia, who was sitting up and looking nearly herself again. The swelling had gone down, and Hoppy was ready to send her home on Sunday. Though still lacking energy, she would be able, he said, to walk around the house, and even go shopping for an hour or two with Mrs. Kershaw.

An enormous relief, he thought. And so was his visit to Russell Jacks, who would be moving to Betty Craig's trim, small house above the hospital, sometime next week. Two triumphs. Two victories.

He'd had a call from Marge Owen, who wanted Dooley for the weekend. Perfect timing, in more ways than one, for that meant he could concentrate more fully on his Easter sermon, two Sundays hence. A call to Rodney assured him that George might be allowed to sit between a couple of officers in the eleven o'clock Easter congregation, assuming the FBI had not yet picked him up. "I reckon they think we've took 'im to raise," said Rodney, who could not fathom the red tape of federal bureaus.

At five o'clock on Friday, as Dooley was packing for Meadowgate, Miss Sadie called.

"Are your ears burning?" she asked, brightly.

"Well, let's see. No, I don't believe so."

"Well, they should be! Louella and I have talked about you the livelong day."

"Miss Sadie, I'm shocked that you can't find anything better to talk about."

"You know what we decided?"

"To string Japanese lanterns around the lawn at Fernbank and have a spring gala."

She laughed with delight. "Guess again."

"Let's see . . . to hire a chauffeur and drive to Charlotte for a day of shopping."

"Never!" said Miss Sadie. "One more guess."

"This is too hard. Wait a minute. You've decided to have me up for lunch."

"Exactly. But you'd never guess the best part."

"Please don't make me try."

"We're going to give Rodney Underwood a little something for the reward fund."

"Well, now . . ."

"A thousand dollars!"

"Miss Sadie!"

"Yes, indeed, and don't even thank me for it. Louella prayed and I prayed and we both got the same message."

"Are you sure about the sum? You're sure he didn't say a hundred? Decimals can be tricky."

"We're sure. With all our hearts, we want you to have your Barnabas back. We're just broken-hearted about this hideous crime. To think this could happen in Mitford, and in broad daylight."

"I'm grateful for your concern . . . more than I can say."

"Then you'll come for lunch on Easter, you and Dooley?"

"Consider it done!" he told his oldest parishioner.

After Dooley had gone, he found the ecru lace cloth that a former bishop's wife had given Lord's Chapel. He would use that over the rose-colored damask that Puny had laundered after Christmas.

He would call Jena at Mitford Blossoms first thing in the morning and order . . . what? Roses, of course.

He polished the brass candlesticks that Walter and Katherine had given him for his fortieth birthday. Forty! He could scarcely remember anything about that turning point, except that he thought he was getting old. Now, he knew the truth. Forty was not old, not in the least. It was sixty that was old, and sixty-one was coming straight at him. He decided not to think further on this sore subject.

He would make something simple to serve before dinner. Perhaps the pâté. But he did not, at all costs, want to seem . . . what was it he did not want to seem?

Forward, perhaps, as if the evening had been too carefully arranged.

He put the tablecloths on, and set out his grandmother's Haviland china, and the napkins. Then he went to his study to plan the rest of the meal. For dessert, he thought, maybe pears. Poached in a sauce of coffee and sugar, brandy, and chocolate.

When should he call? Or, should he knock on her door and invite her in person? He got up and paced the floor, feeling a burning sensation in his stomach. An ulcer, surely! And right before having company for dinner.

Why should he do anything more than simply pick up the phone and call his neighbor? He had certainly done it in the past, without thinking twice. This was not a good sign.

He walked into the kitchen and looked around vaguely. Then he went upstairs and peered down upon Cynthia's small house. He saw Violet sitting on the roof.

Divine intervention!

He went downstairs to his desk. "Cynthia," he said, when she answered the phone, "I've just seen Violet sitting on your roof."

"No!"

"Yes. And licking her paws."

"Oh, how horrid. First the basement, now the roof. I can't keep up with her for a minute. And licking her paws! It sounds like she's killed a bird. I'm telling you the truth, I wish I had a dog!"

That's a thought. "Shall I bring her down for you?"

"No! She can just sit up there till the cows come home. I mean, yes, would you?"

"I'll be right over," he said.

She met him at the back door.

That she looked stunning, he saw at once, would be an understatement. Her dress was the color of a clematis he'd once had, so blue it was nearly purple. He found that it did something extraordinary to her eyes.

"Hello!" she said, smiling. "You're so wonderful to come. I just hate that you'll have to drag my old wooden ladder out, it's heavy as a truck."

There was no way he could not notice her perfume. Like wisteria, something from a garden.

"It's no problem at all. I know right where it is, from the time Violet got caught in the heating vent."

"Where was she when you looked?"

"When last spotted, she was somewhere over your bedroom."

"Do you think it would help to try coaxing her down? I just opened a can of her favorite dinner."

"We could try that."

She dashed into the kitchen and brought out a malodorous brown lump in a dish. Even so, something caught at his heart, for it was supper time for Barnabas, as well.

"Ugh, it's liver," she said, waving it above her head and calling, "Kitty, kitty, kitty."

"I don't believe you have to hold it up," said the rector, taking the dish from her, "I believe the odor will, ah, rise of itself."

"Oh, dear," said Cynthia, straightening her dress and consulting her watch. "Violet, you wretch," she called toward the roof, "come down at once!"

He could say something like, Cynthia, I was thinking you might pop over to dinner tomorrow evening. Of course, it would have to be an early evening, because of services on Sunday. . . .

"Six-thirty!" said Cynthia with exasperation, looking again at her watch. "Oh, dear. I've been invited to the country club tonight."

"Well, then, let me take care of this, and you go ahead."

"That would be perfect, just perfect! How kind of you, how very good. I'll do something for you, I promise."

"But you already have. In fact, I was wondering if you might come to—"

"There's the bell. Would you like to say hello to Andrew Gregory?"

Andrew Gregory!

"Ah, no," he said, hoarsely, "I'll just carry on with the rescue."

"You're so lovely, Father. Just toss her in the back door, I never lock it. Well, then, bye," she said, blowing a kiss his way, and going quickly down the hall to her front door.

He went as quickly to the basement and found the heavy ladder. There was no need to spend precious time calling a vagrant cat.

He carried the ladder to the porch, climbed to the roof, and at once saw Violet curled happily next to the chimney.

He heard the Mercedes engine start and the car pull slowly away from the curb. From where he was standing, he saw Cynthia looking up anxiously, but she didn't see him.

His heart beat dully.

"Violet, you wretch," he said.

❧

There were many things he did not like to feel. But feeling foolish was at the very top of the list. No question.

It had all happened too suddenly. There had been Emma's unexpected comment, and the surprising real-ization that he missed seeing Cynthia. Then he'd impul-sively raced to The Local, for no sensible reason whatsoever, and had ended up doing the whole thing backwards. Clearly, he should have invited first, and planned second. In any case, that was hardly the point. The point was Andrew Gregory. Tall, suave, handsome Andrew Gregory.

After tossing Violet in the back door, as suggested, he went home to a house that felt hollow as a tomb. No maverick dog to leap up with joy at his arrival. No boy with a cowlick that needed wetting down, or hot choco-late to fix, or homework to check.

He would never admit it to Avis, but he put the duck in the freezer. Freezing a fresh, local, corn-fed duck-ling would verge on being a type of moral crime, he supposed.

He paced the living room and looked blankly out the door, then wandered through the dining room and stared at the table, which looked forlorn, somehow, for all the old lace and rose damask.

❧

The cold wind that blew in with flurries of snow on Maundy Thursday made the bare, stripped altar seem even more appalling to the spirit. The congregation left the evening service in silence, not speaking until they passed through the lych-gates facing Old Church Lane.

Father Tim found this service the most dismal in church liturgy, but he also found it to be one of the most crucial. The business of soaking up the joys of Easter without any consideration of the pain of the cross was spiritually risky business, at best.

On Sunday, the wind still blew, but the sun shone brightly. And many of the parishioners at Lord's Chapel felt they had come, at last, through a dark tunnel into new life.

That George Gaynor could kneel at the communion rail on Easter morning added greatly to the rector's personal joy. Rodney and Joe Joe stood behind the prisoner with official solemnity as he took the wafer and cup, then escorted him back to his seat on the gospel side.

FBI agents were to arrive in Mitford on Wednesday, but hardly anyone wanted to see the man from the attic go. The entire village had taken an odd liking to this highly uncommon thief, and the school children had caught the sense of it as well. Letters and cards poured into the jail, with crayon and watercolor drawings that the prisoner taped to the walls of his cell.

Except for clergy, no visitors were allowed, and Cleo had been stationed at the door to discourage the villagers' good intentions.

"Dadgum, I hate to say it," the police chief said, "but I'll be glad to see this brother go. If the feds weren't comin' Wednesday, I'd have to hire on more help."

"How long do you think he'll . . . get?"

"I don't know about these big, fancy jewel jobs," said Rodney, hitching up his holster belt. "My guess is twenty years, more'n likely."

Twenty years, thought the rector. Twenty years out of his new friend's life. On the other hand, he had gained eternity.

❧

The rector said goodbye in the cell, where the two men embraced with some feeling. When George stood back, his face was streaming with tears.

"How long," he asked, laughing, "can I expect this to last?"

The rector could barely speak. "This what, my friend?"

"This . . . bawling."

"May it last always," replied the rector, who knew the worst consequences of a hard heart.

He walked quickly away from the jail, thinking to go home and do some spading around his rose bushes for an hour. But Percy and his crowd of ten o'clock regulars were standing on the sidewalk, waiting for the FBI car to pass on its way out of town.

"I've said my goodbyes," he told Percy.

"Aw, come on and stand with us, it'll swell th' crowd," urged Mule Skinner.

He noticed that people had come out of the shops and were lining the sidewalks on either side of the street.

They saw the car moving toward them, just as Cynthia Coppersmith dashed across from The Local with a string shopping bag. She stood breathlessly beside the rector.

Up and down the street, the onlookers waved silently as the car moved past, its contents kept secret behind dark windows.

Cynthia took the rector's hand, pressed it, then hurried away, as the gray car with the official tag drove slowly around the monument and disappeared from view.

❧

The total collected reward money was $2,400 until Winnie and Joe Ivey came forward with a hundred. At that, the reward committee, composed of Rodney Underwood and Percy Mosely, undertook to have posters printed at the highway Quik Copy, which were soon seen all over town.

"Twenty-five hundred smackeroos," said Mule Skinner. "If that don't flush out those dirty, low-life scumheads, nothin' will."

Rumor had it that Miss Rose Watson was looking for Barnabas herself, as were many other villagers, including Coot Hendrick, who stuck two packs of peanuts in his overalls and headed toward Farmer with his pickup window rolled down, whistling and calling.

༄

"Mayor," said the rector in an early morning phone call, "a thought occurs to me.

"You said the town might keep Uncle Billy in the Porter place if Miss Rose dies. What if Miss Rose deeded the place to the town now, and held a life estate in, say, two rooms and a bath? Would the council consider taking care of them both?"

Two comfortable, well-heated rooms, maintained by the town. Cool in summer, warm in winter, with a good roof and a solid floor, and a commode that flushed every time. In addition, a renovated Porter place, shining on its green lawn across from the monument, and second only in splendor to Fernbank. If someone didn't get to it soon, it would be too late. The whole thing seemed to him the best idea he'd recently generated.

"I'll look into it," said Esther Cunningham, "and get back to you. Have you thought about your speech yet?"

"What speech?"

"Your Festival of Roses speech, of course."

"How's this: 'Roses: I like 'em. Plant some today. Amen.'"

"You can be foolish," she said in her rasping laugh.

"I hope so."

"Joe Joe's been tellin' me all th' excitement about th' man in the attic. I suppose that was a trick you pulled to increase attendance?"

"You're right, as usual. You ought to see the Baptists we raked in the following Sunday."

"Ha, well, you'd do mighty good to get us Baptists singin' those depressin' hymns over at your place."

"Mayor, those hymns are not depressing, they are ancient. There's a difference."

She snorted. "Well, you take Ray, he's ancient *and* depressin'. You know how long we've been married at four o'clock tomorrow?"

"Too long?"

"You got it! Forty-eight years."

"The only thing I've ever done for forty-eight years straight is draw a breath."

"We're havin' a cookout on Saturday and we'd like it if you'd come. All the kids and grans will be there, and th' greatgrans, you name it."

"Why, that's half the town. There won't be a soul left on the street!"

"Well, just come on and don't talk about it," she said.

"I'll give it some thought. Dooley might like that."

"I need you one more minute. I suppose you know about Joe Joe and your Puny."

Aha! No, he didn't. But now he did. "Well, yes," he said, smiling with delight.

"I wouldn't mind knowin' just what you think of her, her bein' an orphan an' all."

"Here's exactly what I think of Puny Bradshaw. She is the finest, hardest-working, most forthright and decent girl on the face of the earth."

"Well!" said the mayor, approvingly. "You know, of course, that Joe Joe was my first gran, and I wouldn't want anybody who isn't . . ."

"Now, Mayor, this sort of thing works both ways. What about *Joe Joe*'s credentials?"

"Joe Joe," she said with fervor, "is a Cunningham!"

In the mayor's view, that explained everything. It had never ceased to amaze him, and others as well, that, of the five beautiful Cunningham daughters and more than twenty grandchildren, there was not a black sheep in the lot. Except for Omer.

"We all remember what Omer did," she said crisply, "but he's over it."

"Let's just say that my stake in this goes nearly as deep as yours," suggested the rector. "I happen to like Joe Joe exceedingly, as a matter of fact. And if this were to take shape, he would be the luckiest man alive. Next to Ray, of course."

"Father," said the mayor, "flattery has never ceased to ring my bell."

❧

"You know what they call me out at th' farm?"

"What's that?"

"Uncle Dools."

The rector, who was on his knees in a perennial bed, looked up and laughed. "Uncle Dools, is it?"

Dooley was standing with his arms crossed and his cowlick shooting up like a geyser. A few days of sun had increased his freckles, and his eyes seemed bluer than ever.

"Yeah, an' ol' Goosedown, she tried that bonehead trick agin of th'owin' me in th' slop, but I stuck on 'er good'n tight and I like to rode th' hair off 'at horse."

"Well, I'll say."

There was a long pause. A bird sang. The rector's heart felt at peace.

"I held 'at baby three times."

"Did you, now?"

"She was grinnin' at me an' all."

He flung the dandelions into a pile as he worked.

"Then she called m' name."

The rector stopped weeding and stood up, feeling the stiffness in his knees. He had a sudden sense that Dooley was sharing a deep confidence. "You don't mean it!"

"Yeah, she did, said, 'Doo-oo-ools,' jis' like 'at. I like t' fell out. She ain't hardly six month old, ain't even got teeth."

"Good gracious," said the rector.

"Nobody heard it but me," the boy told him, wondering if he was free to trust his own ears.

"I believe you, son."

Dooley nodded soberly. Something important had just transpired between them. Father Tim could feel it.

❧

"Spring," said the local gardening column in the *Muse,* "is slowly climbing the mountain to Mitford, wearing a frock of morning mist, and carrying an armful of forsythia. She is shod with ivy and dandelion, and her hair is entwined with sprigs of wolf bane. Unfortunately, she is easily distracted and often interrupts her journey to tarry upon a bed of moss, where she sleeps for days on end."

Laughing, Father Tim put the newspaper down and walked to his open bedroom window. Hessie Mayhew had been reading Coleridge again!

He saw the gray Mercedes parked at the curb in front of his neighbor's house. Good Lord, didn't the man have a home of his own?

He tied the sash of his robe and leaned his elbows on the sill. The air was balmy, inviting, and the sound of the rain as gentle as the whisper of moth wings.

He breathed deeply. Much to do tomorrow. Visit Winnie Ivey who was recovering from a gallbladder operation. Take a copy of the New Testament and Psalms to Homeless. Carry a pound of Jenkins's livermush to Russell, out of the freezer. That brand could only be found in Wesley, and who could ask Betty Craig to make such a trek when she had more important things to do for her cantankerous patient?

Finally, write a demanding letter about the bells. The bells! Now, there was an act of the Almighty.

Had the bells arrived while George Gaynor was living in the attic, he would surely have been discovered and arrested, and God's plan would not have been carried out. Perhaps he should write the English restoration firm and praise them for their endless delay! "Gentlemen, Thanks to your inexcusable delinquency, someone has found new life behind our death bell!"

At noon, go to school and have lunch with Dooley in the cafeteria, as tomorrow was the day parents were invited to share this nostalgic ritual.

Get his medication refilled. Or had he already done that? He couldn't recall. He looked at his watch. Ten o'clock. Time, and then some, for evening prayers.

He realized he had gone over this interminable list to keep his mind off something far more important. What was happening over there, anyway?

He heard his neighbor's front door open and Cyn-

. thia's mole laughter, recognized first at Uncle Billy's art show. He felt frozen to the spot.

"Well, do think about it," Andrew Gregory said.

"Oh, but I already have thought about it," Cynthia responded.

Their voices carried to his room as clearly as if they'd been standing in it. With what seemed enormous effort, he pulled the window down.

I have no claim on her, none at all, nor any reason to be interested in her activities. What's going on here? It was a question that not only had to be asked, it was a question that had to be answered.

❦

"Just tell me one thing," said his neighbor, standing on the other side of his screen door. "Why are you mad at me?"

He was stunned by her sudden appearance, her extraordinary question, and even more, by the astonishing gleam of her eyes. Since he had seen her eyes many times, why was he always so forcibly struck by the intensity of their color?

"Well?" she said, with an openness that disarmed him completely.

"I don't . . ."

"You can tell me," she said, looking at him quizzically.

"But what makes you . . . ?"

"I can just feel it," she said.

"Why don't you come in?"

"Why don't you come out? We could sit on your garden bench. I've been longing to sit on your old bench." She tilted her head and gazed at him with a half smile.

"Well . . ." His heart hammered, which was a feeling he did not like at all, not in the least. Years of not having such a feeling, perfectly content not to have such a feeling, and now this. He felt his throat constrict, so that he croaked when he tried to talk. There was only one thing to do, he decided, until this desperate condition passed, and that was to keep quiet.

In his opinion, it was far too cool to sit on a moss-covered stone bench, but he followed her around to the side of the rectory.

Very likely, he concluded, this was not happening at all. Possibly, he had dozed off on the study sofa, and this was what his subconscious had concocted.

"Just beautiful," murmured Cynthia, sitting down. He was certain that the damp moss would stain her skirt, but that was not for him to say.

"I'd like to draw this little hidden-away spot," she confided. "I can see it from my bedroom window, and even in winter, it has magic."

He nodded, dumbly.

"Please sit," she said, looking up at him and patting the bench.

He sat.

"Aren't we fortunate to have hours like these, when everyone else is working away under some fluorescent ceiling, with no windows to gaze out, and no Carolina junco to come swooping by?"

The little gray bird landed on a branch of rhododendron and preened itself.

"Ummm," he said, still not trusting his voice.

She turned her head and looked at him. "You see, it's nothing you've said or done, really. It's just that I feel things are not . . . the same between us. Perhaps I really shouldn't mention it, but I . . . well, you see, it's important to me." She stared at him frankly. "I'd love to put it right."

He felt he might be able to leap over the hedge and hit the ground, running, in Baxter Park.

"There isn't anything . . ." he began, and was aghast to find he was still croaking.

She gazed at him steadily, trying not to laugh. He felt his face redden.

"You're so funny," she said. "You're like a boy, really."

"Arrested development!" he exclaimed. There! His voice was back, thanks be to God.

A chill breeze moved her skirt against his legs.

"Wouldn't you like to go inside?" he asked, feeling the moss under him like a sodden pew cushion.

"No, let's just sit out here and freeze together." The junco flew in and out among the branches, singing. "Let's see," she said, closing her eyes, "you're mad at me because you had to go up on the roof and fetch Violet."

"Not at all. It gave me a different perspective."

"Then you're furious because when I made fish stew last week, you could smell it cooking and I didn't offer you any."

"I had a cold," he said, sniffing, "and could not possibly have smelled a thing."

Cynthia laughed uproariously. He hadn't thought it a bit amusing. Would this visit never end?

"Timothy," she said, "I have inquired discreetly and was told it's no form of disrespect for a friend to call a priest by his first name."

"That is absolutely correct."

"Only one thing remains to be decided, then."

"And what's that?" he asked, knowing full well that the dampness from the moss had seeped into the seat of his pants.

"Are we friends?"

He thought she looked surprisingly anxious.

"Of course, we're friends. Would I have hauled that ox cart ladder of yours up from anyone else's basement? Or climbed to the roof, reeling with vertigo, if we weren't friends?"

"Oh, Timothy, it's so hard to know how to do in this life. Why, I was terrified to come to your door and demand to know why you were mad at me."

"Why were you terrified?"

"Because I thought you might tell me, you see! But of course, it's obvious that you're not going to tell me anything. Which is fine. Because now it feels better. It feels like it was before."

"Then why don't we have a cup of tea?" he inquired.

"Perfect!" she exclaimed. "I just love having a cup of tea."

❧

"Andrew!" he said, seeing the antique dealer unlocking the door to the Oxford.

"Father, good morning! You're looking well." Andrew greeted him with a vigorous handshake. "And thin, I must say."

"Fit is what I'd like to be, but for now, thin will do nicely, thank you. How are you, my friend?"

"Couldn't be better, actually. Trying to get away for a quick trip to Florida before the spring deluge."

Andrew swung open one of the heavy double doors to his shop and the fragrance of old wood and lemon oil wafted out like incense.

"Come in and have coffee with me. It's been months since we've talked, there's catching up to do! And God knows, I'd like to hear every detail about the man in the attic."

"Not today, I'm afraid. Too many duties call. But soon," he said.

"I'll consider that a promise," said Andrew, dropping the keys into the pocket of his jacket.

"Getting away for a bit of golf?" asked the rector.

"Yes, I think I'll keep the shop open and let one of the Cunningham daughters look after things. Just three or four days, meeting one of my children down there, and taking part in a tournament. Hoping to get your neighbor to go along with me for company; my son and his wife would be taking us in."

"Aha!"

The phone rang in Andrew's office at the rear of the shop.

"Soon, then," said the proprietor, waving goodbye and stepping quickly inside.

❧

When he dropped into the Oxford on Thursday to look at an old book on roses that had been dedicated to Queen Victoria, he found Marcie Guthrie in charge.

That she looked like a carbon copy of her mother from behind was no surprise. It was when she turned around that the surprise came, for the mayor's eldest daughter was astonishingly beautiful. And though she, like the mayor, wore a size twenty dress, she swept along in it with admirable grace.

"Mama says you're goin' to make a speech at the festival."

"I am, that, God willing, but what I'm going to say is quite another matter. Do you think they'd sit still for a warmed-over sermon on sloth?"

"Nope," she laughed, showing her dazzling teeth.

"Well, then, what about plain laziness, the very worst enemy of the rose gardener?"

"I thought Japanese beetles were," said Marcie, wrinkling her brow.

"Is your proprietor off to the links?"

"Left yesterday."

"Drove down with a friend, I hope. It's quite a distance."

"Oh, no. No, he went by himself. And just as well. He was in a stew about something. I'd never seen him like that! Fussy, you might say, like a baby with colic."

The rector felt suddenly joyful. "Speaking of babies, aren't you a grandmother again?"

"I thought you'd never ask!" said a radiant Marcie, who whipped out an accordion-fold photo album that displayed all seven of her grandchildren. "Now, if we could just find someone for Joe Joe," she said wistfully. "He's the only single one I've got left."

Father Tim sat down at a walnut tea table, and with earnest delight looked carefully at every smiling face.

CHAPTER SEVENTEEN

A Surprising Question

While Dooley was getting his homework done on
Thursday night, the rector walked out to the back stoop
and sat on the railing. Surely, there would be freezing
nights to come, and the balm of these last few evenings
was to be savored.

He saw lights in Cynthia's house. He wondered what
she did with her time in the evenings when she was not
going out to the country club. He, too, might have had a
membership at the club; the vestry offered him one
upon arrival. But no, he wasn't a golfer, he wasn't a
swimmer, and when he entertained, he liked very much
to do it at home. So, he'd requested that the funds available for club membership be given instead to a children's hunger fund that he knew to be stable in its
financial ethics. He had never once regretted doing this,
nor had anyone been piqued with him for doing it.

He heard his neighbor's back door slam.

"Violet!" Cynthia hissed. "Violet, you miserable, witless creature, come back here this minute!"

The rector then heard a deafening cacophony of sound, which he recognized as an all-out, three-alarm cat fight.

"Violet!" shouted her mistress, "I will positively murder you for this!"

If only Barnabas were here, he chuckled to himself, those cats would have an instant parting of the ways.

He walked to the hedge. "Cynthia!" he called. "Do you need help?"

Cynthia flew to her side of the hedge in a robe and slippers, her head bristling with the familiar pink rollers.

"Timothy! Violet got out and two toms are killing each other! I've got to get her back inside. She's in heat!"

Good grief, thought the rector, who grabbed the rake propped against the porch and stumbled through the dark hedge.

❧

"You were wonderful," said a wide-eyed Cynthia, sitting in her workroom on what appeared to be a doll-size love seat. "Just wonderful. First, you ran off those marauding toms and then you crawled down the coal shaft to rescue Violet. You will never, ever know how I appreciate this. No, never!" she said, fiercely.

She had poured two glasses of the stunning sherry she appeared to keep just for him.

"You should see yourself!" she said, marveling at the coal dust that covered him from head to foot.

Ha, she should see *herself!* he thought, in those odd slippers and that old robe and curlers sticking up like chimney pots this way and that.

He laughed. "We're a pair, I'm sure. And here I thought you might be . . . traveling this weekend."

"Traveling?" she asked, looking at him intently. "Oh." A pause. "Traveling. Well," she said, obviously flustered, "as you can see, I am not traveling, I am right here at home, where I am perfectly, perfectly happy."

"Aha."

He looked around her small studio. Every inch of wall space was covered with some cheerful drawing or watercolor, or picture cut from a magazine. She had lettered a scripture from the sixteenth chapter of Proverbs that was push-pinned over her drawing table: "Commit thy works unto the Lord and thy thoughts shall be established."

"That," he said, "is a commendable way to do it."

"For me, it's the only way. I don't work at all without committing it to God first. I've done it the other way, and giving it to Him makes all the difference."

Period! The rector smiled. He liked Cynthia's practical relationship with God. It had none of the boldness of Olivia Davenport's glorious faith. It was simple and easy. Cynthia, it appeared, was definitely down-to-earth about heavenly things.

"Well, then," he said, setting his empty glass on a shelf brimming with children's books, "I must go to my young scholar. He's studying for a test tomorrow, and I'll give him a hand if he needs it."

She smiled and tilted her head to one side. "You're lovely," she said.

"And so are you," he heard himself reply.

❦

"What are you grinnin' all over yourself about?" Dooley asked, his eyes bleary with approaching sleep.

"I am not grinning all over myself." He sat on the side of the bed. "Did your studying go well? Did you need me to help?"

"Naw, I got 'at ol' mess figgered out."

"I'll be praying for you tomorrow at one o'clock when your test begins."

"Prayin' ain't goin' t' knock 'at ol' test in th' head."

"You're right about that, my friend. However, praying will help *you* knock it in the head."

Dooley yawned and turned over. " 'night," he said.

" 'night," said the rector, putting his hand on the boy's shoulder.

Father, he prayed silently, thank you for sending this boy into my life. Thank you for the joy and the sorrow he brings. Be with him always, to surround him with right influences, and when tests of any kind must come, give him wisdom and strength to act according to your will. Look over his mother, also, and the other children, wherever they are. Feed and clothe them, keep them from harm, and bring them one day into a full relationship with your Son.

He sat for a long time with his hand on the sleeping boy's shoulder, feeling his heart moved with tenderness.

Then he went downstairs and picked up the phone. "Cynthia, I just remembered something."

"What's that?" she asked brightly.

"I'd like you to come for dinner tomorrow evening . . . if you don't have other plans."

"Why, no," she said. "I'd love to come!"

As he went to the refrigerator, he was surprised to find that his forehead had broken out in a light sweat.

He opened the freezer door and removed the duckling.

When he came home for lunch on Friday, Puny had steamed up the kitchen windows with her cooking projects.

"I'm leavin' you a stewed hen and some p'tato salad for the weekend."

"A million thanks."

He sat down at the counter and peered beneath the top slice of bread on his sandwich. Tofu!

"I never thought to see the day I'd touch that stuff," said Puny, who was watching him out of the corner of her eye, "but I read where it's good for people like you, so eat hearty! You wouldn't believe how it feels when you slice it. Ooooh." She shuddered with disgust.

"I would infinitely prefer a cake of your fried cornbread."

"You can infinitely all you want to, I'm not makin' you any more cornbread for a whole month. I marked th' calendar."

He ate his sandwich with some alarm, but said nothing.

"I seen your dinin' table, it looks like Charles and Diana are comin'. Who're you havin'?"

With some difficulty, the rector swallowed the last of his sandwich and wiped his mouth. "That, Miss Bradshaw," he said with unconcealed delight, "is for me to know and you to find out."

∾

After settling Dooley into his room with a model airplane, he went to the refrigerator. The timing would be perfect for dinner at seven.

To say that he was astounded at what he discovered would be an understatement. Puny Bradshaw had mistaken his prize duckling for a chicken, and stewed it.

❧

"Only if it's decaf," said Cynthia. "Otherwise, I'd be awake till Thanksgiving!"

"We wouldn't want that," said her host, who summarily brought in a silver tray with a pot of coffee, cups, and two dishes of poached pears.

"Oh! I just love pears."

"Cynthia," he inquired, "what *don't* you love?"

She thought for a moment as he poured a fragrant cup of coffee.

"Ummm. People who are never on time. It's so thoughtless, the way they rob us of the hours we spend waiting."

"I couldn't agree more."

"Let's see what else. Garden slugs!"

"Aha."

"Artificial flowers!"

"Ditto."

"Loud music. Stale crackers. Cursing. Complaining." He laughed.

"You'll be relieved to know that I won't ask you such a silly question," she said. "I'd much rather ask you something else."

"Which is . . . ?"

"What were your parents like?"

He poured his own coffee and handed her a dish of pears.

"My mother was a beautiful woman with a loving spirit. She could also be obstinate, strict, and cold at times, but, usually, only toward my father, who was *always* obstinate, strict, and cold." He looked at her with a wry smile.

"My mother was a Baptist, the granddaughter of a

great Mississippi preacher. She was well-read in the Scriptures, had a mind of her own and an arresting wit, into the bargain. When I was an infant, she gave me to the Lord, as Hannah gave Samuel.

"She raised me on Scripture, and the extraordinary thing is, she caused me to love it. Some who're raised that way end up reviling it, because it's taught in the wrong spirit. But who could not love what my mother taught? She was adored by everyone. Everyone except, I regret to say, my father."

His guest stirred cream into her coffee, listening intently.

"My mother, brimming with passion, with love for God and for people—my father, remote, arrogant, handsome, disliked. I remember what my Uncle Gus once said: 'A high-falutin', half-frozen Episcopalian and a hidebound, Bible-totin' Baptist. The North Pole and the South Pole, under the same roof!' Why did they marry? I believe my mother saw in him something tender and felt she could change him."

"Oh, dear," said Cynthia, with feeling.

"At the age of ten or so, I had learned one of the most crucial verses on marriage." He laughed, remembering his mother's frequent allusion to it. " 'Be not unequally yoked together with unbelievers . . . for what communion hath light with darkness?' My father did have a dark spirit, and her brightness seemed to drive him even further into the darkness.

"The church was a terrific issue for years. Mother attended Father's church until, as she liked to say, she was overcome by frostbite. Finally, he quit the church entirely, and Mother returned to her Baptist roots. With me in tow."

He took a sip of coffee from the Haviland cup. His

guest, who was herself a storyteller, seemed transfixed. "What did you think of that?" she wanted to know.

"I liked it. It was like drawing your chair up to the hearth. Church suppers, hymn sings, a sense of family. A great sense of family. I found there something I never found with my father: a kind of unconditional love. But unconditional love with salt, for there was a real honor of God's bottom line. Walnut Grove was a simple church, and it caused me to treasure simplicity. It was also where I very likely developed my early desire to be a pastor.

"I never wanted to rise to bishop. I only wanted to pastor a small congregation, and to weave myself into the life of a parish in . . . in an intimate way."

"I see that you've done that, with wonderful results."

"I don't know. I very often don't know."

"Well, of course, you don't! That's not unusual. I very often don't know if a watercolor is right. I wish I had someone to run to, to say look at this, what do you think? That's terrific, they might say, keep doing it. Or, haven't you made all the heads too big?"

He laughed.

"These pears," she said, "are ravishing, to put it plainly."

He laughed. "One of the qualities I like in you is that you put things plainly."

"What else do you like about me?" she asked, unashamedly licking the sauce off her spoon.

"Now, Cynthia . . ." He felt a mild panic.

"Oh, just say! And then I'll tell you what I like about you."

To think that he might have been sitting here in perfect peace, in his burgundy dressing gown and old slippers, reading or dozing. . . . "Well, then. Are the rules complete candor? Or shall we shade the truth and flatter one another?"

"Complete truth!"

" 'These are the things that ye shall do,' " he quoted from the book of Zechariah. " 'Speak every man truth to his neighbor.' "

"You see!" she said, laughing.

He sat back on the old sofa with the haphazard slipcover. "One of the things I like about you is that you are . . ." He relished a very long pause, as her eyes grew wide with mock expectancy. ". . . fun," he said, smiling.

"Oh, lovely!"

"One of the things I like about you," he continued, warming to his subject, "is . . . your enthusiasm."

"Really?"

"Yet another thing I like about you is your courage."

"My courage?"

"Yes. You haven't told me any stories of your valor, but it's something I sense, nonetheless. Of course, the thing I like most about you is that you're far too kind to make me continue this list. That is, until I get to know you better."

"Done!" she said, scraping the last of the sauce from the bottom of her dish, and licking the spoon a final time. She set the dish on the coffee table and pushed up her sleeves. "Now, to you."

"Do be kind," he implored.

Cynthia made herself comfortable in the corner of the sofa. "One of the things I like about you is . . . you're romantic."

He felt his face flush. "I dare say I've never once thought of myself as romantic."

"But how could you escape thinking it? It's as plain as the nose on your face. Look at the way you love the old writers, especially Wordsworth. And your roses, and the gardens at Lord's Chapel. And the way you set a table with family china, and attend to the needs of your friends . . . and, oh, and go without a car for years on end!"

"That's romantic?" he asked, perplexed.

"Terribly!"

Certainly this sort of evening beat dining at the country club. Why, he might have been talked into playing a rubber of bridge by now, which he utterly despised, or worse yet, doing the fox trot with Hessie Mayhew. There was, however, a price to pay for an evening with Cynthia Coppersmith: He found that he kept feeling his collar grow tighter.

"I could go on," she announced, tilting her head and gazing at him.

"Please don't!" he said. Please do, he thought.

"Why don't we take a walk, then?" His neighbor got up and fluffed her silk dress which he found to be the color of raspberries crushed in a bowl of cream. "What a splendid dinner! I'm fairly stupefied."

He grinned. "That's one way to put it."

They strolled toward the monument, feeling a light chill in the air. He couldn't avoid seeing the reward posters in every shop window they passed, with Cynthia's bold likeness of Barnabas staring dolefully toward the street.

As they went around the monument and walked by the Porter place, he saw that Miss Rose and Uncle Billy had come out and settled themselves in the chrome dinette chairs that held a permanent position at the edge of their neglected lawn. "Well, looky here, Rose, it's th' Preacher!"

"I can plainly see that," snapped Miss Rose, who

was attired in rubber overshoes, a chenille robe, a cotton house dress, pajama pants, and a golf hat. Father Tim was frankly amazed at the style she could bring to such odd apparel.

"Miss Rose, Uncle Billy, I believe you know my neighbor."

"Cynthia Coppersmith!" said Cynthia, extending her hand. "We've met at church. So nice to see you again. I admire your home."

"Don't try to buy it," warned Miss Rose, darkly.

"Preacher, why don't you 'uns come in? Come in an' have a sip of tea Rose made today. You've never seen our place."

"*My* place," said Miss Rose, jabbing him sharply with her elbow.

"Rose, don't act up, now. We got comp'ny."

"Uncle Billy, I don't believe . . ."

"Aw, Preacher, come on and visit a spell. It'd be a blessin'."

The rector looked at his neighbor, who nodded with enthusiasm. "Let's do it! I love old houses."

As they walked up the broken flagstones in the dark, he took Cynthia's arm and whispered: "You might be careful of the refreshments."

She laughed with delight. He knew instinctively that she considered this a grand adventure. How exciting, after all, to go where one must be careful of the refreshments.

❧

Uncle Billy turned on the hall light as they entered the front door, and a great chandelier shone weakly through a layer of grime and dust. "Missin' some bulbs," said their host apologetically.

He heard Cynthia's astonished murmur. They were in a broad foyer with a ceiling that soared two stories high and was ornamented on either side by staircases that, even in the ghostly light, were clearly extraordinary in their design. Faded murals swept up the walls, depicting elaborate gardens and statuary, exotic birds and urns overflowing with fruit. Carved balustrades were missing, with several appearing to lie on the floor where they'd fallen.

In an odd sense, it was a privilege to be in the Porter place, as few had ever been invited and hardly anyone, of late, wished to be asked.

"This is the front hall," Miss Rose said, glowering at her guests.

"Glorious!" said Cynthia. "Absolutely glorious. Who built your home?"

"My brother, Willard," said Miss Rose, in whom the ice suddenly began to melt. "My brother, Willard James Porter. There's his picture." She pointed up the stairs on the right, where a large, wide-framed portrait hung. Even in the dim light, Father Tim recognized the strikingly handsome face of the intense young man in Miss Sadie's silver frame.

"Terribly good looking!" said his neighbor.

In a surprising burst of cordiality, Miss Rose asked if they'd like a piece of pound cake.

"I love pound cake!" said Cynthia.

Now we're in for it, he thought.

"You 'uns go on ahead through th' dinin' room," said Uncle Billy, opening the French doors on their right. "Rose an' me'll bring up th' rear."

Father Tim peered into a vast, dark room with a narrow pathway bordered on either side by towering mounds of musty newspapers.

"You go first," said Cynthia.

He took his neighbor's hand and plunged into the darkness toward a light shining under a distant door.

℞

He saw that she ate the pound cake as if she hadn't had a bite all evening, and did so without inspecting her plate or her fork. As for himself, he broke an infinitesimal piece from the corner of the thin slice, and covered the remainder with his napkin. It was one thing to blindly exercise good manners, he observed, and quite another to exercise reasonable caution.

He saw that the vast kitchen was large enough for an entire studio apartment, especially since it led down a hall to a bathroom. With considerable fixing up, it would make as fine a home as anyone could want.

"My brother," Miss Rose was saying in a loud voice to Cynthia, "nearly married, you know."

"Really?"

"Oh, yes. It would have been the most dreadful thing he ever did, of course."

"I see."

"Caused an uproar."

"Umm."

"Made a fine mess!"

"Oh, dear."

"Nearly broke his faith."

"Oh, no!"

"Set the backbiters on us."

"My, my." Cynthia looked around for help from the rector.

"You 'uns want t' see th' rest of th' place?" Uncle Billy asked.

"We do!" cried Cynthia, jumping up so quickly she nearly upset the table.

His neighbor held on to his hand throughout much of the tour. There were, after all, stacks of newspapers in every room, old pictures, broken furniture, a mirror that had fallen off the wall and scattered glass across the carpet, and even a dozen silver candelabra, black with neglect, sitting squarely in the middle of the floor of an otherwise empty room where the wallpaper was peeling off in sheets.

The young Willard Porter had surely walked through these rooms, admiring their high ceilings and elaborate millwork, the stained glass in every bathroom, the carved balustrades and hardwood floors. He was beginning to wish they hadn't come in to witness the morbid decline of his showplace.

At the end of an upstairs hallway, Cynthia made a discovery. "What is this?" she cried, pointing to a blue door. It was a very small door that appeared to have been put there for children.

"That's my playroom!" said Miss Rose, who had taken off one rubber overshoe because it hurt her corn and was limping down the hall. "My dear brother put that little room up here for his baby sister. Not another living soul could go in there but me."

"Has anyone else *ever* been in there?"

Miss Rose looked fiercely at Uncle Billy. "Bill Watson, have you ever?"

"Nossir, I ain't," declared her stricken husband. "Nossiree bob!"

"Well, we'll just see. I could tell in a heartbeat if anybody's stepped foot in my playroom."

"You ain't stepped foot in there yourself in a hundred years!"

Miss Rose bent down and found a small, rusty key under a broken flower pot by the door, and inserted it into the lock.

The rector heard a soft click, and the little blue door swung open easily.

"You have to get on your hands and knees," instructed Miss Rose, dropping down on all fours, "and crawl in." Cynthia did as she was told.

"Cynthia," said the rector, "are you going in there?"

"Why, of course, I'm going in there! How could I not?"

How could she not, indeed, when it appeared to be a small, black hole in the wall, devoid of any ventilation or light.

"There!" said a satisfied Miss Rose, who reached inside and pulled a chain, illuminating the small space with surprising warmth. "Let's go."

Without any regard for her silk dress, Cynthia wriggled through the little doorway and disappeared.

"Jist foller that overshoe and that stockin' foot," called Uncle Billy.

There were screeches of pleasure, endless sneezes, and uproarious giggles from inside the wall. "Timothy, if I meet the White Rabbit, please take good care of Violet!"

The rector looked wonderingly at his host.

"Ain't that somethin', two growed women carryin' on like that? Don't that beat all!"

"Oh, Timothy, there's a tea set in here! Haviland, just like your grandmother's china! You must come in!"

In the space of a week, he had been on a rooftop and down a coal chute for Cynthia Coppersmith, and that was quite enough for him. He pulled up a battered Morris chair, and sat outside the little door like a cat awaiting a mouse. "You'll have to bring it out here, Cynthia," he called, leaning back and winking at Uncle Billy.

"That's right, Preacher!"

"We can't come out for hours, I'm afraid."

"And Bill Watson," shouted Miss Rose, "don't you dare come in!"

Her husband laughed. "She don't have t' worry about that."

"Uncle Billy, I don't know how you've lasted with Miss Rose all these years."

"Well, I give 'er my word, don't you know."

There. That was the bottom line. The line that hardly mattered to anyone, anymore.

Uncle Billy shook his head. "Y' know, Preacher, th' more things you own, th' more you're owned by things. Rose was always owned by this ol' house and no way out of it, couldn't sell it because of th' way 'er brother fixed it with th' lawyer, and it so big an' drafty, livin' in two rooms, don't you know, lettin' th' oil set in th' tank half th' time, as she don't want t' take charity by burnin' it, but not thinkin' a thing of beggin' food on th' street. . . ."

They heard Miss Rose let out a squawk of delight.

"Th' times I've seen 'er crawl in there, her arthritis jist disappears, she gits like a girl agin."

"We may have your problem taken care of. It's possible that Miss Rose could go ahead and deed the house to the town, with a life estate in a room or two, and one day or another, they'll turn the rest of it into a museum and maybe a concert hall. Your portion would be well-heated, with a good roof, and a nice, modern kitchen and bath. How do you think we can approach her on that?"

"Law, I don't know. She holds on to it like a life raft, and hit's fallin' down on our heads. Th' last time I could git up on a ladder was s' long ago, th' ladder's done half-rotted where I left it."

"Well, my friend, it's something we need to get on with."

"Y' know, Rose has talked about puttin' a statue of Willard in the front yard. If you could git th' town t' do that, it might jist ring 'er bell."

"Aha!"

"But I'd hate t' see a statue of Willard standin' up, it seems too proud. If you was to have 'im settin' down, now, that might work."

"Uncle Billy, you're a thinker!"

"Timothy!"

He peered down at the little door, as his bedraggled neighbor crawled out with something under her arm.

"Look, Timothy! Uncle Billy! It's your ink drawings! A whole stack of them! Miss Rose meant to burn them and forgot!"

✿

"What an adventure," said Cynthia, as they walked home along a deserted Main Street. He was carrying the dust-laden bundle of drawings under his arm, as Miss Rose had insisted that they must reside with Cynthia for the time being. "Hit's f'r th' best," Uncle Billy had said, barely able to contain his joy.

"I'm quite exhausted from having so much fun," sighed his neighbor.

The rector laughed. "We hardly ever hear such a statement in Mitford." He, too, felt a distinct refreshment of spirit.

At the door of her cottage, he handed her the drawings. "I must get to my boy," he said. "Thank you for your company. Tonight has reminded me of yet another thing I like about you."

"What's that?" she asked, smiling at him.

"You're simple."

"I'm perhaps the only woman alive who would be flattered by that remark."

He laughed. "I knew you'd understand," he said, taking her hand.

"Timothy?"

"Yes?"

"Would you be interested in going steady?"

He felt as if the entire front stoop had given away under him, but discovered it was merely his knees. He dared not speak, knowing instinctively that he was in a croaking mode.

"Oh, don't answer now," she said, gazing at him with amusement. "Just think about it."

She leaned forward and brushed his cheek with hers. Wisteria!

Then she turned and went inside. "Goodnight," she said, closing the door.

He didn't know how long he sat on her steps, quite unable to walk the few yards to his back porch.

CHAPTER EIGHTEEN

Something to Think About

When Betty Craig opened the door, she looked worried.

"Father," she said, receiving his weekly delivery of a pound of livermush, "I'm glad you're here. His livermush always cheers him up for a day or two."

"How is he?"

"Ornery."

"Aha."

They walked into Betty's tidy kitchen, wallpapered with geese in blue bonnets. The windowsill was brimming with African violets, and outside the window he saw dozens of bird feeders made from plastic milk containers.

"What has Russell been doing?"

"Sit down, Father, and let me tell you."

Betty, who was one of the most positive people he knew, looked desolate. They sat at her round table, in captain's chairs with blue cushions.

"He gets up in the morning fussing, and he goes to bed fussing. Ida would have done this, Ida would have done that. He hates my cooking and won't take his medicine, and shaves his toenails on the hooked rug. He chased my cat down the hall with an umbrella and . . ."

She looked down at her hands, which she was obviously wringing.

"And what?"

"And peed in the bed twice, for pure meanness!"

"No!"

"Yes, sir," said Betty, whose lower lip had begun to tremble.

"Betty Craig, you are the finest nurse in these mountains. You are caring, sensitive, brave, and persevering. And you are also something else."

"What's that?" she asked meekly.

"Tough! Why, you've nursed men as big as Buicks, and cleaned enough bed pans to sink a ship. How on earth did an old goat like Russell Jacks put you in a shape like this?"

She looked at him fiercely. "I don't know."

"Well, think about it. You nursed Parrish Guthrie in his last days, did you not?"

"I did!"

"Then you can handle a dozen like Russell Jacks, and then some."

She sighed deeply. "I did go off my vitamins about a month ago."

"There! That's it! Take those vitamins, Betty. Tote that barge! Lift that bale!"

"What on earth has got into you, Father?"

"Tell you what I'll do. I'll talk to Russell. I'll tell him exactly what's what, that you'll set him out on the stoop with his suitcase if he doesn't straighten up at once."

Betty looked relieved. "You do that!" she said, blinking back a tear. "And I hope it helps. Because if Mr. Jacks leaves," she said with alarm, "they want me to take in Miss Pattie!"

Russell lay sleeping in a room filled with sunlight and ruffled curtains, with *All My Children* blaring on the TV. The rector quietly turned it off. His last two visits had been hurried. Today, he would spend a full hour.

He sat in a wing chair by the bed and prayed for the old man. With the right opportunities, he could have been another Capability Brown.

"I ain't asleep," said Russell, without opening his eyes.

"Is that right?"

"Nope. I cain't sleep around here."

An old Dooley Barlowe, if he ever saw one!

"Why is that?"

"Noise. Constant goin' an' comin', cat slitherin' around my ankles, phone ringin', neighbors bangin' on th' door."

If he had learned anything in the diocesan counseling workshops, it was that sympathy can be deadly. He changed the subject.

"Russell, I've been meaning to ask . . . do you know if the boy was ever baptized?"

"Nossir. That's th' kind of thing Ida would've knowed. She kept a Bible with such things in it, our married date, when th' kids was born, like that. Ida was a churchwoman and I hate t' think th' times she begged me t' go with 'er."

The old man was silent for a long time, and turned his head away. When he looked at the rector, he was weeping. "I'd give anything on this green earth t' go t' church with Ida now. But I waited 'til it's too late."

How many times had he heard those words from sorrowing parishioners? Too late! Too late to love. Too late to help. Too late to listen, too late to discipline. Too late to say I'm sorry.

"Russell, it's too late to do what Ida wanted, but it's not too late to do what Betty wants." He heard himself speak with unusual severity.

Russell heaved a sigh. "You're right, Father, you're dead right, an' I know it. I'm th' roughest ol' cob you ever seen when it comes t' mindin'. That's why I've fought th' Lord s' long, it meant mindin' 'im if I was t' foller 'im. It's about wore me out, fightin' 'im. Not t' say I don't respect 'im, I do. But I don't want t' mind 'im."

The uneducated Russell Jacks, thought the rector, had just put the taproot cause of the world's ills into a few precise words.

"Well, Russell, when we replace you . . ."

The old man sat up with great force. "You're hirin' somebody else t' do m' work?"

"We'll have to, you know. The way things are going with Betty means you'll probably have to pack up and live at your place. Being without a nurse could set you back a few months, could even send you back to the hospital. All in all, I don't believe the gardens can be let go that long."

Russell threw off the covers and sat up on the side of the bed, which launched a racking cough.

"A mess is what it'll be," he said, breathlessly, "all them bulbs bloomed out and them stems an' leaves dyin' off, and th' weeds comin' in, an' y'r fish pond settin' there all scummed up . . ."

"And you over here wasting energy chasing Betty's cat, when you could be gaining strength." Father Tim looked at him steadily.

There was a long silence, during which Russell Jacks studied his feet.

"Will you hold m' job, Father?"

"Will you hold your temper?"

Russell considered the question. "I'll do it," he said.

"I'll expect it," replied the rector.

Another silence.

"You ought t' git th' boy t' help out in th' church yard when he can. He's gifted at it."

"You know what I'd really like, Russell? I'd like to see that boy laugh."

"He don't laugh. Always was th' soberest little thing you ever seen. 'Course, he was th' oldest, you know, and he's had th' weight of th' world on 'im, lookin' after th' little young 'uns s' much."

See Dooley laugh! On his mental list of things to do, that particular ambition had just gone straight to the top.

Betty Craig knocked lightly on the open door, and came in with a tray. "Time for your medicine!" she said, looking to the rector for a sign of hope.

"*You're* the best medicine this ol' feller could ever have," replied an affable Russell Jacks.

❧

Think about it, she'd told him. Think about it! As if he could forget it for a moment. He urgently wished to call Walter, but could not make himself pick up the phone. Would Walter be shocked? Probably not. Amused? Not especially. What Walter would be was skeptical.

"You're like a' ol' cat," Dooley complained.

"You're laughin' one minute and bitin' my head off the next," snapped Emma.

"Are you takin' your medicine?" Puny demanded to know. Well, no, he wasn't. He'd been meaning to, and he definitely would. He'd do it that very night.

"Grievin' about that dog, are you?" said Joe Ivey, as he trimmed the rector's neck.

It seemed everybody had some comment to make on his behavior these days.

Go steady? At his age? Except for the eleven months he had courted Peggy Cramer, he had never gone steady in his life. What did it mean to go steady, anyway? How in God's name could he know it was something he might like to do, if he hadn't the foggiest notion of what it meant?

And how had all this happened, anyway? He hadn't really meant for anything to "happen." Just dinner occasionally, with the sound of her laughter, and the way she expressed herself so openly, without guile.

The truth of the matter was that he liked her. There! That was it. Nothing more than that. Nothing more than that was needed. Wasn't that extraordinary enough in itself?

He felt oddly excited. So—he liked Cynthia. What was unusual about that? Hadn't he known that? Perhaps. But he had never clearly stated it to himself. The statement of that simple fact felt liberating. He was suddenly relieved.

The relief, however, didn't endure. His everlasting practicality caused him to wonder what he should *do* about liking Cynthia. On the other hand, he reasoned, why couldn't he simply like her, without feeling compelled to do something about it?

When he found that he was pacing the floor of his

study like a windup toy, he went to his room and changed into a jogging suit.

As he headed toward Baxter Park, he glanced through her hedge and saw her sitting on the back stoop, holding Violet. She looked his way.

His heart hammered, and he did something he could not remember doing to anyone in recent years.

He turned his head as if he had not seen her at all, and set off through the park at a dead run.

❧

It was J.C. Hogan who was ringing his office phone at eight-thirty on Monday morning. "I got a letter to the editor I need to answer," said J.C.

"How can I help you, my friend?"

"This kid read my story about the man in the attic, about the prayer you prayed with the guy in the pew, and how you got two birds with one stone, you might say. Wrote me this letter."

J.C. cleared his throat. " 'Dear Editor, What exactly was the prayer the preacher prayed when the man in the attic got saved? My daddy wants to know, and I do too. Thank you.' "

"Do you want me to write it down and drop it by, or just tell you on the phone?"

"Phone's fine," said J.C., breathing heavily into the receiver.

"Well, then. Here it is. 'Thank you, God, for loving me, and for sending your Son to die for my sins . . .' "

"Got it," said J.C.

" 'I repent of my sins and receive Jesus Christ as my personal savior.' "

"Got it."

" 'And now, as your child . . .' "

"As your what?"

" 'As your child.' "

"Got it."

" 'I turn my entire life over to you. Amen.' "

"What's the big deal with this prayer? It looks like some little ol' Sunday school thing to me. It's too simple."

"It's the very soul of simplicity. Yet, it can transform a life completely when it's prayed with the right spirit."

"I was lookin' for something with a little more pizzazz."

"My friend, the one who prays that prayer and means it will get all the pizzazz he can handle."

"Heard anything from th' man in the attic?"

"Not yet. But I expect to."

"Let me know if you do. I wouldn't mind printin' his letters. They'd be a crowd pleaser."

"Consider it done."

"See you at th' Grill."

He had no sooner hung up than the phone rang again. It was Louella.

"Miss Sadie ain't feelin' too good. Now, I ain't sayin' it's her las' breath, but I thought you might ask Jesus to hang on real tight, like He hung on to Hezekiah. You 'member 'bout Hezekiah, don't you, Father?"

"Indeed, I do. He was sick and cried out to the Lord, who said 'I have heard thy prayer, I have seen thy tears; behold, I will heal thee,' and He added fifteen years to the old king's life."

"I hope to th' good Lord He do Miss Sadie like that."

"Tell her she's in my prayers and I'll be up to see her tomorrow. You think she feels like company?"

"Round here, comp'ny's always good medicine. And Father . . . ?"

"Yes?"

"She bin talkin' day an' night 'bout tellin' you her love story. I don' like that talk, like she got to hurry up 'fore she passes."

"Well, then, tell her I'll be up to hear it, and she can count on it."

The phone rang again, immediately. Some days were like this.

"Father?"

"Olivia!"

"I just wanted to say good morning, that I'm thinking of you and hope to be in church next Sunday."

"Thank God!"

"Thank you, as well, for bringing the Eucharist, and being so faithful."

"What does Hoppy say about your progress?"

"I appear to be in a holding pattern. I look a fright most of the time, as you have clearly seen, but my spirits are strong. I believe the heart will come, I just feel it!"

"And how is . . . ah, your doctor's heart?"

Olivia laughed with delight. "Very tender," she said. "And exceedingly large."

"A diagnosis that even I might have made!"

"Keep us in your prayers."

"You're never out."

❧

"You seem worried about something, Father," said Ron Malcolm, who had been a prominent contractor in the area for many years. "It must be the loss of your dog. I know how much he meant to you."

Frankly, he hadn't had time to think of Barnabas, which some would call a blessing. But suddenly, this fact made him feel desperately guilty. Dear Stuart, he saw himself typing, I have given it better than a year, and believe it would be best if I offered my formal resignation right away . . .

"Well, I believe that's all I had to report," said Ron, standing up and looking at him with some concern.

"Thank you, my friend," said the rector, shaking hands. "Give my love to Wilma."

When he was alone, he sat down and put his head on his desk, like a schoolboy. What had Ron come to see him about? He felt as if his mind had been away on some vague errand during the entire visit.

He breathed a sigh of relief as he saw the papers Ron had left in his in-basket. Of course! The architect and Miss Sadie had come to loggerheads about the placement of the dining room. She wanted it to overlook the valley; the architect considered it more feasible to overlook the village. "How could we go wrong?" the rector asked aloud, thinking of the breathtaking beauty of both views.

As he attempted to study copies of the preliminary drawings, he couldn't bring them into focus. They were a blur, and he was shocked to see that his hand trembled as he held them.

❧

"I ain't eatin' n'more of that slop," said Dooley, who was sitting at the counter while the rector cooked dinner.

"Exactly what slop do you mean?"

"That ol' slop at school. Today, they give us meat loaf an' cherry pie."

His all-time school cafeteria favorite! What was wrong with people these days?

"Ever'body packs a lunch, sissies eat slop."

The rector shrugged. "So, pack a lunch."

"Me?"

"You."

Dooley scratched his head.

"Tell Puny what you need, she'll get it at The Local, and you're on your own. In any case, school will be out so soon, you'll hardly have time to fry up your bologna." School out! What on earth would he do with Dooley Barlowe for an entire summer?

Dooley was silent for some time, sitting on the counter stool and swinging his legs. "I got me a friend," he said at last.

"Aha! Tell me more."

"Name's Tommy."

"Tommy! I once had a friend named Tommy. Tommy Noles. Small world."

" 'e's got five birds, eleven ducks, one pig, and three dogs."

"No!"

"I told 'im he could come over here and spend th' night."

"You spoke hastily, but we can discuss it," said Father Tim, sautéing onions for the hamburgers. "What's Tommy like?"

Dooley thought hard. " 'e's got black hair."

"I can just picture him."

"Yoo hoo," someone called through the screen door. His heart galloped. It was his neighbor, carrying a dish covered with a tea towel. "Guess what?"

"Come in and we'll both guess," he said, opening the screen door.

"Hey," said Dooley.

"Hey, yourself," she replied. It had become their standard greeting. "I've changed my mind," she said, turning to the rector. "You don't need to bring me a mole if you catch one. Now, they've turned up in my lawn, the little beasts, and any passion I ever had for moles is over."

"Thanks be to God!" he said, laughing.

"Do you know how many moles Beatrix Potter drew?"

Nobody knew.

"One! Just one! Diggory Diggory Delvet. It seems perfectly clear that one can't build a career on moles."

"Indeed not."

"And while I've decided I can't possibly draw a mole, I did decide to cook one." She handed him the hot dish.

Dooley looked at her with alarm. " 'at's a ol' *mole* in 'at dish?"

"It certainly is! I found it under a bush, with its hideous little fossorial feet sticking up. Waste not, want not, is my motto."

"Cynthia, you wouldn't . . ."

"Oh, I probably wouldn't. But then again, I might." She tilted her head to one side and laughed.

"Let me see 'at ol' mole," said Dooley.

"You wouldn't know a mole if you met it in the street," said the rector, removing the tea towel. Inside the dish was a steaming gingerbread mole, with whiskers, tiny eyes, and little teeth, all made of lemon frosting. He was, of course, wearing a tab collar.

" 'at's funny," said Dooley, laughing. " 'at's pretty funny. Look at 'is ol' feet, ain't they funny!" Dooley threw his head back and laughed uproariously.

Dooley laughing!

Cynthia understood without being told, and her eyes gleamed.

Dooley laughing! His prayer had been answered so quickly, the rector felt his head fairly swim. "Have a glass of tea," he encouraged his neighbor.

"I'd love one," she said. "Dooley, you'd never guess what I did today."

"I don' know."

"Guess!"

"I cain't."

"Of course, you can. Guesses don't have to be right, they just have to be guesses."

Dooley looked at the floor and scraped the toe of his pumps. "Yanked a knot in ol' Vi'let's tail?"

"Nope. Although she certainly deserves it. Two more guesses. It's something I got that I've never had before. And both of them are brown."

"I hate 'is ol' guessin' poop."

"Men usually do, of course," she sighed. "So, I'll tell you. I've got two brown rabbits!"

"You ain't!"

"I have!"

"What'd you git 'em for?"

"To draw! I told Violet that she'd have to start looking for other employment. I cannot draw another Violet book to save my life, and I'm under contract for two more books this year!"

"Where're they at?"

"Dooley, your prepositions dangle terribly. They're at my house."

"Let's go see 'em."

She looked inquiringly at the rector. "I'll just put the lid on, and come with you," he said, happily. Rabbits! He felt as excited as a child.

"I can assure you," the principal had said, folding her arms across her chest, "that if school were not letting out, Dooley Barlowe would be expelled." She glowered at the rector, to make certain her point had been driven home. This was a solemn matter, and he should not, for one moment, forget it.

He hurried to the rectory from Mitford School, as if a dragon were breathing on his heels.

Buster Austin again. This time, in the cafeteria. Not a good, solid licking on the school ground. Oh, no. Nothing that simple and uncomplicated from Dooley Barlowe. It was an out-and-out dog fight in the cafeteria, with black eyes, a bloody nose, and mashed potatoes thrown in for good measure. "And," the principal had said, darkly, "after he threw the potatoes, he followed them with gravy."

What, exactly, had precipitated this brawl? The principal seemed to relish telling him that Buster Austin had called Father Tim a nerd.

Since Dooley had been sent home earlier, and was in his room behind a closed door, the rector decided to take his time about the matter. The day-to-day relationship with the boy was hard enough, much less the crises that arose without any warning whatsoever.

First things first, he thought, dialing the phone in his study.

"Cynthia," he said, "I'm calling because I think you have some wisdom about children, which I lack entirely. My question is this: What, exactly, is a nerd?" He listened intently. "Aha. Well. That's what I needed to know. You've been a great help, as ever. Yes, I'd love to see your rabbit drawings. I'll ring you soon. Yes. Thanks."

So that's what it meant! To tell the truth, he wouldn't mind giving Buster Austin a good hiding himself.

What was he to do about this, after all? Of course, a boy couldn't go around busting noses and slinging mashed potatoes, yet he'd already given him his walking papers once, and now, he'd clearly be required to give them again. The original walking papers had obviously lacked persuasion, but he had no idea what else to do. Hal Owen, perhaps? He'd raised a boy!

He was doing it again. He was pacing the floor in a circle.

Hello, Walter, he said in his ongoing imaginary conversation, Timothy here, I'm leaving in an hour, and I'll see you at the Shannon Airport as we discussed. I hope you've packed your walking stick. When am I planning to return? Walter, I am not planning to return. No, not at all. You see, there's a boy here who's driving me berserk, and a woman who's learned the trick of making my heart pound, and my dog has been violently snatched from me, and the list goes on. No, indeed, I am buying a small cottage, possibly with a thatch. Of course, I've heard that thatch attracts mice. . . .

Blast! He remembered Emma's wedding on Saturday, for which he'd rashly promised to bake a ham and oversee the flowers. For all his high talk and fancy education, he'd never learned to say one simple word: No.

There was a small knock at the door. He most assuredly did not want to see his neighbor. It came again, which made him oddly angry.

He opened the back door, and saw a girl with blond hair and large, gray eyes peering at him through the screen.

"Can Dooley come out?" she asked, wearing an expression of concern.

"I'm sorry, he can't," the rector replied.

"Thank you," she said, and went down the steps and through the hedge to Baxter Park.

Emma's wedding. Miss Sadie's love story. Cynthia's alarming proposal. And now a pretty visitor for Dooley. Was there some sort of epidemic?

He felt a sudden, burning thirst and drank a glass of water. Then he felt too fatigued to stand. He sat on the study sofa for some time. He simply didn't know what to do about Dooley's behavior. He would pray about it, leave it entirely to God, and trust him to control the outcome.

It was dusk when he climbed the stairs and knocked on Dooley's door.

"Yeah," said Dooley. He went in.

"We've got a lot of talking to do to smooth things out. But before that happens, there's something I'd like to say."

The boy looked up. His face was freshly bruised, but it was the old bruise in his spirit that the rector saw and felt.

"Dooley," he said simply, "I'd like to thank you for standing up for me today."

CHAPTER NINETEEN

A Love Story

"Come in, honey, we glad to see a young face aroun' this ol' folks home."

He hugged Louella with one arm, holding on to the gloxinia he'd picked up at Mitford Blossoms.

"What I got t' do wit' that?" asked Louella, who had just lost a finicky Boston fern.

"Set it in Miss Sadie's window, and water it once a week."

"I could jes' set it right here and let it get its own water. See yonder?"

He looked up to peeling paint and a dark stain on the ceiling. "That doesn't look good."

"That leak done filled two dishpans and a Dutch oven. Miss Sadie say let it pour, she don' care, long as we catch it in a bucket. Don' you think if she was plannin' to live awhile she'd be gettin' her a new roof?"

"Well . . ."

"An' if she was plannin' to keep livin', would she be in any hurry to tell you her love story?" Louella shook her head. "This whole thing got me worried."

Miss Sadie was sitting up in bed, against flowered cushions from her divan, looking bright and expectant in a satin bed jacket.

"Father! You've brought your famous gloxinia. Louella, if Father ever brings you a gloxinia, you are officially sick."

"Miss Sadie, you ain't officially sick."

"Oh, well, whatever. Sit down right here, Father." She patted the arm of a chair that had been pulled up to the bed. He put the flower pot on her sunny windowsill and happily did as he was told.

"Well, now, tell me," he said, unbuttoning his jacket, "*are* you sick?"

"Not one bit. I'm just tired. Some people get sick confused with tired. But I know tired when I see it, and that's what I am."

"All those years of eatin' froze' pies and white bread will make you tired," said Louella, putting her hands on her hips. "I'm goin' down and get lunch ready, and it's goin' to be greens cooked with a nice piece of side meat. Greens is full of iron, even if they do smell up the place, and they'll be good for what ails you, ain't that right, Father?"

She winked at the rector and left the room, closing the door behind her.

"She's the most encouragement in the world to me," said Miss Sadie, with satisfaction. "I'd been rattling around in this old house like a seed in a gourd. Now when I sneeze, there's always someone to say 'Bless you'!"

Someone to say bless you, thought the rector. There's a sermon title!

"I'm going to get out of this bed in a day or two and be good as new. But tell me about you. Are you missing your dog?"

"Terribly," he said. "I would never have dreamed. . . ." He cleared his throat, and they were silent for a moment. "I would never have dreamed that an animal could come to mean so much. Perhaps this sounds foolish, but Barnabas really did have a reflective soul. He was companionable in every way."

She looked at him intently. "You say he *was* companionable, and he *did* have a reflective soul. That is past tense." She held her hand out to him. "Life is so short, let's think in the present tense, shall we? I believe with all my heart you'll get your Barnabas back."

She smiled and pressed his hand, which he found immeasurably comforting.

"Thank you, Miss Sadie. You know I've come to hear your love story, if you're in the mood to tell it. All I have to do today is see Evie Adams, so we've plenty of time."

"Evie? What's Miss Pattie done now?"

"Gave the angel birdbath away."

"Oh, dear, that landmark birdbath! The last I heard, Miss Pattie had climbed out on the roof and was singing 'Amazing Grace' in her wrapper. I hope I never get old!"

"I believe you passed up the chance some time ago."

"The nursing home will make a difference, won't it, Father?"

"More than we can know."

"It's wonderful what comes to mind when you really stop and think. Lying here these last few days has helped me settle things. One is, I don't want to call it a nursing home. I know it will be a home, and the people in it will have to be nursed. But the whole thing has such a sad ring to it, we're going to call ours something else. Would you help me think of a name?"

"I will."

A breeze stirred through the open windows of the bedroom, with its high ceilings and cool, hardwood floors. On Miss Sadie's dressing table, Father Tim saw again the old photos in the silver frames. There was the face of the woman so eerily identical to Olivia Davenport. And the brooding, intense gaze of the young man named Willard Porter, whose grand house had been brought to ruin in full view of the whole village.

Miss Sadie took a deep breath.

"Father," she said, "what I'm about to tell you has never been spoken to another soul. I trust you will carry it to your grave."

"Consider it done," he said, solemnly, sitting back in the slipcovered chair, and finding it exceedingly comfortable.

"I've thought many times about where to begin," she said, folding her small hands and looking toward the open windows. "And while it doesn't have much to do with the rest of the story, my mind keeps going back to when I was a little girl playing in these apple orchards.

"You'll never know how I loved the orchards then, and the way the apples would fall on the grass and burst open in the sun. Then the bees would come, and butterflies by the hundreds, and the fragrance that rose from the orchard floor was one of the sweetest thrills of my life."

She lay back against the pillows and closed her eyes, smiling. "Do you mind if I ramble a bit?"

"I'd be disappointed if you didn't."

"I used to carry my dolls out under the trees. If you

walk down the back steps and go straight past the gate and the old wash house and then turn right—that was my favorite place. Louella's mother, China Mae, loved to go with me! Why, she played with dolls as if she were a little girl, herself. She was the most fun, so full of life. I was nine when we moved here from Wesley, into the new house Papa built, and China Mae was twenty. She was my very best friend on earth.

"She was so black, Father! I liked to turn her head in my hands to see the light play on her face, to see the blue in the black!

"She used to call me Little Toad. I have no idea why, I'd love to know. But I'll just have to find that out when I see her in heaven."

"I hope you're not planning to find that out anytime soon."

"Of course not! I'm going to live for ages and ages. I have things to do, you know."

The clock ticked on the dresser.

"Back then, there was a big house in Mitford, right where the Baptist church stands today. It's long gone, now, but it was named Boxwood, and oh, it was a pretty place. Miss Lureen Thompson owned that house, she was like me, an only child; her parents both died in a fall from a rock when they were out on a picnic. Their chauffeur was waiting in the car for them to come back, and they didn't come and didn't come, and when he went to look . . ." Miss Sadie shivered. "It was an awful thing, they say, Miss Lureen was so stricken. You know how she tried to get over it?"

He didn't know.

"Parties! There was always something fine and big going on at Miss Lureen's. And China Mae and I were always invited to come by and sample the sweets before a party. Her cook was as big as the stove, and her cream puffs were the best you ever tasted, not to mention her ambrosia. I have dreamed about that ambrosia several times. She used to make enough to fill a dishpan, because people took such a fit over it.

"Miss Lureen liked to say, 'The firefly only shines when on the wing. So it is with us—when we stop, we darken.' I never forgot that.

"Oh, we all loved Boxwood! It had so many servants hurrying about, and they all seemed so happy in their work. Miss Lureen was good to her people. Why, when her Packard wore out, do you know who she gave it to? Her chauffeur! He fixed it up good as new and drove it back to Charleston when she died.

"His name was Soot Tobin. Black as soot, they said. He was a big, strapping man with a stutter so bad he scarcely ever spoke, but when he did, people listened, colored and white, for his voice was as deep as the bass on a church organ. He made China Mae fairly giddy. 'Most everything he'd say, she'd just giggle and go on, to beat the band. You know, China Mae was not all . . . well, she never grew up, exactly, which is one reason I loved her so. She was just like me!

"One day I came home from school and I could not believe my eyes what had happened.

"China Mae would never have to play with my baby dolls again, for she had one of her own, just her color. It was lying asleep in the bed with her, and had on a little white gown. My mama was standing by the bed looking at that baby, with tears just streaming down her face.

" 'Sadie,' she said to me, 'This is Louella. God has sent her to live with us.' "

Miss Sadie shook her head and smiled at the rector. "Isn't that a surprise? To come home from school one day, and there's your second best friend of life, sent down from heaven?"

He laughed happily. If there was anything more amazing and wonderful than almost anyone's life story, he couldn't think what it was.

"Well, I took after that baby somethin' awful. I rocked her, I bathed her, I pulled her around in a little wagon, I sewed dresses for her, I was as happy as anything to have her to play with and love, and Mama was, too.

"When she got weaned, I started taking her to town. I'd dress her up myself, and they'd say, 'Here comes Sadie Baxter with that little nigger.'

"I never did like to hear that, even as a child. I wanted Louella to be my sister, I played like she was my sister, and then when I'd go to town, they'd say that. So, I stopped going.

"We stayed home and played and I never did miss going to town. Mama hired a tutor for me, anyway. Mr. Kingsley. I declare, he had the worst bad breath in the world, but he taught the prettiest cursive you ever saw, and was real good at history. Mama ordered off for all my clothes and shoes, and China Mae cut my hair, and we went to the doctor and dentist at Papa's lumber yard down in the valley. Or, sometimes, the doctors would drive up the mountain to give us our checkups, and Mama would put on a big spread like the president was coming.

"We called it 'Doctor Day,' and I didn't take to it one bit. I would grab Louella and we would run off and hide in the orchard."

Miss Sadie laughed to herself, with her eyes closed. Father Tim could see that she was watching a movie in which she was both the star and the director. He closed his eyes, too, and quietly slipped his feet out of his loafers.

"When Louella was about three, Mama said she was tired of going off and leaving her and China Mae at home when we marched off to Lord's Chapel. There were only a dozen or so colored people in Mitford, not enough for a church, I suppose. So, Mama said that from now on, we were all going together, that was what God gave us churches for.

"Papa didn't like this one bit, but Mama would not let up on him. She got down the Bible and the prayer book and without a shadow of a doubt, she showed him what was what.

"So, China Mae and Louella and Papa and Mama and me would walk down the road to the old Lord's Chapel that stood on the hill. And we would all sit in the same pew.

"If anybody ever once said 'nigger,' I don't know who it was, for they were scared of Papa. I mean, they respected him, not to mention that he gave a lot of money.

"In a little while, it seemed like nobody noticed anymore, it was just the most natural thing on earth. What they said outside the lych-gates, I don't know, but if China Mae missed a Sunday from being sick, lots of ladies would ask about her.

"Life was better in those days, Father, it really was. When China Mae did the wash in the wash house, and we put the fire under that big iron pot, why, it was an exciting event. China Mae had joy over making the clothes come clean, while people today would think it was drudgery. We kind of celebrated on wash day. Mama would make a pineapple upside-down cake, and Louella and I would make stickies out of biscuit dough and cinnamon and sugar, and after that big load of work was done, we all sat down and had a tea party."

A bird called outside the open windows, and a breeze filled the fragile marquisette curtains. Father Tim caught himself nodding off and sat upright at once.

"You know how the Bible is always talking about the poor? Twice every week, Mama went to see the poor. She would pack a big basket of the best things in the world and put her blue shawl on her head and go off walking to see the poor.

"She never let me go with her, not once, but she taught me some verses from Proverbs, the thirty-first chapter, 'She stretcheth out her hand to the poor; yea, she reacheth forth her hands to the needy. . . . She looketh well to the ways of her household, and eateth not the bread of idleness.' That was her favorite in the whole Bible; she said it was her model.

"Those golden days passed so quickly. I wanted to stay a child forever, but before I felt like I was awake real good, I was sixteen, and it was time to go abroad. Abroad! What a hateful word. I came to despise it. So many girls would have given anything to 'go abroad.'

"When I heard that Uncle Haywood had talked Papa into sending me, I was shocked, I felt betrayed. How could he send me away to another country? Mama was horrified, too, but she said it was for the best. I know I'd complained about Mr. Kingsley's bad breath a hundred times, but I didn't see that as a reason to change my schooling to the other side of the world!"

Miss Sadie opened her eyes. She was silent for a moment, gazing at the faded yellow roses on the wallpaper.

"I can just see Papa now. Right before we were ready to go down to Charleston to take the boat, he came in the front door. I remember all the luggage, the big trunks and the hat boxes, was stacked in the hall, and Papa came storming in and threw his hat on the table. He was burning mad, I had never seen him so mad. The veins stood out on his neck, and the top of his head was red as fire where the hair had thinned.

" 'Cur!' is what he said over and over. He was shouting. I thought a dog had bitten him! But oh, it was so much worse than that.

"Mama tried to make him sit down and drink a lemonade, it was so hot his shirt was sticking to him, it was August. But he wouldn't, and he started up again, saying things like 'scoundrel' and 'scum of the earth.'

"It turns out he'd been driving up from the lumber yard in the valley, and somebody had come speeding by him so fast, that Papa had run his Buick town car into a ditch, causing considerable damage to the beautiful grillework and the fenders."

Miss Sadie looked at the rector. "My papa was a good man, but he was not the kind of man you want to run off the road, and especially not into a ditch. You know, Father, times were different, then, and it was considered almost honorable for a man to hold a grudge against an injustice."

She sighed. "I don't suppose I have to tell you who it was that ran him off the road."

No. No, she did not. Father Tim glanced across the room at the photo of the handsome young Willard Porter, whose dark gaze seemed to pierce the room so forcibly that he might have been present, listening.

"Papa had to borrow a car to drive to Charleston, and in those days, people did not care to loan their cars, so that upset Papa even more. On the way, he talked about what had happened on Lumber Road. He just couldn't seem to get over it. He didn't know who had done it, he hadn't recognized the car, it was a new car, and fancy. And the more he talked about it, the less he acted like himself. Of course, he tried not to talk about me going away, because every time he did, he would cry a little.

"He'd never spent a night away from Mama since they were married, and it was a big sacrifice to give us both up at one time, for she was going with me—to stay 'til I got settled.

"You could have floated that big ol' boat on our tears!" Miss Sadie said, laughing. "And to think—buying all those fancy clothes and hats and steamer trunks, and going to Charleston in August, of all things, and taking that long trip across the ocean in that big storm that broke a freighter in two, and all those tear-stained, homesick letters—just to turn around and come home again, lickety split, in two months!"

"But look what it's given you to remember all these years."

With the only irony he had ever heard in her voice, she said, "Yes. But look what it did to my heart."

Suddenly, an alarm sounded so loudly that it caused his own heart to thunder. "Good Lord!" he exclaimed, thrusting his feet into his shoes and standing up at once.

"That's just Louella," she said, brightly. "Lunch must be ready. Father, dear, would you kindly turn your head and look toward the door?"

He did so, his ears ringing, as she got out of bed and put on her slippers and robe.

"Now you can look!" she said, going to the wall opposite her bed and grasping what appeared to be a drawer pull under a painting. A little door opened in the wall and Miss Sadie stuck her head inside. "Yes, Louella?"

"Miss Sadie!" he heard Louella's mezzo voice boom

up the shaft, "Do th' Father want vinegar on his greens?"

"Father, do you want vinegar on your greens?"

"I think not. A little butter, perhaps."

"Louella, he won't have vinegar, he'll have butter."

"Butter! I never heard of butterin' greens. Miss Sadie, y'all want your tea hot or cold?"

"Which is easier?"

"Cold's done fixed."

"Send cold," said Miss Sadie with some pleasure. "And remember he likes his plenty sweet."

"Ah, not anymore," said the rector, fidgeting.

"Louella, not anymore," his hostess shouted.

"What'd you say?"

"He doesn't like his tea too sweet anymore."

"No sugar," he said, feeling as miserable as if he had just delivered an elegy.

"No sugar in his tea, Louella. Are you coming up?"

"I'm eatin' right here in this kitchen. Do y'all want chow chow for your beans?"

"Yes, indeed," said the rector, pacing the floor.

"Chow chow, Louella, and plenty of it. Don't sound the alarm again, it nearly made him faint. Just knock twice with the broom handle and send it up."

He found that the discussion over lunch particulars had given him an odd twinge in his stomach, but the tea, when it came up on the silent butler, revived his spirits.

❧

"Father," said Miss Sadie, who was sitting up in bed, having finished her lunch, "you can't imagine how wonderful it is to have someone listen to me ramble. Did you ever think that just when people grow old and have so much to tell, that's when people want them to hush? I hope when you grow old, there'll be someone to listen to you ramble."

"I feel blessed to have people listen to me ramble every Sunday of my life," he said happily, folding his napkin and putting it on the tray.

"Oh, pshaw, you're so modest. You never give yourself enough credit, in my opinion. You don't ramble at all, you get right to the point, and it's always God's point, as far as I can see. But, do you know what I appreciate more than your sermons?"

"What's that?"

"The fact that you love us. Yes, that's enough for me, that you love us." She closed her eyes and let out a lingering breath. "Ahhh, the peace. What a blessing. Father, will you come again tomorrow? While I've got the hook in the water, you might say. I don't believe I have the strength to go to the end, today."

"I will. Right after lunch. Don't fix for me tomorrow. I'll bring you a doughnut from Winnie's."

"Just plain," murmured Miss Sadie. "Not fancy."

He went as quietly as he could across the creaking floor, and closed the door behind him.

❧

Miss Sadie was sitting in a slipcovered wing chair by the window, with an afghan over her knees. "I've been thinking all night," she said, "and I don't want to waste a minute."

He sat in the wing chair opposite her and unbuttoned his jacket. "I have until three o'clock, Miss Sadie. My time is yours."

"When Mama and I met Willard in Paris, we would never have dreamed he was the one who made Papa run off the road. He was so nice, so considerate, so genuine.

He had just moved to Mitford from Tennessee, and we learned from his conversation that his family had nothing to speak of. He was a boy who was trying to make the most of his God-given talents, and he was busy inventing things in the pharmaceutical field.

"One thing he'd invented was Formula R, which stood for Rose. Formula R was good to put on burns or wounds. It was an antiseptic, it just worked wonders, but it stung like fire.

"We had the sweetest times together in Paris. My mama was a wonderful judge of character, and while she had a soft heart, she couldn't be fooled. She thought Willard was a fine person. But when we got home, and we started telling Papa about the Mitford boy who befriended us in that faraway place, why, I thought he would have a stroke.

"I couldn't believe the horrible anger that welled up in him, something I had never seen before in my life. He said Willard Porter was trash, the lowest kind, an uneducated, penniless, heathen boy with no future and no breeding, and we were never to mention his name in our house again. He was so mean to Mama, as if she had betrayed him.

"I found out Papa had dealt with Willard after Willard came home from Paris, because, when I saw Willard driving around the monument one day, he acted as if he hadn't seen me.

"All the way over on the boat, I had dreamed of seeing him again, the fact that he lived in my hometown was . . . it was just too joyful for words. And then, to come home to that cold anger and rage, and a papa who hardly seemed the same person . . . .

"One day, China Mae brought me a note. It was folded up little bitty, and hidden in her dress. It was from Willard, and when I saw the handwriting, the same handwriting on the notes that came with the roses in Paris, I remember that my heart beat so wildly, I had to sit down.

"China Mae said, 'Don't you dare faint, faintin' is too white for words.'

"I still have the little note. It said: 'I have made the very worst mistake of my life. The incident on the road was inexcusable, and completely unintentional. I deeply regret that I have caused this strife, and am willing to do anything within my power to remove the memory of it. I have apologized to your father with heartfelt sincerity, but he will not hear me. I do not know what more can be done at this time. Please forgive me. Your faithful servant, Willard James Porter.'

" 'Mama,' I said, 'I think I love Willard.'

"She said, 'Don't even speak of it, don't let your heart think such a thing, it is impossible. This has changed your father in a way I don't understand.'

"Just like when I was a little girl, I stopped going to town. We ordered off for my clothes, just like always, and I didn't even cut my hair. Mama helped me study, and I played the piano and did needlepoint, and read books, and went to church every evening and lit a candle and knelt down and talked to God.

"You would have thought the heavens had been barricaded against me, as if God had said, 'Nail everything up good and tight, in case Sadie Baxter tries to get through.'

"It seemed a long time later that China Mae said someone was building a big house over in town, a big showplace, all white with porches and gables and even a widow's walk, though there was no ocean for hundreds of miles.

"Everybody at church was talking about it, and talking about Willard, how he had sold some of his pharmaceutical inventions, and how he was getting rich.

"Something awful happened to Papa when his name was mentioned at church, or wherever. You would think that the years would soften his heart toward a foolish, unfortunate incident, but it did not.

"You know, Father, looking back, Papa was a lot like Willard. He came from nothing, he had no special education, he was a rough man in many ways, but he refined himself and taught himself to speak well and read good books and travel in polite society, just like Willard.

"China Mae came home now and again, all excited. 'I seen 'im, Miss Sadie,' she'd say, 'I seen your Willard and he jus' th' han'somest man you ever laid eyes on.' He opened up a pharmacy on Main Street where Happy Endings is now. And one in Wesley, and two in Holding.

"I received a letter from him one day, out of the blue. I'd like to show this one to you. Would you be so kind, Father, to step to the dresser and look in the top drawer on the right?"

He opened the drawer and was struck by the scent of lavender that rushed out at him. He found the ivory envelope just where she said it was, and took it back to his chair by the window.

He removed the brittle stationery, unfolded it, and saw that the date at the top was June 13, 1927. He read aloud:

" 'My dear Sadie, I saw you go by yesterday, and though you did not see me, I was very touched by your sweetness and grace. I know it is risky to write to you, and have firmly emphasized to China Mae that you must burn this letter after reading it. I implore you to do so, as I take this liberty with the greatest concern for your happiness.

" 'I once said that when you grow up, I should like to marry you. Today, you are twenty-one, and I believe that is considered by all to be grown up.

" 'As for myself, I am twenty-six, my business is at last going well, and I am beginning to make a place for myself, my mother, and my little sister. For the first time, it is possible for me to marry, and yet it is impossible for me to marry the one I love devotedly and think about night and day.

" 'I do not know your feelings for me, except what China Mae has confided—please, I beg you, do not punish her for speaking out of turn.

" 'I have tried again and again to think of a way to change your father's mind toward me, but I come each time to the same bitter conclusion. He despises me, and anything I might try to do to win your hand would only bring turmoil and despair to you and to your mother.

" 'You may know that I am building a house in the village, on the green where Amos Medford grazed his cows. Each stone that was laid in the foundation was laid with the hope that I might yet express the loving regard I have for you, Sadie.

" 'It is bold to write you so, but I am filled with a longing on this, your twenty-first birthday, that is nearly inexpressible.

" 'I am going to give this house a name, trusting that things may eventually be different between us. I will have it engraved on a cedar beam at the highest point in the attic, with the intention that its message may one day give you some joy or pleasure.

" 'Perhaps, God willing, your father will soon see that I have something to offer, and relent. Until then, dear Sadie, I can offer only my fervent love and heart-felt devotion.'"

Father Tim sat for a time, silently, and then put the letter back into the ivory envelope.

She turned her head and looked out the window. It was a warm, bright spring day. "Such a waste," she said simply.

He waited.

"I prayed for Papa, for God to give him a new heart, like He gave Saul. But He did not. In those days, twenty-one was an old maid, and I believe Papa was sometimes sorry that no one courted me. But there was no one, you see, there was only Willard. And then . . . two or three years later, there was Absalom Greer."

Miss Sadie's eyes twinkled. "Absalom Greer! Another uneducated man! I never could get it right. Which, of course, is why Uncle Haywood wanted me to go off to Paris, France, and then debut in Atlanta, where I'd meet all those fancy boys. He told Papa if I stayed in Mitford I would wind up an old maid—or with dishpan hands, married to a farmer!

"I never did like Uncle Haywood," she said, flatly. "By the way, did you bring my doughnut?"

"Your doughnut!" said the rector, patting his jacket pocket and bringing out a bag that had mashed rather flat. "I'm sorry to say Winnie was out of doughnuts, all she had left was the holes, so I brought you four!"

"Four doughnut holes," said Miss Sadie, solemnly, peering down into the bag. "They can't be very filling, can they?"

She laughed suddenly, and for the first time, he saw the girl she had been. It lasted only a moment, the face of the girl, but it was there, and something in him connected with the young Sadie.

"Absalom Greer worked for Papa at the lumber yard. Of course, I never went down there much, but when I did, I liked it. I had taken to sitting rather gloomily around the house, just to show Papa how wicked he'd been, and how I hadn't forgotten what he'd done.

"He said that what I needed was fresh air and hard work. So, he took me down to the lumber yard, and put me in his office and opened all the windows, and that was the fresh air.

"Then he sat me down with an adding machine and ledgers, and that was the hard work!

"I have made Papa sound like a mean man. But oh, I loved him, and he could be such fun. Some days, he would just relax and laugh and pet me to beat the band. But no matter how hard he tried, he could not teach me to keep those hateful books.

"One day, a young man knocked on the office door and I opened it and there he was—a big, tall boy, as slim as a bean pole, wearing a cap and carrying a Bible. There was a kind of electricity about him. He looked down at me and said, 'Miss Sadie Baxter, are you saved?'

"Why, I declare I didn't know what on earth he was talking about! I looked straight up at him and said, 'Well, I'm not lost!'

"He was the cutest thing, so tall and jovial, he had the heartiest laugh and the nicest smile, and knew how to talk plain talk. I just felt so at home with him, like I had a brother, and he was so excited about the Lord and about the Bible. Once, Papa came in and Absalom was sitting there reading me a Bible story on his dinner break. He didn't miss a beat, he just raised his voice and read louder.

"Papa went and sat down at his desk, he was

amazed. I don't think he knew what to do about it, so he didn't do anything. It kind of made me nervous, but Absalom read all the way to the end of Second Samuel, then got up, put his Bible under his arm, tipped his cap, and went back to work."

Father Tim laughed with delight. That was another picture of the boy who had been delirious with God, the one who had come home from the silver mine and been knocked out of bed one night with a "two-by-four," and had gotten up, at last, to answer God's call.

"Every day at dinnertime—we called it dinner, then, you know—Papa was usually out on the yard, and Absalom would come in and read to me. What a beautiful voice he had, and how hard he tried to polish his diction and improve his speech! It was a wonderful thing to watch, someone with so little schooling, and so much yearning.

"Then came the day he asked if he could court me. 'Ask Papa,' I said, with fear and trembling. I had never been courted in my life, and I was nearly twenty-five years old. My father was the richest man in Mitford or Wesley, and a laborer out of his lumber yard was asking to court me. I didn't see one ray of hope in it.

"I remember I was so excited and upset, I ran to the back door and heaved up, if you'll pardon the expression, Father.

"The next morning, on the way to the yard, Papa was looking straight ahead at the road and he said, 'Sadie, Absalom Greer has asked if he can court you. What do you think about it?'

"I couldn't believe my ears that Papa was asking me what I thought about something. I said, 'Papa, I have prayed about it, and I would like to be courted by Absalom Greer.' My heart beat so hard I thought I would pass out, but I always remembered that China Mae thought fainting was too white for words, so I never did it.

" 'Well, then,' Papa said, 'I am going to give him my permission.'

" 'Papa,' I said, 'thank you for your permission, but what I would covet is your blessing.'

"He must have given it to us, for Absalom was allowed to come to our house, he ate Sunday supper with us before he preached in the evenings, and often, I'd go with him and sit on the front row. We were allowed to drive Papa's town car on special occasions, and once, Papa gave Absalom a beautiful suit that was cut too slim, and it fit Absalom like it was made for him! I'll never forget what Mama said, she said, 'My! You look like a Philadelphia lawyer!' That pleased Absalom so much.

"You should have heard him preach, Father! Why, he'd take the fuzz off a peach. Lord's Chapel hadn't had a fine preacher for a long time, and I was starved nearly to death to hear such wondrous things—about salvation and redemption and Christ's suffering for me.

"Absalom made it all so personal, as you often do, and under his preaching, the Bible came alive for me. He was the one who tried to teach me the great meaning of Philippians four-thirteen."

A banner verse, he thought, smiling.

"But Absalom was like a brother . . . I still loved Willard. Now that I was getting out and about more, I would often see Willard, and the pain of that was very deep. His house was finished, of course, and the most beautiful sight in town—it was more wonderful than Boxwood.

"They said Willard worked all the time; even though

he joined the new country club, all he did was work. He joined the Presbyterian church, and he worked over there, too. Why, he helped them raise enough money for a new building in a little over a year, and in those days, that was something to crow about.

"All this time, Rose wasn't doing well. They didn't know much about her disease, and they still don't, I'm told. But he took such good care of her, and then his mother passed away, and it was just the two of them in that grand house, a lonely man and a confused girl. Father, there were times when my heart was so broken for him that I wanted nothing more than to knock on his door and go in to him, and never leave.

"But something happened after a while, after two or three years of courting Absalom. It wasn't that I no longer cared for Willard, but the caring had worn me out. I was very tired from caring so much and loving so much and hoping."

She took a sip of water from a glass on the window sill.

"Papa and Mama had come to like Absalom, and even though he had no money, and probably never would, they were happy with things, and all the hurt and the anguish seemed . . . in the past. I would not have wanted to upset that delicate balance for anything in the world.

"When I'd see Willard, he would tip his hat to me, though rumor had it that Papa had threatened to kill him if he ever spoke to me. It's a hard thing to have to change your opinion of someone you love, and my opinion of Papa was changing, no matter how hard I tried to hold it back. It was like trying to hold back the ocean.

"The lumber business got awful bad, and I don't think our finances had ever recovered from the money that was spent on Fernbank. You've never seen the little ballroom with the painted ceiling, it's been closed up all these years, but that alone cost a fortune. The man who painted it came from Italy and lived here thirty-four months. And of course, just look at all this millwork. Nobody in western North Carolina had finer, except Mr. Vanderbilt, of course.

"Father, you know how word gets around in a small town, and the word got around about our circumstances, and Willard heard it, and he approached Papa and offered to buy him out. I know why Willard did that, it was one way of saying, here, let me give you a good price for your business and save your face, and make things right after all these years.

"But Papa didn't take it that way. It made him so angry, thinking that Willard pitied him, that we thought he was going to have a heart attack.

"Mama said, 'I am sick and tired of this hateful, evil battle between you and a man who made a foolish mistake and lived to regret it and said so. I will no longer tolerate the dark spirit it brings into this house and into my husband, and into the heart of my child, and I beg you in the name of all that's holy to meet with Willard Porter and face him like a gentleman and settle your differences and ask God to forgive you.'

"That was the single boldest thing I ever heard my mother say.

"Do you know that my father bowed his head and wept? Mama went and stood beside him and put her arm around him and I dropped down at his feet and clasped my arms around his legs, and we all cried together. China Mae was standing outside the door and tears were streaming down her face, and she was praying and thanking God."

Miss Sadie drew a handkerchief from her robe pocket and touched her eyes.

"It's all as clear to me as if it happened yesterday. I remember the fire was crackling in the fireplace, and Papa said we'd need more wood, they were calling for a big drop in the temperature, it was January. He stood up and hugged us both, and Mama said, 'Why not see if you can meet with Mr. Porter now, while your resolve is fresh, and come home to the night's sleep you've been needing for so long.'

" 'I'll do it,' he said, and I remember that I trembled as he rang the operator and asked for Willard Porter.

"He told Willard he had to go to church to take care of something, he was the senior warden, and it would be a fitting place to settle their differences, if he'd care to meet him there.

"It was awkward for Papa, I could tell. Mama was standing beside me, holding onto my arm for dear life, I don't think she drew a breath 'til that phone call was ended.

"I don't know why, but I was very troubled. Mama went to her room to pray and asked me to pray, and I did, I got on my knees beside my bed. Then, I got up and put on my alpaca cape with the hood, and my fur gloves—it was very cold—and I let myself out the front door.

"I just started walking to the church. And even though it was pitch dark, it was nearly like walking from my dining room to the kitchen, it was all so familiar to me. I don't know what I expected, or why I went, I just seemed pulled along. I remember how loud my heart was beating in my ears.

"Ice had formed all along the road, in some places it was slippery and dangerous, and I just kept walking in that bitter cold and grave darkness.

"You know where the old steps are in the stone wall along Church Hill Drive? Well, I went up those icy steps, holding on to the railing, and I could see that Papa's and Willard's cars were parked in the back of the church, because the moon came out all at once."

Miss Sadie pulled the afghan up around her shoulders, and shivered slightly. Father Tim was suddenly aware that she looked very old, something he'd never seemed to notice before.

"When I reached the door, I heard their voices, and they were not the peaceful voices I had longed to hear, they were angry and shouting. Papa was accusing Willard of trying to humiliate him in front of the town, and Willard said he had come to make peace, and he didn't care to hear any more insults and lies.

"The door was standing open and I could see them so clearly. Papa had lit an oil lamp, it was sitting on the little table at the back of the nave, and I remember a strong smell of linseed oil that came off the floors; they'd just been done for a wedding the next Sunday.

"Papa was standing on one side of the table, and Willard was standing on the other. I wanted to rush in and stop them from arguing, but I felt frozen to the spot. I knew that Papa had left the house with the truest of intentions in his heart, but somehow the Enemy had snared him along the way.

"Papa swung his fist at Willard, and Willard stepped back. Papa's arm sent the oil lamp reeling off the table, and it dashed against the floor, and an awful flame leaped up. It was all so sudden, and so horrible, I cannot tell you how quickly that sheet of flame raced across the oiled floor. I felt that the very soul of evil had been unleashed. And still I could not move, though I remember I heard myself screaming.

"I turned and ran home as fast as I could, falling on the ice, and trying to keep to the sides of the road where it wasn't so slick.

"I turned around and looked back once, and I saw the church lighted up inside. It was so horrible, I shall never forget that sight as long as I live. For years I prayed I might die, so that the memory of it would be erased.

"I crept into the house and went upstairs and looked out my window. The flames were already leaping around the wooden walls, and it seemed the fields were lighted up for miles around.

"They said that when the fire truck came, the water was frozen, and there was no way to do anything but watch it burn. Water everywhere was hard as stone, and there was only that searing flame licking the frozen hilltop."

Miss Sadie closed her eyes, and let out a shuddering sigh. " 'They have cast fire into thy sanctuary,' " she quoted slowly from the Seventy-fourth Psalm, " 'they have defiled by casting down the dwelling place of thy name to the ground.' " She rested her head against the cushion of the chair.

The clock ticked in the room, and the rector felt his heart beat dully. How had this small woman contained this large secret for so long?

"My father," she said, keeping her eyes closed, "told the firemen he had gone to church to check the pipes because of the freezing temperatures, and when he arrived, he found it already burning. Willard Porter had left the scene and no one knew he'd been there.

"They suspected arson.

"The grief that I suffered was nearly unendurable, I could not get out of bed. In fact, it was this very bed in this very room. I kept the draperies closed and lived as if in a dream. I felt invalid, and frail; I began to creep about like an old woman. I couldn't confide to China Mae, my best friend, and certainly not to Louella, nor say a word to Mama, whose worry over me nearly drove her to the breaking point. I refused to see Absalom, yet one day, he delivered a note to the house, asking me to marry him.

"Marry!" Miss Sadie shook her head. "I knew at last, full well, that I would never marry.

"My father never revealed the truth to anyone, and he was so gravely stricken with guilt and shame that I thought he might die. The doctor drove up the mountain to Fernbank regularly, we were all so ravaged by our secrets and our sorrows. For me, it wasn't just all that I'd seen, and the knowledge of Papa's deceit, there was also an awful sadness over the loss of Lord's Chapel, the sweetest church in Mitford.

"It was a very long time until I learned that Papa had commanded Willard to leave the scene of the fire, and Willard, for all those years, was willing to protect Papa. He never said a word. He took the truth to his grave in France.

"It seemed that Satan himself had come against us. I thought Louella would never get over the horror of that time. Our faith did not shine through, Father, even my mother was broken by the burden of what she could not understand."

She reached for the glass on the window sill and took another sip of water.

"Papa's business regained its footing, and he rallied to raise the money to build Lord's Chapel on Old Church Lane. He bought your little stone office, which had been an ice house, and gave it to the parish. The rectory was already owned by the church, and standing where it is today. When the time came, Papa gave the pews and the organ, and put the roof on the nave and sanctuary, that was before the parish hall. And he had the gardens dug and planted.

"I feel that Papa would have let me marry Willard, at last, but it was too late. Oh, it was so late. When the war started, of course, Willard went away to serve, and he was killed in France and buried there." She paused, gazing out the window. "And Absalom? Well, I scarcely ever saw him again. I know that his sister, Lottie, could not find it in her heart to forgive me, for I hurt him, and she loved him so.

"When Papa and Mama died, I did perhaps the only independent thing I had ever done in my life." She looked at him and smiled weakly. "I moved across the aisle and started sitting on the gospel side."

She slumped a little in the chair. He leaned forward and reached for her hand, which felt small and cold.

"That's my love story, Father. I'm sorry it did not have a happier ending. The nursing home will give it a happy ending. The building will be given in honor of Mama and Papa. The beautiful fountain out front will be in memory of Captain Willard James Porter. It will be a place of solace and peace, a place for healing."

Father Tim got up from his chair and placed a hand on her fragile shoulder. "Father," he prayed, "I ask you to heal any vestige of bitter hurt in your child, Sadie, and by the power of your Holy Spirit, bring to her mind and heart, now and forever, only those memories which serve to restore, refresh, and delight. Through Jesus Christ, your Son our Lord, Amen."

"Amen!" she said, reaching up to put her hand on his.

❧

"Y'all been talkin' so long, you mus' be dry as two bones."

Louella set a tray on the foot of the bed and handed out tall glasses of tea with bright circles of lemon.

"Thank you, Louella, please sit down. The deed is done."

"Thank you, Jesus!" said Louella, and sat down on Miss Sadie's blue silk vanity bench.

"Have a doughnut hole, Louella," said Miss Sadie, extending the bakery bag. "Father?" she said, offering him one also.

How much harm could the hole of a doughnut do? he wondered, reaching into the bag.

"That," Miss Sadie exclaimed happily, "leaves two for me!" The rector noticed that her color was returning. "Oh, Father, something I've been meaning to ask you. You know that lovely woman who looks like Mama? Olivia Davenport, I think her name is. I'd like to give her Mama's hats; she wears a hat with such style. You know, there's no family to pass them on to, and there are just so many beautiful hats up in the attic, going to waste. Do you think it would be an insult?"

"Why, no. No, I don't. I think Olivia might be very glad to have those hats. Perhaps you could call her and talk to her. I believe she'd welcome hearing from you, she's rather shut in, you know."

"She's going to get a new heart, isn't she?"

"God willing. She's on a waiting list, but she has a rare blood type, and the heart could come from any-where in the world. The trick is getting it to her—or her to it—in time."

"A new heart! How thrilling! I will pray for her, Father, and I'll call her in the next day or two. Could you run them over to her, if she's interested? Would you mind? I could get Luther to take them in the pickup, but he hurt his back and can't drive."

"We'll most certainly work it out," he said, draining the tea glass and standing. He bent down and kissed Miss Sadie on the forehead.

"Take good care of one another," he said. "I'll be in touch."

Louella followed him out the door and closed it behind her.

She walked with him to the foot of the stairs. "Father," she said, speaking in a low voice, "Miss Sadie ain't th' only one got a secret t' carry to th' grave. I got one of my own, and somethin' tells me I better let you have it, jus' in case."

Good heavens, thought the rector. No wonder he had never felt the need to devour mystery and suspense stories. Nearly every day he encountered mysteries and suspense galore.

"If I was you, I wouldn't let Miss Olivia and Miss Sadie get too thick. You know how folks always say 'who was yo' mama and yo' granmaw and where was you born at,' an' all. One thing might lead to another, and 'fore you know it, Miss Sadie might fin' out some-thin' that would put her down, for sure."

He was afraid to ask. "And what is that?"

"That her mama done had a little baby 'fore she married Miss Sadie's daddy. And that little baby growed up and was the granmaw of Miss Olivia."

Louella peered closely at the rector's face.

"Now, don't take me wrong, Miss Sadie's mama, she was a saint, she used to go roun' to th' poor just like th' Bible axe us to. An' th' poor she was mostly

goin' roun' to was that little girl, who didn't live too
far from Fernbank, kep' by a lady from Alabama. That
little girl had th' name of Miss Lydia. Well, she
growed up and had Miss Caroline and Miss Caroline
done had Miss Olivia, an' far as I know, don' nobody
know nothin', they smoothed it out so. You know
what's sad?"

"What's that?" asked the rector, who had heard so
much of sadness today.

"Miss Sadie always talkin' 'bout how she got no kin,
when her own kin livin' right down th' hill—and Miss
Olivia thinkin' she got no kin, either!"

"Louella, thank you for telling me this. Will you
agree with me in prayer?"

"Honey, you know I will!"

"The psalmist tells us that God 'setteth the solitary
in families.' Let's pray that it might please God to make
these two a family, in His own way."

"Cast yo' bread on th' waters . . ." said Louella, grinning broadly.

"And sometimes," replied the rector, "it comes back
buttered toast."

He drove along Church Hill Drive, beside the stone
wall that led to the ruined church. He would never again
be able to look at that hilltop without a kind of sorrow.
His particular job sometimes revealed more to him than
he wanted to know.

There, he thought, as he made the right-hand turn
into Old Church Lane, was where he'd first come panting up the hill in his new jogging suit from the Collar
Button. That innocent time seemed long ago.

He felt a keen anguish over Barnabas, as he drove

slowly down the hill, but reminded himself that, after all, Barnabas was only a dog.

Only a dog? Instantly, he realized where this perverse thought had come from. He'd stood by the cages with his father, surveying in frozen alarm the dead bodies of his entire herd. "There's no use to grieve," his father had said, coldly, "they're only rabbits."

He'd learned that one obstacle to childlike faith in a heavenly father was bitter disappointment in earthly fathers. No, not everyone had that obstacle to faith, which was clearly a favorite of the Enemy, but Miss Sadie had had it, and he had had it and come to terms with it, and forgiven his father, long years ago.

His research for the paper on Lewis revealed this had been a major obstacle for the apologist. One commentator had said, "For years, Lewis had not been able to forgive himself for his failure to love his father, nor had he been able to appropriate God's forgiveness for this sin. But when finally enabled, he was almost incredulous of the peace and the ease he experienced."

He glanced vaguely at the rose arbors that had come into bloom along Old Church Lane. The Rose Festival! He still had no inkling of what to talk about.

The War of the Roses? No, there was enough talk of war in this world.

He would think about it all later, perhaps in the evening when Dooley was asleep. Of course, what he really needed to think about was what to do with Dooley for the summer. And then, there was always what Cynthia had asked him to think about.

He felt oddly relieved to arrive at the office and have the peace of it to himself.

He checked his phone messages and calendar. Meet with the Altar Guild at three o'clock about designs for needlepoint kneelers to replace the ancient leather-covered cushions. Dinner at Wilma and Ron Malcolm's, with Dooley in tow, tomorrow evening. Drop by The Local and pick up a ham to bake for the Newland reception on Saturday. Should he have warned Miss Sadie, who was hoping to be there, that Absalom Greer would be there also?

A note from Emma said: "Winnie expecting you. Olivia fine. Russell behaving. Rabbit food on sale."

As he took the cover off his Royal manual, to type a quick note to Stuart Cullen, he heard a thunderous sound out front, and felt the building shake. There was the explosive whooshing of air brakes, and, in a moment, a loud rap on the door. He opened it to see a truck as vast as an auditorium parked in the street.

"Yes?" he inquired of a large, bearded man with a cut of tobacco in his jaw.

"Bells," said the driver, handing him a clipboard with a delivery slip.

CHAPTER TWENTY

Baxter Park

Puny had set up the ironing board in his bedroom, so she could press the drapes that had been folded over a hanger for two years. Dooley had promised to help her hang them in the afternoon. "I seen that big mess in th' churchyard," she said. "What *is* all that stuff, anyway?"

"Bells. Bells under a tarp, delivered without warning, and nobody to put them in the tower 'til next Wednesday."

"I thought Emma was gittin' married Saturday. That don't look too good with a weddin' goin' on."

"No kidding." He was going through his pants pockets and making a pile for the dry-cleaning truck.

"That ham you got is a whopper. You want me to bake it Friday?"

"I'd be beholden to you if you would."

"I'll use my pineapple glaze that Joe Joe . . . I mean, ah . . . oh well." She flushed beet red.

"Joe Joe, is it?"

"Shoot!" she said, "I didn't mean to let that out."

"And why not? Have you forgotten who prayed for a parade, out of the goodness of his heart?" He was so pleased with her unintentional confession that he could scarcely contain his smug delight.

"I don't think it's right to talk about things like that 'til you know what's goin' on with somebody. That's what Mama said. She courted our daddy a whole year before she talked about it." Frowning, she pulled the heavy, lined drapery panel off the ironing board. "I wish you'd help me put this thing over the chair back, it weighs a ton."

"I've never understood exactly how you keep something like that under cover," he said. He took one end and helped her spread it over the other panels.

"Oh, come on, now," she said, winking hugely at him, "you do know, too. I mean, look at you!"

"What do you mean, look at me?"

"I mean your neighbor is what I mean, ha, ha."

"Ha, ha, yourself," he said, feeling the color steal into his face.

"Somebody said y'all were out walkin' th' other night, right on Main Street."

"Walking on Main Street is hardly keeping anything under cover. Can't two people go for a stroll without causing tongues to wag?"

Puny laughed. "Tongue waggin's 'bout th' only action y'all git over here in Mitford!"

"Now, now. Don't be pulling any of your Wesley high-hat on me, young lady."

"Anyway, I think she's real cute. I like 'er. She's different."

"I agree."

"With what? That she's real cute or that she's different?" Puny's eyes gleamed with mischief.

"I sincerely hope you don't persecute Joe Joe this way," he said, finding two quarters and a dime in a pants pocket. "And speaking of parades, do you find Joe Joe to be a drum and bugle corp, a marching band, or the fire engines?"

"Joe Joe," she said rapturously, "is the Santy Claus at the end, with a big sack of presents, throwin' candy to th' kids."

He was on his hands and knees, searching under the dresser for the dime that rolled across the floor. "That's as lavish a compliment as I've ever heard, I believe."

"He's nice, he's got manners, an' he's got a job. Not to mention good-lookin'."

He stood up, smiling at her. "I agree with all that, and then some. You have my blessing without even asking for it."

"And you," she said, grinning, "have mine."

❧

"Father," said the caller, "Pete Jamison."

"Pete! I'm glad to hear your voice."

"Just wanted to call and check in. I'm in St. Paul. How are you?"

"Good! Can't complain. And you?"

"Not bad. They just gave me an award for the most sales in the first quarter. Considering that this time last year, I had the fewest sales . . ."

"Pete, congratulations. You can't know how I like hearing that."

"Well, Father, you probably won't like hearing this. You know the four things you told me to do when I left that day?"

"Pray. Read your Bible. Be baptized. Go to church."

"Well, I'm going to church. But I've got to tell you that it's full of hypocrites."

Father Tim laughed. If there was ever a popular refrain in modern Christendom, that might be it.

"My friend, if you keep your eyes on Christians, you will be disappointed every day of your life. Your hope is to keep your eyes on Christ."

"Yes, well . . ."

"I will disappoint you, Pete, they will disappoint you, but He will never disappoint you."

"I was about to say to heck with it."

"Don't quit! Are you reading your Bible?"

"Ah, well . . . I was."

"And then you quit."

"You got it."

"Then you can expect to be weak on one of your flanks, and that's precisely where the Enemy will come after you with a vengeance."

"I hear you."

"When are you coming back this way?"

"Soon, I hope. My territory's so big, it's stretching me like a rubber band."

"Keep your faith and you won't snap," said the rector, as Harold Newland walked in with the morning mail and handed him the day's packet. "Excuse me, Pete. Thank you, Harold, see you Saturday." Harold blushed deeply. Right on top, a letter from the man in the attic, with the return address of a federal prison.

"Pete," said Father Tim, "do you have a brother?"

"No, sir. Always wanted one, though."

"You've got one, now. Let me tell you a story."

"Well," Dooley said, slamming his book bag on the kitchen counter, " 'at's 'at."

"That's what?"

"Dern school's out."

"Of course! I'd clean forgotten."

"I tol' Tommy he could spen' th' night t'night."

"We were going to talk about that first. Why did you invite him without talking about it first?"

"I forgot."

Forgot! Well, and so had he. After all these weeks of lamely trying to figure what to do about Dooley when school was out, he'd completely forgotten that, this very day, it was out, period. And here he sat, reading the *Anglican Digest*.

It was enough to make him squirm with guilt, if he'd been so minded. Didn't everybody else have something clearly mapped out for their charges for the summer? Positive things like jobs, and earning money, and opening savings accounts, and sticking to a reading program, and maybe going to camp. Camp! He was astounded that the most obvious thing of all had only at this moment occurred to him. Would he never get this right?

"Put your things away, and we'll have a snack. Then we'll walk up and see your grandfather, take him his livermush."

He heard Dooley bound up the stairs. His face had not shown it, but surely he must be nearly ecstatic with his new freedom. He remembered some of his own ecstasy at the letting out of school and yes, it had to do with friends. Certainly Tommy could come.

Friends, however, could not solve the entire problem of what to do with a summer. For him, those years ago in Holly Springs, there had always been something to look forward to, a project, perhaps, something definite.

He picked up the phone. "Dora," he said to his friend at the hardware, "got any rabbits on hand?"

❧

He had brought home the cage containing one sleek, curious black and white Flemish Giant, and put it on the back porch stoop, when the phone rang.

"Father?" said Miss Sadie. "I've been thinking. School was out yesterday, and I was wondering if Dooley would like a job for the summer? You know there's lots to do at this old place."

"Miss Sadie," he said, "let me talk to him about that. I may put him to work in the church gardens."

When he saw Cynthia at The Local, they stopped to visit by the produce bins. She'd been asked to read from her books at the library, as part of a summer cultural program, and was radiant at the prospect.

Before they went along their separate aisles, she said, "I've been thinking. My basement could use a good clean up. Do you think Dooley would be interested? And we could dig some flower beds in the back, Uncle left it a jungle out there. Oh, and maybe the two of us could build a rabbit hutch. I'd pay him, of course, and teach him to watercolor!"

"Watercolor? Dooley?"

"Well, and why not?"

Why not, indeed?

Later, Hal Owen dropped by the rectory.

"Came to town to pick up a package of serum, hadn't seen you in a while, since we've been skipping the coffee hour. How are you, Tim?"

"Not bad, considering."

"Considering what?"

"Considering that I have a boy who needs proper

guidance, wisdom, direction, instruction, discipline, and last but not least, something to do for the summer."

"That's why I came," said Hal, grinning, and taking out his pipe. "We thought you might let Uncle Dools spend a few weeks at Meadowgate."

When the rector walked back to the hardware to pick up the rabbit food he'd left sitting on the counter, he ran into Dooley's teacher.

"Miss Powell, how did we do this year?"

"I've seen some positive changes in Dooley," she said, smiling. "But he has a way to go."

"And, ah, which way do you think he might be going?"

"Oh, I clearly see an outstanding ability in math, if you'll help him stick with it. He also proved to be a pretty tough slugger on the ball field. And then, there's his singing."

"Singing?"

"Why, yes. We coaxed him into mixed chorus a few weeks ago, I've been meaning to tell you that. He has a marvelous voice, and great timing. It may be a gift."

Dooley singing! How extraordinary.

"Jena," he said, calling his Sunday school supervisor at home, "have we ever thought of forming a young people's choir?"

"Well, we've thought of it, but somehow, it just hasn't happened."

"Would you be kind enough to make it happen?" he asked.

❧

He saw Barnabas at the opposite end of the field, running toward him. "Come on, boy," he yelled. "Come on, fella!" But though Barnabas ran and ran, he remained at the opposite end of the field. He tried to run himself to the great, black, barking dog, but felt as if he were trapped, waist high, in Mississippi mud. In an agony of frustrated longing, he exerted a shuddering effort that seemed to force his very heart to burst.

When he awoke, bathed in sweat, Dooley was standing over his bed, looking stricken. "Why'd you go t' hollerin' f'r 'at ol' dog? 'at ol' dog's gone!" he said severely.

"That old dog is *not* gone!" he exclaimed, with sudden anger.

"You like t' scared th' poop outta me."

"The poop is precisely what you *need* to have scared out of you," he declared, unbuttoning his pajama top. He hated those dreams in which he found himself bound like a mummy, unable to move, his heart pounding like a hammer. "Go back to bed," he told the boy, who was still trying to peer into his face.

"I ain't, 'til you quit hollerin'."

"I've quit, for heaven's sake. Haven't you ever had a nightmare?"

"I've had plenty of them ol' things," said the boy, climbing into bed with him.

"Well, then, you understand." He lay back against the pillows, and glanced at the clock. Four a.m.

"I had one of them dreams th' other night at th' farm. I was dreamin' m' little brother Kenny had fell in th' creek and turned into a fish an' I was runnin after 'im along th' bank, hollerin', 'Kenny, Kenny, come back, don't be a fish, don't leave me!' an' Miz Owen said I woke up Rebecca Jane, but that was all right, she come in and talked t' me."

"Do you miss your brother?"

"Yeah. He was my best friend."

Dear God! Five children wrenched apart like a litter of cats or dogs.

"Tell me about your brothers and sisters."

"There's Jessie, she's th' baby, still poopin' in 'er britches, and Sammy, he's five, he stutters. Then, there's ol' Poobaw . . ."

"What does Poobaw mean?"

"Means he took after a pool ball my mama brought home, had a eight on it, she said it was a keepsake. Poobaw hauled 'at ol' thing around, went t' sleepin' with it, an' that's where 'is name come from, it used t' be Henry."

"What's Henry like?"

"Wets 'is bed, 'e's seven."

He dreaded this. "Do you know where they are?"

"Mama said she'd never tell nobody, or th' state would come git 'em. I was th' last'n t' go." There was a long silence.

If it wrenched his own heart to hear this, how must Dooley's heart be faring? "Have you ever prayed for your brothers and your baby sister?"

"Nope."

"Prayer is a way to stay close to them. You can't see them, but you can pray for them, and God will hear that prayer. It's the best thing you can do for them right now."

"How d'you do it?"

"You just jump in and do it. Something like this. You can say it with me. Our Father . . ."

"Our Father . . ."

"Be with my brother Kenny and help him . . ."

"Be 'ith m' brother, Kenny, an' he'p him . . ."

"To be strong, to be brave, to love you and love me . . ."

"T' be strong, t' be brave, t' love you an' love me . . ."

"No matter what the circumstances . . ."

"No matter what th' circumstances."

"And please, God . . ."

"An' please, God . . ."

"Be with those whose names Dooley will bring you right now . . ."

He heard something hard and determined in the boy's voice. "Mama. Granpaw. Jessie an' Sammy an' Poobaw. Miz Ivey at church, an' Tommy . . . 'at ol' dog . . . m' rabbit . . . Miz Coppersmith an' ol' Vi'let an' all." He buried his face in the pillow and pulled it around his ears.

The clock ticked. Somewhere, through the open alcove window, he heard the rooster crow, the rooster whose whereabouts he couldn't identify, but whose call often gave him a certain poignant joy. Dooley moved closer to him, and in minutes, he heard a light, whiffling snore. He sat up and pulled the blanket over the boy's sleeping form.

He didn't know why he felt this would be a splendid summer for Dooley Barlowe.

❧

When his neighbor came over to see the new rabbit, they sat on the top step of the back stoop. The air was warm and balmy, and a light breeze stirred in the trees.

"Thanks for coming to the library to hear me," she said.

"What makes you think I came to hear you? Didn't you see that I was there to read the *Journal?*"

"Ha!" she said, "you never turned a single page!"

He laughed. "Is that a fact?"

"It is, and you know it."

"Then, while we're into this thanking business, let me say that I appreciate it when you come to hear me, and give the Presbyterians the nod."

"My pleasure," she said, looking directly into his eyes, and smiling. "I suppose I need to be making a decision, soon, about where to join."

"It would be a blessing to look out and see your face."

Dooley came through the back door, slamming the screen behind him. "Hey," he said to Cynthia.

"Hey, yourself."

"They ain't no lettuce n'r any carrots n'r nothin' in there!"

The rector pulled a ten-dollar bill out of his wallet. "Go see Avis and load up."

Cynthia looked after the red bicycle as it disappeared around the corner of the rectory. "Can't we do something about his English?"

"Or his negative attitude? Or his table manners? Or his murderous temper? Or his pain? There are so many things to do something about."

"Overwhelming, is it?"

"Very."

"Let me encourage you, Timothy. I think you've done wonders with him."

"Combed his cowlick, bought him some tennis shoes. It's hard to believe I've done any more than that, really. Trust is the foundational problem, he trusts no one. Jena's doing a good job with him in Sunday school, he's getting some of the basics. I'm just waiting to see where to go from here."

"What about the summer?"

"Overnight, he has a full dance card. I feel the best thing is to send him to Meadowgate for three or four weeks, there's a lot of love for him out there, and farm life will do him good. Then, I'll bring him home to work with me in the church gardens, and try to get your basement cleaned up. As for your flower beds, I can dig those. I've been digging beds for twenty years, so my credentials are solid."

"Excuse me." It was the girl who had come looking for Dooley once before. "Is Dooley home?"

"You've just missed him," said the rector. "But he'll be back in a flash, why don't you stay and wait for him?"

"Thank you," she said, softly.

Cynthia patted the step next to her. "Come. Sit on the steps with us. I've just popped over to see the new rabbit."

"I like rabbits," the girl said, sitting down. She was wearing a sleeveless dress that bared her brown arms, and her blond hair was in French braids. A pretty girl who looked straight out of a Nordic fairy tale, observed the rector.

"What's your name?" Cynthia wanted to know.

"Jenny. See that red roof over there? That's my house."

Another neighbor! And another pair of luminous eyes.

"I'm Cynthia, and this is Father Tim."

"Pleased to meet you," she said. "What's the bunny's name?"

Cynthia laughed. "I wanted them to name him Clarence, but they won't listen to me. Can't you just see him with a little pair of horn-rimmed glasses and tweed knickers? Anyway, he doesn't have a name, yet. As soon as Dooley gets back, we're going to give him one. I have two bunnies."

"Do they have names?"

"Flopsy and Mopsy. It was a busy day and I didn't have the wits to be original."

"This one could be Cottontail."

"It could," said Cynthia, "but I don't think they'll go for it."

When the red bicycle tore around the side of the rectory, Dooley, who was carrying a grocery bag in one arm and steering with the other, looked with amazement at the visitor, and, without slowing down, crashed headlong into the sycamore tree.

❧

The bells continued to sit under a tarp on the lawn at Lord's Chapel, though he tried almost daily to get the crew to install them. They were all working, it seemed, on the golf resort in Wesley. "Putting golf before God!" he said to Ron Malcolm. "Now there's a sermon title, and I ought to be man enough to preach it!"

The earliest they could get to it, they said, was Friday, June 28. They'd get right on it at eight a.m. and by noon, the bells should be chiming.

He noted the date on his calendar. June 28? Why did that have a familiar ring, no pun intended?

❧

He wouldn't put more roses in his own garden this year, but he would certainly put a new bed in the church gardens. He had ordered the memorial plaque from a catalog, and was pleased with the bold, Gothic lettering.

The Souvenir de la Malmaison, with its five-inch pink blooms, had been named in honor of the Empress Josephine's famous gardens, and he'd been intimidated for years by its reputation for being difficult and hard to establish. Well, then, no use to hold back any longer, he told himself, it's now or never.

He also ordered several Madame Isaac Pereire, reputed to be far less temperamental, to climb up the east wall. Even more aromatic than Malmaison, they were said to smell like crushed raspberries. What an extraordinary thing, a rose! He was beginning to feel some inspiration for his talk at the festival.

"Y'ought t' make 'at hole bigger," said Dooley, who was helping him install the roses before he went off to Meadowgate. " 'at hole ain't near big enough."

"How do you know it isn't?"

"I jis' know, is all."

When they were putting the rotted manure in the holes, the rector realized he'd forgotten to bring a second pair of gloves.

"I ain't scared of no cow poop," said the boy, working it deftly into the soil with his hands.

"Good fellow. And what did Jenny have to say the other day?"

"Said she was sorry I got in trouble f'r knockin' Buster Austin's lights out. Said he was askin' for it, he's always goin' aroun' askin' for it."

"Yes, but do you always have to be the one to give him what he asks for?"

"I ain't goin' to, n'more."

"Thanks be to God. And why is that?"

" 'cause."

"Because why, may I ask?"

Dooley took a deep breath. There was a long silence, and then he spoke carefully. "Jis' 'cause," he said.

"Here's the deal," said Walter, who called before the evening news. "Katherine and I have it all worked out. We meet you at the Shannon Airport on July 21. We take a bus to the train in Limerick City, and go up to Sligo, where we stay three weeks in a marvelous old farmhouse near Lough Gill. Then we take a car down to Claremorris and Roscommon, perhaps all the way to Ballinasloe. Margaret says we'll find a few family archives at an abbey in Ballinasloe, but you know how she varnishes the plain truth."

"There's no way under heaven I can do this now, there are too many . . ."

"Timothy, for God's sake! You've been making excuses about this trip for fifteen years! Come now, old fellow, if you wait until you have time, you'll never set foot outside Mitford."

"That's true. I agree with you completely."

"Then, let's do it! Katherine and I could go on our own, of course, but we'd much rather go with you in tow. You know how we've talked about splitting up in three directions during the day, to pursue the family secrets, then coming together every evening at dinner to put it all in one pot. What ground we could cover! It would be an experience of a lifetime, following those crooked turns back to our ancestral castle. Timothy, this is the year for it! Trust me on this."

"Walter, I have a boy now, you know, with a long summer stretching ahead of him like a jet runway. He needs someone to hold down the fort. And his grandfather, recovering from pneumonia, and a parishioner who's waiting for a heart transplant, and a five million dollar nursing home on the drawing board. What's more, I just put in a dozen vastly expensive roses, which will need looking after. You must understand, I simply can't do it. Perhaps next year . . ."

"Cousin, you deceive yourself. There will always be a boy and a nursing home and a case of pneumonia, in a manner of speaking."

He noticed that Walter sounded genuinely disappointed.

"I despise saying no, again and again, to this wonderful dream . . ." His voice trailed off. He was miserably disappointed in his own everlasting inability to get up and go, to take strong action and seize control, and do all the things that other people seemed able to do, and which the world admired so much.

There were times when he felt the Ireland trip was the most possible thing in life, and his heart would lift up and he'd begin to plan and read and even daydream about it. Then, suddenly, it seemed ridiculously impossible, a trivial pursuit in a world of so much suffering and pain. It was vain to go gadding after one's thoroughly dead ancestors and a vague ruin of a castle.

"And another thing," he said, having a sudden revival of energy, "Barnabas is missing, and if that twenty-five-hundred-dollar reward works—as a lot of people think it will—who would be here to welcome him back?" There! That was something Walter could not knock down, not in the least.

"Well, of course," his cousin said, reasonably. "You're right. Katherine will be disappointed, but perhaps we'll screw up our enthusiasm and go anyway, just the two of us. We'll bring the research home and see what *you* can make of it."

"Yes!" he said, immeasurably relieved, "That's a terrific idea. You do the footwork, I'll pore over the papers and the dates and try to make sense of everything, and then, perhaps, we could all go later and fill in the holes."

Why did he have to say that? He could never leave well enough alone.

❧

On June 13, remembering the date at the top of Willard Porter's letter, he took Miss Sadie a birthday card. The walk up the hill warmed him considerably, and he wished for his running clothes, which he hadn't donned in weeks. He must call Hoppy, but fervently disliked telling the truth about the neglect of his exercise and diet program.

He had done so well, for so long, and then he had lost control. A few days off his medication here, a few taboo foods on his plate there, and the first thing he knew, he was again overweight, fatigued, low in spirits, and generally aggravated by the aggressive takeover agenda of his hateful disorder.

When Louella offered him a piece of coconut birthday cake, he responded with such severity that she was taken aback.

"Sorry, Louella, I was snapping at myself, not at you. Please forgive me."

Miss Sadie was breezing about the bedroom, rouging her cheeks, and getting ready to drive to town with Louella to pick up Q-Tips at the drugstore.

"I'm glad to see you got over being tired. Happy birthday!" He kissed her forehead. "May there be many more to come."

"I want all God can give me!" she said brightly. "Oh, and I'm thrilled to say that Olivia Davenport would love to have Mama's hats. But when I told her there were thirty-two of them, she was kind of shocked, I think."

"I'll see that's taken care of in the next few days. Now, what may I do for you on your birthday? I have a half hour or so." He thought she might like a piece of furniture moved, perhaps, or something carried to the basement.

"You've done more than enough, already. More than enough! But if you could spare the time, one day soon, I'd dearly love to know what's carved on that beam in Willard's attic."

He had an odd, sinking feeling when Dooley went to his room to pack for Meadowgate. He could feel it coming; the house already seemed forlorn. What had he done all those years with no dog and no boy, just the everlasting monotony of his own company? He supposed he hadn't noticed very much that he was alone, proving the old adage that "you can't miss what you never had."

He paced the floor of his study, thinking, It's only for three or four weeks, imagine what you can get done around here with no interruptions, no bologna to fry, no hamburgers to fix, no jeans to wash, no homework to help with. He tried to imagine himself sitting with his feet up, reading Archbishop Carey's book, but somehow that didn't seem very interesting, at all.

He heard Dooley thumping down the stairs, dragging a suitcase that was evidently filled with lead.

"What are you taking in that thing, anyway?"

"Jis' some ol' poop f'r Rebecca Jane."

"And what might that be?"

"Jis' a baseball and a dump truck an' stuff like 'at."

"Hal will be here any minute. I pray you'll remember what we discussed."

"Say please and thank you, don't cuss, wash m' hands, don't sass Miz Owen, change m' underwear, make m' bed. That's all, ain't it?"

"No, that ain't all," said the rector.

"An' say m' prayers?"

"Right. Good fellow. And I'll call you twice a week, and try to get out there before too long." He was astounded that he'd just heard himself say 'ain't,' as if it were the most natural thing in the world. It was good that Dooley Barlowe was going away for a while, as he'd begun talking exactly like him.

❦

He'd been right, of course. The house seemed hollow as a gourd. He heard his footsteps echo dully in the hall.

He took two carrots out of the refrigerator and walked to the garage. "Well, Jack," he said, stooping down and putting the carrots in the rabbit cage, "it's just you and me, old boy."

He walked back to the study, and looked at the clock on the mantle. Five-fifteen. Maybe he should run. Puny hadn't come today, so maybe he'd walk to The Local and get something for dinner. He felt ravenous, as he'd skipped lunch, quite without meaning to. He'd worked on his sermon until twelve-thirty, and then the phone had started ringing, and somehow the afternoon had slipped away and he'd come home to say goodbye to Dooley, and here he was, standing in the middle of the floor as bereft as if he'd lost his last friend.

He gazed out on Baxter Park, half-hidden from view behind the rhododendron hedge. The light had stolen softly across the wide, open park bordered on all sides by darkly green hedges. What a treasure, that park, and yet he never used it, nor even encouraged Dooley to go there. A perfect place to sit and read. To sit and think. To have a picnic.

A picnic?

He looked in the refrigerator and found four lemons and made a jar of lemonade. He found cold chicken, and then, a fine wedge of Brie and French rolls. There were berries left from breakfast, and Puny's banana bread that hadn't even been cut.

He put it all into a picnic basket with damask napkins and fetched a starched tablecloth out of the bottom drawer of the buffet.

He stopped suddenly and shook his head. Once again, he had put the cart before the horse.

"Cynthia?" he said, when she answered the phone, "would you like to go on a picnic?" He feared the worst. She was probably off to the country club, perhaps to a dinner dance with a full orchestra.

"You would?" He had certainly not meant to sound so joyful.

❧

Cynthia sat on the tablecloth in her denim skirt and chambray blouse, with a large napkin across her lap. She held her palms up. "Surely it's not raining?"

"No, indeed. That was dew off the leaves. We're not having rain." He poured the lemonade into crystal glasses. How happy he was with his idea, with an idea that was quite unlike his usual ideas. Perhaps he wasn't as thoroughly dull, after all, as he'd felt when talking with Walter.

"Cynthia," he said, raising his glass, "here's to your next book, and all your future books! To your illustrations, may they come alive on the page! To your happiness, to your health, and to your prosperity!"

They drank.

"My!" she said, "that was a toast and a half. Goodness!"

"A picnic, Cynthia, think of it! How long has it been since you were on a picnic?"

"Shall I tell you the truth?"

"Of course. Always."

"Yesterday," she said simply.

He was fairly devastated. To think he'd imagined he was clever and original, and then, to learn it was all merely humdrum and everyday. Andrew Gregory, he supposed, feeling a slow drip on his pants from the perspiring glass.

"Violet and I found a mossy bank on Little Mitford Creek and had deviled eggs and popcorn and tuna on toast."

He was so relieved, he might have shouted. A roller coaster. Being with Cynthia was like being on a roller coaster, his feelings dipped and soared so uncontrollably.

"I sketched ladybugs and moss, it was wonderful. Violet slept in the sun and a butterfly lighted on her ear. Can you imagine?"

He could, but only with some effort. He leaned against the bench, which they'd spread the cloth beside. Surely he'd reached the very gates of heaven, where he found a balmy breeze, a place far removed from the fret of getting and spending, and best of all, someone agreeable to talk with.

❧

They lingered on in the twilight, the evening birdsong loud and vibrant in the hedges.

He knew he would ask her, sooner or later, but each time he thought of it, his heart pounded. "Cynthia," he said, at last, glad for the fading light, "what does going steady mean . . . exactly?"

"Well, it's one of those wonderful things that means

just what it says. You *go* with someone. Steadily! And you don't go out with anybody else."

"I already don't go out with anybody else."

"Yes, but I do. Or did! Or, even might again." She tilted her head to one side, smiling.

"What's wrong with things as they are?" He felt slightly annoyed.

"Things as they are are so . . . unofficial. I never know when I might see you. It would be lovely to have something to look forward to with you, like going out to a movie or having you in for dinner more often, just simple things."

"I don't understand why we have to go steady to do those things."

"Well, of course, we don't have to. It would just be nicer, to know that someone was special, set apart."

He cleared his throat. "You've . . . been seeing Andrew Gregory, I believe."

"Andrew is lovely, really he is. Very gracious and lots of fun. But it's Churchill this and Churchill that, and I can't bear Churchill! He was horrid to his wife, rude to his guests, and cursed like a sailor. And every time we went to the club, I got a terrible knot in my stomach, I'm just not good at that sort of thing. Besides, he likes bridge, and I positively loathe it!" She gazed at him intently.

"You're clearly the most interesting woman I've ever known."

"Do you really mean that?"

"I do. You're easy to be with, you're thoughtful and amusing, you're enormously talented, and yes, very lovely to look at." There. He'd said everything.

Why was this so difficult? She had, after all, asked a simple yes or no question: Would you like to go steady?

Yet, he felt as if he needed to write a full sermon in reply.

"The truth is," he said, "I'm fearful of anything that might interfere with my . . ."

"With your work."

"Yes."

"Typical."

"What do you mean, typical?"

"Men are always afraid that someone might interfere with their work." Now, she seemed annoyed. "You could try looking at it as something to enhance your work, as a welcome diversion that may help you along in your work."

A fresh way of looking at it, he thought, with some surprise.

"You know, the knot that comes with a party at the country club is mild to what I'm feeling right now."

"What are you feeling?"

"So nervous I could throw up. I have never in my life argued for anything like this. It never occurred to me that a simple question would turn into a Platonic debate. After all, Timothy, I did *not* ask you to marry me!" She stood up suddenly, and he rose, also, catching her arm.

"Please! Don't be upset. It was a wonderful question, I should be flattered and grateful beyond words that you asked me. I'm sorry."

Without thinking, he put his arms around her, and drew her close, entering that territory of wisteria which infused even the faint warmth of her breath on his cheek. Her softness was a shock to him, to the place where he kept his heart orderly and guarded, and he realized it wasn't hammering at all, it was completely at peace.

They heard it before they felt it. "Rain!" they cried,

in unison, and, grabbing up the hamper and cloth, fled across the park as it came down in a sudden torrent.

❧

The peace was still there, he thought, lying awake at three o'clock in the morning, listening to the murmur of the rain. It was a palpable thing, this feeling, undefiled by concern or doubt. He prayed for Cynthia, admiring her courage to speak up. "Come boldly to the throne of Grace," Paul had written to the Hebrews. He liked her boldness!

He was filled with a certain excited expectation for the summer, as if his own school had been let out.

❧

It felt as if thunder were vibrating through the bed.

Horrified, he sat up and saw lights flashing wildly around the room. In the sound that filled the air like another presence, he heard an oddly familiar rhythm: cut, cut, cut, cut, cut.

He sprang out of bed and went to the alcove window, but could see nothing more than the flashing light that seemed to be swinging rapidly in circles, like a beacon. Without switching on the hall light, he raced down the stairs to the kitchen window.

A helicopter! In Baxter Park. And people running, and there, just as the light flashed across it, Hoppy's blue Volvo.

Good Lord! Olivia!

He slipped his feet into his garden shoes by the door, and ran toward the hedge and through it, blinded by the light and sickened by the deafening roar.

He saw Hoppy and two others taking Olivia from the car.

"I'm here!" he shouted, fighting the storm of feeling that rose in him.

"Pray!" yelled Hoppy, who had lifted her in his arms. Olivia looked at him and reached out. He was able to touch only her fingertips as Hoppy rushed her to the helicopter door and handed her in to waiting hands. Then, the doctor climbed in, and the door closed.

Someone backed the car across the park, deeply trenching the rain-soaked grass, and almost immediately, the helicopter was lifting, lifting, was in the air, and vanishing over the tops of the trees.

"Philippians four-thirteen, for Pete's sake," he whispered hoarsely to the sudden darkness.

❦

"What a horrid nightmare! What was it all about?" Cynthia came through her hedge with a flashlight.

"It's Olivia. I don't know what the mission is. I pray to God she's flying to her heart." Flying to her heart! A miracle of miracles.

Cynthia took his hand, dropping the flashlight by her side. It beamed on his feet. "Oh, dear," she said, looking down. He had lost one of his untied tennis shoes, the other was covered with mud, his pajama legs were soaked nearly to the knees, and Violet was nuzzling his ankle.

He put his arms around Cynthia, and held her. How good it was to hold someone, especially after the shock of that alarming mission in the park. "So lovely," she murmured against his shoulder, stroking his cheek. "Two dear hugs in one night. It's almost as good as . . ."

"As going steady?"

"Umhmm."

He laughed a little. "Almost, perhaps. But surely, not quite."

❧

It was four-thirty in the morning when he fell to his knees by his bed and began to pray intensely. When he arose from the rug, creaking in his joints and assailed by a burning thirst, he was amazed to see it was six o'clock.

All day, he felt derailed, cut loose from his moorings. The loss of sleep, the accumulating fatigue, maybe it was his age, after all. He had forgotten to call Hoppy, but that was just as well, in view of things. He would see him next week, without fail, assuming Hoppy had returned from wherever he'd gone. If he hadn't returned, he most assuredly did not want to see the new doctor, Wilson, who seemed wet behind the ears.

In the office mailbox, a card from Emma.

"Having wonderful time, do not wish you were here, ha, ha. You should have seen Harold talking to Mickey Mouse, I got a whole roll of snaps. Much love, Emma."

He dropped by the Grill for a late breakfast, comforted by the familiar surroundings and Percy's dependable nosiness.

"I heard that copter set down in th' park last night, it like t' scared Velma to death. Truth is, you look like *you* been scared t' death, you're white as a sheet."

"I come in here to be cheered up, and instead, I get brought down. Do I really look white as a sheet?"

"Warshed out. Gray, like. Sickly . . ."

"That's enough, thank you very much."

"Don't mention it."

He sat in the booth and buttered his toast. Just when he should be gaining a second wind, he was crashing and burning. It seemed a good time to write Stuart Cullen, perhaps even a good time to go see him in person. But he hated the thought of the long drive. Perhaps he would take Cynthia along. There! A brilliant idea. She and Martha would get on famously, and wouldn't Stuart be fairly astounded?

"It's like this . . ." he would explain. It's like what? Well, of course, he didn't know, exactly, so he'd just let Stuart figure it out, and then tell *him*.

J.C. Hogan slipped into the booth with his bulging, half-open briefcase. "When you goin' to have a letter from the man in the attic? I need to fill up some space, advertisin's dropped off."

"A letter from George Gaynor isn't exactly filler. But I just got a letter and you can have it next week."

"Too late. I'd like to get it today, for Monday's paper."

"Let me finish my breakfast. I just came from the office, but I'll go back again."

J.C. got up, jolting the table, and nearly dumping the rector's breakfast in his lap. "Just run it upstairs where I'll be layin' out the center spread."

"I'll see to it," Father Tim said, crisply.

Coot Hendrick slipped into the booth, wearing a red cap from the hardware. "I wish t' God a feller could git 'im a plate of gizzards in this place.

"Gizzards, is it?"

"I was raised on gizzards, like 'em better'n white meat."

"You won't be gettin' no gizzard plate around here," yelled Percy, who could overhear the back booth from the grill.

"Heard anything 'bout y'r dog?" Coot wanted to know.

He dipped his toast in the poached egg. "Not a word."

"I don't think y'r goin' to."

"Is that right?"

"If hit was anybody aroun' here that stoled 'im, they'd've jumped on that money like a beagle on a rabbit. Nossir, I think that dog's long gone."

Percy threw his spatula down and walked over. "Lemme tell you somethin', buddyroe, you say one more word to th' Father 'bout that dog bein' long gone, and you're th' one's gonna be long gone, you hear?"

"You don't have t' git s' bent out of shape," said Coot. "It ain't nothin' but a dog."

"Th' only fella I ever th'owed out of here was Parrish Guthrie. I said that'd be th' only one, and I wouldn't want t' break my promise. Why don't you go on over yonder and set by th' window?"

Coot got up without taking his eyes off the owner and stomped over to the table by the window.

"Don't pay no attention to him," growled Percy. "He ain't got a lick of sense."

"Percy, you didn't have to do that, but I thank you for it. Coot's all right, he didn't mean any harm."

Just then, the door opened with some force, and Homeless Hobbes stumbled in on his crutch. "Father Tim!" he shouted. "Are you in here? I've found your dog! I've found Barnabas!"

The rector bolted from his seat in the booth and stood frozen by the counter.

"He's way up th' hill behind th' creek. They had 'im tied out, I saw 'im with my own eyes. I went up there t' take food t' a sick feller, ol' Barnabas got a load of me and like to barked his head off. Some pretty rough characters come out of that house and dragged him inside."

"How'd he look?"

"I hate t' tell you, he looked starved-like, pore."

"I'm callin' Rodney," said Percy, taking the receiver off the wall phone.

"I asked around about th' jack legs that's livin' there—they say they're bad news, drugs or somethin' else lowdown. One feller said they might be armed. I'd want Rodney t' be plenty careful."

As the few early lunch customers fixed their mute attention on the unfolding drama, Percy held the phone to Father Tim. "He's on th' line."

"Hello, Rodney! Something wonderful has happened. Homeless says he's seen Barnabas at a house up the creek. Yes, yes. A little starved looking, he says. I see. Well, I'll ask him.

"Can you tell Rodney where the house is?"

"I don't think you can get there from here. I'd have t' ride with 'im t' show 'im."

"Rodney, he'd have to ride with you, it's up the hill behind the creek. He says he hears they might be armed, drugs could be involved. Yes. Fine. We'll be at the Grill."

"Anybody wants a doughnut," Percy said to his customers, "it's on th' house!"

❧

He shook hands with Homeless and Rodney. "I'll be at home, then. The Lord be with you."

As the two men left, Percy stared after them. "I know ol' Homeless comes t' town Tuesday nights to go through Avis's garbage, but that's th' only time I ever seen 'im in broad daylight."

❧

It was nearly three o'clock before he saw the police car pull up to the curb, and he was standing at the door as Rodney came up the walk. He saw at once that the mission had not been successful.

"Nothin'," said the police chief. "We got s' dern lost tryin' to find th' way in there, Homeless had walked in before, and when we finally come up on that house, it was tight as a drum. Nobody at home, no dog barkin', nothin'. I hated t' come tell you." Rodney stood with one foot on the top step, looking downcast.

"Well, then."

"We seen two old vehicles on th' place, a car under a tarp, and a van they'd kind of pushed off in th' bushes."

"Did you look at the license plate on the car?"

"I did. Wrote it down on my report. Hang on," he said, going to the curb and taking a clipboard from the front seat. He walked back to the porch stoop, slowly, looking at the report. "Let's see, here. VAT 7841."

"That's it! That was on the license plate of the car that took Barnabas. I forgot all about it 'til this very moment. VAT!"

"Well, all I can do is keep an eye on th' place. I'll send Joe Joe back in th' evenin' and again tomorrow. We'll turn up somethin'. Since you had 'im more'n three days, state law says you own 'im, so they've kidnapped 'im, pure an' simple, and looks like abuse into the bargain. They don't have a snowball's chance."

He felt torn between elation and disappointment. "Thank you, my friend. Keep me posted."

He went into the study and sat on the sofa, feeling a desperate fatigue. He also felt an aching thirst again, which he knew was a warning, but he was too tired to get off the sofa and get a glass of water. "In a minute," he murmured aloud, leaning his head back. "I'll do it in a minute."

❧

On Saturday evening, the phone rang. "Father Tim, it's me. Joe Joe."

"Joe Joe!"

"I went over there and looked around, but I didn't find anything. I tried knockin' on a few doors along the road, but all I could scare up was an old woman and two little kids, they didn't know much. It's spooky back in there, that's where all the liquor used to be made. But don't you worry, I'm goin' again tomorrow, right after church."

Church! He had completely forgotten the crux of his sermon.

"Thank you, Joe Joe, God bless you," he said, going at once to his desk.

There! It was "Tough Times, Tender Hearts," typed rather more neatly than usual, and appearing to be in good order. He turned out the lights and went upstairs. A good night's sleep and the press of Sunday off his shoulders, and he'd be as good as new. Next week, maybe he'd ask Cynthia to go to a movie.

❧

"Nuthin'," said Rodney, when he called after church. "Joe Joe went up there and come back empty-handed. Th' cars hadn't moved, and there was no sign of a dog except a few piles of poop under a tree, I guess where they'd tied 'im up. I tell you what, my instincts got to workin' on this, an' Tuesday, I'm goin' to stake a man out in th' woods around there.

"Maybe us prowlin' around in a police car has run 'em off, but anyway, I smell a rat."

"Smelling rats is your job, and you're mighty

good at it. Remember how you jumped on that candy wrapper?"

"You got to look for th' little things," Rodney said, with dignified authority.

He had no sooner put the phone on the hook than it rang again.

"You comin' out here t'day?"

"Dooley! Well, no, no, I'm not. Not today."

"I thought you might be comin' out."

"I want to get out next Sunday, but not today, we've had a lot of excitement. We think we may have found Barnabas."

"You ain't!"

"Oh, I think we have. We'll see. Rodney's going to stake a man out in the woods to observe the place, it's up on the hill above the creek. Homeless carried food to somebody up there and saw him. Barnabas barked at him, he said."

" 'at's super," said Dooley. " 'at's great!"

"I'll keep you posted. Doing all right, are you?"

"Yep, but Rebecca Jane sleeps all th' time, looks like. I done played 'ith them ol' dogs and rode 'at ol' horse and all."

"Well, let's keep in touch. Are you doing what we talked about?"

"I forgot t' change m' underwear last night."

"Well, then, tonight you get another chance."

"Tell Granpaw hey."

"I will."

"Tell Cynthia hey, and ol' Vi'let and Jack an' all."

"Oh, I will."

"Well, bye," said Dooley, hanging up.

With a warm rush of feeling, he realized that Dooley Barlowe was homesick.

He was getting ready to take a hot shower when the phone rang by his bed.

"Father?" His doctor's voice told him the whole story.

"She's through it! Everything looks good, she's resting. Leo Baldwin is a master. Thank God for Leo. They washed up at eight o'clock last night. I would have called you earlier, but I couldn't, I dropped down on a bed in Leo's office and I was outta here. Today has been hectic, this . . ." His voice broke slightly. "This is a great answer to my prayer, Father, thank you, thank you."

He had never heard his friend sound this way, and he was swept up in the joy of it. "Tell me everything, if you have the strength!"

"We took the copter to Charlotte, put her on a Lear, and flew to Boston. An ambulance was waiting, we were at Mass General in a little under three hours. The donor was a boy, eighteen years old, on a motorcycle, no helmet, closed head injury. Rotten business. They had hooked him to a respirator at the scene, brought him in, did brain scans, there was no blood flow to the brain.

"The emergency room doctor called Leo, Leo talked to the parents, they consented, and Leo called me. What an uncanny, unbelievable miracle! Thousands to one, you know." Hoppy was silent a moment, and cleared his throat.

"She'll be at Mass till we find out whether she's rejecting, probably a couple of weeks, then Leo wants her here in Boston for four to six months."

"That's the bad news."

"I'll fly up whenever I can. Thank God for Wilson, I got him in the nick of time."

"God's timing is always perfect."

"I'm beginning to see that, even about . . . Carol."

"Get the names of the parents who gave their consent; I'd like to pray for them."

"I'll do that."

"When are you coming home?"

"In the morning, the ol' red-eye special. Wilson has probably croaked by now, but he's young, he can handle it. Keep those prayers coming, pal."

"Consider it done," he said, knowing that was one prescription he wouldn't forget to refill.

CHAPTER TWENTY-ONE

The Bells

On Monday, he refilled his medication after a visit to the hospital and breakfast at the Grill, and hurried to the office. Perhaps he should start taking Monday off, like a lot of clergy. But the thought of losing a full day seemed disorienting.

He began his list of calls. "Miss Sadie?"

"Good morning, Father!"

"Remember you asked me to think about a name for the nursing home? I believe the Scripture you want engraved over the front door is Psalm thirty-three, verse twenty-two, 'Let thy mercy, O Lord, be upon us, according as we hope in thee.' "

"You have the best memory! But, of course, you're young."

"Well, then. What do you think of the name Hope House?"

"Hope House? Perfect! Absolutely perfect, Father, I

knew I could count on you. Instead of somebody saying their poor mother has gone to a nursing home, they can say she's living at Hope House!"

"The other matter, the matter of the beam in the attic, well, I haven't gotten to it, yet, but I shall. Now, to the good news. We think we've found Barnabas."

❧

After calling a disgruntled J.C. Hogan to say he'd deliver George Gaynor's letter at lunch time, he called Cynthia.

"What are you up to?" he asked.

"No good!" she said brightly. "Trying to make the crossover from a Violet book to another kind of book is hair-raising. I mean, what if I can't do it? What if I'm meant to do cats for the rest of my life? So, I'm forcing myself along, and I'm drawing a . . . ah, well, to tell the truth, a mouse!"

"From memory, I devoutly hope."

"From life. It's in a cage on my drawing board. I plan to reward it with gouda and let it go in the hedge."

"Cynthia, Cynthia."

"Here's the scoop. The story is about a mouse who lived in the stables where Jesus was born. It's about looking at life from down under, as it were, a mere mouse observing the high drama of a lowly birth."

"I like it."

"It's for children four to eight, so I've even lowered the age of my reading audience. Timothy, I'm scared."

"Don't be. Philippians four-thirteen, for Pete's sake."

She laughed. "I needed that."

"How are the rabbits?"

"Wonderful! They help me so much, I've sketched

pages and pages. I really wanted to do a rabbit book, I think, but I feel strongly led to do this."

"Follow your heart," he said. "And speaking of hearts, Olivia came through the surgery splendidly. She's resting."

"Wonderful!"

"Thank you for your prayers. I also called to say I think we've found Barnabas."

"Timothy!"

"We'll see. So far, a bit of a hold-up, but I'll keep you posted. And I think Dooley's homesick."

"Will wonders never cease?"

"Let's hope not. How about a movie this week?"

"You're really asking me to a movie?" she said, with amazement. "That's instant proof that wonders never cease!"

On Wednesday, a postcard: "I've got a suntan you won't believe. Harold's legs are fried. See you in the funny papers, ha ha. Love, Emma."

From Stuart:

"Thanks for your note. As always, it was good to have word from you. Of course, you may come for a visit and bring Cynthia Coppersmith. Next Tuesday is a conflict, as I shall be away then. Can you come the following Tuesday, perhaps? Martha insists on having you here for lunch, though I have gallantly offered a pricey restaurant. I count my blessings!

"Just give Norma a ring, so it can go on my calendar at the office. Ever yours in His peace."

Rodney called at eleven.

"They're as good as nailed. They're runnin' drugs in and out of there by th' shipload. They keep Barnabas for a watchdog, and when they don't want 'im barkin', they muzzle 'im. Might be a pretty sophisticated operation. Anyway, it's worse than just a bunch of good ol' boys bein' bad."

"What are you going to do?"

"We're goin' in after 'em, that's what. Th' trick is, we got to go in when there's a load of dope settin' in there. Last night, they drove out with th' van, Joe Joe run down to 'is car and called us on th' radio, and by th' time we got th' call in to th' state, they'd disappeared. They may be drivin' it to a truck somewhere right around here, and loadin' it on. I'm goin' to keep Joe Joe out there."

"Be careful, Rodney. I don't like the sound of this."

"Me, either. That's why I'm countin' on you to do one of th' main things th' Lord hired you to do—pray."

What was going on wouldn't bear thinking about, there was no use in it. Instead, he would keep busy, he would call Dooley. He felt rotten that he'd packed him off somewhere, just as he'd begun to set down roots.

How could I have been so thoughtless? he wondered, staring out the window. Very likely, he's staring out his own window right now, marking time until he comes home to Mitford.

"Hello, Marge? Tim here. How's our girl?"

"Beautiful. Precious. Too wonderful for words."

"And how's our boy?"

"Why don't you ask him that, and then we'll talk before you hang up."

"Dooley!" he heard Marge call. "It's for you!"

He heard someone stomping to the phone. "Hey."

"Hey, yourself. What are you up to?"

"I cain't talk, I'm goin' out with Doc Owen. Bye!"

"Well," Marge said, "I guess I'll have to fill you in.

He's busy from morning 'til night, riding Goosedown, shooting baskets with the boy from McGuire Farm, playing with Rebecca Jane, taking off with Hal. I think they're going to deliver a calf this very moment."

"Then he's not . . . homesick?"

"Homesick? Dooley? Maybe for the first five minutes, but he got over it."

A note from Father Roland:

"I must tell you that the pressure here is unrelenting. You say I'm young and it's good for me, but this will surely make me old before my time. How I'd like to come and visit you in that sleepy little village, where I can just see you strolling along Main Street, going your rounds, taking your time. That's surely how God would have us live! My friend, count your blessings, and remember me in your prayers, that I might learn how to better appropriate His peace for labor in the stressful turmoil of a city vineyard."

Hah! And double hah! thought the rector. Going my rounds, taking my time . . . and what sleepy little village? The last time he'd had a decent night's sleep in this village was too long ago to remember.

❧

What if this movie was one of those steamy marathons that would cause them both to be paralyzed with embarrassment? And should he wear his clerical collar or a sport shirt? He had not gone to a movie in well over ten years, and why should he? The last time he had gone, with friends from the parish, he was so astounded at the vile language, casual sex, and equally casual bloodshed that he had left with a pounding headache, declaring, "Never again."

"Cynthia," he said when she answered the phone,

"do you think I should wear my clerical collar or a sport shirt?"

"I think you should wear your clerical collar. After all, your job isn't nine to five, it's twenty-four hours a day, isn't it?"

He felt oddly relieved and happy.

"Ah . . . what movie are we seeing?" he asked.

"A Walt Disney," she said, "I hope you don't mind."

Mind? He was thrilled.

❧

The moment he entered the dark theater, he felt the years dropping away. He was certainly twelve, this was the old Delta Theater, *Flying Tigers* would be coming on the screen at any moment, and the girl with him was Elizabeth Mooney, whose parents were waiting at the diner across the street, drinking coffee. He remembered how badly he'd felt that anyone had to drink coffee for an hour and a half in order to accommodate him in some way.

"Where do you want to sit?" he whispered to Cynthia.

"I like the gospel side," she whispered back. "Toward the front."

If he sat too close to the front, it made him, quite literally, throw up—and how would he explain that?

He steered her just slightly forward of the middle, and they went into the empty row with a box of popcorn, a Diet Sprite, a Coke, and a box of Milk Duds. He had completely forgotten about Milk Duds, his childhood favorite, and though he wouldn't eat a single one, of course, he thought it might be nice to have them, just for nostalgia's sake. He put them in his jacket pocket.

Cynthia settled happily into the plush seat, which, to

his surprise, rocked. "Where are the Milk Duds?" she whispered. "Didn't I see you get Milk Duds?"

❧

There was the scent of wisteria, as if it were blown in on a garden breeze, and her warm laughter at the very places he found amusing, so it was no surprise that he considered reaching over and holding her hand. He discovered, however, that he was incapable of actually doing it.

Lord, he prayed, I'm not used to this "going out" business. Some might tell me to follow my instincts, but I've spent so many years trying to follow yours that I've nearly lost the hang of following mine. So, thank you for being in on this and handling it to please yourself.

There! That put the burden squarely on the Lord, he thought.

At some point during the movie, they looked at each other while laughing at a funny scene, and when he looked back at the screen, he was amazed to find that he was holding her hand.

He couldn't help but notice how perfectly happy she seemed while eating the last of his Milk Duds.

❧

He was saying goodnight on her front porch when a police car pulled up in front of the rectory and someone got out.

Father Tim walked quickly down the steps to the sidewalk. "Hello! Are you looking for me?"

It was Rodney's new man. "Yessir, you're Father Tim?"

"I am."

"I just got it on my radio from Chief Underwood. He thought you'd want to know that Joe Joe's been shot."

❧

The new officer looked as if he were barely out of junior high. "I don't know what happened, sir," he said as they drove to the hospital, "all I got was the report he'd been shot. The chief's up there bustin' that drug house. He took the whole force, just locked up the jail and left."

He heard a certain wistfulness in the young officer, that he was out here chauffeuring a preacher while his peers were risking their lives.

"How is he?" he asked young Nurse Kennedy, who was Joe Joe's first cousin.

"It could have been worse, Father. It only nicked his left kidney, but it lodged in his abdomen. Dr. Wilson is operating now."

"And where, may I ask, is Dr. Harper?"

"In his office."

In his office? Why in God's name wasn't he in the operating room? Obviously, Hoppy was giving far too much responsibility to someone lacking in practical experience. He felt a sudden anger.

"How is he?" Marcie Guthrie burst through the swinging doors that led to an emergency waiting room, wearing a seersucker housecoat and clutching a pink leather Bible.

"He's with Dr. Wilson, Aunt Marcie, but I think he's fine, I really do." Nurse Kennedy gave her stricken aunt a consoling hug.

"I've been afraid of this for years. And Boyd on the road, somewhere in South Carolina! How did it happen?" Marcie wiped her red eyes with a handkerchief.

"I don't know," said Nurse Kennedy, "they just brought him in and left, nobody told me anything about how it happened. They did say something about drugs and a dog."

The rector's heart pounded. "What did they say about the dog?"

"Just that Joe Joe heard it barking."

J.C. Hogan came through the swinging doors, looking grim. "What happened?" he snapped, directing his question to the rector.

"This probably isn't the best time to get the story. Maybe you should talk to Rodney when he gets through at the creek."

"What's he doin' at the creek?"

"I'm told he's over there with his men, doing a drug bust."

J.C. glared at him. "If I'd wanted a story about a drug bust, I would've asked for it. I'm here to get a story on a shooting."

If there was ever anyone whose lights I'd like to punch out, he thought, this is the guy. He could just see the headline in Monday's *Muse,* but it was, of course, misspclled.

"The only one who knows that story is currently in surgery and isn't able to tell it right now."

Red-faced, J.C. looked at Marcie and thc rector, then stormed through the swinging doors.

"That hateful devil," said Marcie. "I ought to sic Mama on him."

❧

Long after midnight, Joe Joe's preacher, Esther and Ray Cunningham, three cousins, two aunts, and an uncle were waiting with the rector in the hallway outside the emergency room. Thinking he heard a familiar voice, Father Tim got up and looked through the glass in the swinging doors, and was nearly knocked against the wall as Puny Bradshaw swept in, followed by an outraged Nurse Herman. "Young lady, to wait in this section, you must be family or clergy. Are you his wife?"

"No, I'm not," snapped Puny, "but I've got a good chance of bein', and that ought t' be enough for anybody who's askin'."

Stopping suddenly, she peered into the faces of a significant portion of the Cunningham clan. "Oh, law," she said, blushing furiously.

Mayor Cunningham rose from the folding chair with all the dignity of her imposing size. "Puny Bradshaw?"

Puny looked so frightened that the rector had to restrain himself from rushing to her side.

"Yes, ma'am?"

The concern of the hour had given the mayor an unusually serious countenance. In addition, she was wearing half glasses, which caused her to look down on the rector's house help with some asperity. "We've heard a lot about you," said the mayor.

"You have?" asked Puny, with a quaking voice.

"And I think it's high time we all met." The mayor's face broke into a big smile as she gave Puny a vigorous hug. Marcie Guthrie followed suit, as did the remainder of the group, including Joe Joe's preacher, who was still in his Little League coach's uniform.

"I can see you're already celebrating," Hoppy said, coming down the hall. "You'll be glad to know the surgery was successful and he's in recovery."

"Praise God!" shouted Marcie.

"The bullet entered the lower left back, went through his ribs, nicked his kidney, and lodged in the abdomen. There were a number of perforations in the small intestine, of course, so it was a tough one, but he had a tough doctor." He stepped aside as Dr. Wilson appeared. The entire group applauded spontaneously.

I'm getting more like Dooley Barlowe every day, thought the rector, seeing the smile that shone on the exhausted young doctor's face. I've been making up my mind ahead of the facts.

Rodney burst through the swinging doors with Cleo. "How bad is it?" The chief's face was scratched and bleeding, and he was walking with a limp. There was a hushed silence.

"Bullet's out, .25 caliber automatic. He's fine," said Dr. Wilson. "You look like you could use some attention yourself."

Everyone stared intently as the chief hitched up his holster and cleared his throat. "They got away," he said, trying manfully to control his feelings. "We surrounded th' house and called 'em t' come out . . ."

"But they won't nothin' in there but warm beer and cold pizza," said Cleo, shaking his head.

❧

"The way it was," said Joe Joe, when the rector visited his hospital room the following day, "was th' chief sent me over to your place to pick up that Almond Joy wrapper and th' truth is, sir, I found somethin' sweeter than candy." He grinned at Puny, who was standing by the bed, and took her hand.

Father Tim laughed. "I've been trying to gouge that out of her for a long time."

"It's hard to talk with this dern thing up my nose," said Joe Joe, "but I want you to know I'm sorry about your dog, Father. Bustin' those low-down snakes was real important to me, but more than anything, I was hopin' you'd get your dog back."

He knew he wouldn't be able to speak, so he said nothing.

"I heard 'im barkin' in there before I went up to th' house. I shouldn't have gone so close to th' house with no backup, but they were bringin' in stuff out of th' van, and I knew if I could get a good look at what it was, I could radio in to th' chief and we could nail 'em. Well, it was cocaine, all right, just like I thought. They were cuttin' it down and puttin' it in little bags for th' street. But somebody turned a light on at th' side of th' house, an' when they saw me, I started runnin' and they started pumpin' that automatic in behind me."

Joe Joe shook his head and sighed. "I managed to get back to my car and call th' station. Cleo came after me, but by th' time th' chief an th' boys got up there, they'd escaped. I feel real bad about it, Father. You don't know how bad."

The rector nodded. "You made the decision you thought was best, and what you learned will come in handy at another time and place."

"He always has somethin' upliftin' to say," Puny informed Joe Joe, with evident pride.

"No, not always. But I hope I can find something uplifting to say to our police chief."

Puny nodded, soberly. "Anybody who shot a tree stump thinkin' it was a man, and then fell in a hole up to his neck will need some upliftin'."

❧

When he awoke at five, the air had been balmy and soft. Now, at barely ten o'clock, it was so cold, he thought of putting on the heater in the bathroom. Not only that, but a dense fog was rolling in that practically shielded the Oxford Antique shop from his view.

He had made a "catch up" list, but lacked any enthusiasm for the project at the top of it. Frankly, he had no earthly ambition to see what was on that beam in the Porter place attic. He did not care to go swimming through towers of ancient newspapers, mounds of broken glass, decades of dust, and a jumble of derelict furniture, especially on a cold, foggy day. However, the bells were to be installed on Monday, and that would not only tie him up, but put him behind, so he supposed that now was as good a time as any.

As he glanced through his desk drawer for a stamp, he saw the extra reward posters he'd stored there, and hastily looked away.

No, he thought, pulling on his windbreaker, I've done my grieving. I'll give the memory of Barnabas to the One who sent him in the first place and be glad of the pleasure of having known that good fellow. Just last night, he'd come across a splendid thing by Shaw. "I like a bit of a mongrel myself, whether man or beast. They're the best for everyday."

When it came to comfortable, everyday companionship, Barnabas had, indeed, been the best. He'd possessed the noblest characteristics of all the breeds he appeared to descend from: the loyalty and intelligence of the Irish wolfhound, the gentle spirit of the Bouvier, and the happy persistence of the sheep dog. If that was what mongrels were all about, then thanks be to God.

There, he thought, putting on his cap. I've made my peace with this cruel thing.

He had his hand on the doorknob when he stopped suddenly, and leaned his head against the door frame, trying to swallow the terrible knot in his throat. He stood there a long time, only to be sorely disappointed with himself that he was, at last, "cryin' over 'at ol' dog."

❧

He followed Uncle Billy to a room that was divided in half by curtains on a clothesline. "That's my side," he said, "an' that's her'n. She went in there a little bit ago, and won't come out 'til supper, most likely. Rose, th' preacher's here."

"I'm indisposed," she said, haughtily.

"He wants t' know can he go up in th' attic and look around?"

"In the attic?" squawked Miss Rose. "Why does he want to go in th' attic?"

Uncle Billy looked at him. "What was it you was goin' up there for? I plumb forgot."

"Well, I've heard so much about how this place was built, I'd like to take a look at how Willard girded those exceptional gables." Underneath the cap, which he'd forgotten to remove, a mild perspiration stood out on his head. He had escaped without telling a total lie.

"Tell 'im to go on, then, but don't stir up the dust."

Uncle Billy grinned, revealing his gold tooth. "Don't stir up th' dust, Rose says."

Looking up into the vast, black hole made his skin crawl. Where was Cynthia when he needed her? Undoubtedly, she would have bounded up these stairs, two at a time, fully expecting to make some thrilling discovery.

"Dear God!" he exclaimed, involuntarily.

"Prayin' about it, are you?" said Uncle Billy.

"Where's the light?"

"Oh, th' light. It's around here somewhere. Yessir, right there it is." A lone bulb switched on and shone dimly against a vast sprawl of gloomy ceiling. "When you come down," said the old man, "I wouldn't mind if you'd cut my corns off for me; Rose has a shaky hand with th' razor. I'll soak 'em good first."

At the top of the stairs, he unashamedly looked back to see if Uncle Billy was still standing at the door. He was not.

The attic was so filled with an odd jumble of debris that he could barely make passage. Why had he not brought a flashlight or asked for one downstairs? There was the beam, exactly where it should be, precisely at the center of the pitch. Surely it was divine intervention, for the bulb cast its light into the vault of the ceiling and shone directly onto the engraved letters.

"W!" he shouted, and heard something scurry across the floor. The *W,* rendered in what appeared to be old English lettering, was followed by an *i,* then an *n.* "Win," he said aloud, squinting into the dimly illumined space. If only he had a stepladder, anything to draw him nearer.

He managed to climb onto the seat of a broken chair set precariously on two steamer trunks that were seated together.

"Winter!" he exclaimed, able to see the lettering more clearly. As the chair wobbled under him, he fervently hoped J.C. Hogan would not allow Hessie Mayhew to write his obituary.

"Winterpast," he whispered, slowly.

Below this word was inscribed "Song of Solomon."

He cautiously descended his makeshift ladder and hurried down the stairs with a sense of excitement. "Uncle Billy!" he called, "bring me your Bible!"

Finding no one to greet him, he wandered along the

musty hallway until he came to the kitchen. Uncle Billy was sitting beside the table, soaking his feet in a dishpan.

"Well, Preacher, I'm ready for m' corn operation when you are."

The old man looked at him with such an expectant grin that the rector rolled up his sleeves and surrendered to the task ahead. Quite suddenly, he remembered hearing about a place where milk truck drivers could still find employment. Unfortunately, it was in Nova Scotia.

The weather was currently doing one of the one hundred and thirty-six things Mark Twain had given it credit for.

The sun was shining gloriously, and the sky was as blue as the egg of a robin, as he set out across Baxter Park in his running clothes. He couldn't remember any recent mission that had pleased him more.

"Miss Sadie," he said, out of breath, finding her on the porch with Louella, "I've been to the attic."

"Come and tell us about it!" she said eagerly, patting the green rocker next to hers.

"Well, then, may I trouble you ladies for a Bible?" he asked, taking his reading glasses out of the pocket of his sweatpants.

"We got one right here," said a beaming Louella, who just happened to have a worn, leather-bound edition lying open in her lap. " 'Course, if you lookin' for some newfangled Bible, you won't find it aroun' here. We jus' keep th' King James."

"My lifelong favorite," he said, taking it from her and sitting down in a rocker.

"Miss Sadie, Willard's letter said he hoped things

would be different for the two of you someday, and that his inscription on the beam would signify his trust in a happier time. I believe he intended for you to stand with him where I stood today, as he revealed the name of the house he hoped to share with you as his wife."

She nodded, and he couldn't help but notice that her cheeks had taken on color.

"The name of the house, Miss Sadie, is . . . Winterpast."

She looked at him for a long moment. "Winterpast," she repeated slowly. "Why, that's a lovely name."

"Willard left a further inscription for you, which leads us to the Song of Solomon." He put his reading glasses on, turned the pages, and read:

" 'For lo, the winter is past, the rain is over and gone. The flowers appear on the earth; the time of the singing of birds has come.' "

Miss Sadie folded her hands in her lap, and looked away. The only sound was, in fact, the singing of birds. She was silent for a while, then she spoke. "It's good to have hope. I'm so glad Willard had hope."

"Many waters, Miss Sadie, cannot quench love. Neither can the floods drown it. That, too, is from the Song."

She looked at him with a small light in her eyes.

"So be it," she said.

How could he have considered taking Monday off? Monday was the diving board poised over the rest of the week. One walked out on the board, reviewed the situation, planned one's strategy, bounced a few times to get the feel of things, and then made a clean dive. With-

out Monday, one simply bombed into the water, belly
first, and hoped for the best.

To his astonishment, the bell crew met him in the
churchyard promptly at eight, and it didn't take long
for his worst fear to be realized. The velvety lawn,
which had lain under a persistent drizzle for two days,
was so thoroughly mucked about with the heaving and
hauling of three vast bells that it soon looked like a
battlefield.

At a little after one o'clock, the bells were chiming.

"Let them ring!" he told the foreman. "Let them
ring!" What a wildly tender thing it stirred in his heart
to hear those glorious bells.

A small crowd gathered, staring with wonder at the
Norman tower that was pealing with music. Andrew
Gregory walked briskly down the lane to offer his congratulations. "I say," he told the rector, "it's been a bit
dry around here without your bells."

J.C. Hogan heard the pealing and came on the run,
and was given an elaborate story of their history, manu-
facture, and recent long sojourn in their homeland.

It was two-fifteen before he went to his office for the
first time that day and picked up the mail from the box,
noting that the bundle seemed uncommonly fat. The
phone was ringing as he unlocked and went in. "Timothy! How grand of you to ring the bells on your birthday!" said Cynthia.

"My what?"

"I think that's just the boldest, most unrepressed
thing to do."

"You do?"

"I'd never have thought you'd have the . . . I've always thought you were so everlastingly modest! What a
surprise!"

His birthday! How extraordinary that he'd forgotten. But, of course, there had been no one around to remind him, and Walter never said a word before the fact, always letting a package from Tiffany's stationery department send his greetings, which usually followed the actual date by several days.

He laughed. "Well, then, now you know the truth. It's my birthday, but you got the surprise."

"There's a surprise for you, too. But only if you come for dinner this evening."

"I'd like that very much. How did you know it was my birthday?"

"It's on the church list I picked up last Sunday in the narthex."

"Ah, well, is nothing sacred?"

He saw that the fat bundle was largely made up of birthday cards, two of which also extended a dinner invitation. There was one from Jena Ivey, which said, "Father Tim, you are dearer to us with each passing year." And one from Meadowgate, signed by Hal, Marge, Dooley, Rebecca Jane, Goosedown, and the six farm dogs, who were all, according to the message, expecting him for an early supper on Sunday.

Emma sent a card with a watercolor of roses, and a Polaroid of Harold and herself on the beach, presumably taken by some stranger she'd snared to do the job. He put it on the bathroom door with a thumbtack, noting that Emma had picked up a jot of weight, while Harold looked a bit spindly.

There was a handwritten note from Stuart, with warm best wishes for a glad heart and good health.

He sat before the stack of cards, feeling a certain comfort.

Then he turned on the answering machine and listened to a lengthy series of well-wishers. "Father," said Winnie Ivey, "I just hate to talk on this thing, but I wanted to tell you how much you mean to everyone. I don't see how in the world any of us could get along without you . . ." He heard Winnie sniffing. "So . . . so, well . . . goodbye!"

What a pleasant lot of activity around an event he'd entirely forgotten!

After dinner, they strolled into Baxter Park and sat on the old bench across from Rachel Baxter's memorial fountain.

"Tell me how you're feeling about Barnabas," she said.

"Terrible, and I think I've finally stopped trying to do anything about feeling that way. It will run its course. You know, if he'd died of old age, that would be one thing. But to have him taken so violently . . . I fear for such dark influences on his spirit."

"But think of the bright influences he found with you. Why, that dog knows more Scripture than most people!"

He laughed, just as the bells at Lord's Chapel pealed the ninth hour.

"Let's suppose the scales weigh heavier on the side of light than dark, and that Barnabas is generously fortified to contend with his present circumstances." She looked at him eagerly. "Like, well, like water lasting a long time in a camel."

He thought about this. It helped a little, and he was thankful. He rested his arm along the back of the bench and touched her shoulder. "Thank you," he said.

They sat silently for a time. In the fading light, the

green of the hedges was as dark as jade. How blessed they were to sit here in this peace, shielded from the suffering of the outside world. "I do hope," Father Roland once wrote, "that you aren't hiding your head in the sand, and sparing yourself the challenge and passion of serving on the cutting edge."

Perhaps, in a small parish, he was spared the passion, but he didn't feel spared the challenge. He was feeling more surely than ever that he was exactly where God meant him to be. All he really needed, he knew, was the endurance to be there with stamina and zeal.

"Do you think you'll stay in Mitford, Timothy?"

"Funny you should ask. I want to. But I feel . . . worn, somehow. Thin soup. I can't seem to do at least one of the things that would help renew my energies."

"And what's that?"

"Take a break. I'm afraid Pastor Greer nailed me one evening. He asked if I was too tired to run and too afraid to rest. And the answer is, yes. Yes, and I'm confused and ashamed about that, about my seeming inability to take charge of my own life."

"I understand."

"You do?"

"Oh, yes," she said, without elaborating.

It occurred to him that he hadn't heard anyone say "I understand" in a very long time. He was suddenly aware of the warmth of her shoulder through the silk shirt.

"Will you drive over with me next Tuesday to see the bishop and his wife? We're going to talk about this very thing, and I'd enjoy your company." The truth was, she'd make the long drive seem a grand holiday.

She looked at him in the frank way he found so appealing. "Next Tuesday? I don't know. I'm trying to get the first draft of the new book out to my agent, to see what she thinks. If you'll pray for me, then of course, I can get it all finished, and in the mail, and go see the bishop with you."

"Consider it done," he said, feeling a surge of happiness.

CHAPTER TWENTY-TWO

A High Command

Viewed from the site of the burned church, where Hope House would be built, the valley spread below like an emerald carpet, dotted with gardens that stocked the coolers of The Local twice a week.

Already, the Silver Queen corn had started coming up the mountain every Tuesday and Friday, to be unloaded into the wooden bins. And, as always, the villagers could be counted on to clean out the entire truckload in a single day, so that everybody knew what everybody else was having for dinner.

He was happy to stand in line at the sidewalk corn bins holding his paper bag, though, inevitably, someone offered him their place toward the front of the queue. No, he did not want to move through the corn line quickly, he wanted to savor the little hum of excitement that always came, and the fellowship, and the laughter.

He wanted time to get a good look at Avis Packard's

face as he peeled back shuck and tassel to display seed-pearl kernels. "Ain't a worm in 'em. You find a worm, you got yourself a free ear."

Miss Rose came, intently looking for worms, while Uncle Billy sat on the bench by the street lamp and told his latest joke to a captive audience. Winnie Ivey closed the bakery and filled a sack for herself and her brother.

While Louella hunted for a dozen perfect ears, Miss Sadie sat in the car, which she had pulled onto the side-walk in front of the library next door, and Percy Mosely walked across the street in his apron to pick up the bushel Avis had earmarked for the Grill.

A tourist once asked a local, "Is there a festival in town?"

"Nope, it's just that th' corn's come in."

"How quaint! Perhaps I should get some."

"Don't know if I'd do that," the local cautioned, darkly. "They say it sours if it travels in a car." Mitford did not like to sell its early corn to outsiders, who, they said, would only overcook it, and couldn't appreciate it, anyway.

Having picked up a bushel for the bishop's wife, he drove around the monument with his neighbor, who looked dazzling in a dress the color of jonquils, and headed toward Wesley as the bells chimed nine o'clock.

"Once you go around the monument," he said, "it's another world."

"I'm excited! Do you know I've hardly been outside the town limits since I came here last fall?"

He laughed. "That happens to some of us. I've hardly been outside the town limits since I came here more than twelve years ago."

"Perhaps this is the day that will start to change."

"I'd like to think so. Old age and creeping provincialism are a dire combination."

"Did I tell you how much I liked your sermon on Sunday?"

"You did not, or I would have remembered it."

"Well, it was glorious. You were very bold, I thought, to preach on sin. Hardly anyone wants to hear sin preached."

"Mainstream Christianity glosses over the fact that it isn't just a question of giving up sin, but of doing something far more difficult—giving up our right to ourselves."

He made the turn onto the busy highway toward Wesley, which always, somehow, seemed a shock to his senses. "The sin life in us must be transformed into the spiritual life."

"How?"

"Through sacrifice and obedience."

She smiled ironically. "How do you think that will be received by those of us who come to sit in a comfortable pew, and find a hot seat instead?"

"They'll just have to go across the street until I've finished preaching on that particular subject."

She laughed with delight. "You're different these days."

He laughed with her. "I pray so," he said.

❧

"Timothy!" Stuart Cullen came down the steps with his arms outstretched.

"Stuart, old friend!" said the rector, as they embraced.

"You've come a long way, and relief is on the table," the bishop assured him. "And who is this beautiful woman?"

Cynthia took his outstretched hand.

"This is my neighbor, Cynthia Coppersmith. Cynthia, Bishop Cullen, my seminary confidant, esteemed friend, and—thanks be to God—my bishop."

Cynthia curtsied a little. "Oops, I'm sorry. That was involuntary."

He laughed. "You're a century or so off, Cynthia, but I appreciate it, nonetheless." Still holding her hand, he drew her toward the front door.

The rector saw that Stuart's sandy hair was beginning to mingle more freely with gray, and there were furrows in his brow that he hadn't noticed when they met some months ago. Even so, he was still surprisingly trim and boyish, with an unaffected charm that never seemed to diminish. He felt a great warmth toward this man who had been an ongoing part of his life.

"Come inside, please. We've laid on the family silver, and Martha's rolls are just coming out of the oven. Your timing has always been excellent, Timothy."

As they entered the foyer, the rector saw something he hadn't been able to see as Cynthia sat on the passenger side. It was one of those infernal pink curlers, bobbing jauntily behind her right ear, as she greeted the bishop's wife.

During lunch, he did everything he could think of to apprise her of the curler, to no avail.

He decided he wasn't very good at sending nonverbal signals, and gave up halfway through the veal chops. He remembered his father had been made responsible for telling his mother whether her slip was showing before they set out for church. Any runs in her stockings? Too much rouge? Any labels protruding in unsightly places?

He recalled that his father had taken this job rather seriously, and seemed to enjoy it, though he had no earthly idea why.

❧

In the study, Stuart Cullen sat in a leather wing chair and looked at the rector with his warmly direct gaze.

"Tell me everything, Timothy."

"I've tried to organize my thinking, so I could spare your time."

"Please. Let that be my concern. I've set all else aside until a meeting in my office at six."

"Well, then. Things haven't changed dramatically since my letter more than a year and a half ago. I seem to be paralyzed at times with such fits of exhaustion, that I end up merely plodding on, and my sermons reflect it. I should say my spirit reflects it, and it's carried out into my preaching.

"I'm reminded of the time the vestry was invited to the home of a new parishioner, someone fairly wealthy, by most standards.

"Most of us were pretty excited about the banquet that would likely be spread." He laughed. "Well, we sat around 'til nine in the evening eating stale crackers and a cheddar so hard it broke the cheese knife."

When the bishop smiled, fine lines crept around his eyes.

"I feel that's what I'm serving. On every side, God's people look for—and deserve—a banquet, but they're getting thin rations. 'Feed my sheep,' he said. That's a direct commission.

"The love of the people at Lord's Chapel is clearly there for me. The church is growing, our obligations are settled on time, and soon we'll build one of the finest nursing homes anywhere. Looking at it from the outside, it seems everything is all right."

He was silent for a moment. "I think what I want to say, Stuart, is that I want it to be more than all right. It must be more than just . . . all right. That's where I am. And I don't know where to go from here."

"Cynthia seems to think your sermon on Sunday was a great deal more than thin rations. Even on first meeting, I trust her judgment. She appears to have a lively faith."

"Yes, well . . ."

"Surely you don't expect your sermons to be preached from the mountain every time? You know as well as I that we must also preach from the valley."

"I do know that. But the times on the mountain have been too few. I have, in many ways, disappointed myself, and if that's so, then surely I'm disappointing others. It's hard to put it clearly, Stuart, but I feel . . . flat."

"That's putting it clearly."

"Somehow, things seem to have taken a turn about the time of the diabetes."

"Diabetes? You never told me you have diabetes."

"Oh, well," he said, shrugging, "it's the non-insulin-dependent variety, nothing to worry about. I didn't want to trouble you with something unimportant."

"Martha's sister is diabetic. And believe me, it's not unimportant. It's a critical dysfunction."

"Oh, but nothing that diet and exercise can't address. Martha's sister is probably insulin dependent."

"She is now," Stuart said, "but she was once precisely where you are. It erupted suddenly into something far more serious. This concerns me."

The last thing he wanted to do was give his bishop any grave concern. That was not why he had come.

"Are you completely fastidious about taking your medication, about your exercise and diet?"

He couldn't tell a lie. "No. I'm not."

"Timothy. For God's sake."

"I'm feeling as miserably guilty as I should, and I want to promise you that I'll become fastidious again—at once. What I don't want to do is let us confuse this issue with the deeper issue."

"I'm not convinced that this issue isn't part of the deeper issue. Bodily fatigue, which nearly always accompanies this hateful malady, can wear down the spirit. And how can the Holy Spirit work with a vessel that's leaking as fast as he can fill it?"

"If I know you," the bishop continued, kindly, "you are not resting. You are not recreating. You haven't been on vacation in a very long time, as I recall."

"Yes. That's right."

"What have you been facing, recently? Let's look at the last few months."

"A boy, I've been given a boy, he's nearly twelve. Dooley." He missed Dooley, he realized suddenly. "That's been . . ."

"Rough."

"Yes. For an old bachelor like me. Then, the jewels, of course. All that was morbidly unnerving, though the results, as I told you on the phone, were glorious.

"And Barnabas—my dog—was snatched from me on the street, and a man has been shot over the whole affair."

"I'm sorry . . ."

"Not to mention a parishioner and friend who's just had a heart transplant against some very dire odds."

"So. No recreation of any sort, and a series of stressful circumstances superimposed over your usual round of duties and the symptoms of diabetes. Has sleeping been a problem?"

"The worst."

"Seen your doctor lately?"

"Not lately. He's been very caught up with the transplant logistics."

"Lousy excuse. No good! See your doctor immediately."

He nodded. "You have my word."

"Now, I want to exercise my authority as your bishop and ask you to do something else. I want you to go away for two months."

"But there's the boy, and—"

"I'm not interested in the boy, or in any other condition or circumstance that presently exists in your life. That sounds cold and hard, but it's neither. You are my interest, not because you're my friend, but because you're exceedingly valuable to this diocese, and I very much want to keep it that way.

"You've always known how to take care of everybody and everything but yourself. I can say that freely because I'm afflicted with the identical weakness, and, trust me, it is a weakness. I'm blessed with a wife who monitors me, but you have no monitor. If you're going to extend your life in the body of Christ, Timothy, you must act at once to restore, to revive, to refresh your energies.

"You tell me you've gone stale, but the sound health of your parish disproves it. 'Wherefore, by their fruits ye shall know them,' Christ said. That's how I know you, my friend, by your fruits. You haven't let Him down, you haven't let me down, and you haven't let your parish down. But you've been letting yourself down—shamefully."

He was suddenly chilled and peevish. He wished he had never come. Why hadn't he kept his own counsel, made his own determinations? To be scolded like a child was a rude shock, and he felt his skin grow damp with a disagreeable sweat.

"Do you think I like to speak to you this way?" Stuart asked. "I do not. But it must be done. If you need money to go away, that will be taken care of at once."

"It isn't money."

"I recall that your mother left you a considerable sum, if you haven't given it all away."

"Not all," he said, coloring.

The bishop waited a moment. "Tell me . . . what about Cynthia? Does she mean something to you?"

"Yes. I think so."

"You seem uncertain."

"I'm not uncertain about whether she means something to me; I'm uncertain about what that implies."

"You mean whether it could imply marriage?"

"Yes. And if so, is that what would be right and good at this stage of my life, and good for her . . ."

"I think she feels tenderly toward you."

He realized it felt better to discuss Cynthia than to hammer away at his backsliding. "She asked me to . . ." he cleared his throat, "to go steady."

Stuart laughed heartily. "Why, that's wonderful! That's terrific!"

He waited, impatiently, for the laughter to stop. Blast! Why had he brought it up?

"That must have taken some courage on her behalf."

"She said as much."

"What was your answer?"

"She asked me to think about it—and I'm still thinking."

Stuart's eyes shone with happy amusement. "When you've thought it through, I hope you'll let me know the outcome. I like her, she's tonic. And that is, after all, what you seem to be needing."

They had veered off course, and it was clearly up to him to veer back. "Are you suggesting that I carry on? That I take a break and carry on?"

"I am. Since your letter a few months ago, you haven't done anything differently. Its time to do something differently, to rest, to seek God's heart on this matter with a fresh mind. I'd like to see you settle your affairs quickly, and be off. We can put Father John in your pulpit, if that's agreeable. He'd be like a hand slipping into a glove, and you can trust him not to turn the place upside down in your absence."

"Very well," he said, smiling. "You've pushed me to the brink once again."

The bishop chuckled as the two men stood and embraced. "But I only do it once every thirty-five years!"

So it had been thirty-five years since his friend had helped him make the decision about Peggy Cramer.

"Stuart," he said, as they stood for a moment at the door of the study, "I'd like to do something rather unorthodox."

"I trust your orthodoxy enough to trust your unorthodoxy."

"I'd like to put an old Baptist preacher in my pulpit now and again. He has a lot to say to us, I believe, and I trust him. He's self-taught and has pastored several country churches for many years. His theology is sound as a dollar, and his spirit is fervent in the Lord. I believe the very oddity of it would cause many to listen who haven't had ears to hear."

"Do it, then."

"Thank you. Now, where do you and Martha want the corn?"

✿

He was relieved that Cynthia didn't look at him, but at the dashboard of the car, which she addressed with great feeling. "I cannot—no matter how hard I try—believe that you did not tell me that stupid curler was banging around back there. I could have died when I found it! There we sat, civilized as you please, and that stupid curler sticking in there. What's worse, it was on the side next to the bishop!"

"It was only Stuart," he said, mildly.

"But why didn't you say something?" wailed Cynthia.

"I tried to. I did! I kept pointing to my head, I thought that might . . ."

"I thought you were scratching your ear, for heaven's sake!"

"I have never been fluent in body language."

"When you were in the study, Martha just reached over and said, 'Do you know, that's exactly where I always forget and leave one, myself,' which was the most dreadful lie, since she's never rolled her hair in her life, it's straight as a stick!"

If he dared even glance at her from the corner of his eye, he would howl with laughter.

"Timothy, you're laughing at me, I can tell! Your stomach is jiggling! Why not come right out with it, and laugh your head off, then? Go on, you're most cordially invited!"

He cleared his throat, unable to speak.

"I mean, what if your fly had been open?"

"I beg your pardon?"

"Well, think about it! If your fly was standing

open in broad daylight, don't you think I'd have informed you?"

He had to admit that was a sobering thought. "Cynthia," he said, still looking attentively at the road, "I'm sorry. I'm truly sorry. I did try to tell you. Forgive me."

A long silence. "Oh, poop! I do forgive you." She sat back in the seat, as if exhausted. "Will I never get it right?"

"I think you have it far righter than most people, as a matter of fact."

"You do?"

"Indeed, I do. And so does the bishop. He says you're tonic. Tonic! Is that the cruel judgment of a man who was appalled by the sight of a mere hair curler?"

Though he wasn't inclined to be careless at the wheel of a car, he reached over and took her hand.

"Well . . ." she said, brightening.

❧

He awoke in the night and found himself drenched with sweat, his pajamas clinging wetly to his legs. Water! That's what he wanted. He was burning with thirst.

With great effort, he sat up, then forced himself to go to the bathroom and fill his empty glass. Dear God, he felt strangely weak and bereft.

Tomorrow, he would begin the medication with a vengeance and would be up and running by six. It would be good to get on schedule again. He recalled how terrific he'd felt during those early months of running, seeing Mitford from a new perspective. Life changing!

He put on another pair of pajamas and went back to bed, speaking aloud from the Psalms, to the still room: "Withhold not thy tender mercies from me, O Lord; be pleased, O Lord, to deliver me . . ."

An image of Cynthia in the dazzling yellow dress came to him just before he slept.

He stopped by the hospital in his running clothes, and spent a half hour with Joe Joe, who was eager to come home. Then he ran by to see Russell and Betty Craig, who appeared to have struck a happy truce. After a light breakfast at the rectory and a brief visit with Puny, he went to the office to do what the bishop had asked him to do.

"I'm sorry, Father," said the nurse when he called, "but Dr. Harper is out of town for a week. Dr. Wilson would be happy to see you, I could work you in . . ."

"No, that's all right. I'll wait for Dr. Harper. Better put me down right after he returns."

"Let's see. I don't have anything the week after he gets back, but if we have a cancellation, I could call you."

"Excellent! Do that," he said.

There. He had a full prescription on hand, he had taken his medication, he had run, he had eaten a sensible breakfast and cut back on caffeine, and he had called the nurse. All that was easy enough. It was the other, the planning of the two-month sabbatical that he dreaded.

As odious as the prospect seemed, he was, however, grateful. Another sort of bishop might have trusted him to take care of the problem on his own. But Stuart had used his authority to issue a command, and he had been absolutely right. His bishop had done what he hadn't the gall to do himself. That feeling of being stuck to this place like moss on a tree, like lichen on a stump, would have to be gotten over.

"Hello, Walter? Timothy. Is this a good time? Well,

then, if it isn't too late to get in on the trip with you and Katherine, I'd like to come along." There was a stunned silence. "Walter? Walter! Hello?"

❧

Had the Enemy tricked him all these years into believing no one could do without him?

Wasn't Russell in the best of circumstances? Didn't Olivia have a new heart, and wasn't she improving daily, with no signs of rejection?

Wasn't Lord's Chapel enjoying an especially smooth state of affairs just now, with as little wrangling and backbiting as he'd witnessed in years?

Wasn't the Sunday school gaining momentum and fulfilling a need? Wasn't the new youth choir gearing up for a full program in the fall?

And wasn't Miss Sadie in better shape than ever, with the secret off her heart and Louella under her roof?

He searched his conscience for anyone who might need him. In a day or two, he would approach Miss Rose about the life estate and whether they could move ahead at once—after resolving, of course, the statue of Willard.

There would be no final drawings of Hope House for some time, and, when they came, Ron Malcolm was infinitely able to judge them fairly and make interim decisions with the vestry.

Emma would be back any day and could handle things without him. Father John would be an agreeable fellow, if a bit lazy. Cynthia would take the rabbit in, surely. Puny would continue to cook and clean on the two days the vestry paid for, very likely causing Father John to think he'd died and gone to heaven.

Perhaps, just perhaps, if he promised to bring her a

Waterford goblet, Hessie Mayhew would chip in to turn the sprinkler on the roses in the memorial garden.

But what about Dooley? The last thing he wanted was for Dooley to feel uprooted and pulled apart.

"I'd like to have a boy," said Cynthia, looking brave. "I could . . ."

"You could what?"

"Draw him!"

"Aha," he said, unconvinced.

"I've had a boy in my life, my husband's nephew. His mother died, and Elliott and I took him in while he was in college. David and I got to be the fastest of friends and comrades, he was such a blessing to me when Elliott was away for weeks and months at a time. You've never met him, but you shall."

"I appreciate your offer, but God hasn't yet shown me what to do about Dooley."

"He will show you, of course, so just relax, why don't you?"

Relax? Yes. Well, that was a good idea.

❧

The door to the office swung open.

"They got 'em," Rodney said, proudly. "Down in Holding is where they nailed th' scumheads. Th' law down there had up a roadblock, checkin' licenses. This little ol' boy on th' force remembered hearin' th' statewide when it went out, and recognized 'em. They'd painted their van an' all, but he was on to 'em. Pulled 'em over for a dead headlight, radioed in without 'em knowin' it, and three cars of Holding's best jumped over there like blue ticks on a coon. Dadgum!" said Rodney with considerable joy, hitching up his holster. "That was the biggest bust Holding ever did, a whole vanload of dope."

"Barnabas. What about . . . ?"

"Nope. Sorry. That's th' bad news," said Rodney, taking off his hat. "No sign of your dog. I tell you, Father, that might be just as well, if you know what I mean."

He didn't know, exactly, and probably didn't want to.

❧

"Hey," said Dooley, coming to the phone.

"Hey, yourself. How's it going?"

"Great."

"Tell me about it."

"Me'n ol' Kenny McGuire rode th' hair off 'em horses this mornin'. Then we played softball with 'em boys down at th' pond, and whipped 'em s' bad they was about t' bawl. You comin' agin Sunday?"

"I wouldn't miss it."

"I want you t' see me ride Goosedown. I got 'er t' likin' me s' good, she's jist like a little ol' baby or somethin'."

"Speaking of which, how is Rebecca Jane?"

"Cryin' after me s' bad, I have t' git out of th' house. Dools this, Dools that. You know how 'at is."

"Oh, I do, I do," said the rector.

To some, he thought as he hung up, that might have sounded like an ordinary conversation. But in fact, it was music, yes, music to his ears.

❧

During the announcements at the eleven o'clock service, he drew attention to the meeting of the Altar Guild and the meeting of the lay readers, and issued another plea for youth choir recruits.

He tried to drum up business for the Baptists, who

were having a lawn sale for foreign missions, and the Presbyterians, who were having a bake sale for hymnals.

"Are there any other announcements?" he asked.

"Why, yes," said Hal Owen, coming to the steps in front of the altar with something in his hand, "I'd like to announce, on behalf of the entire congregation, that we're sorry to have taken so long to celebrate your birthday."

He felt his face grow warm.

"You see, we had to wait for everybody to get their Frequent Flyer points together, so we could give you this envelope. It will take you nearly anywhere you care to go . . . and we'd appreciate it if you'd come back."

As he took the envelope, the congregation applauded enthusiastically. "I don't know what to say," he blurted.

Hal grinned. "Oh, just anything that comes to mind will do."

"Hallelujah!" he exclaimed, through the lump in his throat.

❧

"I don't know how to tell you this," said Emma, who had gotten a tan, stepped up the amount of henna in her rinse, and was wearing earrings that looked like small hands of bananas.

"Just start at the beginning," he advised.

"I'm goin' back to bein' a Baptist," she declared flatly.

"Emma, you definitely got too much sun. Baptists quite often become Episcopalians, but Episcopalians seldom ever become Baptists. You will be going against the tide."

"Peedaddle on th' tide. Harold and I talked it over and we decided it was foolish for him to head off in one direction on Sunday and me to head off in another. Because the truth is, Harold will never be an Episcopalian."

"True, Emma, true."

"He said for me not to mention this to you, but if he had to keep singin' that ol' stuff in our hymnbook, he'd jump out the window."

"That would be a sight for sore eyes. Headfirst, I take it."

"Now you want to hear the good news?"

"I'm always ready to hear good news."

"I'm goin' to keep workin' just like I've been doin', keepin' the same hours and all. That part won't change a bit."

Blast.

"And I'm goin' to report to you on how the Baptists do things. It will be a big help around here. For example, do you ever see First Baptist hurt for money? No way! That's because they don't have any of this 'tithe on the net or tithe on the gross' business. Baptists do it on the gross, just like the Bible says, period."

Perhaps he would jump out the window, headfirst.

"Anyway, Esther will take the collection home on Sunday and bring it to me on Monday. In the winter, I told her to carry the money bag under her coat, and in the summer, stick it in a book bag under some library books. You never know, these days."

"Absolutely!"

She leaned over her typewriter and peered at him. "Are you all right? You look pale. When's the last time Joe gave you a trim? Have you been seein' your neighbor? Oh, and how's her cat—don't cats make you sneeze? I drove by your house this morning and saw her yard. You should offer to mow it."

Very likely, Emma Garrett was the penance he'd been ordained to pay for the delight of employing Puny Bradshaw.

❦

"So Rose said t' me, she said, 'Bill Watson, I'm goin' t' give you a piece of my mind,' and I said, 'Just a small helpin', please.' " He grinned broadly at the rector.

"Yessir, I told Rose what you said about givin' th' house to th' town, an' them givin' her a nice, modern place all fixed up in th' back, and she said th' only way she'd do it was if the statue was like Sherman or Grant or one of them, don't you know. That's when I said he ought t' be settin' down, and she like to th'owed a fit."

Uncle Billy chuckled. "Preacher, I took Rose f'r better or worse, but I declare, she's s' much worse than I took 'er for!

"Maybe we ought t' let 'er have that statue standin' up. I dread another winter, don't you know, with th' wind a blowin' through th' cracks, and th' oil a settin' in th' tank."

The rector doubted that Miss Sadie would be able to drive past such a statue without a shudder, but that was not the issue. "It might be possible to have at least one room modernized by winter, with a bath to go with it, if we can agree on this matter right away."

"Law," said the old man, "I'd dearly love to have me a hot bath, if Arthur'll let me set in a tub."

"Why don't we move forward with the standing version. If we carry on too long about whether he sits or stands, you might go out of here lying down."

"You hit the nail on th' head. Why don't you do th' talkin' and I'll do th' duckin'?"

❧

"We can move ahead on the Porter place," he said to Esther Cunningham when he dropped by her office. "If I were you, I'd have some renderings done right away, so Miss Rose can feel involved, or she could change her mind on the whole thing. The D.A.R. crowd ought to know about statues and monuments and who does that sort of thing. Of course, we'll need to talk with her attorney at once, and I'd hope we could have them in a snug room and bath by winter."

"We'll start by dumpin' all th' Rose Festival proceeds in the restoration fund." The mayor's face had started to blotch with red spots, as it usually did when she was excited. "This thing's goin' to cost a king's ransom; we'll have to depend on some big shots around here to help get it done. How about if you. . . ."

"Don't go appointing me to raise any money. I can see it in your eyes."

The mayor laughed heartily. "You're quick."

"I have to be quick to dodge the bullets you'd fire if I gave you half a chance."

"Speakin' of—our boy's lookin' good, wanted mashed potatoes and gravy for supper last night. Puny carried him a bowlful."

"What do you think about that girl?"

"She calls herself a Bradshaw, but she's Cunningham through and through. We love 'er to death. Ray says he wouldn't take a war pension for the way she cuts up and sasses him."

"Well, maybe now that she's got Ray, she'll leave off sassing me."

"I wouldn't hold y'r breath," said the mayor.

It was Olivia.

"Father, I just called to say I love you."

"You did? Why, what a wonderful thing to hear." He felt as if someone had poured a bucket of warm water over him. Love! Sometimes, the very sound of that word conjured the feeling itself.

"I'm missing your sermons. Hoppy gives me a report when we talk, but sometimes he forgets the point!"

He laughed happily. "Let me mail you my sermons each week, shall I? The Holy Spirit often sends more than you'll find typed out, but at least, it will be something from home."

"Thank you! I have a proposition."

"Don't keep me waiting."

"How would you like to fly to Boston with Hoppy and spend a few days? It would be such good medicine to see you. And you could meet Leo. You'd enjoy each other so much. It would be lovely!"

After nearly thirteen years of staying put, it was suddenly "Come to Ireland!" "Come to Boston!" Feast or famine.

CHAPTER TWENTY-THREE

Homecoming

"Are you in the mood to have your bed dug?" he asked through the screen door.

"Why, yes!" she said, turning around from the stove.

"Good, because I'm in the mood to dig it."

"Come in and have a cup of tea, the kettle's hot, and I'll get dressed. My, you're an early riser. For heaven's sake, stop looking at me," Cynthia said, fleeing from the kitchen in her bathrobe.

He took a spoonful of tea out of the canister, put it in the silver caddy, poured boiling water into the mug, and sat down on the stool by the wall phone. It was nice to have a change of scenery, to get up and sit in someone else's kitchen and look out someone else's back door. For another change, he'd rested well, and, since it was Saturday, hadn't set the alarm. Then he had run along Church Hill by the orchards, and looked down upon the village in its spring finery. He had felt such a tenderness of heart for the little town tucked so neatly at the foot of the hill, that he had stopped to sit on the stone wall.

Sitting on a stone wall, idly gazing, scarcely thinking. Stuart Cullen would have been proud.

"There!" said Cynthia, who had caught her blond hair in a yellow bow, and was wearing blue jeans, a sweatshirt, and sneakers. He thought she didn't look a day over twenty.

"Any word from your agent?"

"She called last night. She'd like to see more people in it, not just animals. So, I was thinking. Would you be a wise man?"

"Me being a wise man would be a foolish contradiction. Is this drawing to be from life . . . or the other?"

She laughed. "It depends. If you'll go to a party at the Sturgeons' with me, it will be from life. If you refuse to go, it will be from . . . the other."

❧

Digging a bed was no job for the fainthearted, he thought, especially when it was a king-size bed.

"Just dig around here," she said, walking it off in her sneakers, "and then come around like this." She paced the circumference of what might have been a small ballfield.

"Cynthia," he said, wiping his brow, "that is not a bed, that is your entire backyard."

She pushed her glasses up on her nose and peered around.

"A job for a backhoe!" he exclaimed, hoping to make his point. "A John Deere tractor! A team of mules!"

"Oh, well, whatever you think, then," she said, cheerfully.

He dug the long, narrow bed near the sidewalk, away from the shade of the oak tree. "Do you have something we can break up the clods with, and then rake it fine?"

She came back with a motley assortment of her dead uncle's garden tools, which, he reasoned, should be in grand condition, since he'd never used them. She plunked them down proudly at the edge of the bed.

"Well, then," he said, unable to identify little more than an ancient bulb planter. "Let's just break up the clods with our hands, I see you've got good gloves. Then we'll rake it. How's that?"

"Perfect!" she said, with redeeming eagerness.

"What are you going to put in?" he asked, as they knelt side by side and went to work.

"Canterbury bells. Delphinium. Foxglove. Cosmos. And in the fall, double hollyhocks. Gobs and gobs of things!"

Just then, he heard an oddly familiar sound, somewhere. What was it? Still on his knees, he raised his head to listen.

It was the great and booming bark, as deep as the bass of the organ at Lord's Chapel.

Before he could rise or turn around, he was knocked sprawling into the loam of his neighbor's perennial bed, and a warm and lavish bath was administered at once to his left ear.

Barnabas had come home.

He rolled on his back, shouting with joy and trying to get up, but Barnabas immediately stood on his stomach, finding it a good base from which to administer a bath to Cynthia's face. "Timothy!" she shrieked. "Say a Scripture and step on it!"

" 'And we know that all things work together for good to them that love God!' " he shouted.

Barnabas sat on the rector's stomach and sighed.

There he lay in the dirt, with an enormous, mud-caked dog sitting on top of him, while his astonished neighbor was thrashed by a wagging tail the size of a kitchen broom. He laughed until the tears came.

"I'd like t' have a Kodak picture of this deal," said a voice overhead.

He looked up into the face of Homeless Hobbes.

"This critter was at my door at daylight this mornin.' He was s' starved, I give 'im half a cake of cornbread and it was gone in one bite. Then I poured up last night's soup and he eat that. I give 'im two Moonpies and he chased 'em down with a bucket of water. I was doin' m' wash and had t' wait f'r my shirt t' dry, so I put a rope around his neck and staked 'im to m' cot. In a little bit, we come on up here, an' when he heard you talkin', he like t' pulled me down, so I let 'im go."

Father Tim got to his feet and embraced his friend from the creek, as Barnabas collapsed into the dirt with a contented moan. "Homeless, meet my neighbor, Cynthia Coppersmith. Cynthia, meet Samuel K. Hobbes."

"Mr. Hobbes," she said, throwing her arms around him, "you will surely get a blessing for this!"

"I believe I just got my blessin'."

Father Tim examined Barnabas as well as he could through the muddy coat. "Looks like he's been on the road for a while. See here, his feet have been bleeding, not to mention he's a bag of bones under all this hair. I'll have to get him to Hal this afternoon."

Barnabas home! How unbelievable, how extraordinary. He felt as if some part of him had been returned, like an arm, perhaps, or a leg. He felt strangely, suddenly whole. What was needed was something to suit the occasion—shouting, maybe, or anything loud and recklessly fervent!

Just then, Violet strolled around the side of Cynthia's house, and Barnabas shot away from him like an arrow to its mark. The blur of white raced across the grass and disappeared down the coal chute as Barnabas filled the air with sufficient noise to suit the occasion.

❧

Homeless sat at the kitchen counter while the rector brewed a pot of coffee and an exhausted Barnabas lay sleeping by his food bowl at the door.

"It's a treat to have you in my kitchen, for a change," he told his friend from the creek. "You know, you've brought me something I thought I'd never find again."

"That brings up m' own point," said Homeless. "Somethin' I lost has been found, too."

"And what's that?" asked the rector, leaning against the sink.

"My faith. It looks like it's come back. An' t' tell th' truth, it's a whole lot stronger than it was when it left."

"I'm glad to hear it. You don't know how glad."

"Well, I took down th' New Testament you brought me, an' I said, I b'lieve I'll just crack this open f'r a minute—I knew I didn't want t' go gettin' no religion out of it, nossir.

"So I baited me a hook and I put it on my fishin' line and went 'n sat on th' creek bank, an' done somethin' I hadn't done since I was a boy—I tied th' line on m' big toe. You know, that makes sense, you don't have t' mess with a pole. That way, when you get a bite, you know it, and all y have t' do is just pull 'er in. Time savin'!

"So I was settin' there an' I commenced t' read, and first thing you know, I was dead into it. I'd catch me a crappie, take it off th' hook, bait up again, and go back t' readin'. I done that all day, and by th' time I'd fried me some fish and eat a good dinner, it come to me plain as day that m' faith was back. God Almighty had put his hand on me again after all these years. You know what I figure?"

"What's that?"

"I figure what can y' lose? Jesus said, 'Verily, I say unto you, he that believeth on me hath everlasting life.'

"Well sir, what if that's a lie? If it's a lie, then you live in sin, and die in sin, and the worms consume y'r flesh, anyway. But if it's th' God's truth, like he says it is, you win. Y'r sins are forgiven, you get a clean start, and when you die, you live for eternity.

"It seems t' me that's a deal a man cain't pass up. Number one, it's free. Number two, you cain't lose." Homeless grinned happily. "It's a good feelin'. Kind of like I've found a home."

"Your heart is saying you're not homeless, any-more."

" 'Course, I don't know what I'm goin' t' do about it, yet."

"Just enjoy it!" said the rector. "You'll know soon enough. And when you're ready, we'll talk about it, if you'd like."

"Dandy!"

He poured coffee into a mug for his guest. "I don't have a drop of cream, but there's sugar."

"I give up cream when I give up likker. No connection, that's just th' way it fell out."

"You know, they'll be wanting to present you with that twenty-five hundred dollars right away."

"Well, I ain't takin' it," Homeless said, blowing on the steaming coffee. "But I've got a idea."

"Keep talking."

"Up on th' hill behind th' creek is a lot of folks who need it worse'n I do. There's little bitty babies in there that don't get fed right, an' old people that needs medicine and a hot meal. They're people that slip through th' cracks, somehow or 'nother. I'd like t' see that money go in an emergency fund t' help th' ones that need it th' most.

"Give ol' Fred money t' buy 'is own britches instead of wearin' mine to look f'r work. Buy that little ol' Pritchard baby somethin' t' wear, instead of it runnin' around naked. Get ol' woman Harmon a pair of shoes, she's been half-barefooted f'r two winters. Maybe have a free supper once a week, I'll do th' cookin'."

"I guess I thought there'd be social service agencies in there."

"There's this kind of social service and that kind of social service, if y' know what I'm sayin'."

"I know."

"So, if th' reward money's goin' t' be doled out anyway, I'd like t' see it go in a special fund, somethin' we could get to without a lot of flimflam. Maybe we could call this fund th' Creek Bank."

"What a grand idea, in every way!" Barnabas looked up when he heard his master laugh. "See there, old fellow, what you've done? You've helped buy Fred a new pair of pants."

❧

"Homeless man refuses check for $2,500," read the *Muse* headline on Monday.

That the story touched hearts throughout the newspaper's circulation base was no surprise. The surprise was the additional money that poured in, bringing the total to $3,800 in just one week.

The front-page headline on the following Monday gave an update: "Creek Bank Overflows."

"Right there," said Mule Skinner, "is th' single best headline J.C. Hogan ever wrote."

❧

He was doing everything right, including using the food exchange system, which he found to be the very soul of aggravation. But somehow, he didn't feel right. He noticed that his hand shook on several mornings as he read the paper, that his vision blurred occasionally, and his thirst was more pronounced. While all of that had happened before, with no dire consequence, he was relieved that Hoppy would check it out in just two days.

Perhaps the time when he felt most stable and at peace was when he'd wake in the middle of the night and feel Barnabas at the foot of the bed. The comfort of that was so great, that it seemed to alleviate some of the other, milder disorders. Lying awake, he often wondered how a vacation in a foreign country, sleeping in strange beds, and eating strange food, could possibly make one feel better.

He wrote George Gaynor and gave him a complete update on all church doings, including one death and two new members of the nursery.

"Who're you writin'?" asked Emma.

"The man in the attic."

"Do you think I ought to send him some fudge?"

"That's a splendid thought."

"I'm makin' Harold a big batch tonight, he's so skinny I have to shake th' sheets to find him. I'll just make a double batch, and mail it tomorrow. Do you think they'll X-ray it for files or razor blades or whatever?"

"Probably."

"If they're doin' their job, they will," she said with authority. "Do you know what we sang Sunday?"

"What's that?" he muttered, looking in his desk drawer for some glue to repair his bookend.

" 'Amazing Grace.' "

"Aha."

"If Episcopalians would sing that more, instead of all that stuff with no tune, you'd be amazed how people would flock in."

"Is that a fact? I suppose you think a Baptist wrote that hymn."

"Well, of course a Baptist wrote it, they sing it all th' time."

"My dear Emma," he said with obvious impatience, "that hymn was written by an Episcopal clergyman."

"He was prob'ly raised Baptist," she said, huffily.

❧

Esther Bolick was standing at the front door of the rectory, with a cake carrier. Instantly, he knew that he must not, at all costs, let her give him whatever it contained.

"Father?"

"Esther, come in!"

"Oh, I can't," she said. "I've left the car running, and Gene's home waiting for his supper, but I was baking today, and I know how you like my orange marmalade cake, and so I baked one for Gene's birthday tomorrow, and one for you, and oh, I do hope you like it, because I think it's the best I've ever made!"

There. That did it. Looking into those bright and expectant eyes, he knew that he could no more refuse that cake than he could run along Church Hill Drive stark naked.

He paced in front of the refrigerator for a full ten minutes after Esther had gone, finally deciding he must get it out of the house at once.

There was no answer at Cynthia's. Russell? Russell and Betty! No, no. He was going to Meadowgate day after tomorrow, and he'd take it out there. Knowing that cake as he did, he recalled that it would only get better with time.

"Well, then," he said, weakly, staring at the refrigerator.

❧

Barnabas had not gotten through that hateful experience without scars, he concluded. When he dropped a book on the hardwood floor of the study, the dog shot from beneath his wing chair, trembling with fear, and bounded up the stairs to hide under the bed.

He called Meadowgate. "He'll get over it," said Hal. "Give him six months or so for his nervous system to heal, and just keep doing what you're doing. Is he taking the vitamins?"

"Like candy."

"He's been through a tough time, very likely made his way from Holding all the way to Mitford, which was no picnic. Got any plans for your Frequent Flyer points?"

"That's something I need to talk with you and Marge about on Wednesday."

"If you want to leave the boy with us while you take a break, you know you can. He's starting to be pretty responsible around here. He fed the dogs this morning, helped me clean out the kennels, and ran an errand for Marge. He's a neat kid."

"I was going to wait until I got there to tell you, but I'm planning a trip to Ireland."

"Will wonders never cease? You've been talking about that for years."

"Time to put up or shut up. But I want you to know that other arrangements could be made for Dooley. This may be for a couple of months . . ."

"Umm, well . . . he's got some roots going down here. I don't believe I'd disturb them, Tim."

"I don't want to say anything to the boy, yet."

"Come on out, then. I've got a sick horse on the next farm and it doesn't look too good—colic. I may have Dools with me, but we'll catch you around supper time."

"Thank you, my friend. Thank you."

"Don't mention it," said Hal Owen.

❧

He was suffering from his usual evening exhaustion, which he had recently begun to identify as "old age." Perhaps he needed to join Barnabas in a vitamin program.

At a little after nine, the phone rang. It was Stuart.

"Am I interrupting anything?"

"Absolutely nothing of consequence, I'm sorry to say." He was, in fact, very sorry to say it. He would prefer to announce that he'd been reading Archbishop Carey's book or doing sit-ups, something profitable.

"I've just spoken with Father John. His mother died late last night. Quite sudden, the family is devastated. He's going home in the morning to spend some time with his father, who isn't well. I'm sorry about this for many reasons, not the least of which is the jumble it may make of your trip. You *are* planning a trip?"

"Oh, indeed! The congregation has given me a vast

store of Frequent Flyer points and I'm planning to go to Ireland with Walter and Katherine."

"Bravo! Well done! It will just take a jot of time to work out plan B."

"Father Douglas? Would he be available?"

"Father Douglas is writing a book and won't budge from his PC."

"Aha."

"Let me think through this, and I'll get back to you. How's Cynthia?"

"I must call and find out. I've been meaning to do that."

"Yes, please do that, Timothy," said the bishop. "He who hesitates is lost, especially where women are concerned. By the way, I'm thankful to have your news about Barnabas."

When he hung up, he noticed that the receiver seemed heavy, like a barbell.

He turned out the lights in the study, then went to the kitchen and opened the refrigerator door.

There was that blasted cake carrier. Thank God, it wasn't a see-through carrier. One glimpse of that cake, and he'd be dead meat. This way, it might contain a lump of coal, for all he knew.

Barnabas was already sleeping at the foot of the bed when he came upstairs.

As he took his socks off, he noticed his feet and ankles were oddly swollen, something he'd never noticed before. Had he been on his feet a lot today? No more than any other day. He remembered going with a parish group on an intensive three-day bus tour of gardens in Vermont. His ankles had swelled exactly like this. "It's the walking," said his curate. "It's the sitting," said the choir director.

❧

"I don't like it," Hoppy told him on Tuesday afternoon, and proceeded to run a series of uncomfortable tests. The rector decided he'd wait to hear the results on Wednesday morning, then head to Meadowgate. The bulletins would be done, the Evensong posters had just been reprinted, and he, as well as Barnabas, could do with the country air.

He returned to the office after seeing Hoppy, and sat staring at the door. He made an effort to pay attention to his calendar, and saw the dreaded words "Rose Festival," which he'd marked in for this coming Friday and Saturday. Had he prepared anything to say? If his life had depended on it, he couldn't be certain whether he had or not.

He looked at the book-lined walls, which seemed to be closing in on him, and then at Barnabas, snoring in the corner.

No, it wasn't Barnabas he heard snoring, it was the sound of his own breath coming in short, hollow gasps. He sat there, praying. Then, with the only ounce of energy he could summon, he left the office, forgetting to lock the door, and walked home.

He saw Cynthia in her yard as he came around the corner of the rectory.

"Hello!" she said, cheerfully, popping through the hedge in a denim smock and jeans. "I'm looking forward to this evening. Around six-thirty, they said, I hope that's OK. You'll like the Sturgeons, I promise."

Those fish people. Six-thirty? What was she saying?

"You look a bit fagged out, Timothy. Would you like a cup of tea or a sherry?"

"No," he said, curtly.

"Well, then," she murmured, backing away with a bewildered look, "I'll just see you at my house around six-fifteen?"

"I'll be there" he said vaguely, going up his back steps. Be there for what? He would find out later. Right now, he wanted a glass of tea, water, anything, something cold.

He let the leash drop and heard Barnabas dash into the hall and bound up the steps with it clattering behind him.

He saw the tea container in the refrigerator door, but the sight of the cake carrier was suddenly so compelling that he couldn't take his eyes off it. Something cold! The cake would be cold. And sweet. Dear God, he was wrenched with a craving for something sweet, if only one bite. Surely one small bite couldn't hurt.

He took the carrier out gingerly, as if trying to prevent an alarm from going off and announcing his indiscretion to the neighborhood.

His hand shook as he snapped off the top and stood staring at what Esther Bolick had done in an act of innocent generosity. Then, without thinking about it any further, he cut a large slice, ate it standing over the sink, and went back for another piece.

At four o'clock, feeling somehow revived, he sat in his wing chair in the bedroom. He was trying to get dressed for the evening, but something was wrong, he told himself, looking at his feet. Possibly, it was his shoes. He seemed to be wearing one black loafer and one brown loafer. Was that it? He wasn't sure. Perhaps it was something worse, something more grave than shoes.

He studied the situation, keeping his eye on the

clock, and was finally interested to see that he had not put his trousers on. He was sitting there in his shorts. He knew this was true because he could see his legs quite plainly.

"Pants," he said aloud. He looked in his closet and found something that felt like pants. It was not a jacket, it was definitely pants, folded over a hanger.

Water. He had meant to drink water, but had somehow forgotten. First, he must get his pants on, though he couldn't understand how it might be done. They seemed to be upside down. He saw that he couldn't stuff his feet in through the cuffs, that wasn't right, he knew that wasn't right. He would sit down and think about it, he decided, dragging the pants behind him and going to the chest of drawers.

He would need . . . what would he need? Cuff links? The Spurgeons just might dress up for this affair. Charles Spurgeon had said, "Christianity rests upon the fact that Christ is risen from the dead, His sovereignty depends upon His resurrection."

He was thrilled that they'd be visiting the Spurgeons. In fact, Spurgeon was among the saints he had wanted most to meet in heaven.

The room seemed still as a tomb, suspended in time. He knew at last that he could not keep running, he was getting out of breath, he was hurrying too fast, it was all too much, he could not go on.

He felt for the foot of the bed and worked his way around to the side. Then he pulled the covers back and got in, still wearing his shoes and clutching his pants, and breathing the Invitation, "The gifts of God for the people of God, take them in remembrance that Christ died for you, and feed on Him in your hearts by faith, with thanksgiving."

He was not surprised to see that the Spurgeons were having fish for dinner. But he was surprised to see the Lord sitting at the table when they walked into the high-ceilinged room. He felt his heart hammer in his breast.

"Timothy, I have a purpose for this time in your life."

"Yes, Lord," he replied, and at once the hammering ceased and a sweet peace invaded him, and he was floating.

He lifted up through the roof of the rectory and over the village, and saw the monument that anchored the little town, and Lew Boyd's Esso, where Coot and Lew were looking up and waving to him as he passed.

He saw that he had great wings, the wings of a butterfly, that they were an iridescent yellow and purple, and as smooth as velvet. The air rushed under him like a caress, he was buoyed along without effort, and found that the movement of his wings wasn't for the sake of keeping him aloft, but was for joy's sake alone.

He passed over the town, over the green and rolling countryside, and in the distance saw a ribbon gleaming in the light. It was a river, a broad, winding river, and on the other side, there was a small church.

He flew down, attracted to a single flower in the churchyard, and lighted there.

Then the procession came, with everyone dressed in white, led by a man who was bearing a wooden cross.

He placed the cross in a newly dug hole near the church door, and dirt was cast into the hole, and the children brought flowers and pressed their roots into the damp earth around it.

Then the man lifted his hands and prayed, thanking

God for new life and for hope. The butterfly flew to the cross, and lighted there.

"As He left the shroud of death," said the man, "and rose to new life, so this butterfly, which was once trapped in a cocoon, has become free. Go in new life with Christ. Go, and be as the butterfly."

The butterfly lifted its wings and flew. It soared above the church, in the sunshine. It saw the river again, and a cool, sudden breeze, the kind found in the brewing of a storm, moved in from the west.

The butterfly passed over the town anchored by the monument, and over Fernbank sitting on the hill in the orchards. Then there was the red roof of the little house next door, and the slate roof of the rectory.

His head felt thick, as if he had been drugged, or struck a blow. Uneasily, he rolled over and saw someone sitting in the glow of his bedside lamp, looking at him.

Cynthia put her hand on his forehead. He could not speak, nor could he understand her when she spoke. "Timothy," she said, "I'm here."

CHAPTER TWENTY-FOUR

In New Life

"Profound dehydration," said Hoppy. He had pried the rector's jaws open and was looking at his tongue and mouth. "He's not responding. He may have had a stroke."

"No," Cynthia said softly. She heard a siren somewhere.

"Or his sugar may have dropped off the cliff. I'm going to give him a little dextrose now. I told the ambulance to follow me, just in case. Go down and make sure they find us; it's a new driver."

When she came back up the stairs with the ambulance attendants, she was shocked again to see the eyes which could not see her.

❧

"His dextrostick was off the top of the scale. I think I know what's going on," Hoppy told Nurse Kennedy, coming along the hall behind the stretcher. "I want those lab results immediately."

"But, Doctor, there's nobody—"

"I don't want to hear 'nobody,' " he snapped. "You do what has to be done. Pronto."

"Yessir."

"I'm praying," said Cynthia.

He turned to the older nurse, who was waiting calmly for his directions. "Herman, he needs fluid and lots of it. Run a liter of half-normal saline wide open, then cut it back to 500 cc's 'til we get the report."

"Yes, Doctor."

❧

He was walking up a flight of stairs. They seemed to narrow to a point, with an opening at the end as small as the eye of a needle. A brilliant light shone beyond the opening. He didn't know whether he could make it through. . . .

❧

"Well, pal."

He opened his eyes and stared at the doctor's face, finding it an unutterably welcome sight.

"Well, what?" he croaked, glad for the sound of his own voice.

"You took a dive."

"No kidding."

"You've gone and gotten yourself the real thing."

"Meaning?"

"The Big One. You'll have to start giving yourself shots and peeing on a strip of paper. The nurses will be teaching you how to give yourself insulin, and I've ordered a glucometer so you can follow your blood sugar."

"Bad news."

"The good news is, you're alive. Not always the usual after several hours in nonketotic hyperglycemic coma."

With some effort, he realized that the good news was—he wouldn't have to make a speech at that blasted Rose Festival.

❧

Though he was feeling fine, he was strictly forbidden to have visitors.

"Except your neighbor," said the doctor, without further comment.

He learned, to his surprise, that he would be up and around and better than new in only a few days, so there was no obstacle, after all, to his trip. There would be certain inconveniences, yes, like a daily shot that he'd have to administer himself, extreme caution with his diet, and plenty of exercise, none of which promised to enrich foreign travel.

In the meantime, Father Douglas was found to be willing to stir from his PC after all, and agreed to deliver both sermons for the coming Sunday. Father Lewis in Wesley had cheerfully offered to celebrate.

By the second day, he'd received seven arrangements, a gloxinia, and a topiary, giving him the pleasure of knowing that Jena Ivey, at least, was profiting from his condition.

Cynthia came, wearing something emerald-colored and flowing. "A bedtime story," she said, opening a manila envelope containing her new manuscript. "See what you think." She made herself comfortable on the foot of his bed and read aloud the story of the mouse in the manger.

What did he think? Merely that it was beautifully written, thought-provoking, and charming, not to mention touching, funny, and destined for certain recognition.

"All that?"

"All that and more."

"I've heard that sickness softens the heart, but it's made yours positively expansive!"

"Thank you for being there," he said, taking her hand.

"When you didn't come to fetch me for the Sturgeons, I thought you'd stood me up. I knew you hadn't been thrilled about going anyway. So I waited and waited and you didn't come, and finally, I popped through the hedge and knocked on your door and there was no answer, but Barnabas was in the kitchen, barking his head off. I called, but couldn't find you. I looked in the study, the garage, all over. And then I went upstairs, and found you in bed clutching a pair of pants in your hand."

"You did?"

"And with your shoes on!"

"The usual, then."

She laughed. "But I could tell you weren't sleeping. You looked so odd, and you were sweating and your mouth was moving, though nothing was coming out. I called the hospital and Hoppy wasn't there, and I said it was an emergency, so they found him and sent him to your house, thanks be to God!"

He pressed her hand tightly. "I can't remember anything at all. Nothing. The last thing I remember was eating Esther's cake."

"Esther's cake?"

He looked at her helplessly. "I hope you won't say anything to Hoppy."

He saw the concern in her eyes. "I promise. But let it be a lesson to you, for Pete's sake."

"Will you come again tomorrow?"

"Yes," she said, leaning down to brush his cheek with her lips. At the door, she turned around and waved. He thought she looked for a moment like a wistful child. "Sweet dreams," she said, tilting her head to one side.

The faint scent of wisteria on his pillow was a comfort.

❧

"I wouldn't be kissin' any Blarney Stone, if I was you," said Puny, plumping up the cushions on the sofa. "When you think of how many folks has put their mouth on that thing, it gives me th' shivers."

"I have no intention of hanging over some precipice to kiss a rock," said the rector, who was taking his prescribed midday rest in the study. "Instead, I will devote that time to shopping for one Puny Bradshaw and shipping her a surprise."

"As if I didn't have enough surprises," she said tartly, dusting the mantle.

"Like what?"

"Like Joe Joe gittin' shot, and you gittin' in a coma and half dyin'. That's been keepin' me plenty surprised, thank you, not t' mention busy."

"Speaking of busy, would you keep doing the splendid things you do, for the priest who takes my place while I'm in Ireland?"

"I might" she said cautiously. "I'd have t' check 'im out. I don't work for gripers, complainers, or hypocrites, not to mention bossy, mean, or stingy people."

"A good policy. I wish I could say the same. If I'm

still away when school starts, would you be able to live here and take care of Dooley 'til I get back?"

"Well . . ."

"Just think, Joe Joe wouldn't have to drive all the way to Wesley to court you, he could just walk down the street."

She flushed.

"Think about it. It would nearly double your salary, and all you'd need to cook for the boy would be bologna, which, if the priest is young enough, he'd probably like, too."

She sighed. "I wonder why th' Lord is always dishin' out preachers t' me."

❧

Dear Friends:

When I left Mitford several weeks ago, you couldn't see me, but I could see you. Thank you for coming out to wave goodbye.

Especially, I want to thank the kids who cared, and sent those wonderful drawings to the jail. I've been allowed to put a few of them up in my cell, and you'd be surprised to see how much they mean to the other inmates. In this grim and oppressive place, the bright colors stand out vividly, but more than anything, it's a joy to see the freedom in your drawings. They are spontaneous and genuine, and seem to give a certain hope to people who are clearly destitute of hope.

I'm pretty isolated from contact with the other inmates, as I work in the laundry with just five other men. The exercise yard is about the size of the grassy area around your town monument. I go every evening after supper and try to keep myself in shape. Mostly, it's good for clearing my head, as I often feel a real panic about being here.

They told me I'd have to keep an eye on my watch and my shaving kit, but that nobody would steal my Bible. If they could imagine the riches to be found in it, they'd all be after it, and that's what I'm praying for.

I don't know what I can say in this letter, I don't know what is being censored, but I feel pretty certain they will let me say this:

I found something in Mitford that I never believed existed. After I prayed that prayer with Father Tim and my new brother, Pete Jamison, God changed my life. Then He demonstrated His love through you.

Thanks for the shoes. The casseroles. The cakes. The pies. And your prayers. Please write me if you can.

Sincerely, George Gaynor

The rector lowered the latest edition of the *Muse* into his lap. The mail clerks at that prison had their work cut out for them.

❧

"It's Mr. Gregory," announced Puny, wiping her hands on her apron.

He knew he should have shaved this morning. "Ask him to come in!"

He heard Andrew's footsteps coming briskly down the hallway. "A bachelor's paradise!" he said, seeing the book-lined study, the view of Baxter Park, and the bright face of Puny Bradshaw. He inhaled deeply, enjoying a fragrance that clearly had its source in the kitchen.

The rector got up and gave his favorite antiquarian a forceful embrace. "Sit down at once, my friend, and tell me everything. I haven't seen you in . . . when have I seen you? You'd think that since we're across the street from each other, we'd meet more often."

"Life, Father, life," said Andrew, sitting down in a wing chair and unbuttoning his jacket. "It is far too hurried."

"Even in Mitford."

"Particularly in Mitford, I sometimes believe. How are you feeling? Are you going to push along all right?"

"Oh, I think so. A bitter inconvenience, nothing more."

"Would y'all like a cup of coffee or a glass of tea?" asked Puny. The rector thought she looked a picture in her new apron and dress, and her red hair caught up with a green ribbon.

"Tea!" Andrew responded eagerly. "No sugar, if you please."

"I'll have the same," said the rector. He was tenderly amused to see that Puny, who appeared to be in awe of their handsome visitor, curtsied slightly as she left the room.

"Where on earth did you find such a gem?"

"Sent from heaven!"

"Speaking of heaven, I have a new shipment of books from a priory in Northamptonshire. Very rare. Exceptional. One day they won't allow such treasures out of the country. There's a very early *Imitation of Christ.* I thought you'd like to come and have a look."

"I shall. It's a good thing books aren't bad for this aggravating condition, or I'd be a dead man. Any more sales on Uncle Billy's drawings?"

"Why, yes. Four more, and I took him an envelope only yesterday. He likes cash, you know, not checks, and I fear he may be keeping it under his mattress."

"Not a bad move, considering the times."

Andrew laughed. "I read George Gaynor's letter in the paper. And only yesterday, I heard that two of the three British-side dealers have been arrested in Norwich. Fascinating circumstances, really; I've tried to keep up with the account in the newspapers. Inspected all my table legs, but not one is worth a farthing!"

"What can you tell me about Ireland?"

"Ireland? Only a bit. Hopeless Anglophile, you know. Of course, there's been a big trend to Irish antiques, but they're not my cup of tea. Too primitive. Why do you ask?"

"I'm going in a matter of days. Thought you might have some suggestions. We'll be staying in Sligo."

"Ah! rough country. Undeveloped. But spectacularly beautiful, I'm told. Take a raincoat, mud boots, a waterproof watch . . ."

Blast, he thought, why bother to go to such a place, at all?

"Your tea, sir," said Puny, who had put the rectory's best damask napkins on the tray and used their finest cut-glass water goblets.

Andrew took a sip of tea and pressed his mouth with the starched napkin. "I haven't seen much of your neighbor. Is she still about?"

"Oh, very much about."

"Clever lady."

"Yes. Yes, she is."

"Terribly attractive."

"Rather pretty, yes."

"Funny, actually."

"I agree."

"I can't seem to make any headway with her, however. I suspect you know her a bit, being next door. Any suggestions?"

Tall, suave, trim, urbane Andrew Gregory was asking *him?*

He thought for a moment.

"Oh, she'd probably enjoy being invited to more of those fancy country club affairs, perhaps to play bridge, that sort of thing," he lied. Forgive me, Lord, he prayed, I promise I won't do it again.

✼

As Puny saw Andrew to the door, the phone rang.

"Hello," he said. He heard someone breathing. "Hello?"

"I prayed that prayer," said a hoarse voice, and hung up.

"Was that by any chance Joe Joe?" Puny asked, eagerly, hurrying into the study.

"No, it wasn't. I'm not sure who it was." The voice had been oddly familiar, but no . . . no, it couldn't have been who he was thinking.

"You don't know who it was?"

"I didn't recognize the voice, exactly, and then they hung up."

"Wrong number!" said Puny, setting the glasses on the tray and taking it into the kitchen.

✼

Absalom Greer looked at him steadily. "My brother, if I step into your pulpit, some of your flock will be gone when you return."

"So be it."

They were sitting on the steps of the country store, on a day so hot that both had taken their jackets off and rolled their shirt sleeves up.

"You know I'll preach on sin."

"Preach on it, then."

"I'll preach a personal relationship with Jesus Christ."

"I fervently hope so."

"And I'll preach the cross."

"That's what we all need to hear. May God bless you, my friend."

"And may he bless you, Timothy. I didn't know when I quit my little churches last week to get a rest, that th' Lord would hitch me up again before he let th' traces fall." The old pastor laughed, happily. "I'll see that Lottie dresses me proper and I'll keep my shoes shined and a handkerchief in my pocket."

"That's more than I usually manage. How thankful I am that your schedule allows this. It was a sudden inspiration in the middle of the night. I believe the Holy Spirit put it on my heart. Can you hold out for two months?"

"When it comes to preachin', I'd a lot rather hold out than hold it in. I'll answer this call at your place, then I'll quit."

They stood up, and Father Tim clasped the pastor's hand with both of his. "We'll go through the order of service until you get the hang of it, and the bishop will provide someone to celebrate."

"This is pretty unorthodox, you know," Absalom said.

"I trust the orthodoxy of it enough to trust the unorthodoxy," replied the rector, returning his gaze and smiling.

❧

The trip to the airport had become a dilemma. Joe Ivey, Mule Skinner, Ron Malcolm, and Hal Owen had all volunteered to drive.

Emma, however, had insisted, which settled that consequential matter.

"Well, of course, you must leave Barnabas with us," said Marge, when they talked on the phone.

"But you've done—you're doing—so much already," he protested, sincerely.

"Just think of all you do for us, Timothy!"

Frankly, he couldn't think of anything at all.

In his last sermon, he made every effort to prepare the congregation.

"Pastor Greer warns me that some of my flock will have leaped over the wall by the time I return. But I challenge you to remain in the fold, and to hear what he has to say, and to ponder it in your hearts. I haven't made this decision lightly, nor has the bishop been casual in giving his blessing. There will be some awkward moments, very likely, for Pastor Greer doesn't know our order of service, but I want you to pray for him, and give him the right hand of fellowship, and keep a strong hedge around yourselves until I return."

Some of his flock looked at him quizzically as he greeted them on the church lawn. No one liked change, and why in heaven's name couldn't he have brought in Father Douglas, whom they at least knew? What did it matter if his sermons were largely tepid? He was comfortable, they were comfortable, and surely any bishop worth his salt could have talked him into leaving his book, which probably wasn't going to be very exciting, anyway. Or Father Randall, now there was someone who'd pep the place up and make a contribution, though there was always the question of his unfortunate preference for guitar music at the eleven o'clock. And what about this preacher being a Baptist, for heaven's sake? They only hoped he would not raise his voice and shout, or worse yet, issue an altar call.

In the cool of the evening, he walked to Fernbank

with Barnabas, taking his time on the hill, and found Miss Sadie and Louella sitting on the porch, fanning.

"Ladies, what's up?"

"What's up is that we're looking for company," Miss Sadie told him. "Louella and I were just talking about how nobody visits on Sundays like they used to. What on earth do you think people *do* if they don't visit?"

"They go to the mall," said the rector, out of breath. He sat on the steps with Barnabas, who was glad for the cool steps on the east side of the house.

"Surely not!"

"However, the old customs haven't vanished entirely. After all, here I am."

"Let Barnabas come up with us," said Miss Sadie, who was still in her church clothes.

Louella drew away from Barnabas. "Thass th' biggest dog I ever seen. I lived in houses ain't as big as that dog."

Barnabas collapsed at Miss Sadie's feet and yawned contentedly. "There now! What a treat! Louella, do you suppose we ought to get a dog?"

"Oh, law!" Louella was speechless.

"Well, Father, you should know that we're all in a dither about Absalom Greer coming to supply us while you're gone. I think that was a very odd thing to do, but I'm excited about it."

"You're right. It was a very odd thing to do. But I think the oddity of it will have its effects. Will you give me a report on how things are going now and then? I'll leave you an itinerary, with addresses and phone numbers. And I wanted to say I'll write you ladies every week. That's a promise."

"You've spoiled us, Father. You really have. Nearly thirteen years and barely missing a Sunday except for special meetings of the diocese, and that awful winter when the flu kept you down."

"You know to call Hal or Ron if you need anything, and Esther Bolick and Emma will look out for you. Why, after a day or so, you'll be saying, 'Father who?' "

"A likely story!"

"You know Olivia will be coming home soon," he said. "Perhaps you'd care to call her."

"Oh, we bin talkin' 'bout that!" said Louella. "Miss Sadie goan have her up to try on all those fine hats, and I'm goin' t' fry her some chicken that will melt in her pretty mouth, yessir."

"And we'll sit at the dining table, won't we, and use Mama's china?"

"Aw, let's just set in th' kitchen where it's comfortable, and not put on airs for Miss Olivia. Let's just treat her like family!"

"Why, Louella, that's a perfect idea. What will we have with the chicken?"

Father Tim got up and went to Miss Sadie's rocking chair. He leaned down and kissed his eldest parishioner on the forehead, then turned and gave Louella a kiss on her warm cheek. "Keep up the good work," he said. "Remember I'll write you every week."

He hurried down the steps with Barnabas, and out into the drive, where he stopped and looked back, grinning. "Stay out of trouble!" he said.

❧

"Let's have a romantic dinner by candlelight," suggested Cynthia, who had dropped by his office on her way to The Local.

"That sounds good. But I had another suggestion, if you're interested."

"Try me!" she said, tilting her head and looking pleased with life.

"Why don't we take a drive in the country?"

"I love to drive in the country!"

"On my motor scooter."

"On your motor scooter? That little red thing?"

"The very same. We can take a picnic."

"Where would we put it?"

"Well, I don't know. I haven't thought it through."

"Obviously not."

"But I will, I will think it through. I'll devise a plan, and you'll be stunned by the brilliance, the wit, the . . . foolishness of it!"

She laughed with delight. "I love it when you talk like that! The minute you devise your plan, let me know more. Anything I can pick up for you at The Local?"

"Nothing, thanks," he said, seeing her to the door.

She was on the sidewalk when he called to her. "Cynthia?"

"Yes?" She turned around and smiled.

"I'll miss you," he said.

❧

He was dreading it, dreading it all. He had not been on an airplane in nine years, and to fly across the ocean was suddenly unthinkable. Travel always sounded wonderful when one considered the end, but to consider the means was quite another story. Walter and Katherine had gleefully reported that the farmhouse had featherbeds, but as he recalled from boyhood days at his grandfather's, featherbeds contained more than feathers. He recalled hearing faint chewing sounds that lasted the livelong night.

Then there was the issue of where the bathrooms

were. They believed both rooms had baths *en suite,* but then again, one of the baths—and guess whose it would be?—just might be a step or two down the hall.

He sat in his chair in the bedroom and looked at the results of his feeble packing effort. He wouldn't leave for four days yet, but he thought it best to start working on that aggravating project now.

"Timothy," he said aloud, causing Barnabas to look around curiously, "you have a rotten attitude about this trip. Back up and start over! Thank you, Lord, for the opportunity to go to this wonderful part of your world, thank you for making provision through the sacrifices of so many people, and for bringing it all together in a way that is clear evidence of your grace.

"Thank you for a good home for Dooley and Barnabas, may you bless the Owens exceedingly for their care for us. Forgive me for being dark-spirited about what is certainly a privilege, and enable me to take care of every need before I go. And, Lord, show me what to pack."

❧

"Leave this packin' alone!" said Puny. "You are makin' a mess. You have two pairs of underwear in here and nine handkerchiefs. You have three pairs of cuff links and no French cuff shirts." He was alarmed to see how she was undoing what he had so carefully done.

"You jis' go on and let me handle this. I packed for my grandpaw all th' time when he was travelin' with a revival tent. He was neat as a pin. He said he got compliments all th' time about the way he turned hisself out. What's this?"

"That," he said, irritably, "is my diabetes case."

"Ugh," she said, looking inside. "Needles! What's this?"

"Those are the strips to dip in my urine, to test blood-sugar levels."

"Do you have something to pee in?"

"Puny . . ."

"Well, think about it. You might need a little jar. You could git over there in that foreign country, and you don't know what you might have to pee in."

"Put in a jar, then," he said.

"I'm so glad you got Mr. Greer, an' another preacher ain't movin' in here. I hope you don't mind that I prayed about it."

❧

They had parked the car on the dirt road, climbed through a barbed wire fence, crossed a meadow brimming with daisies, and climbed a green knoll dotted with buttercups. They spread the quilt where pines and blue spruce cast a cool shade.

He lay down, put his hands behind his head and looked up at a sky filled with vast, cumulus clouds. He felt as if he might have been journeying to this very place for the duration of his sixty-one years. Surely, this was destination enough. Could Ireland be any greener? Its hills any nobler?

"Is this heaven?" inquired Cynthia, who was also lying on her back, looking up at the clouds. "Well, of course it is! Just look over there to the right, you see that chariot with an angel driving it? Look, Timothy, do you see?"

One thing he liked about his neighbor. It didn't take much to entertain her.

"I was looking at the face of Beethoven, myself."

"Where?" she asked eagerly.

"Straight up. See that wild mane of hair?"

"Why, that's not Beethoven at all," she said with urgent sincerity. "That's Andrew Jackson!"

He surprised himself by laughing so hard he couldn't stop. Nor did he want to. Being joined by his neighbor in this foolish collapse made it even better.

When the spasm had passed, Cynthia fetched a handkerchief out of her skirt pocket and blew her nose with some abandon. "Doesn't it feel grand to laugh over nothing?" she wondered. "Why don't we laugh more?"

"I think we forget," he said, wiping his eyes.

"How can we possibly forget to laugh, when it feels so good, and cures so much? How can we possibly?"

He had no answers. Ever since he was a child, he had been prone to forget about laughing.

"When I was a girl, I used to get tickled in chapel. I must tell you that it was the most delicious laughter I ever enjoyed in my life, because it was so forbidden. But oh, it was terribly painful, too. I would laugh 'til I hurt, and the tears would be streaming down my cheeks, but I had to keep all the rest of it inside, because if one single little bit of laughing slipped out, well, you know."

"Sudden death!"

" 'Dear Cynthia,' they said, 'she sits in chapel and cries, what a tender heart! Oh, dear'."

He smiled. How good to lie on his back and talk of nearly nothing, and feel the breeze now and then, and hear the bawling of a calf, and the song of the juncos in the hedges. He could not remember when he had been so supremely contented.

He reached over and took her hand, and turned his head to look at her. He thought that if he dared kiss her, he would devour her. He would kiss her lovely cheek and the tip of her nose, her forehead and her hair, he would not be responsible, he would come undone. It seemed dangerous merely to breathe.

"Timothy, look at that funny cow staring at us."

He raised his head slightly, and froze. "Do not move," he said. "That is a bull."

"Oh, for heaven's sake," she whispered, "this happens in comic books, not real life. Will we be gored?"

He did not feel confident about sitting up, but he felt less confident about lying down. So he continued to hold his head up, gazing at the bull somewhere over its left flank, feeling that the eye contact was not advisable.

"I think that what I should do is stand up slowly, and then you should run for the woods."

"I'll take the basket," she volunteered in a low voice. "I will not share my raspberry tart with that oaf."

He forced himself into a sitting position. How would J.C. handle this story? In the obituaries or on the front page?

The bull looked at him with consuming interest, as he managed to stand, albeit unsteadily. His knees had nearly gone out. "OK, run," he said evenly to his neighbor. He heard her do that very thing.

Were Frequent Flyer points refundable? he wondered.

The bull gazed at him steadily. Then, it lowered its head and turned to lumber down the hill to a shade tree at the edge of the meadow, without looking back.

The rector picked up the quilt and trudged to the edge of the woods to meet Cynthia, who was standing by a pine tree, shaking with laughter.

"Its stressful in the country," he said, grinning.

✿

"I vote that the best picnic lunch of my life!" she declared. "The best cold chicken, the best French bread, the best cheese, the best raspberry tart!"

"I agree with all of that!" he said, trying to ignore his increasing appetite for holding her in his arms.

She took a small sketchbook out of her skirt pocket, and a box of pencils. "I don't suppose you'd care to put one corner of the quilt over your head?"

"Not particularly. Why, for heaven's sake?"

"I'm starting on the wise men, and this is my very last chance at you, you know. All you have to do is sit over there and pull the quilt up around your head, like this."

"That's all? How long will it take?"

"Five minutes! I'll hurry. Then, when I get to my drawing board, I'll use the sketch as a model for the watercolor." She peered at him. "Actually, if you get on your knees, it will be easier."

"For who?"

"For me, I think. Here, get on your knees, and I'll fix the quilt like a burnoose, sort of." She took the raffia that he'd used to keep the napkin wrapped around the bread, put the quilt over his head, and tied it.

"There!" she said approvingly, "You look just like you've come from afar!"

He was relieved that the ordeal was nearly over, when he looked up to see an old man and woman coming along the path leading from the woods to the knoll. They were carrying burlap sacks filled with newly dug ferns, an occupation pursued by a number of locals.

As oddly stricken as if he'd been caught thieving chickens, he could not seem to budge from his knees, nor remove his burnoose. "Good afternoon!" he called, weakly. They paused, looked at him quizzically, then turned and hurried back into the woods.

"An' that feller's a preacher!" he heard the man say to his wife.

❧

They sat on the grassy knoll until the shadows lengthened over the quilt. They had found peace here today, and laughter, and he was thankful.

"Cynthia," he said, quietly, holding both of her hands, "I've thought about it."

She tilted her head and gazed at him. There was a happy light in her eyes which spoke her own thoughts.

He had decided to be simple and direct. "I can't make that decision yet," he said. "I'd like to think about it while I'm away. But if that's asking too much, then you've only to . . . deny me the privilege of thinking about it anymore, at all."

She listened without speaking, but her hands clasped his tightly.

"I won't try to kid you. I honestly don't know what I want to do. All I know is that I want the decision to be right and good. If I were younger, it would be an easier decision. But I've been so one-track minded, for so long, that I don't know if I can run on two tracks without causing a collision."

She smiled, nodding.

"I care very much for you, Cynthia." He had a sudden foreboding that he might begin to croak, so he was silent for a while, simply looking at her.

He saw in her spirit such a tender willingness that he was touched. She had a gift for touching him—with laughter, with delight, with deep feeling, with hope.

"At first," she said, quietly, "I was hurt that you didn't answer right away. But I think I've come to understand you better just recently, and I feel good about what you're saying. Yet, there's something in me that says, you fool, you've been pushy and presumptuous, he doesn't care for you any more than all the other people he's so lovely to, and you'll frighten him off if you don't back away, and then . . . and then the path through the hedge will grow over . . ."

The path through the hedge will grow over.

Hadn't she been the one with the courage to blaze that path in the first place?

He took her into his arms and held her close, and kissed her hair. They were silent for a time. Then he kissed her cheek and the bridge of her nose. "We must not let the path through the hedge grow over," he said with feeling.

❦

"Good mornin', good mornin', good mornin'," said Mule Skinner, coming through the door in an orange and turquoise shirt with an Indian blanket motif.

"I follered that shirt in th' door," said Rodney, who was behind him, "and you're under arrest."

"What for?" said Mule.

"For disturbin' th' peace."

"You want to arrest somebody, pick on that feller right there," said Mule, pointing to J.C. Hogan in the back booth with Father Tim.

"What'd he do?"

"Forgot t' run my ad this week, an' it a half page."

J.C. was sopping his toast in sausage gravy. "I'll run it next week, and give you a free one th' followin' week."

"That's no more'n anybody at the Wesley paper would do," said Mule, who had often threatened to take his real estate advertising elsewhere.

"So, how about if I give you two free ads?"

There was a stunned silence.

"Go for it!" said Rodney.

"Deal," said Mule, incredulous.

"Quarter pagers," said J.C.

The rector grinned. How accustomed he'd grown to the simple familiarity of friends in this small place on the map. Mitford had given him an extended family, with cousins galore, and no two alike.

"The usual," Mule told Percy, "an' squeeze th' grease out."

"I'll squeeze you some grease—on your bald head."

What would he find in Sligo? Considering that half of Mitford had Irish blood, with a liberal dose of Scottish thrift, what he'd find might not be so different, after all. He hoped there would be a warm place like the Grill, in the village near the farmhouse.

"Percy," said J.C., "there's somethin' unusual about these grits."

"Oh, yeah?" Percy said suspiciously.

"They're real good 'n thick an' got plenty of butter, th' way I like 'em."

Percy beamed. "I never used t' eat grits, but now that I've started eatin' 'em of a mornin', I make 'em th' way they taste good t' me."

Was something different about J.C.? Father Tim wondered. Maybe so, but he couldn't put his finger on it.

"Th' only thing is," said J.C., "this gravy's got lumps the size of banty eggs."

The rector finished his coffee and got up from the booth. "Boys, I've got more to do than I can shake a stick at, and Emma's picking me up at the crack of dawn tomorrow. Hold it in the road 'til I get back."

They all got out of the booth and stood up. It wasn't every day that one of their own went off to a foreign country.

Mule slapped him on the back. "Don't take any wooden nickels, buddyroe."

"Drop us a line," said J.C., "but keep it short and axe th' big words."

Rodney shook his hand. "Take it easy, Father. I'll miss all th' business you've been givin' me lately."

"God bless you," said Percy, choking up. "And put y'r money back in y'r pocket, it's on th' house."

There, he thought, untying Barnabas from the bench leg on the sidewalk. It's official. I'm really going to go through with this thing.

❧

They walked down to see the place where Dooley was currently catching his fish bait, down into the cool, sweet-scented woods where the only sounds were birdcalls and running water. How thankful he was that Dooley Barlowe could have this golden time in his life. It would provide nourishment the rest of his days.

"So, I wanted to come out and say goodbye," he said, squatting down on the creek bank beside the boy.

"Goodbye, y'rself," said Dooley, slapping the water with a stick.

"I'm going because I need to, son, not necessarily because I want to. And I want to say that I'll miss you." He tousled the boy's hair.

"You don't need t' miss me," said Dooley, looking at him frankly. "I got plenty t' do. I prob'ly won't miss you."

"Well, heck. I was kind of hoping you would."

"Oh, I might, once in a while, y' know, if I don't have nothin' else t' do."

"That's fair enough. Hal and Marge say you're doing all right out here, keeping up your end. They're old friends, and they mean a lot to me, so I thank you for helping them."

"They need help," Dooley said, flatly. " 'at ol' Rebecca Jane, she cries a lot an' all, and crawls around eatin' dog food outta Bonemeal's dish, and peein' in 'er pants, an' Doc Owen, he don't have nobody t' help 'im clean out th' horse poop, 'n look after th' kennel. He even gits me t' help 'im deliver calves."

He had never seen Dooley looking so proud. And he could have sworn he'd grown an inch or two just since he saw him ten days ago.

"You'll learn something from Hal Owen."

"You know what 'e told me?"

"What's that?"

"He said I could be anything I want to be."

"That's true. You can."

Dooley slapped the water with the stick. "Anything?"

"Anything."

There was long silence, broken by the call of a cardinal seeking its mate.

"The Owens will take you in to visit your grandpaw. You're good medicine for him, you know. And I'm hoping you'll keep an eye on Barnabas."

"When you comin' back?"

"In September. School will have started, and Puny's coming to live with you. I'll be back by the time you've made your first A in math."

"I like ol' Puny."

"Puny likes you."

"Has Jenny bin around, lookin' f'r me?"

"No, not that I know of. She's a pretty girl."

"Yeah." He jabbed the stick into the moss on the bank.

"Something on your mind, Dooley?"

He hesitated. "I bin prayin'."

"You have? Tell me about it."

"Is it all right to ask for dumb stuff?"

"I sure hope so, I ask for a lot of dumb stuff."

"I mean, like, help me do it right when Doc Owen asks me t' do somethin' in th' barn, or hand 'im somethin' when a calf is comin' . . ."

"That's not dumb stuff. God wants us to ask Him for help. And speaking of how to do something right, you know what God has to say to you, Dooley?"

Dooley looked startled. "What's 'at?"

"In the Thirty-second Psalm, He says, 'I will instruct you, Dooley, and teach you in the way which you should go. I will guide you with my eye.' "

"Did he put my name in like 'at?"

"He did. Just like He put my name in, and the Owens' name, and Cynthia's name. The Bible speaks to everyone who trusts Him."

"I cain't set here jabberin'," Dooley said, leaping to his feet. "I got t' feed 'em ol' dogs. You want t' come?"

"I'm right behind you."

The boy set off at a trot, up the winding path that led to the barn and the kennels. Then, he heard a booming bark, and saw Barnabas race to Dooley, who threw his arms around the black dog and rolled to the ground with him, shouting his name and laughing.

❧

One thing he could say for his secretary. If he'd had any reservations about this trip, any dread of going, the ride down the mountain to Holding with Emma Garrett had made him positively ecstatic about getting on the plane—and the sooner, the better. She had queried him so relentlessly about what he had packed or forgotten to pack, that he finally admitted that he didn't know any of the answers, that Puny Bradshaw had packed absolutely everything—with his blessing. She was mortified that he'd allow anyone else to do something so personal. How could he be sure what he'd end up with over there across the ocean, and no running home to get it?

When he saw that the first leg of his journey would be on a small aircraft that looked like a bathtub, and was patently made of tin, he did not flinch. Never mind that he had heard horror stories about small planes crashing into people's bedrooms, or that they could be as airless as bread boxes.

He took his luggage out of the trunk of Emma's lilac Oldsmobile and, staggering under the weight of the suitcase and the suit bag, gave her a kiss on a cheek wet with tears, and vanished into the terminal building.

❧

He sat looking out at the runway, which was baking in a fierce summer sun. He was the one who was leaving; why did he feel rejected, somehow? Why had they all let him go? Now, here he was, forced to do this thing, to travel thousands of miles away, across an entire ocean, and have an adventure—whether he wanted one or not.

The little plane took off with a rattle and groan so ferocious, he felt the whole thing would come apart under him. If this was the so-called, much-touted technological age, how had they failed so miserably to make a plane that didn't do its job any better than this?

He held on to the leather briefcase in his lap, the one

the vestry had given him years ago for Christmas. What had he forgotten, after all? He was mildly alarmed that everything seemed to be taken care of, that there were no loose ends. And why on earth should that be alarming? For the simple reason that it happened so seldom in one's life that it encouraged suspicion, that's why.

He opened his briefcase and pulled out a folder with a legal pad and a pen, and began to make notes about a sermon topic that had occurred to him only yesterday. There. That felt better. Next, he'd make a list of things to write home about, like how had the Rose Festival done? He'd forgotten to ask. And would someone make sure the new bathtub at the Porter place had a rail to hold on to? And when Cynthia heard from her agent about Uncle Billy's ink drawings, would she let him know at once? And had he put the premium increase notice on the Mortlake tapestry in his desk drawer, or given it to Ron for the next vestry meeting? He was surprised at the list he could make if he just put his mind to it.

He happened to look out the window.

They were flying over lush, rolling countryside, with his own blue mountains to the right. He thought it might be the most beautiful thing he had seen in a very long time.

There was a peaceful farm with acres of green crops laid out in neat parcels, and a tractor moving along the road. There was a lake that mirrored the clouds, and the blue sky, and the shadow of the little plane as it passed overhead.

Away toward the mountains, there was a ribbon of water flung out on the land, glittering in the sunlight, and beyond the river, a small, white church with a steeple catching the brilliance of the sun.

He closed the folder in his lap.

"Go in new life," came unbidden to his mind.

He felt as if he were emerging from a long, narrow hallway, from a cocoon, perhaps. He felt a weight lifting off his shoulders as the little plane lifted its gleaming wings over the fields.

Go in new life with Christ, he said silently, wondering at the strangely familiar thought.

Go, and be as the butterfly.

Visit America's favorite small town—
one book at a time

Welcome to the next book,

A Light in the Window

CHAPTER ONE

Close Encounters

Serious thinking and crossing the street, he once said, shouldn't be attempted simultaneously.

The red pickup truck was nearly upon him when he saw it. The shock of seeing it bear down with such ferocious speed sent him reeling backward to the curb, where he crashed in a sitting position. He caught a fleeting glance of the driver, talking on a telephone, as the truck careened around the corner.

"Father Tim! Are you all right?"

Winnie Ivey's expression was so grieved he felt certain he was badly hurt. He let Winnie help him up, feeling a numb shock where he'd slammed onto the curb.

Winnie's broad face was flushed with anger. "That maniac! Who was that fool, anyway?"

"I don't know. Perhaps I'm the fool for not looking where I was going." He laughed weakly.

"You're no such thing! I saw the light, it was still yellow, you had plenty of time to cross, and here comes this truck roarin' down on you like a freight train, and somebody in it talkin' on a phone."

She turned to the small crowd that had rushed out of the Main Street Grill. "A phone in a truck!" she said with disgust. "Can you believe it? I should have got his license number."

"Thank you, Winnie." He put his arm around the sturdy shoulders of the Sweet Stuff Bakery owner. "You've got a special talent for being in the right place at the right time."

Percy Mosely, who owned the Grill, ran out with his spatula in his hand. "If I was you, I'd ask th' good Lord to kick that feller's butt plumb to Wesley. Them poached eggs you eat are now scrambled."

The rector patted his pockets for the heavy office key and checked his wallet. All there. "No harm done," he assured his friends. The incident had simply been a re-grettably dramatic way to begin his first week home from Ireland.

Though he'd spent the summer in Sligo, he found on returning that he hadn't, after all, missed summer in Mit-ford. His roses bloomed on, the grass lay like velvet under the network of village sprinklers, and parishioners were still leaving baskets of tomatoes on his porch.

As he came up the walk to the rectory, he heard a booming bark from the garage. It was the greeting he had missed every livelong day of his sojourn across the pond.

Since returning home less than a week ago, he had awakened each morning to see Barnabas standing by the bed, staring at him soberly. The inquiry in the eyes of his black Bouvier-cum-sheepdog companion was simple: Are you home to stay, or is this a joke?

He walked through the kitchen and opened the garage door, as Barnabas, who had grown as vast as a bear during his absence, rushed at him with joy. Laying his front paws on the rector's shoulders, he gazed dolefully into the eyes of his master, whose glasses fogged at once.

"Come now, old fellow. Slack off!"

Barnabas leapt backward, danced for a moment on his hind legs, and lunged forward to give the rector a great lick on the face that sent a shower of saliva into his left ear.

The victim dodged toward his parked Buick and crashed onto the hood with his elbow. " 'Sing and make music in your hearts,' " he recited loudly from a psalm, " 'always giving thanks to the Father for everything'!"

Barnabas sat down at once and gazed at him, mopping the garage floor with his tail.

His dog was the only living creature he knew who was unfailingly disciplined by the hearing of the Word. It was a phenomenon that Walter had told over the whole of Ireland's West Country.

"Let's have a treat, pal. And you," he said to Dooley's rabbit, Jack, "will have beet tops." The Flemish giant regarded him with eyes the color of peat.

The house was silent. It wasn't one of Puny's days to work, and Dooley was at football practice. He had missed the boy terribly, reading and rereading the one scrawled message he had received in two long months:

I am fine. Barnabas is fine. Im ridin the hair off that horse.

He had missed the old rectory, too, with its clamor and quiet, its sunshine and shadow. Never before in his life as a rector had he found a home so welcoming or comfortable—a home that seemed, somehow, like a friend.

He spied the thing on his counter at once. It was Edith Mallory's signature blue casserole dish.

He was afraid of that.

Emma had written to Sligo to say that Pat Mallory had died soon after he left for Ireland. Heart attack. No warning. Pat, she said, had felt a wrenching chest pain, had sat down on the top step outside his bedroom, and after dropping dead sitting up, had toppled to the foot of the stairs, where the Mallorys' maid of thirty years had found him just before dinner.

"Oh, Mr. Mallory," she was reported to have said, "you shouldn't have gone and done that. We're havin' lasagna."

Sitting there on the farmhouse window seat, reading Emma's five-page letter, he had known that Edith Mallory would not waste any time when he returned.

Long before Pat's death, he'd been profoundly unsteadied when she had slipped her hand into his or let her fingers run along his arm. At one point, she began winking at him during sermons, which distracted him to such a degree that he resumed his old habit of preaching over the heads of the congregation, literally.

So far, he had escaped her random snares but had once dreamed he was locked with her in the parish-hall coat closet, pounding desperately on the door and pleading with the sexton to let him out.

Now Pat, good soul, was cold in the grave, and Edith's casserole was hot on his counter.

Casseroles! Their seduction had long been used on men of the cloth, often with rewarding results for the cook.

Casseroles, after all, were a gesture that on the surface could not be mistaken for anything other than righteous goodwill. And, once one had consumed and exclaimed over the initial offering, along would come another on its very heels, until the bachelor curate ended up a married curate or the divorced deacon a fellow so skillfully ensnared that he never knew what hit him.

In the language of food, there were casseroles, and there were casseroles. Most were used to comfort the sick or inspire the downhearted. But certain others, in his long experience, were so filled with allure and innuendo that they ceased to be Broccoli Cheese Delight intended for the stomach and became arrows aimed straight for the heart.

In any case, there was always the problem of what to do with the dish. Decent people returned it full of something else. Which meant that the person to whom you returned it would be required, at some point, to give you another food item, all of which produced a cycle that was unimaginably tedious.

Clergy, of course, were never required to fill the dish before returning it, but either way, it had to be returned. And there, clearly, was the rub.

He approached the unwelcome surprise as if a snake might have been coiled inside. His note of thanks, which he would send over tomorrow by Puny, would be short and to the point:

Dear Edith: Suffice it to say that you remain one of the finest cooks in the county. That was no lie; it was undeniably true.

Your way with (blank, blank) is exceeded only by your graciousness. A thousand thanks. In His peace, Fr Tim.

There.

He lifted the lid. Instantly, his mouth began to water, and his heart gave a small leap of joy.

Crab cobbler! One of his favorites. He stared with wonder at the dozen flaky homemade biscuits poised on the bed of fresh crabmeat and fragrant sauce.

Perhaps, he thought with sudden abandon, he should give Edith Mallory a ring this very moment and express his thanks.

As he reached for the phone, he realized what he was doing—he was placing his foot squarely in a bear trap.

He hastily clamped the lid on the steaming dish. "You see?" he muttered darkly. "That's the way it happens."

Where casseroles were concerned, one must constantly be on guard.

"Edith Mallory's lookin' to give you th' big whang-do," said Emma.

Until this inappropriate remark, there had been a resonant peace in the small office. The windows were open to morning air embroidered with birdsong. His sermon notes were going at a pace. And the familiar comfort of his old swivel chair was sheer bliss.

"And what, exactly, is that supposed to mean?"

His part-time church secretary glanced up from her ledger. "It means she's going to cook your goose."

He did not like her language. "I am sixty-one years old and a lifelong bachelor. Why anyone would want to give me a whang . . . why anyone would . . . it's unthinkable," he said flatly.

"I can tell she thinks about it all th' time. Besides, remember Father Appel who got married when he was sixty-five, right after his social security kicked in? And that deacon who was fifty-nine, who married th' red-headed woman who owned the taxi company in Wesley? Then, there was that salesman who worked at The Collar Button . . ."

"Spare me the details," he said curtly, opening his drawer and looking for the Wite-Out.

Emma peered at him over her glasses. "Just remember," she muttered.

"Remember what?"

"Forearmed is forewarned."

"No, Emma. Forewarned is forearmed."

"Peedaddle. I never do get that right. But if I were you, I'd duck when I see her comin'."

I've been ducking when I see her coming for twelve years, he thought.

"One thing in her favor," said Emma, recording another check, "is she's a great hostess. As you have surely learned from doin' your parties, a rector needs that. Some preachers' wives don't do pea-turkey, if you ask me. Of course, if anything's goin' to happen with your neighbor, and Lord knows, I hope it will—you ought to just go on and give 'er a nice engagement ring—then Edith would have to jump on somebody else."

"Emma," he said, ripping the cover off the typewriter, "I have finally got a handle on the most important sermon I've written in a year . . ."

"Don't say I didn't warn you," she replied, pressing her lips together in that way he loathed.

At noon, Ron Malcolm appeared at the door, wearing boots caked with dried mud and a red baseball cap.

Being away for two months had given everyone the rector knew, and Mitford as well, a fresh, almost poignant, reality. He had scarcely ever noticed that Ron Malcolm was a man of such cheering vigor. Then again, perhaps it was the retired contractor's involvement in the nursing-home project that had done something for the color in his face and put a gleam in his eyes.

"Well, Father, we're off and running. Jacobs has sent their job superintendent over. He's having a trailer installed on the site today." He shook the rector's hand with great feeling.

"I can hardly believe it's finally happening."

"Five million bucks!" Ron said. "This nursing home is the biggest thing to happen around here since the Wesley furniture factory. Have you met Leeper?"

"Leeper?"

"Buck Leeper. The job superintendent. We talked about him before you left for Ireland. He said he'd try to get by your office."

"I haven't met him. I'll have to walk up—maybe Wednesday afternoon."

Ron sat down on the visitors' bench and removed his cap. "Emma around?"

"Gone to the post office."

"I think it's only fair that I talk to you straight about Buck Leeper. A few months ago, I told you he's hardheaded, rough. I know I don't have to worry about you, but he's the kind who can make you lose your religion."

"Aha."

"His daddy was Fane Leeper, so called because a preacher once said he was the most profane man he'd ever met. Fane Leeper was also the best job superintendent on the East Coast. He made three contractors rich men, and then alcohol got 'im, as they say.

"You need to know that Buck is just like his daddy. He learned contractin', cussin', and drinkin' from Fane, and the only way he could get out from under the shadow of his father was to outdo him in all three categories."

Ron paused, as if to let that information sink in.

"Buck's on this job because he'll save us money—and a lot of grief. He'll bring it in on time and on budget, and you can count on it. Out of respect to you, Father, I talked to Jacobs about sending us another man, but they won't send anybody but Buck on a job this size." He stood up and zipped his jacket. "We'll probably hate Jacobs for this, but before it's over, we'll thank him."

"I trust your judgment."

Ron opened the door and was backing out with his hat in his hand.

"You might look softhearted, Father, but I've seen you operate a time or two, and I know you can handle Buck. Just give 'im his rein."

The rector looked out at the maple across the street, which had taken on a tinge of russet since yesterday. "I can't imagine that Mr. Leeper will be any problem at all," he said.

"Timothy?"

It was Cynthia, his neighbor, peering through the screened door of the kitchen, her hands cupped on either side of her eyes. She was wearing a white blouse and blue denim skirt and a bandanna around her blond hair.

"You look like Heidi!" he said to his neighbor. Though she admitted to being fiftysomething, there were times when she looked like a girl. Again he was struck by the fresh, living way in which he saw people, as if he had lately risen from the dead.

She walked past him, unfurling the faintest scent of wisteria on the air. "You said to think of something we could do to celebrate your return."

She went to the stove and lifted the lid on the pot of soup he was making. "Yum," she said, inhaling. Then, she turned to him and smiled. Her eyes were like sapphires, smoky and deep with that nearly violet hue that always caught him off-guard.

"And have you thought about it?" he asked, afraid he might croak like a frog when he spoke.

"They say walls have ears. I'd better whisper it."

He had completely forgotten how easily she fit into his arms.

Going to a town council meeting was decidedly not what he wanted to do with his evening. After two months away, he hardly knew what was going on. And he was still feeling oddly jet-lagged, shaking his head vigorously on occasion with some hope of clearing it. But he would go; it might put him back in the swing of things, and frankly, he was curious why the mayor, Esther Cunningham, had called an unofficial meeting and why it might concern him.

"Don't eat," Esther told him on the phone. "Ray's bringin' baked beans, cole slaw, and ribs from home. Been cookin' all day."

"Hallelujah," he said with feeling.

There was a quickening in the air of the mayor's office. Ray was setting out his home-cooked supper on the vast desktop, overlooked by pictures of their twenty-three grandchildren at the far end.

"Mayor," said Leonard Bostick, "it's a cryin' shame you cain't cook as good as Ray."

"I've got better things to do," she snapped. "I did the cookin' for forty years. Now it's his turn."

Ray grinned. "You tell 'em, honey."

"Whooee!" said Paul Hartley. "Baby backs! Get over here, Father, and give us a blessin'."

"Come on!" shouted the mayor to the group lingering in the hall. "It's blessin' time!"

Esther Cunningham held out her hands, and the group eagerly formed a circle.

"Our Lord," said the rector, "we're grateful for the gift of friends and neighbors and those willing to lend their hand to the welfare of this place. We thank you for the peace of this village and for your grace to do the work that lies ahead. We thank you, too, for this food and ask a special blessing on the one who prepared it. In Jesus' name."

"Amen!" said the assembly.

The mayor was the first in line. "You're goin' t' get a blessing, all right," she told her husband. "Just look at this sauce! You've done it again, sweet face."

Ray winked at the rector. There, thought the rector, is a happy man if I ever saw one.

"How's your diabetes, Father?"

"It won't tolerate the torque you've put under the hood of that pot, I regret to say."

"Take doubles on m' slaw, then," said Ray, heaping the rector's plate.

"You know what we're here to talk about," said the mayor.

Everybody nodded, except the rector.

"I don't want it to come up in a town meetin', and I don't want it officially voted on, vetoed, or otherwise messed with. We're just goin' to seek agreement here tonight like a family and let it go at that."

She looked at their faces and leaned forward. "Got it?"

Linder Hayes stood up slowly, thin as a strip of baling wire. He placed his hands carefully behind his back, peered at his shoes, and cleared his throat.

"Here goes," said Joe Ivey, nudging the rector.

"Your honor," said Linder.

"You don't have t' 'your honor' me. This is an unofficial meetin'."

"Your honor," said Linder, who was a lawyer and preferred the formalities, "I'd like to speak for the merchants of this town who have to make a livin' out of the day-to-day run of things.

"Now, we know that an old woman dressed up in party hats and gumboots, directin' traffic around the monument, is not a fit sight for tourists, especially with leaf season comin' on.

"You say she's harmless, but that, in fact, is not the point. With her infamous snaggle tooth and those old army decorations, think what she'd look like if she came flyin' out of th' fog wavin' at cars. She'd clean th' tourists out of here so fast it'd make your head swim."

"And good riddance," said the mayor testily.

"Madam Mayor, we've fought this tourist battle for years. We've all moved over to give you plenty of room to do your job, and you've done it. Your faithful defense of what is good and right and true to the character of this town has been a strong deterrent to the rape and plunder of senseless development and reckless growth."

"But . . ." Linder gave a long pause and looked

around the room. "Two Model Village awards will not suffice our merchants for cold, hard cash. That ol' woman is enough to make babies squall and grown men tuck tail and run. Clearly, I don't have to make a livin' off tourists, but my wife does—and so, incidentally, do half your grandchildren."

"We're in for it," muttered Joe Ivey. "I should've carried a bed roll and a blanket."

"Linder," said Esther Cunningham, "sit down and take a load off your feet."

"Your honor . . ."

"Thank you, Linder," the mayor said, measuring each word.

Linder appeared to waver for a moment, like a leaf caught in a breeze. Then, he sat down.

"I'd like us to look at a couple of things before we open for a brief discussion," said the mayor. "First, let's look at my platform. There is no such thing in it as a middle plank, a left plank, or a right plank. It's just one straight platform. Period. Joe, why don't you remind us what it is?"

Joe stood up. "Mitford takes care of its own!" He sat down again, flushed with pride.

"Mitford . . . takes . . . care . . . of . . . its . . . own. That's been my platform for fourteen years, and as long as I'm mayor, it will continue to be th' platform. Number one. Miss Rose Watson may be snaggle-toothed and she may be crazy, but she's our own. Number two. Based on that, we're goin' to take care of 'er.

"Number three. Directin' traffic around the monument is the best thing that's happened to her since she was a little girl, as normal as you and me. Uncle Billy says she sleeps like a baby now, instead of ramblin' through that old house all night, and she's turned nice as

you please to him. Directin' traffic is a genuine responsibility to her. She takes pride in it."

"She does a real good job," said Ernestine Ivory,
who colored beet red at the sound of her own voice.

"What's that, Ernestine?" asked the mayor.

"Miss Rose does a real good job of directing traffic.
'Course that's just me . . ."

"That's just you and a lot of other people who think
the same thing. She's very professional. I don't know
where in th' world she learned it.

"Now, here's what I propose, and I ask you to consider
it in your hearts. Every day from noon to one o'clock, traffic drops off and Mitford eats lunch. My stomach starts
growlin' right on th' button, like th' rest of this crowd.

"I propose we let Miss Rose direct traffic five days a
week, from noon 'til one, which'll give her just enough
cars to keep her happy.

"Now, Linder, I have to hand it to you about those
cocktail hats and funny clothes, so I propose we give 'er
a uniform. Navy hat, skirt, and jacket from my old days
in th' Waves. Be a perfect fit. I was skinny as a rail,
wasn't I, doll?"

Ray gave the mayor a thumbs-up.

"Ernestine, I want you to go with me to dress her in
th' mornin' at ten o'clock, and Joe, how about you
givin' her a nice haircut. We'll bring 'er up to your shop
about eleven."

"Be glad to."

"Father, I wish you'd make it your business to pray
about this."

"You have my word," he said.

"And Linder, honey, I really appreciate the way
you're lookin' after the merchants. God knows, somebody needs to. Any questions?"

Before anyone could respond, the mayor pounded her desk with a gavel. "Meeting adjourned. All in favor say aye."

"I declare," said the rector, walking home with Joe Ivey, "every time I go to a meeting with Esther Cunningham, I feel like somebody's screwed my head around backwards."

You'll be coming home to a new Dooley, Marge had written just before he left Ireland. When he read that, his heart sank. He had managed to grow fond of the old Dooley.

He's actually learning to speak English, his friend wrote from Meadowgate Farm. *Just wait; you'll be thrilled.*

He couldn't say he had been thrilled, exactly, on seeing his twelve-year-old charge again. First, the cowlick had miraculously disappeared. When he left for Sligo in July, it had been shooting up like a geyser; now, it simply wasn't there, and frankly, he missed it. Then, he noticed that Dooley's freckles appeared to be fading, an upshot that he especially regretted.

He also found a new resoluteness in the boy that he'd only fleetingly glimpsed before, not to mention the fact that he was putting the top back on the catsup and the mayonnaise. How could so much change have taken place in two short months?

"I refuse to take credit," Marge told him on the phone from Meadowgate the morning after his return. "It's all that wonderful spade work you'd already done, laced with a strong dose of cow manure and fresh air. Last weekend, he helped Hal deliver a colt, which was like a shot of Miracle-Gro to his self-confidence. Furthermore, I'm crushed to tell you that Rebecca Jane took her first step to . . . guess who? Uncle Dools!"

I have planted, Apollos watered, but God gave the increase, the rector mused as he approached the rectory from the council meeting. Joe Ivey had offered him "a taste of brandy" if he cared to walk up the stairs to the barber shop, but he declined. He could hardly wait to get home and into the old burgundy bathrobe he'd sorely missed in Ireland.

After a quick trip with Barnabas to the Baxter Park hedge, he took a bottle of mineral water from the cabinet, and the two of them climbed the stairs.

"Dooley!"

"Yessir?"

Yessir? He walked down the hall to the boy's room and found him sitting against the head of his bed, reading and absently scratching his big toe. The room seemed remarkably well-ordered.

"How's it going?"

Dooley looked up. "Great."

"Terrific." He stood in the doorway, feeling an awkward joy. "What's the book?"

"Dynamics of Veterinary Medicine."

"Aha."

"See this?" Dooley held the book toward him. "It's a picture of a colt being born. That's jis' the way it happened last weekend. It's the neatest thing I ever done . . . did. I want t' be a vet. Doc Owen said I could be one."

"Of course you can. You can be whatever you want to be." He stepped into the room.

"I never wanted to be anything before."

"Maybe you never saw any choices before."

"I never wanted to be an astronaut or a rock star or anything, like Buster Austin wants t' be."

"That's OK. Why rush into wanting to be something?" He sat down on the bed.

"That's what I thought." Dooley went back to his book, ignoring him but somehow comfortable with the fact that he was there.

"So, how's Buster?" Only months ago, he and Buster Austin had been the darkest adversaries, with Dooley whipping the tar out of him twice.

"Cool. We swapped lunches today. He likes 'at old meatloaf you make. I got 'is baloney."

"Done your homework?"

"Yessir."

Yessir. It rang in his ears like some foreign language. "How's the science project coming? Are we finishing it up Sunday evening?"

"Yep. You'll like it. It's neat."

Since he came home from Ireland, he'd been peering into Dooley's face, searching it out. Something was different. A wound had healed, perhaps; he was looking more like a boy instead of someone who'd grown old before his time.

It had been nearly a year since Russell Jacks, the church sexton and Dooley's grandfather, had come down with pneumonia and was rushed into emergency treatment. The boy had come home with him from the hospital, and he'd been here ever since.

One of the best things he had ever done was bring Dooley Barlowe home. Yes, he'd been trouble and calamity and plenty of it—but worth it and then some.

"I hear you went to see your grandpa every week. Good medicine."

"Yep."

"How is he?"

"That woman that's lookin' after 'im, she says he's

doing good, but he ain't had any livermush since you left . . ."

"Uh-oh."

"And he was riled about it."

"We'll take him some. And I'll see you at breakfast. Has Jenny been around?"

"I ain't into 'at ol' poop, n' more."

The rector grinned. There! he thought. There's my old Dooley.

In his room, Barnabas leapt onto the blanket at the foot of the bed, then lay down with a yawn as the rector stepped into the shower. While the raftered room in the Sligo farmhouse had been perfectly comfortable, the long passage down the hall to the finicky shower was another story entirely. As far as he could see, it might be months before the thrill of his own bathroom, *en suite,* began to wane.

He felt as mindless and contented as a steamed clam as he sat on the bed and dialed his neighbor.

"Hello?"

"Hello, yourself."

"Timothy!" said Cynthia. "I was just thinking of you."

"Surely you have something better to do."

"I was thinking that my idea of how to celebrate was too silly."

"Silly, yes, but not too silly," he said. "In fact, I was wondering—when are we going to do it?"

"Ummmm . . ."

"Saturday night?" he asked, hoping.

"Oh, rats. My nephew's coming. I mean, I'm delighted he's coming. You must meet him. He's very dear. Saturday would have been so perfect. Could we do it Monday evening?"

"Vestry meeting," he said.

"Tuesday I have to finish an illustration and FedEx it first thing Wednesday morning. Could you do it Wednesday around six-thirty?"

"Building committee at seven."

"Darn."

"I could do it Friday," he said.

"Great!"

"No. No, wait, there's something on Friday," he said, extending the phone cord to the dresser where he opened his black engagement book. "Yes, that's it. The hospital is having a staff dinner for Hoppy, and I'm giving the invocation. Would you come?"

"Dinner in a hospital? That's suicide! Besides, I can't stand hospitals. I nearly died in one, you know."

"No, I didn't know."

"And I don't know how you ever will know these things unless we can figure out a way to see each other. What about Sunday evening? That's usually a relaxing time for you. Sunday might be lovely."

"I'm helping Dooley finish his science project. He has to hand it in Monday morning." A nameless despair was robbing him of any contentment he had just felt.

"I could meet you on the bench by your German roses at six o'clock tomorrow. We could do it there and get it over with."

But he didn't want to do it and get it over with. He wanted to linger over it, to savor it.

"You're sighing," she said.

"It's just that there's so much going on after being away for two months."

"I understand," she said simply.

"You do? Do you really?"

"Of course I do."

"I'll call you tomorrow. Let's not waste it on the garden bench."

"All that lumpy, wet moss," she said, laughing.

"All that cold, damp concrete," he said forlornly.

"I hope you sleep well." He could hear a tenderness in her voice. "Jet lag really does persist for days."

"Yes. Well. So," he said, feeling immeasurably foolish, "blink your bedroom lights good night."

"I will if you will."

"Cynthia?"

"Yes?"

"I . . ." He cleared his throat. "You . . ."

"Spit it out," she said.

He had started to croak; he couldn't have uttered another word if his life depended on it.

"I'm not going to worry anymore about being too silly. It's you, Timothy, who are far too silly!"

His heart pounded as he hung up the phone. He had nearly told her he loved her, that she was wonderful; he had nearly gone over the edge of the cliff, with no ledges to break his fall.

He went to the window and looked down upon her tiny house. He saw the lights blink twice through the windows of her bedroom under the eaves. He raced around the bed and flipped his own light switch off, then on again, and off.

"Good Lord," he said, breathlessly, standing there in the dark. "Who is the twelve-year-old in this house, anyway?"

The last book in the Mitford Series is coming from Viking in Fall 2005

Light from Heaven

ISBN 0-670-03453-3

For more works by Jan Karon, look for the

At Home in Mitford
ISBN 0-14-025448-X

A Light in the Window
ISBN 0-14-025454-4

These High, Green Hills
ISBN 0-14-025793-4

Out to Canaan
ISBN 0-14-026568-6

A New Song
ISBN 0-14-027059-0

A Common Life:
The Wedding Story
ISBN 0-14-200034-5

In This Mountain
ISBN 0-14-200258-5

Shepherds Abiding
ISBN 0-14-200485-5

Jan Karon books make perfect holiday gifts.

Paperbacks from Penguin:

The Mitford Years Boxed Sets

6-Book Set:
ISBN 0-14-771779-5

3-Book Set, Volumes 1–3:
ISBN 0-14-771203-3

3-Book Set, Volumes 4–6:
ISBN 0-1 -771728-0

Patches of Godlight: Father Tim's Favorite Quotes
ISBN 0-14-200197-X

Hardcover Books from Viking:

Esther's Gift: A Mitford Christmas Story
ISBN 0-670-03121-6

The Mitford Snowmen: A Christmas Story
ISBN 0-670-03019-8

Christmas in Mitford Gift Set
(*Esther's Gift* and *The Mitford Snowmen*)
ISBN 0-670-78349-8

The Trellis and the Seed
ISBN 0-670-89289-0

The Mitford Cookbook & Kitchen Reader
ISBN 0-670-03239-5

A Continual Feast
ISBN 0-670-03364-2

All the Mitford books are available in hardcover editions.
For more information visit www.penguin.com

At Home in Mitford
ISBN 0-14-086501-2

A Light in the Window
ISBN 0-14-086596-9

These High, Green Hills
ISBN 0-14-086598-5

Out to Canaan
ISBN 0-14-086597-7

A New Song (Abridged)
ISBN 0-14-086901-8

A New Song (Unabridged)
ISBN 0-14-180013-5

A Common Life
ISBN 0-14-180274-X

The Mitford Years Boxed Set
ISBN 0-14-086813-5

Shepherds Abiding
ISBN 0-14-280033-3

Jan Karon for Children

Jeremy: The Tale of an Honest Bunny
ISBN 0-670-88104-X (hardcover)
ISBN 0-14-250004-6 (paperback)

Miss Fannie's Hat
0-14-056812-3 (paperback)

The Jan Karon Story Hour
The Trellis and the Seed, Miss Fannie's Hat,
and *Jeremy: The Tale of an Honest Bunny*
ISBN 0-670-06001-1 Audio CD

In bookstores now from Penguin Group (USA)
Visit the Mitford Web site at www.mitfordbooks.com

All of the Mitford books are available in hardcover
and can be ordered from us or your local bookseller.
To order books in the United States: Please visit
www.penguin.com or write to Consumer Sales,
Penguin Group USA, P. O. Box 12289, Dept B, Newark,
New Jersey 07101-5289. VISA, MasterCard, and
American Express cardholders call (800) 788-6262 or
(201) 933-9292.